Mind Games

For Angela Heard.
A greatly missed friend who always
wanted me to write thrillers.
This one's for you, Angie.

Grateful thanks to (in alphabetical order): Howard Barmad; Jennifer Bloch; Lynn Curtis; Sara Fisher; Gillian Green; Jonathan Kern, for helping in so very many ways; Rose Klayman of the *Miami Herald*; Kate Miller; Detectives Paul Marcus and Paul Scrimshaw of the Miami Beach Police Department, who shared their knowledge and world with kindness and great patience, even though I showed up at the *worst* possible time for them; Herta Norman, as always for her crucial daily 'reviews'; Judy Piatkus; Helen Rose; staff at the Sheraton, Bal Harbour. And extra special thanks to the 'Tarlow connection' – Alison R. Tarlow, M.S., Scott J. Sale, Sharon Tarlow and, as always, Dr Jonathan Tarlow (this time as much for sailing expertise as medical!).

*

As always in my novels, all characters and situations are purely fictitious. So, in this case, (though the locations are certainly real) is the Florida weather.

Retrieve File

Filename:	<u>**My Journal**</u>
Current Dir:	c:\wpwin\sundries
File Info:	14912 Bytes
03/29/98	23:08

File Password Protected

File:　　　　c\wpwin\sundries\jrnl

Password:　　<u>H-A-T-E</u>

　　　　　　　　<u>O</u>K　　　　Cancel

Cathy's Journal
Tuesday, March 31, 1998

I see their faces, see them smile at me, and I remember what they've done to me, know how they *really* feel about me.

I hate them. I really *hate* them.

I don't think I can stand it much longer.

CHAPTER ONE

FRIDAY, APRIL 3, 1998

The Robbins' housekeeper, Anita del Fuego, arrived at work same time as every morning at the house on Pine Tree Drive: six-thirty. She enjoyed the short walk from the K bus stop, liked the cool fragrance of the tall double line of pines that bisected and gave the exclusive Miami Beach road its name. A morning person by nature, Anita was singing softly as she let herself in through the side entrance, hung her bright floral polyester jacket on its hook, took down the white pinafore – fresh washed and pressed, just the way Señora Robbins liked her to wear – and changed into her white, soft-soled nurse's shoes. Still singing, she made her way into the kitchen – and stopped.

Something was not right.

The house was too quiet and too dark. The blinds in the kitchen were shut and there was no aroma of fresh-perked coffee. Señor Robbins always made the first pot about a half-hour before Anita got to work; sometimes she found him still peaceably sitting at the kitchen table, though more often than not he was either upstairs getting dressed or had already left for business. Whichever, the *señor* always opened all the blinds and drapes on the first floor before the housekeeper's arrival.

Not today.

Anita went out into the hallway and listened. Quiet. It was way too quiet.

She lifted her wrist close to her face to peer at her watch, checking that she hadn't made a mistake about the time. The watch said six-thirty-five. High time for young Cathy to be up and about, getting showered and dressed for school.

Her skin prickled. She had a bad feeling.

'*Ridículo*, Anita,' she rebuked herself, softly. All this was, probably, a case of everyone oversleeping, and when she went upstairs and knocked on Cathy's door she would find her lying curled up on her side under her comforter, the way she always slept.

Encouraged, Anita started up the stairs. That was all this was. First she would wake Cathy, then the girl could go rouse her *momia* and *papá* … Or maybe Señor Robbins had left the house *real* early to go to the market for his restaurants, too early to make coffee and open the drapes – and the *señora* had forgotten to set her own alarm clock. That was all.

So why did she still have such a bad feeling?

Cathy was not in her bed. The bathroom door was open.

'Cathy?' Anita called softly.

No answer.

She went to the door and looked inside. The shower curtain was open and dry, and the pale pink bath towel was neatly folded over the warming rail.

Anita's palms grew clammy. She didn't know why she was so afraid, but something was gnawing at her mind, growing by the second, something dark and nasty, something she had a powerful urge to run away from. She opened her mouth to call out a second time, more loudly, then shut it again, silenced by the stillness and that feeling inside her head.

Cobarde, she chastised herself. Coward.

She turned around, left Cathy's empty room and walked along the corridor to the *señor* and *señora's* closed bedroom door. She knocked, twice, tentatively. The silence grew heavier. She knocked again, gripped the door handle in her fingers, felt its coolness against her own rising heat. For another moment she wavered – and then she opened the door.

It was very dark in the room. The thick drapes were still closed. Anita took two steps inside and stopped, waiting for her eyes to grow used to the dimness.

Slowly, the bed came into focus. She could see vague shapes. Humps and lumps. Black waves. Motionless waves. Anita stood very still, trying to listen past the air-conditioner's hum.

She began to tremble.

There was a smell in the air.

It was unmistakable. Hot and animal, somewhere between the scent of her own monthly *regla* and the heavy odour she smelt whenever she saw her cousin Bobby who worked at the meat market.

A sick sound of revulsion was muffled against her lips even as it emerged, squashed flat by her right hand. Seconds passed. Still scarcely daring to move, still half-blind, Anita tilted her face slightly towards the windows. To open the drapes she would have to walk across the room, to pass the bed and those humps beneath the quilt that looked so black in the dark.

Turn on the light.

Anita backed up to the door, found the switch with her left hand.

And flicked it.

And saw that the blackness covering the bed was not a quilt after all.

It was what she had smelled.

Blood.

Spread over the three of them and over the sheets and pillows. Sprayed up over the headboard and the wall and the lampshades on both bedside tables.

Anita opened her mouth to scream, but nothing came out. The black, sick sensation was swamping her, suffocating her, sucking her in, like the corkscrew spiral of a tornado drawing everything into itself. Her whole being seemed engulfed in that twisting funnel, was being sucked down, down into a black, narrow, contracting hole. *All dead, all dead*, the only words, the only halfway coherent thoughts spinning down with her.

Three corpses.

The middle one stirred. Sat up.

Anita's scream began then, and did not stop. It came from deep inside her, from within that narrow whirling bore of terror, came twisting, surging, gushing, roaring out through her mouth into the death silence.

As Cathy Robbins, her blue eyes almost bright against her bloodsoaked cheeks and forehead, her golden hair matted and darkened, lifted both her arms towards Anita in speechless supplication.

The housekeeper stared at the girl's mouth, saw that it, too, was red.

Still screaming, Anita del Fuego turned and ran.

CHAPTER TWO

He left Martinez, Riley, the ME, the Crime Scene guys and the Assistant State Attorney with the distraught Mrs del Fuego and the deceased, and took the vigil with the living for himself. Detective Samuel Becket had been with the Person Crimes unit of the Miami Beach Police Department for six years, and had seen his share of homicides, but the sheer horror never diminished so far as he was concerned. Sam knew that his sense of motivation for solving those violent, most inhumane crimes was as undiluted as ever, but he still – when he was in a position to have a say in the matter – got the hell away from the grisly end of things first chance he got. Sergeant Kovac having appointed him lead investigator for this particular case, Sam was, as it turned out, in that position today.

In Miami Beach, in his experience, death didn't come much grislier than this. Arnold and Marie Robbins – an affluent, middle-class, middle-aged couple in the restaurant business – dead in their kingsize Miami Beach bed with their jugulars sliced and their fourteen-year-old daughter lying snuggled up between them, alive and unharmed.

Physically unharmed, anyway. As to the rest, Cathy Robbins was now tucked up between white hospital sheets in Miami General, being taken care of by the best there was: In Sam's book, anyhow.

'How's she doing?' he asked his father.

'How should she be doing?'

Dr David Becket and his son both turned and looked

11

through the glass into the private room where Cathy Robbins was lying, eyes closed and perfectly still. Her left arm, resting on top of the covers, showed a healthy Florida tan, but her face was so white it seemed almost translucent.

As a detective, Sam knew full well that – theoretically at least – being a family member placed indisputably at the murder scene made the girl a possible suspect. He knew it, and he'd seen in the eyes of both Sergeant Kovac and Al Martinez that they knew it, too. But ever since joining the force, Sam had developed a habit of silently, privately, splitting himself down his emotional core, one half Sam-the-cop, the other half Sam-the-man. Right now, Sam-the-man was looking at a child-woman who had just been extracted from hell on earth, and thinking about what she might have endured, and his heart was going out to her.

'Has she spoken?' he asked his father.

'Not really,' David Becket said. 'A word or two, nothing to help you.' He paused, his open, expressive face clearly revealing his dismay. At fifty-six years of age, a paediatrician with a sideline as a volunteer general practitioner on West Flagler Street in downtown Miami, he'd seen more than his fair share of anguish, yet he had never learned to tame the acuteness of his own imagination. His patients suffered from sickness or drug abuse or violence or depression, and David felt their suffering. It was exactly what he had been warned to guard against all those years back in medical school, but it was probably at least part of the reason they flocked to him day after day, night after night, in the hospital and in the 'freebie' clinic he shared with Fred Delano and Joan Melnick. It was also part of the reason his wife Judy, still fretting after all these years, periodically asked him to give up that practice because of its inherent physical and emotional dangers.

'Where did Mrs Dean go?' Sam asked. Anita del Fuego had told them that Cathy Robbins' next-of-kin now was her mother's sister, Frances Dean.

'She's resting in another room,' David answered. 'I gave her something to help her. She stayed with her niece for a while, but one of the nurses saw she was about to crack and got her out of the room.'

'Do you know if Cathy said anything to her?'

'Not as far as I know.'

'How long till we can try talking to her?'

'Hard to say,' David said. 'Who's we?'

Sam heard the caginess and understood it. 'If the aunt agrees, probably me with a counsellor from the Child Assessment Centre.' He saw his father's nose wrinkle in disapproval. 'She's our only witness, Dad. You know we'll be gentle.'

'You're investigating her parents' murders,' David said grimly. 'How gentle can you be?'

Sam gave a small, weary shrug. 'Can I sit with her? I mean just sit.'

'I have no problem with that, so long as it's just sitting.'

'Can't do much more until Mrs Dean gives the okay.' Sam paused. 'I know you'd like us to leave her alone, but it isn't going to happen.'

'I know it.'

'I'll wait as long as I can, Dad.'

'It's her you have to wait for, not me.'

Sam looked back through the glass. 'At least she's not catatonic.'

'At least,' David said wryly.

'How long would you like me to tell the CAC counsellor to wait?'

'I have no idea.' It was David's turn to shrug. 'I never found my mother and father slaughtered in their bed.'

Close up, the girl looked even paler, even more vulnerable. Her blonde hair was still damp at the roots from washing. A tiny speck of dried blood lay, like a final testimony, a horror freckle, at the base of her right ear lobe. Sam restrained his impulse to wipe it away. He looked at her left hand – no traces remained beneath her fingernails. If they had been polished that, too, had been removed, either by the police surgeon or by hospital personnel. Sitting on his hard plastic chair, Sam's mind conjured up pictures of Cathy Robbins' shower, of the unspeakable trauma of having her parents' lifeblood scrubbed off her flesh, and then swiftly, urgently, he pushed the images away. His father was not the only one in their family with a too-vivid imagination; if Sam had not been adopted, he'd have assumed it flowed through their gene pool.

13

'Hi.'

Sam jolted in his chair. Cathy Robbins had opened her eyes and was looking at him. Her eyes were very blue, their pupils dilated, perhaps from the sedative she had been given soon after she'd been found.

'Hello, Cathy.' He didn't ask her how she was feeling, knew it would be both cruel and pointless. 'I'm Detective Sam Becket from the Miami Beach Police Department.'

'Two Beckets,' she said softly.

Nothing too fuzzy there. 'Dr Becket's my dad,' Sam told her.

'How come?' Borderline interested.

It was a question Sam had answered more times than he could count. A natural enough question given that Sam was an African-American and David was a Caucasian Jew. 'Adopted,' Sam said.

'Me, too,' Cathy said, and closed her eyes.

She didn't speak again until late that evening, long after Sam had gone. A nurse was in her room, putting down a jug of fresh water.

'Did it really happen?' Cathy asked her.

The nurse understood what she meant, but everyone had been alerted to be careful about what they said to Cathy Robbins, and so she froze for a second or two, saying nothing.

'Okay,' Cathy said, and shut down again.

CHAPTER THREE

Grace Lucca could not remember the last time she'd felt quite so relaxed, even on a Sunday. Weekends tended to be gentle family affairs for most of her neighbours on the Bay Harbor Islands, the two miniature, self-contained communities that lay between exclusive Bal Harbour and North Miami. A number of the people who lived around Grace were professional men and women with children of various ages. At weekends they pursued civilized amusements; they shopped, barbecued, shot baskets, tinkered with the boats some of them kept moored right outside their backyards.

Grace had a mooring of her own, but though she thought about buying something small someday, she hadn't done so yet. If she had, she doubted she'd find time to do much more than look at it. For one thing, as a child and adolescent psychologist, she seemed to have developed a bad habit of being unable to turn down patients in real need whatever the day or hour, and for another, she was less able than she ought to be to shut down from work.

This particular Sunday had started out differently, though. Both the afternoon appointments Grace had scheduled had been postponed, the weather was especially fine, and she'd woken up feeling remarkably laidback. She'd taken a muffin, juice and coffee back to bed with the *Herald* and *New York Times*, dozed off in the midst of the Travel section, woken up to find that Harry had burrowed right under the covers with her, and then she had gotten up to take a shower, do some overdue laundry and put together a sandwich. Now, a little after one o'clock, she was sharing a *real* Sunday afternoon with Harry, sitting out on their deck, her long legs dangling over the side, bare toes brushing the water. That felt good. The whole package felt good. Doing nothing, just sitting and gazing at the pretty, almost smugly secure Bal Harbour scene across the water.

Harry – a handsome, self-possessed, ten-year-old West Highland terrier – shifted a little, tucked his white-haired compact body closer in against Grace's right thigh, and wagged his stubby tail.

'Is this good or is this *good*?' she asked him

The phone rang.

Grace sighed.

The machine picked up. From the deck, through the screen doors, she heard her own voice asking for name, number and message, then the high-pitched whistle and click as recording began, then a stranger's voice, deep and unfamiliar.

She looked down at Harry. 'Do I go listen or do we go on sitting here?' He snuck in even closer, keeping his little dark eyes on the water, and she fondled his ears. 'I know,' she said. 'But it could be important.'

Harry grunted as she got to her feet and shook the water off her toes. They'd been a good team from the start, Grace and Harry, from their Miami beginnings in the ground-floor beach apartment that they'd escaped from in a hurry after it had gotten invaded by crabs, through the plush, too swanky Miami Beach condo from which Harry had come too perilously close, more than once, to taking a dive from the terrace. But then Grace had found this little house on the island, tucked between two somewhat grander but no lovelier houses, and she and Harry had come home to pure white stone, arched windows, a red, Mediterranean-style tiled roof, their own twin palms and fiery bottle brush tree and, best of all, the deck.

Grace had known right away that the house would work out well, too, as a professional environment, and it had. The parents who brought their children to her and left them in her care appreciated, for the most part, the fact that it looked and felt safe and clean. From her standpoint Grace set great store by comfort and ease, which was why when the weather was fine – as it almost always was in south-east Florida – and unless a patient had some kind of problem with being outdoors, they could sit out in the fresh air on the deck or inside the screening on the lanai – and having Harry around tended to help relax most of the children Grace spent time with. Lord only knew many of them needed all the relaxation she could offer.

The phone message, from a detective of the Miami Beach Police Department, sounded urgent enough for her to return the call right away. The number was for a cellular phone, and Detective Sam Becket picked up after just two rings.

'Detective, this is Grace Lucca. I just got your message.'

'I appreciate your calling back so fast, doctor.' His voice was rich and gentle. He sounded, Grace thought, quite illogically, very unlike a policeman.

'No problem. What can I do for you?'

'My father tells me you have a talent for breaking through to badly traumatized kids.'

'Your father?' Grace tried ransacking her memory.

'Dr David Becket. I believe you've worked together.'

'We sure have.' The craggy face of one of the gentlest paediatricians she knew sprang into Grace's mind, and she smiled into the receiver. 'It's kind of him to have said that about me.' She paused. 'So what's the story, detective?'

Becket filled her in on the Cathy Robbins tragedy.

'Cathy's out of the hospital now,' he told her, rounding off, 'staying with her aunt – her mother's sister – but she still won't talk about what happened.'

'Not surprising, under the circumstances.'

Becket explained that his father, Frances Dean – the aunt – two counsellors from the Child Assessment Centre and a psychologist resident at Miami General had all failed to elicit any response from the young teenager.

'You realize there's no guarantee she'll talk to me either,' Grace pointed out.

'Of course not,' Becket agreed, 'but my father thinks she just might.' He paused. 'We have to find out what she knows.'

'It might not be much,' Grace said.

'Whatever it is, however small, we need to know,' he persisted, sounding more like a cop.

Grace took a moment, glanced down at Harry, on his back

17

on the floor near her feet. Harry liked staying close as much as possible. She wondered, fleetingly, if Cathy Robbins liked dogs.

'Is her aunt okay with this?' she asked the detective.

'She says so.'

'This afternoon too soon?'

'Sooner the better,' Becket answered.

'Any rules about what she tells me?'

Becket took a moment before answering again. 'No rules. This is an unofficial request, Dr Lucca, and I'm making it because no one else has made any headway.'

'You realize that my concern will be for Cathy, not your investigation?'

'I do. But I'm hoping whatever you learn may help us all.'

'So Cathy Robbins is not a suspect?'

'Not at this time,' the detective answered, and Grace knew he was being careful. 'Right now, so far as you're concerned, she's strictly a victim.'

She grabbed a pen from the Donald Duck mug on her desk. 'I'll need an address.'

Becket gave it together with Frances Dean's phone number, and thanked her. Grace wrote down the details, replaced the phone on her desk and looked out of the window. Outside it was still sunny, but the warmth and ease had drained out of her afternoon. She had dealt with victims of rapes and violence and all kinds of terrors, both real and imagined, but this was her first homicide.

Down by her feet, Harry rolled off his back and grumbled.

'You said it,' she agreed.

CHAPTER FOUR

Marie Robbins' widowed sister lived on Granada Boulevard in the heart of Coral Gables, the Spanish-styled city that was one of Dade County's oldest neighbourhoods. It was a single-storey, handsome, grey and white house with shutters at the windows and a front garden lush with palms, banyans, and a pair of beautiful floss silk trees.

Frances Dean looked much as Grace had expected her to. Wrecked. Silver-grey hair that was probably normally elegantly coiffed, was today straggly; what make-up she'd made the effort to apply had been smudged again through weeping. A black dress that might, in better circumstances, have made her look a sleek and quite attractive fifty-some-thing, today gave her a sallow, shrunken appearance. Grace wondered how Mrs Dean had lost her husband. It seemed unlikely that any disease, sudden collapse or accident, however harrowing, could have been quite as shattering a mind and body blow as the one that had now wiped out her sister and brother-in-law.

'Cathy's resting,' Frances Dean said soon after Grace had arrived, offered deep sympathy and been offered, in return, a seat on a soft white couch in her living room. 'Or meant to be.' She shook her head. 'Poor child. I don't think she's really slept, as such, since it happened.'

'How about you?' Grace asked, gently.

'I don't sleep very well at the best of times.' Frances Dean remembered her manners. 'May I bring you some coffee, Dr Lucca?'

'I'd love some.' Grace didn't really want coffee, but she

was aware that any activity, however trivial, was often preferable to the newly bereaved than just sitting and staring. 'If it's not too much trouble?'

'No trouble at all.' She rose from her armchair and walked unsteadily towards the tall, generously proportioned doorway that led to the hallway and, presumably, the kitchen and sleeping areas of the one-storey home. She paused, just short of the door, and turned back.

'Would you like me to fetch Cathy right away, doctor? Or would you prefer to talk to me for a while first?'

'Whichever you prefer,' Grace said. 'Whichever may be easier.' She knew that nothing was easy, nor going to be.

'I'm here, Aunt Frances.'

The voice came from directly behind Mrs Dean, its owner invisible to Grace from where she sat. It was a young voice, soft and even.

Mrs Dean turned around. 'Cathy, honey.' She extended her right hand to touch her niece but – though Grace felt it was probably not a deliberate snub – the girl, wearing a white T-shirt and blue jeans, kept her own arms by her sides and walked around her aunt into the living room.

Grace stood up. Her heart was beating fast and she felt unusually nervous.

'Hello, Cathy,' she said. 'I'm Grace Lucca.'

The girl stopped three feet away. 'The shrink.'

'That's me.' Grace smiled at her.

'They kept sending shrinks to talk to me in the hospital. I didn't feel like talking, so they all went away again.'

'Cathy —' Frances Dean stopped, looking uncomfortable.

Cathy turned her face towards her aunt. 'It's okay, Aunt Frances.' Her tone was kind, as if she felt that the older woman needed more gentle handling than she did. 'I think I'm ready now.' She looked back at Grace. 'Maybe it was the hospital. I just couldn't seem to say anything much there.' She gave a strange, jerky little shrug. 'I tried, but I felt like I was going to choke.'

'And now?' Grace asked.

'I'd like to try.'

It was more than Grace had expected, but she knew that her relief had to be premature.

'I was getting some coffee for Dr Lucca,' Frances Dean said, still over by the doorway. 'Would you like something, Cathy?'

'Uh-uh.' Cathy shook her head. 'No, thank you, Aunt Frances.'

Her aunt left the room. Grace sensed she was glad to escape.

'Shall we sit down in here?' she asked. 'Or would you rather go outside?'

'I'd like to stay here, if that's okay?'

'Of course it is.'

Grace sat first, allowing Cathy the opportunity to choose her distance. Many patients, younger or more mature, liked to sit as far away from her as possible at their first encounter. Cathy chose the other end of the same couch. It seemed to Grace a reserved, but not unconfident action.

'What do I call you?' Cathy asked.

'Whatever you're comfortable with. My name's Grace.'

'Not doctor?'

'Not unless you prefer it.'

'Okay.'

Cathy settled down, tucking her legs under her, and Grace allowed herself a first close look. She was quite lovely, the untouched kind of loveliness that only young teenage girls – very young women – often possess for just a brief time. She was very slender, almost fragile, though her arms looked taut, perhaps well-muscled from sport, and she had long, straight golden hair and clear blue eyes, the left iris flecked with a dot of melanin. It was a pretty, yet somehow bland face, one that, under normal circumstances, Grace might have assumed had yet to be touched by significant life experiences. Given what had happened to Cathy Robbins in the past forty-eight hours, however – whatever, exactly, that was – the psychologist's immediate assumption was that it was the face of someone blocking out, or even concealing, the truth.

Someone. Daughter of slain parents. Witness of unimaginable horror.

'I don't have much to tell you, doctor.'

Grace found that she had, inadvertently, been holding her breath, and exhaled. 'Grace,' she reminded, gently, easily.

'I'm sorry.'

21

'Don't be. It doesn't matter what you call me.' Grace paused. 'Tell me what you can, Cathy.'

'About what happened?'

'If you can. Or how you feel. Whatever you want. Anything.'

'There really isn't much,' she said.

Grace waited. The blue, clear eyes regarded her for a long moment, then turned away and gazed into nothingness. The young lips parted, then closed again. No words came out. Cathy shifted a little, exposing her right forearm. There was a Band-Aid on it.

'Would it help if I asked you some questions?'

'I don't know.' The eyes remained averted. 'Maybe.'

Grace's brain, well trained in the posing of simple, key questions, scrambled and came up blank and oddly panicky. She thought perhaps she'd made the mistake of indulging in satisfaction because Cathy had agreed to try and confide in her, and now she felt afraid of failing the girl.

'I was asleep,' Cathy said suddenly, rescuing her. 'In my room.'

Saved from her own vacuum, Grace came to attention.

'Something woke me.' Cathy frowned, wrinkling her smooth forehead. 'I don't know what.'

'A sound?'

'Maybe. I don't know.' The eyes showed the strain of recall. 'I remember the time. It was just before four. It was still dark.'

Grace heard a stirring from outside the room, looked across and saw Frances Dean standing in the hall, the coffee tray in her hands. For a moment or two, she remained there, indecisive, torn, perhaps, between not wanting to interrupt and wanting – or not – to hear. She turned away, vanished out of sight. If her niece had noticed her, she gave no indication.

'I lay in my bed for a while – I'm not sure how long.' Cathy paused. 'I was scared.' She looked back at Grace. 'Don't you want to know why I felt scared?'

'Do you know why?'

'No.' Cathy swallowed. 'Or I didn't know then, anyway.' She paused again. 'I guess I know now.'

*

She'd said she had little to tell, and Grace supposed that from the Miami Beach Police Department's point-of-view it *was* precious little. From a psychologist's stand-point, however – from Cathy's stand-point – it was everything and more. Too much more.

She said she remembered going into her parents' bedroom and finding them dead. They were already dead, she told Grace, her voice dull, almost a monotone. It was a quality Grace had encountered several times before in badly traumatized patients, as if they felt that by keeping all the feelings and reactions suppressed, jammed down tight, they might be able to keep control of them.

'I don't remember any more after that,' Cathy went on. 'Until Anita woke me up and started screaming.' She looked right at Grace. 'How could I have gone to sleep?' she asked, and for the very first time a glimpse of horror showed through the blandness. 'How did I get into that bed? How did I *do* that?'

Grace saw that she badly needed an answer. It wasn't the first time she'd had none to give a patient crying out for help, but that made it no less painful or frustrating.

'I don't know,' she said.

CHAPTER FIVE

Sam Becket was a surprise to Grace. His father, the doctor, was a middle-aged, stockily built Caucasian Jew of no more than five feet ten who tended to wear even fine clothes as if he'd crawled straight out of bed into them. The detective was at least six-three, African-American, rangy but noticeably powerful even in his conservative dark suit. Intrigued as Grace was, however, origins and family backgrounds were not on the agenda for either her or Becket that afternoon. The late Marie and Arnold Robbins and their daughter were of much more pressing concern.

'It's only a first impression, of course,' Grace said, 'but I think that Cathy may genuinely not know anything that's going to be particularly helpful to your investigation.'

It was just after seven p.m. and she was facing the detective across a file-stacked desk in one corner of the large open-plan office that housed the Person Crimes unit inside the attractive, modern white Miami Beach Police Department building on Washington Avenue in South Beach. It was a small, over-crowded but workmanlike space, its only real colour splashing out of a Florida Grand Opera poster for *Aida*.

'I realize that you're going to have to talk to her yourself again,' she went on, 'and maybe you will get more details from her in time. But as to whether they'll help you find the person who did this, I don't know.'

'At least she's started talking.'

'So far as that goes,' Grace qualified carefully. 'She's still in deep shock.'

'Do you think she's blocking?' Becket asked.

'Of course she is.' Grace took a long look at his lean face, trying to gauge what she was up against, wondering how much she was going to have to spell out. *She's blocking the way her mother looked with her throat cut, or what it felt like to lie down between her butchered parents and to hold their bloody bodies ...*

'How can she not?' Becket asked.

His voice was soft, his dark brown eyes bleak. Policeman or not, maybe he was his father's son after all. Grace let herself relax just a little.

'When will you talk to her again?' she asked. In her ideal world, a victim like Cathy Robbins ought not to have to confront a single police officer unless she elected to, but, not entirely unlike Chicago – Grace Lucca's home town – Miami was a million gruesome miles away from Utopia. She might not like it, but she had to accept that before this was over, Cathy would face any number of inquisitors; so better, perhaps, that she should at least begin with the son of a gentle, caring, clever man.

'Tomorrow,' Becket answered. 'Can't hold off any longer.'

It was still Sunday, but the unit was a fairly busy place. There were three other men coming and going, sometimes working at desks, sometimes speaking to each other, occasionally coming to have a swift word with Becket or simply to drop papers under his nose. In his capacity as lead investigator on the Robbins case, he explained to Grace, it was vital that every grain of gathered information should come to him as soon as possible, and although it was only Day Three of the investigation, tension was clearly visible in his eyes and in the frown lines creasing his forehead. Still, busy as he was, Detective Becket still seemed ready to fetch coffee for the two of them and to tell Grace all that – and more than – she wanted to know about the murders.

The actual weapon, he said in strict confidence, had not yet been found, but Marie and Arnold had both been slain with a fine, acutely sharp blade that the ME had immediately suspected of being some kind of scalpel. A search of the house on Pine Tree Drive had subsequently yielded an old, hand-stitched, purpose-made leather pouch containing an equally old and quite valuable set of hallmarked solid silver surgical instruments, each in its own separate stitched narrow compartment – with one compartment empty. According to Frances Dean, the instruments were a family heirloom left to Cathy by her late father, Marie's first husband.

'Was he a surgeon?' Grace asked.

'A physician,' Becket answered, 'but his father was a surgeon.'

'So if the missing scalpel was the weapon,' she mused, 'the murderer might have known about the pouch?'

'It's a possibility. The house wasn't ransacked. We don't feel there was anything random about the killings.'

'But you said there was a break-in?' Becket had said something earlier on the telephone about a forced window at the rear of the house.

'Maybe,' he said now.

Grace looked across the desk, querying.

'That was how it looked.'

'So what's changed?' She saw indecision in his expression. 'Is this information you can't share with me?' She gave him a second or two. 'I do understand, detective, but you must realize that confidentiality gets a pretty high rating in my line of work, too.'

Becket studied her for a moment before making up his mind. 'The crime-scene people think the window may have been broken from inside the house.'

Grace waited again. He offered nothing more, but the implication seemed perfectly clear to her.

'You think someone wanted it to look as if it was broken from outside?'

'It's a possibility,' he said again. 'Though if that was the intent, they did a poor job.'

'Mightn't it have been broken before?' Grace asked. 'In the past?'

'It might,' he said. 'It might also be unconnected.'

'What does the housekeeper say?'

'Mrs del Fuego says she has no knowledge of the window being broken before Thursday, but she can't be sure because it's not a room she went into every day.'

Grace thought about Anita del Fuego and the impact of

coming suddenly upon that kind of mayhem. 'How's she doing?'

'Coping,' Becket said.

'That's a word I mistrust,' Grace said. 'I hear it all the time.'

'Still, coping's what people do, isn't it?' the detective asked her. 'They cope – they get by. They survive.'

'Of course.' She gave a small grimace. 'They also bottle up nightmares, wall themselves up.'

'Storing up problems for the future,' he said.

They were both silent for a moment.

'Cathy looks like she's coping,' Grace said, 'but we both know she isn't. She can't be. It isn't possible.' She noticed suddenly that Becket was looking at her intently, and she bristled slightly. 'Do I have a smudge on my face?'

'I'm sorry.' He paused. 'It's just the similarity.'

'I don't understand.'

'Between you and Cathy Robbins.' He saw her startled expression. 'You're really quite alike, physically, Dr Lucca.'

'Are we?' Grace said coolly. 'I didn't notice. Looks were not uppermost in my mind when I was talking to Cathy.'

'No, I don't imagine they were,' Becket said. 'I'm sorry.'

Grace had learned the tough way, as had many of her professional contemporaries, to slap down references to her appearance by colleagues, male or female. Her own blue eyes and straight blonde hair were certainly irrelevant here, yet Cathy's fairness and fragility were clear in her mind; and with them, overriding the youthful femininity, the absence of character-defining features that had troubled Grace briefly when she'd met the teenager. She knew from photographs that her own face, even as a young child, had already testified to her personality, and it had taken her years of practice to learn to mask private feelings or reactions that were better kept within. Cathy Robbins' face was a little like a poorly executed portrait; pretty but too blank. Grace thought it might be symptomatic of the effects of her desolation, like an empty wasteland left by a bomb strike, but it was much too soon to be sure of that.

'The window,' she said abruptly, bringing herself back to the police findings. 'Do you really think it might be an inside job?'

27

'We have to consider it.' Becket was careful again.

'The housekeeper?'

'With her mother and children until she left for work. We're checking.'

'Who else has keys to the house?'

'The aunt – Mrs Dean.'

Grace was sceptical. 'Marie Robbins' sister?'

'She knew about the surgical instruments,' Becket said.

Grace thought about the bereft woman. 'I don't think so.'

Becket waited a moment. 'What about the girl?' he asked, quietly.

Grace's head went up sharply. 'What about her?'

'What were your first impressions of her? Generally.'

The surge of anger she felt startled Grace. 'No way,' she said. 'No *way*.'

'It's another possibility,' Becket said, remaining quiet. 'The instruments belong to her.'

'Only because they were left to her.' Grace reminded herself that it was obvious that Cathy would need to be ruled out as a suspect, and that the detective was just doing his job. 'If I'm any judge,' she said, trying to stay calm, 'Cathy's involvement is purely as victim, nothing more sinister.' There was a knot tightening in her stomach. 'She's a traumatized, grieving adolescent, Detective Becket, not a killer.'

'Do you know how many killings are attributed to fourteen-year-old girls in this country these days, especially stabbings?' Becket wasn't scoring points. He looked the way he felt. Sad. Sick at heart.

Anger and dismay gave way to sudden suspicion. 'When did you learn about the window?' Grace enquired.

Becket understood her meaning instantly. 'After I asked you to meet with Cathy, Dr Lucca.'

Grace had no choice but to accept what he said, but felt compelled to go on in the teenager's defence. 'She's very fragile.'

'Emotionally, of course.'

'Meaning?'

'I noticed a number of school trophies in the house. For running.' The detective paused. 'Not that physical strength necessarily played a great part in these killings. Marie and

Arnold Robbins both took sleeping tablets before they retired on Thursday night – they'd have been in no condition to fight.'

'Oh God.' Grace tried not to picture the possible scene.

'If it's any consolation,' Becket told her, 'my own instincts are with yours.'

'You don't believe Cathy did it either.'

Becket shrugged. 'One of my problems is I never want to suspect a young person – especially not a kid as patently vulnerable as this. But you must have come across your share of violent adolescents, doctor – you know as well as I do that kids can kill.'

'Of course I know,' Grace said, more heatedly than she meant to. 'On the streets, with knives and guns and broken bottles and stolen cars.' She fought to sound logical. 'But with a *scalpel*? Have you ever come across a fourteen-year-old girl who's taken a surgical instrument and sliced her parents' throats?' She looked across at the detective, trying to read him again, to imagine the paternal influences of David Becket, wise, kindly paediatrician, on this powerful-looking street cop. 'What does your father say about this?'

'We haven't talked since Cathy was discharged from the hospital, but I'm sure if he were here listening, he'd be in complete agreement with you.' Becket looked around the room, which had, for the moment, emptied out. His face was very grim. 'But then, the idea of the child-woman parent killer isn't an image my father would find easy to conjure up.'

They were both silent again for a moment. A telephone rang on another desk, then stopped.

'You said you haven't found the weapon yet?' Grace asked.

'Not yet.'

'Was there any physical evidence taken from Cathy?'

'Sure. But given the circumstances, I wouldn't expect to find anything either way. They were parents and child – prints, fibres, hairs, skin traces would have been all over each other, all over the house.'

'And she must have been covered with their blood,' Grace said quietly.

'Yes,' Becket said.

*

29

Grace went home, fed Harry, made herself a bowl of pasta and sat in front of the TV, staring at, but not really seeing, what was on the screen.

There was one thing she did keep on seeing, in her mind's eye, over and over again, a small, nagging, trivial thing like a smudge of dirt on a pair of sunglasses that only went away completely when one got around to cleaning the lens.

The Band-Aid on Cathy Robbins' arm.

It hadn't just come back to Grace since getting home. She'd thought about it more than once during her meeting with Becket, had wanted to ask if he knew what lay beneath the sticking plaster – had wanted the assurance that it was not a cut that might have been inflicted with a scalpel. But the fact was she hadn't dared ask.

Which seemed to her now to indicate that she was taking sides. Which was bad news, unprofessional news under the circumstances. She was not, after all, even Cathy's psychologist. Neither the girl nor her aunt had approached her – the introduction had been effected unofficially by a third party.

Yet by not asking Detective Becket about that Band-Aid, Grace knew she was already withholding the seedling of a suspicion.

Why? The answer was simple.

Because Cathy Robbins had touched her.

Which meant that Grace was going to have to be careful. Stand back a little.

Becket had said that she and Cathy were physically alike. Grace wondered now if she herself had, perhaps subconsciously, noted a resemblance between the teenager and her own Nordic-rooted looks inherited from her mother. She wondered if that superficial link had perhaps evoked echoes of her own troubled childhood; wondered if all that had, somehow, impacted on her in some way, perhaps even tilting her objectivity a little.

Surely not. She hoped not.

But a small warning voice in her mind was already making her wish that Becket's father had not suggested his son call her. That she had never heard of Cathy Robbins.

CHAPTER SIX

MONDAY, APRIL 6, 1998

It was past midnight when Sam got back to his South Beach home a few short blocks from the police department – the close-to-miraculous apartment he'd managed to acquire four years earlier in a deal that had raised a few eyebrows at work, but which no one had ever suggested was anything other than the kind of dumb luck any one of them might have hoped for.

The building he lived in was a pink-and-white curvy Art Deco guest house on Collins Avenue between Ninth and Tenth Streets. Sam had passed it often enough without a second glance since joining the department, but his first close encounter had come about when an old college friend now living in New York City had taken a room there. Sam had paid a visit and gotten into conversation with the owner, a guy who'd known better times. It seemed the roof was in bad shape and the whole top floor, and the only real question was whether he was going to go under financially before the authorities closed him down. Sam had fallen in love with the place, and had made a deal whereby he had agreed to take care of the renovations and make the building passable for the inspectors, provided the whole floor – along with the roof – became his private, permanent home.

Taking an ice-cold beer and the still-hot dish of conch-filled tamale he'd picked up on the way back, Sam headed up to the roof now. It was still not much more than a small square of concrete, cluttered by a cooling tank, satellite dish and pipes, yet it was his favourite place for hanging out and unwinding at night. Lit by glints of neon and starlight, removed from the tourist hustle that spread out nightly from Ocean Drive, it was also his number one rehearsal venue. A borderline opera fanatic, Sam possessed a rich enough baritone to get him regular leading roles with S-BOP – the South Beach Opera – a local group of more than adequately gifted enthusiasts. Any day now, the guys were going to be holding auditions for their summer production of *Il Trovatore*, and Sam was just itching to get his teeth into the part of the Count di Luna – always providing, of course, that the others were prepared to go on tolerating his frequent no-shows. It was a measure of their respect for his voice and his passion, he supposed, that they had put up with an unreliable black cop singing traditionally white roles for so long – that, and the weird-but-true fact that Sam knew most of the baritone roles written by Verdi, Puccini, Mozart, Wagner and even Gounod, off by heart – even weirder given that the only foreign language he actually *spoke* with any fluency was Spanish.

He was taking his first bite of tamale when his phone rang. He could hear it through the open trapdoor that led from the fire stairs to the roof.

It rang four times before his machine picked up – he already knew that it wasn't likely to be work, because his pager was still in his pocket. A minute later it rang again, for two rings this time, then stopped. And began again.

Ma was the only person who did that, the only person who knew that if Sam was there – even if he was dead on or off his feet, or up on the roof, or in the shower or, if he was damned lucky, in bed with a lady (when had *that* last happened, by the way?) – her simply coded rings would drag him to the phone sure as a hand on his collar.

He looked at the tamale and at the beer, then tilted up his face and grabbed a swift fix of Miami night sky, determined to relax.

Why in hell was his mother calling after midnight?

Sam was up on his feet and down the stairs and back in his living room in about five seconds flat. He played back the last message.

'It's after midnight, Samuel Becket, so where are you?'

Accusing, like only Judy Becket knew how to be. Her adopted son might be thirty-four years old, six foot three and a police detective, but she still figured she ought to be informed of his whereabouts after the witching hour.

'This is your mother.'

Sam grinned at the machine.

'If you get home anytime before three, call me. Don't worry about waking me because I can't sleep, and don't worry about waking your father because I turned off the bell in our room.'

Dad hated her doing that in case a patient needed him.

'And don't worry – I'll turn it on again when I go to bed.'

Meaningful pause.

'Which I won't do till I hear from you.'

The message ended. Newly alarmed, Sam punched out the number. Judy Becket picked up on the first ring.

'Ma? What's wrong?'

'What should be wrong?' Cool as a cucumber.

'Ma, you just left a message saying—'

'So you were there,' she pounced on him.

'I just got in,' Sam defended.

'Very convenient.'

'Ma, what's the matter? Telling me to call any time up till three in the morning – you almost gave me a heart attack.' He paused. 'Is Dad all right?'

'Your father's fine – it's me you should be worried about.'

'Why? Ma, *why*?'

'Making me stay up half the night.'

Sam's worry dissipated instantly. 'What do you want, Ma?'

'I need to know about Friday.'

'Friday?' He was momentarily confused. The coming weekend was Easter, which meant they were four days from Good Friday, but liberal as his mother was, he felt sure she wasn't referring to that. Yet in the more than fifteen years since he'd left home, during which time he'd gotten married, become a father and gotten divorced, he couldn't recall the Jewish Sabbath ever being a big issue with his parents.

'You've forgotten.'

'Apparently. What's happening on Friday?'

'Just a little thing like Passover,' Judy said, 'nothing important.'

Sam winced. 'Seder night.'

'Bingo,' his mother said. 'Give the boy a prize.'

'I don't know if I can make it Friday.' He steeled himself.

'Why doesn't that surprise me?' Sardonic.

'You know how it is, Ma.'

'I should do by now.' A pause. 'And I wouldn't be making such a fuss if it mightn't be the last chance for us all to get together before Saul's barmitzvah.'

'Saul's barmitzvah's almost a month away, Ma.'

'But he's reading the Four Questions on Friday night.'

'He always reads the Four Questions.'

'This is different,' Judy Becket insisted. 'He wants you to be here to hear him, give him confidence.'

'Saul has plenty of confidence.'

'You haven't seen him lately. He's nervous, Sam.'

'That's normal, Ma. Everyone gets nervous before their barmitzvah.'

'You didn't.'

'Sure I did.'

'So will you come?'

She always did that to him, let him think she'd moved away from a topic, then veered suddenly back, nailing him.

'I'll try, Ma.'

'You know how important Pesach is to your father.' Another tack.

'Of course I know,' Sam said, fighting to stay patient, 'but I'm dealing with a double homicide right now, and a young girl's been orphaned, and Dad knows all about her, just ask him – so chances are I may not get to you till late on Friday.'

'Can't you —?'

It was time to hang tough, so he rode straight over her. 'But I'll try to make it in time for the after-dinner singing, okay?' He paused, taking in the disapproving silence. 'Okay, Ma?'

'Okay.' There was a shrug in the word.

'Will you go to bed now?'

'I'll go to bed, but I don't suppose I'll sleep.'

'Then at least you'll rest.' He remembered something. 'Would you tell Dad in the morning that I met with Dr Lucca?'

'That's the child psychologist, isn't it?' Judy asked.

'Uh-huh. Tell Dad I liked her.' He paused again. 'And don't forget to switch the phone back on in the bedroom, Ma.'

'I've been a doctor's wife for twenty-eight years, Samuel

34

Lincoln Becket, and I still have all my faculties, thank you very much.'

Sam smiled into the phone.

'Good night, Ma.'

He went back to the roof. The tamale was cold, so he drank the rest of the beer and lay down on the beach lounger he often used as a bed on warm nights. He loved this semi-dark, this living, breathing night, felt less lonely up here than down in his far more comfortable, air-conditioned, but oh-so-empty bedroom.

He stared up into the neon-and-star canopy and thought about Cathy Robbins and all the horror she'd woken up to that early morning, and then he thought about Dr Grace Lucca and the small shock of *something* that had stirred him when she'd first walked into the department. All that Scandinavian poise and cool balanced out so well – so *damned* well – with something much warmer lurking underneath the surface. And calm, too, even in the midst of her outrage. That was, he supposed, what made her the good child psychologist his dad said she was.

Sam went on night-sky-staring and let the day slip away, let himself think, instead, about the woman who had become his mother so many years ago, about the many parts of her. That little show of archetypical Jewish mom belonged to the genuine chicken-soup side of her, the side that had wept right through his barmitzvah and graduation, but it wasn't the real Judy Becket, not the one kept carefully tucked out of sight for the most part, emerging only in redoubtable splendour at times of need. The one who had kept a constant iron vigil at his ICU bedside after he'd been shot for the first time, not shedding a single tear until he was off the critical list. The one who had, above everyone – even David, his beloved adoptive father – refused to let him go under when Sampson had died and Althea had blamed him for their loss. Judy Becket was a strange, remarkable woman in so many ways. It was only in untroubled times that she allowed herself to wear the mantle of fretful mother, and even if she was a *nudnik* at times, Sam loved and respected her all the more.

The pain of that greatest of all losses was still with him, would never go away, not if he lived five hundred years, but the loneliness seldom really troubled him now. He filled his life to bursting – with work, mostly, and family, and, when time allowed, with opera – so it was only on those nights when he couldn't get to sleep in his empty bed that it drove its awful, nagging ache into his bones. And it wasn't much to do with not having a woman beside him – Lord knew he'd experienced loneliness of a different kind often enough with Althea lying stiffly awake, an inch or two away in physical terms, but a thousand spiritual miles apart. It was missing Sampson. It was the absence of a child – of his son – in his home. That small, light, compact body whose physical warmth and whose spirit, even in sleep, had seemed to heat Sam Becket right through to his core.

Loss. It wasn't the word for being deprived of Sampson Becket.

Maybe the word just hadn't been invented.

CHAPTER SEVEN

Grace had just returned from an emergency session with an eight-year-old assault victim when Sam Becket called again.

'I spent the morning at Frances Dean's house.'

'And?' She felt the tension rise inside herself.

'And nothing.'

'I can't say I'm surprised,' Grace said.

'Me neither.' Becket sounded tired.

'What's up?' she asked.

'Nothing. Unless you like making a bereaved sister feel like a suspect.'

'How was Cathy?'

'In bad shape.' Becket paused. 'Would you see her again?'

'Does she want to see me?'

'Her aunt seems to think so.'

Grace took no more than a moment.

'Then of course I'll see her.'

She worried as she drove over the MacArthur Causeway on her way to Coral Gables. There was nothing too unusual about that; she always worried in the early stages of dealing with traumatized youngsters, and it was a soundly based, perfectly rational fear. The fear that no matter how gently she went about her business, she might end up just stirring the pot, forcing the terrors clinging to the bottom and sides up to the surface too soon, whereas maybe if she left things alone, the stew might taste duller for a time, but at least it might still be edible. Grace might have pulled up Detective Becket for talking about 'coping' the day before, might have pointed out

37

the dangers of blocking, but there were times, she knew, when a certain amount of suppression of agony was just what helped drag a human being through a crisis.

She had to accept that, because she had done it herself. Grace had suppressed and blocked and blanked out and 'coped', *and* survived – and emerged with a life more than worth living.

Nothing looked any different in Frances Dean's tidy, elegant living room, but the woman herself looked ten times worse than she had less than twenty-four hours earlier.

'The police won't leave us alone,' she told Grace, keeping her tremulous voice low so that her niece might not hear. 'They were here all morning, searching the house.' Her grey-blue eyes widened. 'Searching my home, as if I might have something to hide. Marie was my sister, for the love of God – my *sister.*'

'It's just routine,' Grace told her gently. 'Loss of privacy's one of the terrible things about this kind of investigation, Mrs Dean. The police don't have any choice – they have to examine every detail.'

'What sort of detail?' the other woman protested, twisting the lace handkerchief in her hands. 'Marie and Arnold were murdered in *their* house, not mine – in their *bed* —' She made a small, trembling, reflexive gesture with her right hand that might, Grace thought but was not certain, have been a signing of the cross. 'They think I might have killed them, don't they?' She stared wildly at the psychologist. 'They do think that, don't they?'

'No, they don't.' Grace spoke decisively. 'I've talked to Detective Becket, and I know he doesn't think anything of the kind. It's normal procedure, as I said. You and Cathy are the closest surviving relatives, and she was in the house when it happened – they have to go through these motions.'

'It's going to be too much for her,' Frances Dean said, abruptly. 'I'm afraid it's going to break her.' She shook her head desolately. 'It's so unfair. All those years of misery her mother and she had to —'

She stopped, clearly regretting her words. Grace waited a moment for her to go on, but it was obvious she'd clammed up. 'What misery?' she prompted, very gently.

Another shake of the head. 'Too much to tell. Too much, and irrelevant anyway.' The older woman's chin came up a little and she looked directly into Grace's face. 'I woke up last night, late – I guess I must have slept a while for once —' Her voice grew even more hushed. 'I woke up and Cathy was standing next to my bed looking down at me. She didn't say anything, she wasn't crying, she just stood there and stared – not really *at* me, more *into* me, if that makes any kind of sense?'

Grace nodded, said nothing.

'The child is almost destroyed,' Frances Dean went on, quietly but desperately, 'and if those people keep on coming back and trying to make her go over it and over it, I don't know what —'

She stopped, suddenly, her face turning towards the doorway, and Grace, too, heard the soft tread of Cathy approaching. Swiftly, she reached out and touched Mrs Dean's hand. 'Any time you want to talk.'

Cathy came in. She was wearing jeans again, with a loose-fitting white cotton blouse and loafers.

'Hello, Dr Lucca.' She paused. 'Grace.'

Grace smiled up at her. 'Hello, Cathy.'

The girl's aunt stood up. 'I'll leave you to talk.'

Cathy stayed where she was.

'Would you mind if we went for a walk, Grace?'

'I'd like that,' Grace said.

Cathy looked towards her aunt. 'You don't mind, do you, Aunt Frances?'

Frances Dean managed a small smile. 'Why would I mind? A little fresh air might do you some good. We were going to go out this morning,' she explained to Grace, 'but then the police came.'

They walked along Granada Boulevard, strolling, taking their time, passing the big, handsome houses and their exotic gardens, made a left on to Coral Way and then turned on to the path that ran beside the Coral Gables Country Club. It was warm and balmy; just ahead of them a pair of cyclists were wheeling their bikes along the road, and on one of the grey concrete tennis courts two couples were playing and laughing.

It was a normality that felt oddly out of reach even to Grace. Cathy walked in a calm enough straight line, her arms swinging a little, her hair loose around her shoulders, her face betraying nothing, but it wasn't hard to sense the wall of horror that moved with the teenager everywhere she went.

'I can't seem to escape,' she said, still walking, not pausing or looking at Grace. 'I do all the things I have to do – I try to eat what my aunt puts in front of me, and I go to the bathroom, and I go to bed and sleep some, and then I get up and it all starts again. But none of it feels like me doing it.'

Grace just walked and listened.

'Detective Becket asked me again if I could remember anything else, but I told him I can't.' Cathy stopped. 'I told him I want to remember, but that's a lie. I don't want to remember anything more, if there is anything.' Her pupils dilated, darkening her eyes. 'I get flashes about what I saw.'

'Flashbacks, you mean?' Grace asked.

'Not really,' Cathy said. 'They're faster than that. Over and gone before I even know what they were.' She shrugged. 'It's not just because of what happened to my parents. I've had them for years.'

Grace remembered what her aunt had said inside – something about years of misery for Marie and Cathy.

'The flashes,' she said, carefully. 'What are they like?'

Cathy shook her head. 'They're nothing.'

She stopped talking and began walking again, faster now, and beside her Grace increased her stride to keep up. Abruptly, Cathy turned and crossed the narrow road without looking, and a young man rollerblading had to swerve to avoid hitting her. He called out to her angrily, but she didn't appear to notice. Grace paused to cross more cautiously, then quickened her pace again to catch up.

'I'm sorry,' Cathy said, not slowing.

'No problem.'

'It's good to be outside,' Cathy said, then stopped walking again. 'I'd like to run, Grace. Would you mind if I ran? I know I can't run away, but I feel as if it might help.' Her eyes were very blue in the sunlight, very intense. 'Would you mind?'

'I think it's a good idea,' Grace said, easily. 'Want me to come along, or do you want to run alone?'

'Alone. If that's okay?'

'Sure it's okay. Mind if I wait for you here?' Grace nodded towards the edge of the golf course beside them. 'I'd be glad to sit down for a while.'

'You're very nice,' Cathy said, and then, as an after-thought, added: 'I'll be more careful – I won't get knocked down or anything.'

'Go run,' Grace said.

She watched the teenager run to the end of the road, then, as she disappeared from view, forced herself to sit down on the grass and try to relax. Grace was aware that there was some risk in what she was doing – that for all she knew, Cathy Robbins might just keep on running and not come back. But at the same time, Grace also realized that Cathy desperately needed the release and, perhaps, the simple freedom. And even though she was right in saying that there was no escape, and even though it was perfectly true that there could be no escape from her nightmare for Cathy Robbins for a very long time, there was probably less harm in trying for a quick burst of freedom than in just sitting and letting it all roll over her.

She came back, cheeks flushed, breathless, at least physically better for the exercise. 'That felt good,' she said, stretching out her muscles. 'Thank you.'

'I didn't do anything,' Grace said.

'You let me go without making a fuss. I might have done anything – I might have run straight under a bus.'

'You told me you wouldn't.'

'And you trusted me.'

They headed back to her aunt's place at a comfortable pace, neither of them saying much. Grace wasn't about to push Cathy into disclosing anything she was reluctant to, not at that time, anyway, though she did ask her, before they parted, if Cathy wanted to see her again.

'I don't mind,' she said.

'Just to talk,' Grace told her easily, 'about anything you want to.'

'I don't want to talk about what happened.'

'That's okay. We wouldn't need to. You could come to my house. We could talk about your mother, if you felt you

41

wanted to – we could talk about good, happy times.' Grace paused. 'You could tell me some more about those flashes.'

'They're nothing,' Cathy said, as she had when she'd mentioned them earlier, but her eyes veered away as she said it.

'I get them, too,' Grace told her. 'At least, I think I probably get something similar. I think of mine as snapshots – they come and go very fast, but they're quite clear.'

Cathy shook her head. 'Not mine.'

Grace gave a swift, easy shrug. 'Maybe they're not so similar.'

The girl looked at her for a moment. 'I think I would like to talk to you some more, Grace. If you don't mind.'

'I wouldn't have suggested it if I did.'

'If I do come,' Cathy said, cautiously, 'I don't have to talk about stuff I don't want to, do I?'

'That's what I said.'

'Only I went to a therapist once before.' She paused. 'I didn't like her much.' She was still watchful. 'I didn't feel I could trust her.'

'It happens,' Grace said.

'She's very intuitive,' Grace told Sam Becket later on the phone.

'I noticed that, too,' he said. 'Any progress?'

'Not the kind you're hoping for.'

'Pity.'

'How about your end?'

Grace could almost hear Becket considering his words.

'Our people have analysed some ashes we found in the Robbins' garbage incinerator,' he said, finally. 'Apparently they may have been from a fabric similar to the nightgown Cathy was wearing when she was found with her parents.'

'Which means what?' Grace had a bad feeling.

'I'm not convinced it means anything at all, except that someone in the household burned some voile fabric, and obviously we're going to be trying to find out who that was, and why they did it.' Becket paused. 'But one theory on the squad is that Cathy might have stabbed her parents, burned the nightgown she was wearing, then showered and put on a fresh gown before lying down with Marie and Arnold and waiting for the housekeeper to arrive.' He heard the shocked heaviness in Grace's silence. 'Personally, I think the theory's full of holes.'

'Glad to hear it.' Grace knew she sounded stiff. 'None of it rings true to me.'

'I didn't think it would,' Becket said.

Uncertain if that was a slight or encouragement, she went on. 'I've spent a little more time with Cathy now, and everything I've observed to date convinces me that she's a sad, bewildered, haunted child who loved her mother and stepfather.'

'Actually,' Becket said, 'Arnold Robbins adopted Cathy.' He paused. 'Has she talked about her relationship with them?'

'No, not really. No protestations of love or devotion. It's all too deep, too real for that. Cathy Robbins doesn't seem to have any idea that she has to prove her love for her parents.'

'Any chance she might just be a fine actress?'

Grace bit down the urge to answer sharply. 'If my instincts are at all sound,' she answered steadily, 'the Cathy I was with this afternoon was not play-acting.'

'Let's both hope your instincts are very sound,' Becket said, quietly.

CHAPTER EIGHT

TUESDAY, APRIL 7, 1998

Cathy arrived at Grace's house just before a quarter to three in the afternoon, it having been arranged with Frances Dean that she would come in a cab, and that her aunt would come to collect her at four.

'I'm sorry to be early,' Cathy said at the front door. She was unsmiling, her eyes and mouth betraying her nervousness.

'No problem.' Grace kept her voice low, mindful of the twelve-year-old boy waiting for her. She'd left him out on the deck with Harry, but he was an inquisitive child with a tendency to wander around and, almost certainly, to eavesdrop. 'If you don't mind waiting, I'll try not to be too long.'

Grace drew Cathy through the entrance hall and into the den, a cosy room lined with books, photographs and paintings by former child patients, most of them colourful and hope-bringing. 'I shouldn't be more than fifteen minutes. Will you be all right in here?'

Cathy was already looking at one of Grace's favourite paintings, of a vivid red balloon floating free in a pure blue sky, only a white dove for company.

'I'll be fine,' she said, not looking away from the painting.

Grace closed the door quietly, and left her.

The twelve year old collected by his mother and his case notes filed away, Grace grabbed a dish of cookies from the larder and a jug of juice from the refrigerator, and, with Harry trotting alongside, took Cathy out to the lanai.

'We can go out on the deck if you prefer,' she told the teenager, 'but this is more comfortable.'

44

'This is fine,' Cathy agreed. 'And no bugs.'

They sat on a pair of shabby old cane chairs, made bright and welcoming by blue and white cushions, the cane itself scuffed and bowed by scores of restless young bodies and feet and all the more homely for the abuse. Harry, having investigated the new visitor and been duly ruffled and scratched between the ears, came and lay down, as usual, at his mistress's feet.

'He's a cool dog,' Cathy said.

'Yes, he is.'

'I've never had a dog.'

'Would you have liked one?'

'I don't know,' she said. 'I guess.' She paused. 'I can't imagine Aunt Frances having a dog in her place.'

Grace smiled. 'It is immaculate.'

They sat awhile. Cathy drank some juice and nibbled at a cookie. A crumb fell to the side of her chair. Harry stood up, went over and licked it up. Cathy looked to Grace for assent, then dropped the rest of the cookie. Harry-the-Hoover made short work of it, then lay down beside Cathy.

'You're in,' Grace said.

'What kind of dog is he?' Cathy asked.

'A West Highland Terrier.' Grace paused. 'So, is there something you'd like to talk about, Cathy?' Starting out was difficult with many patients, but with children it tended to be tougher, given that none of them ever saw her for the first time entirely of their own volition.

'I don't know,' Cathy said.

'How are you feeling?'

She shrugged. 'Oh, you know.'

'Not really.'

'How would you feel?'

'I don't know,' Grace said.

'If your parents were murdered, and you found their bodies,' Cathy responded with a degree of hostility, 'how would you feel?'

It seemed a perfectly normal reaction to Grace. She'd often felt, when she asked those first awkward questions in her effort to start the ball rolling, that she sounded too much like those news reporters who badgered people after hideous tragedies.

45

She decided to answer honestly. 'I don't get along with my parents.'

'Oh.' Cathy digested that. 'Would that make it better or worse?'

Grace shook her head. 'Hard to say.' She paused. 'Hope I never find out.'

'Me, too,' Cathy said.

They sat quietly for another minute.

'I got on great with Mom and Arnie.' Cathy's voice was softer.

'I'm glad,' Grace said.

'Me, too,' Cathy said again.

Grace let her take her time. Her head was down, so it was impossible to see her eyes, but she was chewing her lower lip.

'I can't believe it's happened,' she said after a few moments. 'I mean, I was there – I saw them.' She stopped again and swallowed hard. 'I keep waiting for them to come and get me from Aunt Frances' place. I hear cars stopping outside, and I go to the window, and I keep expecting to see my mom.' She looked up, and her eyes were bright with tears.

Grace said nothing, just pulled out a bunch of tissues from the box on the cane table between them, and gave them to her. A shrink couldn't function without a clock and a box of Kleenex, one of her first tutors had told her. Grace had never found it easy to follow the timer on the table routine; she understood its use, but personally found it offensive and intrusive. Which didn't mean, of course, that she didn't keep a close eye on time when with a patient. Time control had many functions, after all, one of them being that the end of a session – and the note-making that followed it – was supposed to spell a temporary end to her own involvement in a patient's world. Healthy and essential and undoubtedly sensible, Grace accepted, but as was the case for many of her colleagues, that ending was often an illusion for her.

'Do you want to talk about your mother, Cathy?'

Cathy shook her head.

'It might help,' Grace said.

'Might it?' The teenager sounded doubtful.

'It helps some people.'

'I'm not going to forget Mom,' Cathy said.

'I'm sure you won't,'

'Or Arnie.'

'He was your adopted father, wasn't he?'

'Yes, he was.' Cathy paused. 'I called him Arnie because —'

Grace waited a moment before prompting. 'Because?'

Cathy licked her lips. 'Because I didn't want to call him Dad or anything, because of my first father.'

'Your first father died, too, didn't he?'

Cathy nodded. 'A long time ago.'

'How old were you?'

'Five.'

'Do you remember him?'

'Not really.'

Grace watched her. 'You mentioned flashbacks, Cathy.'

She shifted in her chair uneasily.

'Are you uncomfortable talking about that?'

'Yes.'

'We don't have to, if you don't want to.'

'Okay.'

'Maybe another time.'

'Maybe.'

Cathy picked up her glass of juice, and Harry, down by her side, sat up, poised for action if she took another cookie.

'Can I give him some more?' she asked.

'So long as you have some too.'

Grace watched Cathy break up a Pepperidge Farm Brownie, eat one small fragment, then pass the rest to Harry a piece at a time. She was gentle with him, didn't tease him with it. Grace always paid attention to the way young people were around animals.

'Are you finding it hard to eat?' she asked, after a while.

'A little, I guess.'

'It's a normal reaction,' Grace said, 'though some people react to grief by eating nonstop.'

'Aunt Frances keeps telling me I'm going to get anorexic.' Cathy pulled a disparaging face. 'But she's not eating any more than I am.'

'You should both stick to easy things. I always find sandwiches are easier than real food when I'm churned up.'

Cathy seemed about to speak, then hesitated.

'What did you want to say?' Grace asked.

'You said – yesterday, when we were out walking ... You said you had flashes, too.' Cathy paused. 'You said you called them snapshots.'

'Because that's the way they seem to me.'

Cathy was wary, feeling her way. 'Did something bad happen to you, Grace? Is that why you get them?'

She answered steadily. 'My childhood wasn't easy. I'm okay now, but I guess we all carry our past around with us in different ways.'

'I hate mine,' Cathy said. 'My flashes, I mean.'

Grace noted the swift clarification, made lest she thought Cathy might be referring to her own childhood. She'd mentioned yesterday that she'd suffered from them for years. That, combined with what Frances Dean had said about her past, made Grace itch to try taking her back, but she knew she was going to have to take this slowly. Cathy Robbins wanted to talk, that much she was pretty certain about, but it was going to have to be in her own time.

'The police came to my aunt's house again,' she said, suddenly.

That startled Grace. 'When?' Becket hadn't said anything yesterday about plans to go back.

'This morning,' Cathy answered.

'What did they want?'

'They asked us a lot of questions.' Cathy paused. 'Aunt Frances got real upset. She told them to leave me alone.'

'You aunt wants to protect you.'

'I know. Detective Becket said I could go, but I heard Aunt Frances tell him it was monstrous for them to be treating me like a suspect.' Cathy looked down at Harry, fondled his ears. 'I guess I shouldn't have been listening.'

'I don't blame you,' Grace told her. 'I don't like it when people talk about me behind my back.'

Cathy looked back up at her again. 'You don't think they do suspect me, do you, Grace?' Her voice was deceptively soft, but the plea was clear behind her eyes. 'You don't think anyone thinks I could do something like that, do you?'

'I doubt it very much.' Grace was determined to be straight.

'I didn't really get why my aunt was so upset,' Cathy went

48

on. 'I mean, I thought Detective Becket was being nice, but she just got more and more uptight, you know?'

'I can understand why she would.'

Silence ruled again. Grace let it go on for a while, mentally drawing a pencil line beneath that topic, before broaching the next. Their hour was ticking by. Despite her reluctance to think too much about time, Grace had learned to tell, without glancing at a watch, how much of a session was left. They still had plenty in hand, but she had in mind to finish early and maybe go out on deck with Cathy and Harry, simply to hang out for a while. She didn't want to overtax Cathy, didn't want to put her off coming back. Still, there was one more avenue she wanted to try opening before they stopped.

'You told me yesterday that you went to a therapist once before.'

'Yes.'

'You said you didn't trust her.'

'Did I?'

'Yes.'

Cathy hesitated. 'She taped everything I said.'

'You didn't like that.'

'No.' She paused. 'You're not taping me, are you, Grace?'

'No, I'm not.'

Cathy eyed the notepad on Grace's lap. 'You haven't written anything down.'

'I don't always. Sometimes I like to,' Grace explained, 'if there's something important I'm worried I might forget. But I have a pretty good memory, on the whole. After you go, I might make some notes, and then next time – if you want to come again – you might see me taking a look at what I wrote last time.' She paused. 'Is that okay with you?'

'I guess.'

She seemed to accept what Grace had said, but the uneasiness had crept back in and Grace could sense her starting to put up shutters, knew that by bringing up the subject of her former therapist, she had entered high-risk territory. She decided to veer back to safer ground before suggesting they called it a day.

'I hope you feel you can trust me, Cathy,' she said.

'I hope so, too,' she answered.

Five minutes later, Frances Dean arrived, earlier than scheduled, seeming edgy and anxious to take her niece away. Grace was frequently left after sessions feeling uncertain of a patient's – or their parents' or guardians' – faith in her, unsure of whether they would, given a choice, actually return for more. It always mattered to her a great deal.

If she was honest with herself, however, she wasn't sure if she always cared quite as much as she did about Cathy Robbins.

CHAPTER NINE

WEDNESDAY, APRIL 8, 1998

Sam Becket and Detective Al Martinez stood out in the back-yard of a Coconut Grove house a little after noon. It was humid and unpleasant and the air was full of small insects, but Sam was glad to be outside for a while, away from the scent of blood. He wondered, for a moment, why Beatrice Flager, the victim, a fifty-two-year-old divorced psychotherapist, had not put up a lanai or any kind of bug screening – though no amount of insect-proof mesh could have protected her from whoever had pierced her left temple with a fine, sharp weapon of some kind.

'So what do you think?' he asked his partner.

'You're the main man on this one. What do you think?' Martinez had a round, kindly face, sharp, dark eyes and wavy hair. A slightly built man who only reached Sam's shoulder, he was a man of strong opinions, quiet and calm until roused when, once in a while, he turned into a pitbull.

'Too soon to tell.'

'I'll bet the wad it's the same perp.' Martinez's accent was light, but his vocabulary tended to stray from refined to street tough.

'I'm not a betting man,' Sam reminded him.

The call from Elliot Sanders, the ME who'd come out to the house on Pine Tree Drive five days earlier, had surprised Sam. First, it was a pure coincidence for the same doc to have taken both cases. Second, if an ME noted a possible connection between cases in separate jurisdictions, the police investigators usually only heard about it after the weekly Dade

51

County medical examiners' meeting. Even then, if a potential link had been spotted, Sam would have expected to have to wait for the other police department – in this case the City of Miami PD, who policed Coconut Grove – to be ready to share any relevant information with Miami Beach. Dr Sanders, however, was a big, broad man who did his damnedest to see commonsense prevail. He'd seen the similarity to the Robbins' killings immediately, had seen no point in not alerting the guy in charge of the Miami Beach case, and had convinced the local investigators to let Becket and one colleague drive over to take a look.

Startled and intrigued by the development, Sam and Martinez had wasted no time accepting the offer. It looked, Sanders said, as he'd hinted to Sam on the phone, like another scalpel wound.

'Think it could be the same weapon?' Sam asked now, as the ME came out of the house to join him and Martinez.

'Wouldn't like to say.' Sanders mopped his brow with a large handkerchief and lit a cigarette. For a physician he broke way too many health rules, smoking every chance he got, carrying too much weight and drinking too much whisky, but most people who knew him agreed that for a man who spent so much of his life around cadavers, he was a whole lot of fun.

'Time of death?' Sam asked.

'She's been dead about eight hours, give or take.' Sanders checked his watch. 'Sometime around four a.m.' He fanned himself with a pad of paper. 'Air's like soup today. Mind you, it's not much better in there.'

'Air-con's busted.' Martinez had been nosing around, trying to find out whatever was up for grabs without raising hackles. The victim, he'd learned, had been found by her next-door-neighbour after the second of her two clients for that morning had knocked on her front door to ask if she knew where Flager was. The client, a Cuban teenager, had been questioned and allowed to leave, and the neighbour, in a state of semi-hysteria, was currently back in her own house being nursed through a cup of tea by one of the patrol officers who'd been first on the scene.

'What else do you have, doc?' Sam asked the ME.

'You want to take another look while I tell you?' Sanders

52

grinned. Sam Becket's comparative squeamishness with messy corpses was well-known to him and his fellow examiners – though at least in this case there was less blood splashed over the place itself than there had been in the Robbins' bedroom. There was a short trail of the stuff ending three feet from the couch where Flager's body lay; probably the blood that had dripped from the blade before it was wiped by the killer. As yet, no trace had been found either of the weapon itself, or of whatever had been used to clean it. There was also no sign of forced entry – the back door having been wide open – and the only apparent property damage was a smashed up computer.

'Don't sweat it, Becket,' Sanders told Sam, 'we can stay out here.' He glanced at his notes, though there was nothing in them that wasn't still at the forefront of his mind. 'One puncture, clean through the temporal artery.'

'So someone had to get up real close,' Martinez said.

'No sign of a fight,' Sam added,

'She's on the couch,' Sanders said, 'so she might have been sleeping.'

'The TV wasn't on,' Sam commented. 'Most people fall asleep on their couches in front of the TV.'

'You don't,' Martinez pointed out. 'You're always zeeing up on your roof.'

'That's a beach lounger, not a couch,' Sam said. 'Anyway, I aim to fall asleep up there.' He paused. 'Maybe she wasn't alone on the couch.'

'Possible,' Sanders agreed. 'Snuggled up close to someone with a scalpel in their pocket.'

'If they were dressed,' Martinez said.

'She was dressed,' Sam said.

'Coulda hidden the scalpel under a cushion,' Martinez suggested.

'You're sure it was a scalpel?' Sam looked at Sanders.

'So far as I can tell right now. Certainly a scalpel-like instrument, same as on Pine Tree.'

'So maybc thc same instrument,' Martinez said. 'The one that belonged to the Robbins girl.'

By three p.m. activity inside the house had begun to dwindle and Sam knew that Sergeant Rodriguez, his Miami PD counterpart, was unlikely to want him or Martinez around much longer. The technicians had finished dusting, every conceivable photograph had been taken, the body had been thoroughly checked for crucial trace evidence that might have vanished en route to the morgue, and then it had been taken away. The Miami Police team were engaged in examining the psychotherapist's client files and calling at other houses along the Coconut Grove street – though everyone knew it was unlikely anyone would have heard or seen anything useful at four in the morning. Anyway, the hour aside, with no gunshots and no apparent fight to play with there was less than no hope of finding a witness – after all, a scalpel sliding comparatively smoothly into a possibly sleeping woman's temple didn't make a whole lot of noise, and the sound of a computer being smashed wasn't likely to rouse anyone outside the house.

Martinez found Sam in Flager's bedroom just after three-thirty. 'They think the air-con was broken deliberately.'

'So she'd have to keep her windows open.' Sam shook his head.

'Should've known better than to open the fuckin' door,' Martinez said.

'Any prints on the air-con unit?' Sam asked.

'Not even a smudge.' Martinez looked at Sam. 'So what's the link between the Robbinses and Flager?'

'We don't know yet that it's the same weapon,' Sam reminded him.

'Two scalpels in a week?' Martinez was sceptical.

'Yeah, I know.' Sam didn't believe in coincidences either.

They left Sergeant Rodriguez and his squad sifting through the remnants of Beatrice Flager's life and death, and drove over to Coral Gables to check on Frances Dean's and her niece's whereabouts the previous night.

Mrs Dean's answer was predictable.

'We were here, at home – where else would we have been?'

They were standing in her living room. Frances Dean had not offered either of the detectives a seat, and Sam thought he well understood her desire to have them gone as swiftly as possible.

'Are you sure that Cathy was here all night, ma'am?' Martinez asked.

'Of course I'm sure.' Frances Dean looked baffled.

'Were you sleepin' in the same room as your niece, Mrs Dean?'

'No,' she answered, 'but then again, I wasn't sleeping at all, which is why I'm certain that Cathy was in her bedroom all night.'

'You were awake all night, ma'am?'

Sam was letting Martinez run with it. Personally, he saw no good cause to doubt her word. Frances Dean looked like hell.

'I don't think I've slept more than a handful of hours since my sister and her husband were murdered, detective,' she told Martinez. 'My doctor gave me some pills, but I don't like the way they make me feel.'

'So you would have known if Cathy had left her bedroom, or maybe the house?'

'Yes, I would.' Frances Dean looked up at Sam. 'What is this about?'

'Just routine,' Sam said. 'Would you mind if we ask your niece a few questions now?'

'I would mind very much,' Frances said heatedly, then lowered her voice to a distressed hiss. 'Are you people *trying* to push that poor child right over the edge? Because you're going about it the perfect way.'

'One more question, Mrs Dean,' Sam said. 'Have you heard of a woman named Beatrice Flager?'

'No, I don't think so. Who is she?'

'A psychotherapist,' Sam answered.

'I know her.'

Sam, Martinez and Frances Dean all turned around and saw that Cathy, barefoot and wearing a blue sundress, had come into the room. There were dark rings beneath her eyes, Sam noticed right off, that he didn't recall seeing before. Otherwise, she looked composed. He wondered how long Cathy had been in or outside the room, listening to them. Being barefoot, it was perfectly reasonable for her to have come in unnoticed, but there was something about the silent, almost deceitful way she had slid into the room that he found disturbing. It also raised some extra doubt about Frances Dean's claim that she would have known if Cathy had left her room or the house, since there was clearly more than a passing chance that she could not have known any such thing.

Sam looked at the girl's upturned face. 'Hello, Cathy,' he said. 'Would you like to sit down?'

'No, thank you.'

They all went on standing, all stiff and uncomfortable except for Martinez, who was always telling Sam Becket that he was too friggin' tenderhearted to be a cop.

'The detectives were asking where we were last night.' Frances Dean, voice still quivering with anger, was clearly determined to preempt the officers' next move. 'I told them, of course, that we were in our beds.'

Sam and Martinez both watched Cathy and said nothing.

'Why did you ask that?' Cathy asked Sam. 'And what does it have to do with Mrs Flager?'

'She was killed last night,' Martinez answered.

'How?' Cathy's face gave little away.

'She was stabbed.'

'Oh God.' Suddenly she grew very white. 'Oh, God, that's horrible.'

'Wouldn't you like to sit down now, Cathy?' Sam asked her, gently.

Without a word, she sat, very slowly and quietly, on her aunt's sofa. Frances Dean sat down beside her, close but not touching, her attitude protective.

Sam and Martinez, not invited to sit, remained standing.

'Why are you —?'Frances halted in mid-sentence, her face even paler than it had been, her eyes widening with new horror as she stared up at Sam. 'What does this woman's death have to do with us?'

'Like we said, ma'am,' Martinez answered, 'just routine.'

'I don't believe this.' The aunt shook her head in disbelief. 'I don't believe any of this.'

'It's okay, Aunt Frances,' Cathy said.

'You say you knew Beatrice Flager?' Sam asked the teenager.

She nodded. 'A little.' Her voice was very quiet now, almost too soft to hear. 'I know she was a therapist.'

'How do you know that, Cathy?' Martinez asked.

'I saw her one time.' She glanced sideways at her aunt, taking in her tightly compressed lips and shocked eyes.

'Professionally?' Martinez asked, and she nodded.

'Do you mind telling us why?' Sam asked.

'*I* mind,' Frances said.

'No, it's okay,' Cathy told her again, then looked up at Sam. 'I went because Arnie – my father – wanted me to.'

'Why did he want you to see a therapist?'

'Don't answer that.' Frances stood up. 'I'm sorry, I don't think my niece should answer any more questions.'

'I don't have anything to hide, Aunt Frances.'

'I know you don't.' Frances didn't look at Cathy, kept her still angry eyes firmly on Sam's, ignoring Martinez. 'Does my niece need a lawyer, Detective Becket?' She shook her head again. 'I can't believe I'm really asking that question, but it suddenly seems the right thing to do.'

Sam looked at her. She'd seemed so frail earlier, and yet as soon as the impact of what was going on – of why they had come to her house again – had hit her, Frances Dean had seemed almost to grow in stature and strength. He felt a kick of admiration for her, and hoped he would have no reason to cause her any more pain.

'The questions are just routine, ma'am,' Martinez said again.

She turned her eyes back to him. 'Is it *routine* to harass a child who's just lost her parents, detective? A child who's still going through hell?'

Martinez stayed calm, the way he almost always did.

'Yes, ma'am,' he said, 'under the circumstances, I'm afraid it is.'

'Then your routines are very savage,' Frances said.

'I can't disagree with you,' Sam said quietly.

Retrieve File

Filename: My Journal

Current Dir: c:\wpwin\sundries

File Info: 15305 Bytes

03/31/98   23:52

File Password Protected

File:	**c\wpwin\sundries\jrnl**
Password:	<u>**H-A-T-E**</u>
	<u>**OK**</u> **Cancel**

Cathy's Journal
Thursday, April 9, 1998

She shouldn't have done it to me.
She ought to have minded her own
business.

She was always a bitch, anyway.

CHAPTER TEN

THURSDAY, APRIL 9, 1998

Grace was in the kitchen, sharing a coffee break at around eleven o'clock with Teddy Lopez – the young man who kept house for her several times a week and who took care of Harry when she could not – when Sam Becket telephoned.

'There's been a development I think maybe you should know about, Dr Lucca,' he told her.

'What kind of development?'

She was using the cordless phone at the kitchen table, and sensing business – which, from his three years' experience of working with the doctor, he knew meant privacy – Teddy picked up his coffee cup and went out on to the deck to finish it there.

'This may well be unconnected,' Sam said, 'but given that we've already had to talk to Cathy and her aunt about it, I figure I should mention it to you.'

He told her about the new murder, told her that the victim, a psychotherapist named Beatrice Flager, had seen Cathy Robbins as a patient in the past. The news shook Grace up more than a little. When the detective told her, in strict confidence, that there was a possibility that the weapon had, once again, been a scalpel-type blade, she felt the chill of goosebumps parading up her spine.

'Did you know that Cathy had seen a therapist in the past?' Sam asked.

'She mentioned it to me,' Grace answered as evenly as she could. 'She didn't tell me the therapist's name.'

'We know it was Mrs Flager,' he said. 'Cathy volunteered the information herself. Do you know why she saw her?'

'No, I don't.'

'And if you did, you probably wouldn't tell me.'

'Probably not,' Grace agreed.

'Anyway,' Sam went on, 'we had to pay Mrs Dean and her niece a visit yesterday to ask a few more routine questions, and the lady got pretty upset —'

'What kind of questions?' Grace broke in.

'Just routine.'

'You said that already,' she said. 'Did Cathy get upset, too?'

'Briefly,' Sam said. 'But after that she seemed quite calm, on the face of it. Anyway' – he went on again, smoothly, as if she hadn't interrupted him – 'I was thinking that it might be useful if you could get in touch with them again.'

'Useful for whom?'

Sam heard the crispness in her tone. 'I'm not sending you in as a police spy, Dr Lucca.' There was a smile in his voice.

'Are you sure?'

'You seem to have gotten through to both Cathy and her aunt, that's all,' he said lightly. 'And I have a feeling that however calm she might have seemed, Cathy could use all the help she can get.'

'You don't expect me to report back to you then?' Grace asked.

'Are you always this suspicious, doctor?'

'Pretty much,' she answered.

'Maybe you have just cause,' Sam admitted.

Grace's cheeks were warm as she put down the phone. She knew it was partly guilt that had made her attack him just now. Guilt for not mentioning what had started running through her mind the instant she'd heard about Beatrice Flager.

What Cathy had said about the therapist she'd been to once. *I didn't feel I could trust her. She taped everything I said.*

All the way through that conversation with Becket, Grace had wanted to ask if the psychotherapist's records had been tampered with in any way. If her tapes, or transcriptions, had been stolen or destroyed. But she hadn't asked, had not said a word.

'Doctor-patient confidentiality,' she muttered out loud.

Which was, of course, a perfectly reasonable excuse. But still Grace was aware of a silent struggle already going on in her mind between her loyalties to Cathy Robbins and to the law.

The awareness was uncomfortable.

She was in her office searching for Frances Dean's telephone number, and Harry, in the mood for a game, was trotting around the room with his red ball in his mouth, when the phone rang again.

'Grace, it's me.'

'Hi, sis.' Grace found the number, and sat down. 'What's up?' Her sister, Claudia Brownley – who, with her husband and children, divided her time between their homes in Fort Lauderdale and the Keys – rarely called during working hours. 'You okay?'

'Yes and no,' Claudia said. 'Papa called.'

'Frank phoned you?' Grace had stopped calling her father Papa the day she and Claudia had left their parents' home in Chicago more than sixteen years earlier. Frank Lucca *never* telephoned either of his daughters.

'Mama has cancer,' Claudia said. 'She has to have surgery.'

'What kind of cancer?'

'I'm not sure. "Women's stuff", Papa said.' Claudia paused. 'He wants us to go home.'

Grace sat back in her chair, closed her eyes and took a breath. There was a small thud as the ball dropped out of Harry's mouth. She opened her eyes. The white terrier was sitting, gazing up at her expectantly.

'How do you feel about that, sis?' Grace asked quietly.

'I don't know how I feel about it,' Claudia answered. 'How about you?'

'I guess I don't know either.'

Grace didn't even know how she felt about their mother having cancer. She had been conscious, even while asking it, that the first question out of her mouth had been 'What kind of cancer?' rather than 'How bad is it?' But then, she and Claudia didn't have the kind of relationship with their parents that would make them drop everything and fly back home

66

because of illness. The truth was, they didn't have *any* kind of relationship with either Frank or Ellen Lucca.

Darkness and cold had brought Grace and Claudia to Florida all those years ago. And the need to stay close to each other. Claudia was the elder sister by a little over a year, but in childhood it had generally been she who had come to Grace for comfort and strength after she'd caught a beating or something worse from their father. It had always been Claudia, the gentler, more compliant sibling, who'd been the magnet for Frank Lucca's rages and passions, while Grace – younger, more impulsive, more avid for learning and less pliable – had seldom seemed to inflame him.

Not that there had ever been much logic in Frank's choice for target practice. Lord knew he gave the impression that he'd grown to hate his wife, Ellen, yet he took out most of his loathing and sexual frustration on little Claudia, who physically resembled *him*, rather than on Grace, who – like Ellen – was fair and blue-eyed and ought therefore, one might have thought, to have been the one to spark him off.

Years later, Grace tended to refer to having followed Claudia to Miami, as if she had been the leader, but in reality that was far from true. It had all been Grace's idea, from the day she'd made friends with a girl named Betsy in her class at school in Chicago, who had a doting aunt and uncle who lived in the warm sunshine of Miami Beach. Grace began fantasizing about going to Florida, far away from their father, the abuser, and their mother, whose own crime was that she had never lifted a finger or even raised her voice to help protect her children.

Gradually, fantasy became reality. Grace confided in Betsy, enlisting her sympathies, persuaded her to ask her relatives to find out for her where two teenage girls could live, cheaply but safely, and then, the information in hand, had proceeded to work out a deal with their parents.

If Frank and Ellen didn't try to stop them leaving, Grace and Claudia would not report them to the authorities. Frank called it blackmail, but Grace said it was just compromise. It was her first experience of using psychology to resolve a bad situation, and she knew it had really only worked out because their parents didn't give a damn about her or Claudia, but it was a heady experience nonetheless – especially when she watched sixteen-year-old Claudia strengthen and blossom almost as soon as they left concrete, steel, icy winds and Frank, and reached palm trees, blue ocean, sunshine and freedom. No *way*, the new Claudia said, was Grace quitting school, because she, Claudia, was going to find a job and work hard to make sure that Grace – who'd always been smarter and more ambitious than she was – could finish high school and go to college.

Neither of them had ever laid eyes on Frank since fleeing Chicago and they had seen Ellen Lucca only once, back in the winter of 1992, when she had arrived unannounced on a Greyhound bus, bruised and weary and in need of a break from her husband – but even then all she had really wanted to do was load her daughters with guilt for running out on her. She truly seemed to feel that none of the responsibility had been hers, to believe that it had been their *duty* to take the pain and fear and to stay home for her sake.

No logic there either, Grace had learned, and that became a useful tool to take with her into the world of psychology and counselling: the awareness that in the recesses of the heart and soul there was little logic, scanty justice, and no rules whatsoever.

'Just how sick did Frank say Ellen is?' she asked Claudia now.

'He didn't say,' Claudia answered. 'He was very vague. I asked if I could talk to Mama, but she couldn't come to the phone – or he wouldn't let her.' She sounded calm, yet her tone was shot through with traces of old bitterness. 'I asked him what surgery she had to have, and he wouldn't say, so I asked him straight out if it was a hysterectomy, and that put the lid on it.'

'He got mad?'

'Not exactly. He got offended, said something about he'd done his bit by telling me, and now it was up to us, but he thought we should come.' Claudia paused. 'I'd say what he wants is for someone to shoulder the burden, take care of Mama after her operation.'

'Well, that someone can't be you,' Grace said quickly, hoping to quash any feelings of guilt even before they were born. 'You have Daniel and the boys to take care of, and you can't afford to risk getting sucked back into that old hellhole just because Frank Lucca makes one phone call in a decade.'

'I know that, Grace,' Claudia said, softly. 'I didn't say I'd go.'

'Good,' Grace said, a little sickened by the force of anger that had just welled up out of her. She shut her eyes again, thought about Ellen, pictured her sick and afraid and having to face coming home after surgery to her shitbag of a husband. 'Oh, God,' she said, violently, and opened her eyes.

'Grace, are you okay?'

'Yes. I guess.' She knew she didn't sound okay. 'Just facing the fact that I'm trying to stop you from feeling guilty about Ellen, but I'm not even sure I can switch my own feelings off.'

'You're human, too, Grace,' Claudia pointed out, calmly, then paused. 'So what do we do now?'

'I think we should wait a while,' Grace said. 'With Easter in a couple of days, we probably couldn't get a flight to Chicago if we wanted to. Anyway, we both have commitments.' Cathy Robbins' face came into her mind, and she remembered the phone number in her hand. 'Matter of fact, sis, there's someone I need to call right now.'

'That's fine,' Claudia said. 'Are you still up for this weekend?'

Grace thought about the prospect of two days and nights with her sister and brother-in-law and their sons down in Islamorada, and warmth coursed through her.

'I wouldn't miss it,' she said.

Frances Dean was evasive on the telephone, bordering on hostile, but Grace had the feeling that was probably because the older woman was now associating her with Sam Becket and the rest of the Miami Beach Police Department – and with Beatrice Flager's murder plainly raising the temperature of suspicion towards her niece, Grace could hardly blame Frances for that. Nor could she, Grace supposed, somewhat grudgingly, entirely blame Sam Becket for doing what the taxpayer paid him to do.

Out of the blue, something came back to her. The niggly feeling she'd had last Saturday after she'd noticed the Band-Aid on Cathy's arm and failed to ask Becket about it. Now Grace had just been given the perfect opportunity by Frances Dean to abandon this case, to forget all about Cathy and Marie and Arnold Robbins, to legitimately walk away from a girl who might – who just *might* – have murdered three people, one of them her own mother.

The thing was, Grace simply did not believe that. And even if she did, it was not in her province to prove Cathy Robbins' innocence or guilt. If she was going to continue with an ugly situation that was likely to turn even uglier, Grace was going to have to stick around to help Cathy come to terms and deal with what had happened to her.

Even if what had happened to her was becoming a killer.

CHAPTER ELEVEN

FRIDAY, APRIL 10, 1998

Grace had to break through two barriers next morning in order to set up her new session with Cathy. First she had to persuade Frances that, no matter what she might be feeling about the way the investigation was being conducted, Grace was still on her niece's side. Second, she had to obtain police permission to use the specific location she had in mind for this next meeting. The Robbins' house on Pine Tree Drive was officially still a crime scene, cordoned off from normality, but it was where Grace felt she most wanted to speak with Cathy – provided the teenager agreed.

She did agree. Grace had been almost certain she would.

'So long as we don't have to go back to that room,' she said.

'We most certainly don't,' Grace assured her.

Going back to the scene of the horror was not Grace's reason for wanting to take Cathy to the house. She was aware that one of the traumas adding to the girl's load was the fact that she had been wrenched, from one moment to the next, out of her home. As if the manner of losing her parents had not been horrifying enough, Cathy had simultaneously lost that other major anchor. Home was where people needed to go to lick their wounds, to begin to recover. In her aunt's house – however well-meaning Frances Dean was trying to be – Cathy couldn't be herself. She had her aunt's own grief and immaculate rooms to be considerate of. She had a room of her own to go to, to be alone, but it was not *hers*. Grace was in no way underestimating the potential trauma of making this first journey back into what had surely, in her mind, now become a house of horror. Yet that last event, that last nightmare, represented only one night; Cathy Robbins had lived within those walls for years. She needed, Grace thought, to touch base with her roots, with herself, and going back with someone sufficiently detached to let her react the way she needed to, might, Grace hoped, be good for her.

Sam Becket, too, thought it a good idea. He'd brought up the notion with her aunt at one point, in the hope that returning to the house might jog something in Cathy's memory, but Frances Dean had rejected it ferociously. He was glad she had given her consent to Grace.

'I guess she doesn't consider you family enemy number one,' he said on the phone, after giving her police permission to enter the crime scene.

'I guess she doesn't think I'll just be taking Cathy home to try and trap her,' Grace said. 'Not that that's why I think you would have taken her there.'

'Why do you think I would have?' Becket asked.

'To get closer to the truth,' Grace answered.

'Isn't that what you're hoping to do, Dr Lucca?'

'In a way.'

The house was a big, but not too grand, mock Tudor, with plenty of landscaped space around it. Grace noted three different kinds of palm trees, bougainvillaea, jasmine, roses, a smooth, immaculately maintained front lawn – the image of tranquillity – until the partially torn crime-scene tape and careless litter of soft drink cans and discarded coffee cups reminded her of the brutal reality.

They entered from the side, moved through the kitchen and into the hallway. Grace didn't need to watch Cathy's face; the tension was coming off her in palpable waves. The first pangs of self-doubt and guilt hit Grace hard.

'Where do you want to go to feel safe, Cathy?' she asked.

Her answer was instant. 'The backyard.'

'Let's go.'

Grace followed her back through the side entrance and around to the rear of the house, and right away she understood. It was the kind of backyard any teenager would like to live with. It was big and private, its perimeters lined with shady palms and a lovely Jacaranda tree. The lawn was good-sized, there was a great, tempting pool with a diving board, a stone barbecue, table and chairs, a couple of swing-seats with canopies and a hammock. There was also a pool-house at the end of the garden with a second barbecue, and Grace guessed that Cathy had spent a lot of time down there with friends. If she had friends. Grace realized, abruptly, that she'd seen or heard no evidence of any youngsters coming to her aunt's house, or calling. Not that that proved much; Grace knew very well that death of all kinds caused some people of all ages to keep their distance.

'This is a great backyard for parties,' she said, softly, watching Cathy's face, glad that here, at least, the memories seemed to be happy.

'My parents threw a few,' she answered, 'when Arnie wasn't working at the restaurants. He loved parties.'

'What about your mother?'

'Not so much. Mom was quieter, you know?' Cathy paused. 'No, I guess you don't.'

'I'd like to hear, if you want to tell me.'

'Can I take off my shoes, dunk my feet in the pool?'

'It's your pool,' Grace said. 'You don't need permission.'

'I feel like I need to ask before I do anything these days.'

'Not with me.'

Cathy took off her sneakers without untying her laces. Grace did the same, and they both sat down on the edge of the pool. Cathy was wearing shorts and a halter neck top; Grace wore tan slacks, but wished she'd put on a pair of shorts instead. The water felt great. Cathy gave a long sigh. It sounded like relief.

'What?' Grace asked.

'It feels the same,' she said.

'It is the same.'

'Nothing's the same,' she said.

Grace couldn't argue.

They sat silently for a while.

'I would like to hear about your mother,' Grace said, at last.

'What do you want to know?'

'Anything.' Grace knew better than that. 'Were you good friends?'

'I guess.' Cathy stared into the blue water. 'Mom wasn't really fun, you know? Though she could be, sometimes, when she let herself go. Arnie was fun. Mom was quieter.' She paused. 'I said that already, didn't I?'

'That doesn't matter.'

'She worried a lot,' Cathy said.

'What about?'

'I don't know.'

'Didn't she confide in you?'

'Did your mom tell you private stuff?' It was the same kind of retaliatory question she'd come back with near the start of their last session, before she'd started to settle down a little.

'My mother only told me private stuff when it suited her.' Grace was still sure that straight was the only way to go with Cathy. One of her first tutors had taught her that it was okay to refer to her own life experiences with a patient so long as the focus remained firmly on them.

'Is that why you became a shrink?'

'It may have been part of the reason.'

Grace had told Sam Becket that Cathy was an intuitive person. Fourteen going on twenty-four, the psychologist thought now, and wondered if that acuteness was going to help or hinder her position with the Miami Beach Police Department.

'I think my mom just wanted to protect me,' Cathy said, abruptly.

'From what?'

'From bad stuff.'

There it was again. *Years of misery*, her aunt had referred to briefly, cryptically. And the flashes that Cathy hadn't wanted to talk about. Or had thought she ought not to talk about.

They sat quietly again for a few minutes. Cathy drew circles in the water with her big toes. Grace felt the sun on her face, the slight breeze in her hair, and let herself relax a little. They had time.

'You heard what happened to the therapist, didn't you, Grace?'

Grace had decided not to refer to the Flager killing unless Cathy brought it up first. She had anticipated that Cathy probably would.

'Was Beatrice Flager the therapist you told me about?' she asked, carefully. 'The one who taped you.'

'Yes.' Cathy hesitated. 'I didn't kill her.'

'I didn't imagine you did,' Grace said, matter-of-factly.

'Detective Becket and one of the other officers wanted to know if I'd been in Aunt Frances' house all night Tuesday.'

'I know,' Grace said.

'Did you tell him what I said about Ms Flager?'

'No.'

'Why not?'

'For one thing, I didn't think it was relevant.'

Cathy hit the surface of the pool harder with her left heel, making a splash and sending droplets flying over them both. Grace didn't mind.

'Is what I tell you the same as stuff I might tell a priest?' Cathy asked. 'I mean, don't you have to tell, if the police ask you?'

'Like the sanctity of the confessional, you mean? Yes, more or less,' Grace answered. 'It's called doctor-patient confidentiality. That means that I'm not allowed to disclose things you've told me, unless you give me permission to talk about them.' *Or unless you're likely to harm yourself or anyone else*, she added silently.

'Even if you think I've done something really bad? Like killing three people?' Cathy's voice was hard, but the fear beneath the bravado was audible. She stood up suddenly. 'I think we should go back inside again.'

'Are you sure you want to?' Grace got up, too.

'No.' Cathy shrugged. 'But now I know I can escape out here, I'm willing to risk it.'

'And we can just leave anytime, too.'

They went back the way they'd come, into the kitchen. Cathy wanted to look in the refrigerator. She said that she wanted something cold to drink, but Grace felt she was probably hoping for a quick fix of the way things had been. Ice boxes were personal things, favourite foods laid out in specific ways. Grace wasn't sure what might be worse for the bereaved teenager: finding that her family refrigerator had been emptied by strangers, or finding it much as it had been.

75

It was well-stocked, and visibly tough on Cathy. There was a whole bunch of stuff in there that Marie or the housekeeper had probably brought back from the market not long before the killings; and there were plastic containers of soup and pasta sauces with stickers labelled **Arnie's** that Grace supposed had been brought back from one or other of the restaurants.

Cathy stared at the contents for about a minute. Grace wondered what it was she was seeing in her head. Her mother taking out eggs and milk and bread and making French toast? Arnie opening one of those bottles of white wine that stood in the ice box door? The family sitting round the kitchen table, eating brunch? Maybe she was replaying an argument, or maybe she was thinking that she'd never seen Marie cooking breakfast or any other meal, that maybe the housekeeper had done all the cooking – or maybe Arnie had brought his restaurant skills home with him each night? Under different circumstances, Grace might have asked Cathy to tell her what she was seeing in her family ice box, but at that moment it just didn't seem like the right thing to do.

Cathy closed the door quietly. 'I need to get out of here.'

'Okay,' Grace said. 'Out of the house, or just the kitchen?'

'I'd like to go to my room.'

'Alone or with company?'

'Not alone.' She said that fast, fearfully.

'Let's go.'

The problem was she had to pass her parents' bedroom to get there. Grace didn't need to be told which room it was – it was obvious from Cathy's body language, by the way she stopped breathing and averted her face and accelerated past the tall, white door, that that was the place she was not ready – might never be ready – to go back into.

Her own room was at the end of the corridor. She opened the door, went in fast and sank down on the single bed.

'Want the door closed or open?' Grace asked, standing just inside.

'Could you close it, please?'

Grace shut it quietly. 'If you do want some time alone, I could wait right outside.'

'No,' Cathy said. 'Maybe next time.'

It felt like an intrusion. That was curious, Grace thought,

76

considering that her entire professional life was exactly that, an ongoing invasion into other people's privacy, a gradual process of worming her way into a patient's mind. Frankly, though, no matter how skilled at that she might have become, what she achieved at the end of the day was mostly edited highlights – the parts that the patient *chose* to show her. Cathy Robbins might have just invited her into her bedroom, but the visit to the house had still been at Grace's suggestion, and she was acutely aware that she was now treading on intensely intimate territory.

It was a fairly typical fourteen-year-old girl's bedroom. Remnants of childhood. A Raggedy Ann doll in a small chair. A collection of cuddly animals. A set of Laura Ingalls Wilder books. Evidence of growing teenage influence. Two posters, one of Brad Pitt, another from the movie *Titanic* with Leonardo di Caprio. A stack of CDs that seemed to embrace ballet, rock and rap. The running trophies that Sam had mentioned. Photographs. Of Marie and Arnold and of herself. One of her with a dark-haired, pretty girl.

'Who's that?' Grace asked.

'My friend, Jill.' Cathy paused. 'She came to see me on Sunday, after you left. She stayed about a half-hour, and then her dad came to take her home.' Bleakness touched her eyes. 'We've talked on the phone a few times since then, but I don't think her parents want her seeing me right now.'

'That's a pity.'

Cathy shrugged.

Grace looked back at the photographs. 'Do you have a picture of your first father?' She recalled that was how Cathy had referred to him.

'No.' She was still sitting on the bed, staring around the room. 'They took my diary.'

Grace stayed where she was. She had hardly moved since closing the door. It was enough that she was in here with Cathy, ruffling the atmosphere a little; she didn't want to stir it up too much, not at this time, anyway.

'Why would they want my diary, Grace?'

'I don't know.' Grace paused. 'Was there much private stuff in it?'

'Not really,' Cathy said. 'I keep my journal on my computer.'

77

'Is that here?' Grace couldn't see any computer equipment. She shook her head. 'I took it with me to my aunt's house. It's a notebook model.'

'I'm sorry they took the diary,' Grace said.

'No big deal.' Cathy stood up, wandered over to the window, looked out over the backyard. 'I guess I'll never get to live here again, will I?'

'I don't know. Would you like to?'

'Maybe.'

'Do you think your aunt might be willing to move?'

'No.' Cathy was still looking out of the window. 'I asked her. She said she couldn't bear it.'

'I'm sorry,' Grace said again.

'Maybe she's right. I don't know if I could stand it either.'

Grace looked back at the photographs of Cathy with her mother and Arnie. They looked happy. She wondered about the absence of a photograph of her biological father, and decided he was a subject worth trying to address again.

'You told me you don't remember much about your first father.'

'I don't.'

'Did your mother talk much about him to you?'

'My mother never talked about him.' Cathy turned around, looked straight at Grace. 'He made her unhappy, I know that.'

'What about you? Did he make you unhappy?'

'I don't think so.' Cathy bent down and picked up Raggedy Ann. 'Aunt Frances told me about Mom being miserable. She never said anything to me herself.'

'Didn't you ask her?'

'A couple of times.' She tugged idly at a few strands of the doll's stringy red hair. 'Mom said she wanted to forget about it.'

'What else did your aunt tell you about it?'

'Not much.' She dumped Raggedy Ann back on her chair, and the doll tilted over to one side. 'I'd like to leave now.'

'This room or the house?"

'Can we just go, please, Grace?' She looked at her pleadingly.

'Of course we can.'

Grace realized suddenly that she was standing in front of the door, and that maybe Cathy might feel trapped. Quickly, she stepped to one side and opened the door. Cathy started out past her, then stopped and turned, went back to the doll, bent down and straightened her. As she passed Grace again, already bracing herself for the walk back through that corridor, there were tears in her eyes.

Grace wondered, as they left the house, got into her Mazda and buckled up, if the visit had helped or hindered Cathy. She was always questioning her own ideas and decisions, especially during the difficult early weeks of getting to know her patients. She asked loaded questions, raised taboo subjects, watched new walls go up, saw all kinds of distress, and frequently experienced dreadful guilt. There was no escaping the fact that bringing Cathy home had, at least temporarily, made her feel a whole lot worse rather than better. And yet Grace knew, just as decisively, that it had had to happen sometime, and she also knew that this was probably just the beginning. *Not your fault, Lucca*, she could almost hear that old tutor telling her, in one of her gentler moments. *You didn't create the unhappiness in Cathy's family. You didn't murder her parents.* No, of course Grace had not done those things. But she had chosen her profession. She had chosen to meddle in people's lives and minds.

She didn't waste much time these days questioning her motives for having become a psychologist. She did know, absolutely, that there was not even a hint of prurience in her curiosity about people – but she was, undoubtedly, a deeply curious woman who wanted very much to help.

There were times, however, when Grace was not at all sure that she succeeded.

CHAPTER TWELVE

Grace had promised to call Sam Becket after seeing Cathy, in case the visit to the house had thrown up something relevant to the investigation. At least, she was grateful to realize, she could tell him in all honesty that she'd found out nothing to help the department in any way.

'Would you mind,' he asked, 'if I dropped by to see you later?'

'Of course not. Why?'

'I have some findings of my own that might just help you.'

At a quarter past eight that evening he called again to say that he'd been held up by some urgent work. 'I guess we ought to leave it for another time.'

'That's up to you,' Grace told him, 'but I tend to be a late-night person.'

'How late is late?' Sam asked.

'Any time up to midnight.'

'I hope it's going to be a lot earlier than that,' Sam said.

It was almost eleven-thirty when he finally knocked at her door.

'Are you hungry, detective?' Grace asked, sizing him up. 'You look hungry.' *And exhausted*, she thought but did not say, noting the sagging broad shoulders, tired eyes and unshaven jawline.

'As a horse in the Sahara,' Sam said. 'I only remembered an hour ago that I was supposed to have dinner with my family this evening.' He grinned wryly. 'My mother's pretty mad at me.'

'She must be used to it by now,' Grace said, 'with a doctor

for a husband and a cop for a son.' She paused. 'How'd you like to share some *Cacciucco* with us?'

'What's *Cacciucco* and who's us?'

'Us is me and Harry.' Right on cue, the West Highland came trotting into the entrance hall. 'This is Harry.'

'Hey, Harry.' Sam bent down and put out a hand, and the dog came and sniffed at him. 'Do I pass muster?'

'Most people do,' Grace told him, and led the way into her kitchen, which, like the food she best loved cooking, evoked the Italian half of her heritage. She might have written off her father a long time ago, but her ancestry had always fascinated her.

'Sit down, detective, and I'll show you what *Cacciucco* is.' She indicated the big rustic wooden table with its matching hand-carved chairs.

'Thank you, doctor.' Sam sat down wearily, watching Grace go to the stove and light the gas under a large copper casserole. 'I know you said you were a late-night person, but surely you must have eaten dinner by now?'

'That was hours ago,' she said easily. 'Haven't you ever heard of midnight snacks?'

'Heard of them?' Sam said. 'Hell, doctor, I wrote the recipe book.'

Grace smiled. 'If we're going to share a midnight snack, do you think we might graduate to first names?'

'Suits me.'

He smiled back, saw her lift the lid off the pot and give things inside a gentle stir. It was hard not to register how cool and sexy the psychologist looked in her lightweight denim jeans and pale blue cotton T-shirt. He hadn't really noticed the delicate, feminine curves at their previous meeting. He did recall noticing everything that hadn't been covered up by her business suit – the good face with its cool-*un*cool blue eyes, the almost-Deneuve-nose, the warm lips and the long legs – but the twin topics of their conversation, homicide and grief, had hardly been conducive to that kind of thinking.

'It sure smells good,' he said, turning his attention to her cooking and sniffing the air. 'Fish soup?'

'It originated as a poor man's fish soup, but I think it tastes pretty damn good, too.' She grinned. 'See what a modest cook I am?'

'When you're right, you're right,' Sam said. 'That's one of my mother's sayings. Though when it comes to me and her, it's not often me who's right, at least not according to her.'

'Better not tell her you're eating my dinner instead of hers,' Grace said.

'Damn right,' Sam said.

Fifteen minutes later, the kitchen table simply laid, glasses filled with Chianti and his first taste of Grace's fish stew en route to his famished stomach, Sam began to feel restored.

'So how Italian are you?' he asked.

'Half Italian, half American. How about you?'

'Nothing Italian about me,' Sam said.

Grace dipped a hunk of bread into the thick, aromatic soup. 'You don't mind my asking, do you? Only I remember your father mentioning you – his son – a couple of times, and I knew you were a cop, but that's all.'

'You mean, he didn't say what colour I was?' Sam teased. 'Actually, I don't think it would ever occur to him. I think he stopped noticing I was black a couple of years after he and Judy adopted me.'

'When was that?'

'1972. When I was eight years old. About a year after my parents and sister died.' He paused, swallowed some more wine, looked across the table at Grace, saw empathy in those keen blue eyes, and figured he didn't mind expanding a little. 'We lived in Coconut Grove – my father was a cop, too, with good friends up in Opa-Locka. March 24, 1971, my daddy, off-duty, decided we should all take a drive up and see them. That just happened to be the day after a police sergeant up there had shot a black bystander at a robbery. A riot started that evening.'

Grace thought about all she'd been told about the great Miami riot of 1980, the by-all-accounts terrifying ugliness that she and Claudia had missed by less than a year. 'You got caught up in it?'

'Not exactly,' Sam said. 'We were still at our friends' place when it started to get bad. I remember they wanted us to stay, but my father was determined to get back home. He said he was going to stay clear of trouble, go a long way around if he had to, but you know how it is with a riot – the trouble spreads, fans out like fire.' He shrugged. 'Anyway, we did get caught up in it, on the outskirts.'

Grace waited silently.

'I never saw exactly what happened,' Sam went on. 'I'd fallen asleep next to Angela, my little sister, in the back of the car. I only woke up for about a second before it happened.' His eyes darkened, his voice grew quieter. 'I heard people yelling – then suddenly my father swore and my mother gave a kind of a scream, and something hit the windshield – I found out later it was a stone.' He paused. 'I guess my father lost control of the car. We smashed into a tree. He and Angela were killed outright. My mother died a few hours later.'

Grace thought about a seven-year-old boy hurtled into so much horror and grief, and felt her heart contract. 'What happened to you?'

'I had some cracked ribs and a busted leg, but that was all.' He gave a small, bleak smile. 'David Becket was doing volunteer work at the hospital up there when we were brought in. He took care of me in the hospital, and a few days later his wife Judy came in to visit with me. They found out I didn't have any family left to speak of, and asked me if I wanted to go live with them.'

'Just like that?'

'Almost,' Sam said simply. 'David always said it was like love at first sight for them both. They fostered me for just over a year, and then they adopted me. I'm the descendant of a runaway slave from Georgia; David's and Judy's parents escaped from the Nazis in Europe – maybe that gave us something in common, I don't know.'

'Did you have many problems?' Grace asked.

'Some, of course. Changing schools – changing lives. Pretty heavy stuff for a kid.' Sam's eyes were hazy with recall. 'They talked to me a lot during the year they were fostering me about the bad stuff they knew we might all hit up against if I became their son. Judy was more down-to-earth about it. David was an idealist. To him, there was really nothing to consider, certainly nothing we couldn't surmount if we were together.'

'David's a wonderful man,' Grace said softly.

'Judy's no slouch either,' Sam said. 'Have you met my mother?'

'Not yet. You have a brother, don't you?'

Sam nodded. 'Saul.' Another smile. 'He's thirteen, about to be barmitzvah.' He speared a piece of squid. 'Now that's an endurance test I can relate to.'

'You had a barmitzvah?' Grace smiled at the notion.

'Did I ever.' He shook his head at the memories of Hebrew lessons and the ordeal of having to stand up in synagogue to be counted. 'It was Judy's idea more than David's, but they both took a lot of time making sure it was what I wanted, too.'

'And you did?'

'I wanted to be their son,' Sam answered simply. 'Whatever that took.'

'Did you convert?'

'No. David and Judy never wanted me to feel I was turning my back on my parents' religion – they were Episcopalian – or our culture. They found this real broadminded rabbi who understood and who was willing to teach me and let us go through the whole thing in temple, but I guess it wasn't really kosher according to Jewish law.' He grinned. 'Probably still kosher enough to make me the only barmitzvahed, Friday-night-candle-lighting, Bahamian-black-Episcopalian police detective living in South Beach.'

'Do you light candles?' Grace asked, intrigued.

'To be honest, hardly ever.' His grin became a grimace. 'And since it's Passover, and this evening was our Seder, and I'm definitely going to be *persona non grata* with my mother for missing out, I guess that's another thing not to confess to her.' Sam dropped a piece of shrimp for Harry, who promptly set up a new sentry post between their chairs. 'How about you, Grace?' he asked. 'Has your own mixed bag brought you many complications?'

'None that have much to do with the fact that my father was a second-generation American-Italian-Catholic and my mother third-generation Swedish-American-Protestant.' Grace shrugged. 'Plenty that had to do with what they were like as human beings.'

Sam looked at her keenly. 'Not an easy start?'

'Worse for my sister than for me.' She paused. 'They were

84

an ill-matched, unhappy couple, and their greatest combined gift was for spreading their own misery over us.'

'Does your sister live here, too?'

'Claudia lives part-time in Fort Lauderdale, part down in the Keys. Matter of fact, I'm driving down to Islamorada on Saturday morning for the weekend.'

'Do you like the Keys?' Sam asked.

'Sure, though I couldn't spend too much time down there.'

'Me neither,' Sam said. 'I like the buzz of a city around me.'

'The mix seems to suit my sister and her family well,' Grace went on. 'My brother-in-law's an architect who loves to fish, so he figured the Upper Keys were the perfect location for them to build their own house – most of his clients tend to be in south-east Florida.' She paused. 'I think Claudia's at her happiest when they're living on Islamorada. Probably because it's the farthest she could get from Chicago.'

'Chicago?' Sam queried.

'Where our parents live,' Grace said.

She waited until after Sam had finished eating before asking, as she brewed some fresh coffee, what he'd wanted to talk to her about when he'd first asked if he might call on her. The fleeting disappointment in his eyes let her know that he'd been just as relaxed, had been having just as much of a good time as she had.

'It was something we uncovered,' he answered, slowly, 'that I figured, as Cathy's psychologist, you probably ought to know.'

They already knew, he went on, that Cathy had visited Beatrice Flager as a client – she had admitted that much herself – but if there had been a file with her name on it in one of Flager's cabinets, it had been either removed by the therapist herself or had been stolen by person or persons unknown by the time the police had become involved.

'Like most people these days, though, Ms Flager kept a full set of records on computer.' Sam paused. 'The equipment was smashed when we got to her house, but according to our experts, unless the person doing the smashing really knew what they were doing, they wouldn't have easily been able to destroy information on the hard disk itself.'

The coffee was ready, and Grace asked Sam if he minded moving outside on to the deck. 'I don't know why, but I always try to take the tricky stuff outside,' she said as they carried out their cups. 'Maybe it's something to do with the water, maybe I'm subconsciously trying to toss my troubles into it and watch them float away.' She saw him watching her. 'Or maybe it's just a pretty spot.'

'Bit of both, I'd guess.'

'I'm going to kick off my shoes and dunk my feet in the water.' Grace did just that, sat down on the edge and thought about the way she and Cathy had done much the same at the side of the Robbins' pool that afternoon.

'Looks good,' Sam said, and did the same. His feet, Grace noted, were compact for such a tall man. As he had indoors, Harry came right over and lay down between them. For a few moments, they stayed quiet.

'Want to tell me what was on the disk?' Grace asked Sam, at last. 'Or are you too beat? It's pretty late.'

'I feel great, if you're okay?'

'I'm fine,' she said. 'I told you, I'm a late-night person. But this is such grim stuff, isn't it? I mean, you need to take a break for a few hours.'

'I don't need a break. It's not my own grim stuff, after all.' His eyes were fixed on the dark water. 'Not my pain.'

Something in his tone – just a whisker of something, nothing more – and a tiny flicker in his eyes alerted Grace to the probability that Sam Becket knew all about great pain – something perhaps even greater, she thought with a flash of insight, than what must have crushed him as a child. For the briefest of moments she let herself wonder about that, then pushed it away.

'So what did you find?' She saw no point putting off the moment.

'We found Cathy's file. It was pretty short. She only went to see Beatrice Flager one time, and that was because Arnold Robbins made her go. Robbins told Ms Flager that he was very concerned about his daughter.' Sam took a sip of coffee.

'Why was he concerned?'

'Typical adolescent stuff. Withdrawn, sluggish, problems keeping friends. Low self-esteem, generally. Robbins seemed

genuinely worried.' He paused again. 'He told Flager that
Cathy had been for counselling a few years back, before she
and her mother had come to Miami —'

'I thought Cathy had always lived here?'

'Not according to the therapist's files,' Sam said, 'though
Arnold didn't tell Flager where they'd relocated from.'

Grace took a moment to sort through what she could, from
the confidentiality standpoint, share with him. 'You probably
noticed that there were several family photographs in Cathy's
bedroom at the Robbins' house, but none of her natural father.
She says that she doesn't remember him.'

'Maybe that's true,' Sam said. 'I gather he died when she
was five.' He paused. 'I was two years older than Cathy when
my family died, so I can't really judge.'

'I guess not.' Grace drank some coffee and gazed out over
the water at the Bal Harbour lights. 'So according to Beatrice
Flager's records, what happened when Cathy went to see her?'

'Not a great deal. Ms Flager felt that Cathy didn't want to be
there, that she resented the whole encounter. She wrote in her
notes that Cathy objected to her wanting to tape their session –
is that normal, Grace? Do you tape sessions with your patients?'

'Not usually, though some psychologists do and sometimes
it's mandatory.' Grace paused. 'Cathy did tell me about that,
by the way. About having been to a therapist who'd taped
everything she'd said. She told me she didn't like it.' Grace
looked more closely at Sam, wanting to be sure he understood
the point she was making. 'I mean, Cathy was quite open with
me on that score – it came up because she was checking me
out, making comparisons between me and her last experience.'

'Did she tell you what she did after the session with
Beatrice Flager?'

'No.' Grace hesitated. 'I thought she only saw her once?'

'That's right,' Sam confirmed, 'but Flager added some
more notes to her file after Arnold Robbins called her to bring
her up to speed.' He paused. 'Robbins said that Cathy had a
temper tantrum when she got home – and that she cut the
heads off all the goldfish in Marie's fish tank.'

'Really?' Grace was shaken. 'Cathy did that?'

'According to the notes she denied it, then flew into another rage and smashed some ornaments in her bedroom. Arnold and Marie were both sufficiently alarmed to take Cathy to the family doctor, who ordered some blood tests.' Sam looked up from the water and into Grace's face. 'The tests showed that Cathy had taken – ingested, the notes said – cannabis.'

'What did Cathy say?'

'She denied that, too, but no one believed her.' Sam shook his head. 'In the circumstances, how could they?'

Grace stayed out on the deck for a while longer after Sam had left. Beatrice Flager's notes about Cathy's disturbed adolescent behaviour had dismayed her deeply, and however sympathetic Sam Becket might seem to her plight, it wasn't hard to see how this had to be damaging the teenager's credibility with the rest of his department and perhaps with the State Attorney's office, too.

Up until now – at least to her and, she sensed, Sam Becket – Cathy had been, above all else, a victim.

Now, suddenly, they were being forced to look at her as a young person who had allegedly cut the heads off goldfish.

Grace sat on the edge of the deck again and stared down into the water, trying for a few moments to visualize Cathy doing such a thing. Briefly imagining her patients in the midst or depths of their traumas was a thing she had trained herself to do over the years. A degree of detachment was essential, of course, to a psychologist, but absolute detachment had frankly always been impossible for Grace, especially since most of her work involved children – how in the name of God could anyone stay unaffected by those suffering, messed up young psyches?

She gave up trying to imagine the sensitive girl who'd been so gentle with Harry mutilating living creatures, and thought instead about her taking cannabis. That, at least, was not so hard to envisage, nor were the reasons she might have done so: a desire to escape or simply to feel better than she had at the time.

Even so, breaking a few ornaments, taking cannabis from some outside influence – and even decapitating her mother's goldfish – were all still light years from the murders of her parents and former therapist.

*

The telephone rang just as she was climbing into bed and Harry had burrowed down, as he did every night, into the base of her duvet.

'Grace, it's Sam.'

'What's happened?' She felt a jolt of alarm.

'Nothing. Nothing's happened.' He paused. 'Ah, shit, I've woken you, haven't I? I knew I should have left it till morning.'

Grace glanced at her clock and saw that it was almost three o'clock.

'It is morning, Sam,' she said. 'And you only left an hour ago. Anyway, I wasn't sleeping. Too busy thinking.'

'Me too. About Cathy?'

'Of course.'

'You still don't think she did it, do you?'

'No, I don't,' Grace said.

'Me neither,' Sam said. 'Though things could look better for her.'

'I guess they could.'

'Actually I didn't really call to talk about Cathy – I called to thank you. For the *Cacciucco* and the hospitality.'

'It was no trouble. The soup was made. It was a pleasure sharing it.'

'For me, too.'

Grace smiled into the dark. 'It's nice of you to call.'

'Must be my mother's training.'

'Must be.'

'I'll let you get some sleep then,' Sam said.

'What about you?' She realized suddenly that he sounded anything but tired. In fact, he sounded wired. 'It was my coffee, wasn't it? I knew I made it too strong.'

'It was great. But I am wide awake, so I thought I'd spend a little quiet time trying to nail down some other connection between the Robbinses and Beatrice Flager.'

'That would be good,' Grace said.

'Up until the therapist was killed, there was a fair chance that the Robbins' deaths might have been business or money-related – maybe something heavy that Arnold Robbins got into through his **Arnie's** chain.'

'But Beatrice Flager getting murdered put paid to that?'

'I'm not ready to stop looking yet,' Sam said.

Grace hesitated for a moment. Late as it was, there was still an unasked question gnawing away at her. 'You mentioned, after the first killings, finding some burned fabric that might have been Cathy's nightgown.' She tried to pick her words carefully. 'Was there anything else?'

'Such as?'

'I don't know. Anything the police surgeon found on her.'

Another brief silence crept between them.

'You're asking about the Band-Aid on her arm, aren't you?' he said.

Grace winced at his acuteness. 'Yes, I am.' Her face grew warm. She was grateful he wasn't here to see it.

'Cathy said she stumbled against a tree trunk the day before the killings, scraped her arm.' Sam paused. 'We confirmed that, Grace. It wasn't a cut from a scalpel. Nor anything to do with the broken window, if that's what you were thinking.'

Grace hadn't even considered the window.

'If it was bothering you,' he asked, 'why didn't you ask me about it before?'

'I don't know,' she lied.

She knew he didn't believe that; he realized that she had, in some confused way, been reluctant to stir up more trouble for the teenager – or that, maybe, she simply hadn't wanted to risk having to contemplate another possible strike against Cathy.

She also felt that – as a man rather than as a cop – he understood.

CHAPTER THIRTEEN

SUNDAY, APRIL 12, 1998

It had been an almost perfect family weekend on Islamorada until Grace had checked her messages on Easter morning and heard Frances Dean telling her that the police had taken Cathy in for questioning, and that Sam Becket had as good as told her it was time to get her niece a lawyer. Grace didn't know exactly when the message had been left, but when she had tried calling back there was no answer.

'She wouldn't be calling me if she weren't desperate,' she told Claudia – physically so much like their father, with her pale olive skin, brown eyes and smooth, dark hair, cut in a bob that swung with every movement.

They were sitting on the porch drinking Cokes while Claudia's husband Daniel Brownley barbecued on the deck, their boys horsed around in the water and Sadie – the wire-haired dachshund who had come to the Brownleys three years before – flopped in the shade, her brandy-coloured eyes darting back and forth between the youngsters and the chicken legs on the barbecue. (Harry and Sadie got along famously, and Harry liked to travel and thoroughly *dis*liked Grace's packing any size bag and leaving home without him, but she had to attend a seminar on Key Largo that Monday – and Lord only knew that a hotel banqueting suite filled with shrinks was no place for Harry – and so he'd been left in the tender care of Teddy Lopez.)

'Do you want to go home?' Claudia asked, keeping an eye out for Robbie, her youngest at six, who tended to overstretch himself in every activity in the vain hope of keeping up with Mike, his eight-year-old brother.

'I would if I thought there was much I could do to help,' Grace said. 'But if Cathy's in custody, I won't be allowed to talk to her, and though of course I'll try Frances again later, I don't think it's a psychologist she either wants or needs.'

'What does she want?'

'An ally. Someone to prove that her niece is innocent.' Grace gave a small sigh of regret. 'I'm no miracle worker. I wish I were.'

They had gritted their teeth that morning and tried calling their parents' home in Chicago to check on Ellen's condition, but there'd been no answer, and for a while the sisters had sat quietly – too quietly – allowing irrational guilt to ebb and flow, until Daniel had put a finish to it, at least for the time being.

'You want to go to Chicago?' he'd asked them, straight out.

As an architect, Daniel Brownley – a tall, angular man with myopic green eyes and slightly rounded shoulders from years spent hunched over plans – tended towards straight, clear lines in thought and deed as well as in his designs. It wasn't that he didn't fully comprehend and empathize with the convolutions of hearts and souls, but for Daniel, if there was a true, linear approach to a problem, then that was what he chose to try first.

'Not really,' his wife had answered.

'Not in the least,' Grace had said, for her own part.

'Do you figure you ought to be helping Frank out?'

'No.' Grace led that time.

'Ditto,' Claudia followed.

'Is there something you could be doing for your mother?'

'Hard to tell, unless we talk to Papa again.' Claudia, for one, had no more clear-cut answers.

'So you'll try calling him again later or tomorrow,' Daniel had concluded, practical as always, 'and in the meantime you can help me hide the boys' Easter eggs.'

'How about we hide them in the house this time?' Claudia suggested.

'I don't think so,' her husband disagreed. 'They'll smash things, we'll get mad and then we'll feel guilty and they'll hate us.'

'But they already know all the hiding places outdoors,' Claudia pointed out. They'd been playing the same game since Mike's third Easter.

'So they'll feel smart for finding them so easily,' Grace had said.

She left next morning without having reached either Cathy's aunt or Frank Lucca, but arrived at the Westin Beach Resort on Key Largo with enough time to spare before the start of the seminar to try calling Sam Becket in Miami.

To her surprise, she got him first time.

'Glad you called,' he said.

'How come you brought Cathy in?' Grace got straight to the point. 'Has something happened since Friday night?'

'Not really,' Sam answered, 'except for my sergeant, captain and chief all deciding that her recent history was grounds for asking her a few more questions.'

'That's it?' Grace was angry and sounded it.

'That was the reason for wanting to talk to her some more.'

'And you still don't have a shred of hard evidence against her?'

Sam's sigh came across the phone line. 'She hasn't been charged with anything, Grace.'

'Not yet,' she said, coolly. 'I take it she's been released?'

'She was never arrested.' He paused. 'She's in the hospital right now.'

'What happened?' Grace gripped the phone more tightly.

'She's okay,' Sam said hastily. 'She got sick to her stomach during questioning, then passed out, so we got her over to Jackson Memorial right away.' He paused. 'Her aunt got very upset, wanted to move her to a place in Coral Gables, but we compromised on a private room at Miami General.'

'I hope that wasn't too much trouble?' Grace said coldly.

'No one was anything but gentle with her,' Sam said. 'My dad went in to see her, and he tells me she's going home tomorrow. Check with him if you don't believe me.'

'I wasn't suggesting you got out the rubber hoses, Sam.'

'I know you weren't,' he said, quietly. 'Believe me, I hated every second of that questioning. No one enjoys this kind of case – no one on our team, anyway.'

Grace believed him.

In the knowledge that David Becket would most assuredly be taking good care of Cathy and that there was no purpose to be served by her speedy return to Miami, Grace headed for the conference room on the first floor, and the first session of the day – a lecture and debate on Factitious Disorder by proxy. The disorder – also commonly known as Münchhausen's Syndrome by proxy, or MSBP – was a highly complex, emotive syndrome for all concerned, not least for the psychiatrists and psychologists confronted with both the sufferers and their young victims; in the past five years Grace had personally encountered two children abused and endangered by their mentally sick mothers.

'Grisly stuff,' a male voice said just behind her during the recess as she grabbed a much-needed cup of coffee.

She turned around. A tall, slim man of around forty-five, in a rumpled beige linen suit, stood looking at her. His name tag read Dr Peter Hayman.

'As often as I hear the stories,' he said, 'they still give me the chills.' His eyes, behind slightly tinted spectacles, were brown and couched in sun, laugh or frown wrinkles. 'Peter Hayman,' he said.

She put down her cup and saucer and shook his hand. 'Grace Lucca.'

'I know.'

'How come?' She hadn't pinned on her name tag. She'd never liked being labelled unless there was a good reason.

'You've been seeing the child in the Robbins murder case, Dr Lucca.' Hayman caught the wariness in her eyes and explained: 'Your name was in one of the newspapers.'

'Which one?'

'I'm not sure. Could have been the *Herald*.'

'It wasn't.'

'Maybe the *Sentinel*.'

'I'd be mad if it was in either,' she said.

'I know.' Hayman spoke quietly, with implicit understanding. 'Poor kid has more than enough on her plate without that kind of intrusion.'

'Yes, she does.' Grace paused, frowning. 'Was there a photograph of me?'

'Where?'

'In the newspaper. You seem to have recognized me.'

'You're very cautious, Dr Lucca.' Hayman smiled.

'Where privacy is concerned, yes, I am.'

'There was no photograph,' he said. 'I noticed your name on the registration list when I collected my name tag, and made it my business to ask about you.'

'Why did you do that?'

Peter Hayman glanced around. 'Could we go somewhere a little less jammed?'

'Where did you have in mind?'

If Hayman found Grace's continuing caution offensive, he didn't show it.

'Just a swift stroll – get out of the air conditioning for a few minutes, maybe? Someplace less noisy where we can talk without being overheard.'

'What is it you want to talk about, Dr Hayman?'

He took a moment before he answered. 'An old case of mine.' He seemed to search for the appropriate words. 'One that's thrown up a few possible parallels with the Robbins case that I think you might find interesting.'

'What kind of parallels?' Grace was suddenly off-balance.

'This is something that might help,' Hayman said.

'Help who?'

'Cathy Robbins.'

As it turned out, there was no time left for further conversation before the end of the coffee recess, so it was lunchtime before they took their stroll outside the hotel, through shady mangroves down to a boardwalk overlooking Florida Bay. It was a perfect Keys afternoon, warm and balmy with a light breeze, the shallow water a tranquil vivid blue; a setting infinitely more suited for day-dreaming or siesta than for discussions about murder.

Peter Hayman came to the point. In his capacity as a psychiatrist, he explained, he had, a few years back, been asked to see a young patient on the Florida west coast – somewhere in the vicinity of St Petersburg, he said with careful vagueness – accused of shooting his parents.

'No one's accused Cathy Robbins of any crime,' Grace asserted crisply.

'Not yet,' Hayman said, calmly. 'But reading between the lines, there seems every possibility that they might, given time.'

'I think you've read too much between the lines.'

'Maybe. I still see no harm in sharing a few facts with you that strike me as salient. Taking confidentiality into account, that is,' he added.

Grace kept silent.

'Would you like to sit down?' Hayman asked.

'I'm happy to stand,' she said. 'We'll be sitting all afternoon.'

'I often wonder why they don't take seminars like ours out to the beach,' the psychiatrist mused. 'All those cold, air-conditioned rooms, everyone uncomfortable as hell, with paradise right outside the window.'

'Too comfortable. Hard chairs and cold air keep us awake.'

'Not always.' Hayman smiled.

'You had something to tell me?'

He wasted no more time. The young man in his case, he told Grace, had fallen under suspicion because of general behavioural problems and because he was known to have taken illegal drugs, but as Hayman had come to know him, he'd come to the conclusion that those violent acts – even taking drugs into account – were completely at odds with his character.

'The two obvious major differences between that case and what I know about the Robbins case,' Hayman said, 'are that my patient's parents both survived, and that the father was affluent and locally influential enough to keep the affair out of the public arena.'

'I'm puzzled that you seem to feel you know so much about the Robbins case.' Grace's antennae were bristling with fresh suspicion. 'I don't believe that too many details about the family have appeared in any newspaper.'

'No, they haven't,' Hayman agreed. He registered her cold expression. 'I'd better come clean.'

'I'd say so, if you want to continue this conversation.'

'I'd like to.' The psychiatrist paused. 'It's very simple. I read and saw and heard just enough about the case and the young woman concerned to strike some chords in me. On the strength of that, I made a few calls to Miami, asked the right people a few questions.'

'Which people?'

'I can't answer that.' He shrugged. 'I can confess to you that my interest is in part quite selfish, inasmuch as it relates to a subject I'm currently researching in some depth – in fact, if you hadn't shown up here today, Dr Lucca, I was thinking of getting in touch anyhow.'

'Go on.' Grace's curiosity, if nothing else, was piqued.

'Obviously I can't give you any precise details about what I did, ultimately, come to learn about those west coast shootings.' Hayman paused again. 'But I can tell you that I came to realize that what I was dealing with was a very strange variant of Factitious Disorder by proxy – MSBP, as I still tend to call it.'

'I don't understand.'

'A mother who – rather than creating symptoms of *physical* illness in her child so that he might have to undergo tests and treatments – deliberately fabricated her son's psychosis.' Hayman saw from her fascinated, horrified expression that he'd more than captured Grace's attention. 'It took me a while, too, I assure you, Dr Lucca.'

'But what are you saying about the shooting?' she asked, confused and appalled. 'That the son was driven by his mother to attack her and his father? Or that the mother pulled the trigger herself and set it up to look as though her son had done it?'

'I can't really answer those questions,' Peter Hayman said, 'other than to tell you that the MSBP element started long before the shootings.'

'The mother making it look as if her son was mentally sick?'

'In that instance, yes.' He shook his head. 'I'm not saying that it necessarily has any relevance at all to your Miami scenario – just that something about the case rang some warning bells in my head.' He paused. 'There was a great deal of suffering for that family – the teenager involved went

97

through all kinds of hell. I just felt it wouldn't hurt to share my experience with the psychologist caring for Cathy Robbins.'

'Except, of course, that in her case both her parents are dead.'

'Doesn't make it impossible,' Hayman said.

CHAPTER FOURTEEN

'Your mother's mad at you,' David Becket told Sam when he dropped by for a cup of coffee on Sunday evening.

'Ma's always mad at me,' Sam said easily.

'Your father's the one who's really mad at you,' Judy Becket said.

'What's up with you, Dad?' Sam asked, surprised.

David shook his head and grunted.

'Dad's mad at you because of the girl in the hospital,' Saul Becket informed his older brother. 'He told Ma not to say anything to you about it, but you know Ma.'

Sam was aware that Judy was still claiming to be pissed with him for being too busy to make it to the Seder the previous Friday, but he was also aware that she understood perfectly well that if he could have made it in time, he would have. His father's anger was a rarity.

It was just after ten o'clock, and they were all sitting around the living room in the house in Golden Beach that the Beckets had lived in for more than twenty-five years. The TV was turned down low because David wanted to watch the news but Saul was supposed to be working on a school assignment. There was a shabbiness about the room that Judy – a petite, trim woman with brown, silvering curly hair and intelligent hazel eyes – sometimes complained about, but the truth was she loved every soft, snug inch of the battered old furniture she and her husband had lived with since before they'd become parents. Every scuff and scratch on Judy Becket's mahogany cabinets and bookcases reminded her that she and David had brought up two happy sons who'd always felt free to enjoy their home rather than treat it as a showcase.

'Cathy Robbins is doing okay, isn't she, Dad?' Sam asked his father.

'Compared to what?' David answered, dryly.

'I know,' Sam said, quietly.

'You may know, Sam, but do you really understand?' David's tone was quiet, but full of rebuke. 'Do you understand that she collapsed at the station yesterday because she'd already bottled up a whole ocean of stress, and she just couldn't take one more question – one more outrageous accusation?'

'No one's —'

'Don't tell me no one's accusing her of anything,' his father interrupted heatedly, 'because you and I both know better than that.' He shook his greying head. 'Your brother's right – I am mad about this, and I'm sad and I'm tired, too, about the things that have been happening to this child.'

'What makes you so sure she's innocent?' Judy asked her husband.

'Instinct makes me sure.' David shrugged. 'My eyes – my ears. My experience. I look at her and I listen to her, and I see and hear a little girl who's lost her mother and father. Who's seen and touched their dead bodies, for God's sake.' He took off his spectacles and rubbed the bridge of his nose, a weary but still angry gesture. 'And instead of going and looking for the real maniac behind these slayings, the Miami Beach police – including my own *son* – are harassing this poor child.'

Sam leaned forward. 'Dad, I do understand, believe me. I feel the same way.'

'But you were there, at the questioning.'

'Sure I was there,' Sam said. 'I'm the lead investigator – it's my case. There were questions that had to be asked.'

'Did they have to be asked there, in the police station, with your chief and a lawyer present?' David wanted to know. 'Couldn't they have been asked in her aunt's house, with someone who loves her beside her?'

'No, they couldn't,' Sam replied. 'Dad, three people have died —'

'I know,' David broke in again. 'And Cathy Robbins is the common denominator between them, I know that too. But

100

maybe if you and your chief and your other colleagues looked a little further than the ends of your noses you might find someone else who fits the same bill. And hasn't it occurred to you that maybe there's someone out there who just *wants* it to seem like Cathy could be the killer?'

'Who would want to do such a dreadful thing?' Judy asked. 'If she's as sweet and innocent as you seem to believe.'

'I can't imagine,' David answered. 'But then, I'm just a middle-aged Jewish doctor, not a shrink or a detective.'

'Middle-aged enough, maybe,' his wife suggested, 'to stop giving your son a hard time for doing his job the only way he can.'

'I'm not giving him a hard time,' David said.

'Could have fooled me,' Judy retorted.

'Dad's giving us all a hard time,' Sam told his mother. 'The department, the system. And I can't say I blame him. If I were in his place, having to try to fix up a fourteen-year-old girl distressed enough by questioning to need to go to the hospital, I'd feel the same way.'

'Do you think she did kill her mom and dad, Sam?' Saul, a young, male, carbon copy of his mother, who'd been staying quietly under cover of his school books, sounded more anxious than curious as he asked Sam the crucial question. It was one thing living close to a city where you knew that too many kids carried knives or guns, but it was another thing entirely when you thought about a girl from a nice, regular-sounding family – a girl just one year older than yourself – doing what the TV news people at the Coconut Grove crime scene had all-too-graphically described.

'I don't know, Saul,' Sam said, troubled by the fear in his brother's voice and eyes. 'I honestly don't know.'

'What does Grace Lucca think about it?' their father asked.

'Why don't you ask her?'

'You've talked to her about Cathy, I'm sure.'

'Yes, of course.' Sam paused. 'Grace says she doesn't think Cathy's guilty of anything. Frankly, though, I think she feels the way I do.'

'Which is?' David asked.

'I don't *want* Cathy to be guilty,' Sam said. 'I hope like hell she's innocent.'

101

'But you're not sure?' Saul asked.

'Not as sure as I'd like to be, no.'

Judy Becket was sitting up a little straighter than she had been.

'So you and Dr Lucca are on first-name terms already?' she asked.

CHAPTER FIFTEEN

MONDAY, APRIL 13, 1998

Grace's first stop when she drove back into Miami on Monday morning was at Miami General. After ten minutes talking to David Becket, she felt comforted to know for sure that his intuition was still riding in tandem with her own.

'I think she's a good kid,' the doctor told her over two cups of machine coffee near the nurse's station on Cathy's floor. 'For what it's worth, I've told my son what I think.'

'I don't think Sam really disagrees with you,' Grace said.

Becket's face was sad. 'Sam doesn't want to disagree with me,' he said. 'That's a little different.'

Cathy was out of bed, sitting in a chair by the window. She was paler than the last time Grace had seen her, but otherwise not markedly changed.

'How're you doing?'

'I'm okay.'

'I hear you're getting out of here later.'

'So they tell me.' Cathy turned her face away and gazed out through the glass at nothing in particular.

'Aren't you ready to leave?'

'Depends on where I'm going next, doesn't it?'

'Back to your Aunt Frances' house, I guess,' Grace said.

'Or back to the police station.'

Her voice was dull, but one didn't need to be a psychologist to recognize the fear and bitterness behind the words.

'Has anyone been in to talk to you?' Grace asked.

Cathy turned around. 'The cops, you mean?' She shook her head. 'Not yet – but I guess that's because Dr Becket wouldn't let them.' She smiled for the first time. 'He was pretty mad at them, you know. He's an okay guy.'

'You know he's the detective's father, don't you?'

'I know. Weird, huh?'

'What do you think of Detective Becket, Cathy?' The instant the question was out of her mouth, Grace was unsure of her motive for asking it.

'I don't know.' Cathy shrugged. 'He's okay, I guess.'

'For a cop,' Grace said.

'I guess.' Cathy paused. 'His dad likes you a lot.'

'Does he?'

'He told me I could trust you.'

'That was nice of him.' She looked into Cathy's eyes. 'Do you believe him?'

She didn't answer right away.

'I guess,' she said again, finally.

It was afternoon before Grace was able to surface for long enough to put a call in to the Person Crimes office. Another detective named Martinez told her that Sam was likely to be snarled up for the rest of the day, yet less than fifteen minutes later he called her back.

'I only have a minute, but I thought it might be urgent.'

'Not exactly urgent,' Grace said, 'but I would appreciate another meeting, if you can find the time.'

'Dinner okay?' he asked. 'I don't know how long I'll have, but we could share whatever time I can grab.'

Grace considered for no more than a second.

'Fine by me.'

They met up at a small seafood restaurant near the northern edge of South Beach – Sam's choice, since it was home territory for him. It was a quietish place, devoid of razzmatazz and obvious tourists, but still buzzy enough for earnest conversation not to be easily overheard.

'You realize I want to talk about Cathy,' Grace said right after they'd sat down, keen to be open with him and not misunderstood.

'What else?' Sam said. His eyes were gently humorous.

They ordered – stone-crab claws and swordfish – and then

104

Grace told him about Dr Peter Hayman's case history, which had been scratching major holes in her thoughts now for more than twenty-four hours.

Sam knew something about both Münchhausen's and MSBP, but his first response after hearing about the west coast shootings and Hayman's findings was much the same as her own initial reaction.

'Lord knows I'm willing to listen to any theories you want to run by me,' he said, 'but surely in this case the possibilities are a little limited, with Cathy's mother dead?'

'That's what I said at first. Then I got to thinking.' Grace paused. 'Don't forget this is a Münchhausen's-*type* disorder Hayman is talking about, so its scope may be way beyond anything we've come across before.' She drank some water. Her wine glass was filled with Chardonnay, but she wanted a clear head until she'd told Sam everything she needed to. 'Don't misunderstand me,' she went on quickly. 'I know how off-the-wall this may very well be, but I've been thinking about it a lot since Dr Hayman approached me, and I do think it's worth considering.'

'I'm listening,' Sam said.

'Who's to say – purely hypothetically – that a woman might not be sick enough to be prepared to endanger herself – maybe even to die – in the act of proving her child psychotic?' She paused, took a close look at Sam, trying to see how he was receiving this so far. 'And taking that even further, who's to say that she might not have paid someone to help go on framing Cathy even after she and Arnold were dead and gone?'

'That's a hell of a hypothesis,' Sam said.

'I know it is.' Grace was getting morose. 'Especially since both Münchhausen's and MSBP sufferers want the attention that comes from either being sick or having a sick child.'

'So getting yourself killed in the act would be pointless.'

'I guess it would. Except —'

'Except we're not exactly talking about Münchhausen's.'

'No.'

Sam mulled over his thoughts for a moment. 'Do we have any idea what causes MSBP? Is it one of those things that comes prepacked in our genes, or is it triggered by something?'

'We don't know exactly what causes either syndrome. We know that they're factitious disorders, and that the symptoms a regular sufferer presents are real to them. They're not malingerers – just desperate to be cared for in a hospital setting.'

'The cry for help syndrome?'

'Almost certainly. And for attention. They have an uncontrollable need to be investigated and treated – sometimes even to undergo surgery, no matter how much pain or unpleasantness that means they have to endure.'

'Sounds like a kind of masochism,' Sam said. 'Which makes MSBP a type of sadism, doesn't it?'

'I think it's a lot more complex than that, and a whole lot sadder.'

Sam took another minute. 'My father said something yesterday that meshes with what I think you're getting at. You said Marie might have paid someone to go on framing Cathy. Dad thinks we should be trying to find someone who wants it to look as if Cathy Robbins might be the killer.'

'A straightforward frame, you mean?'

'Anything but straightforward,' Sam said. 'But I really find it hard to believe a mother could do something so evil to her own child. She'd have to be some kind of monster.'

'Or very sick,' Grace said.

'Like this young man's mother in Dr Hayman's case.'

'Maybe.'

Sam thought about it again. 'Is it always mothers who get MSBP?'

'Almost always, though fathers do suffer, too – and I've read cases of nurses who've harmed children in their care being diagnosed with MSBP, though personally I have some doubts on that score.'

'Anyway, it gets us nowhere, since Arnold Robbins died too,' Sam said.

'And her natural father died years ago.'

Sam shook his head. 'I have to say I think this theory's a non-starter, Grace. And even supposing there were a grain of truth in it, how in hell would you go about trying to prove it?'

'I was hoping you might want to help do that. At least by broadening the investigation.'

'The investigation's still open.' Sam glanced around,

lowered his voice even further. 'So's my own mind, but I do have to say that more than a couple of people in my unit are pretty much convinced that Cathy's guilty and that her aunt's been covering up for her.'

'But you still have no more proof, do you?' Grace had less intention than ever of giving up.

'Nothing solid, or Cathy would have been charged.'

'Surely it's in everyone's best interests for you *all* to keep an open mind.' She paused. 'Maybe I could talk to your chief about this theory?'

'I don't think that's such a great idea,' Sam said.

'Because it's off-the-wall?'

He smiled wryly. 'You said it, not me.'

'Maybe you could talk to him about it instead?'

'Maybe.'

'One thing you could do for me,' Grace said.

'And what's that?' The wryness was still there.

'Marie's first marriage – Cathy's natural father.'

'What about them?'

'No one wants to talk about them. I've been getting curious, and I think a little more knowledge might equip me better to help Cathy.'

'You want me to see if I can find out something about that?'

Grace nodded. 'I'd be grateful.'

'I'll put out some feelers,' Sam said.

For the first time since they had sat down, Grace relaxed, took a long sip of wine. It tasted good. She looked around the restaurant. It had been almost full when they'd arrived, but somewhere along the line more than half the diners had left.

'So,' she said.

'So,' Sam said.

'What do we talk about now?' She remembered what he'd said that afternoon about not having long to spare. 'Or do you need to get out of here?'

'I have time,' he said. 'Unless I get a call.'

'Do you have your pager with you?'

'Always.'

'Always?'

He grinned. 'Afraid so.'

His eyes half closed when he smiled that time, giving him a

lazy, warm look that was a thousand miles removed from the cooler, sharper, very clear-sighted expression he seemed to wear most of the time in his official capacity.

Grace liked both looks.

They pushed Cathy Robbins temporarily to one side and started the tentative business of getting to know one another a little better – something, Grace felt, they were both certain by now that they wanted to do. She told Sam some more about her childhood with Claudia in Chicago, and their disastrous relationship with Frank and Ellen Lucca, and Sam told her that he'd been married once, to a woman named Althea, and that the marriage had ended in divorce.

'A bitter one, I'm afraid,' he said softly.

'Do you have children?' Grace asked.

Sam took a moment before answering.

'We had a son,' he said. 'His name was Sampson.'

Was. The word hung in the air.

'He died,' Sam explained. 'He was run down by a drunk driver.'

She saw the veins in his neck tauten, read the nightmare replaying behind his eyes, felt – and rapidly quelled – the urge to reach for his hand.

'He was three years old.' Sam's voice was steady but very low. 'My wife blamed me. I wasn't with Sampson when it happened, and she was, but Althea still blamed me.' He gave a small shrug. 'So did I.'

'Why, if you weren't with him?' Grace put the question gently.

'Exactly because of that,' Sam answered simply. 'Because maybe if I had been with them, it might not have happened.' He paused. 'Correction. If I'd been there, it would most certainly not have happened. I'd have been holding on to Sampson's hand more tightly, so when he pulled away I'd have been able to keep ahold of him. Althea wasn't very strong. And she was very tired that day – she'd had a lot of sleepless nights, worrying about me.'

'Do you blame yourself for that, too?'

'Of course I do,' Sam said.

*

They took a stroll through South Beach before parting. It was a pleasant evening, not too warm or humid. They walked slowly, close but not too close, and though Sam was about eight inches taller than Grace, they kept pace easily, naturally. Ocean Drive was alive and kicking as it was every evening of every week, young and not-so-young people – some colourful, some ordinary, some downright wacky-looking – blading or just walking, some talking animatedly, some just watching, drinking, smoking, hanging out outside Casablanca and the All Star Café, or staring at the Versace house. Sam and Grace were both mostly silent now, but her mind at least was full of images of Cathy Robbins – growing ever more bitter and afraid – and fantasy pictures of Sampson Becket at least half grown: a boy who, had he lived, would probably have begun by now to look like his daddy, tall, lean, broad, gentle tough guy.

Sam walked Grace back to her Mazda, parked outside the restaurant.

'Going back to work?' she asked, unlocking the driver's door.

'Not tonight,' he answered. 'Not unless I have to.'

She looked up at him. 'Paperwork for me, I'm afraid.'

'Like that as much as me, do you?'

'Do I ever.' She smiled.

'I'm going to wander back to my place,' Sam said, sounding lazy, 'and then I'm going to head up to my roof, which is where I like to hang out, and I'm going to sing a couple of arias and give my neighbours something to bitch about.'

'You're a singer?' Grace was surprised, and sounded it.

'Oh, yeah,' Sam said, and grinned. 'I'm not great, but I'm not too bad either – but even if I was the worst baritone in south Florida, I couldn't give it up. Singing and listening to opera's what I love to do more than anything.'

'I like to listen, too.'

'Like?' Sam shook his head. 'No such word when you're talking about opera, Grace Lucca. Love or hate. Nothing in between.'

'Perhaps I need teaching how to listen.'

'Perhaps you do,' Sam said.

CHAPTER SIXTEEN

WEDNESDAY, APRIL 15, 1998

The whole of Tuesday and most of Wednesday flew by for Grace with scarcely enough time to draw breath let alone spend it worrying about Cathy Robbins. Patients and paperwork aside, she had a minor flood to deal with that stemmed – according to Ramon, the plumber, one of Teddy Lopez's many friends – from some pipework running between Grace's bedroom floor and kitchen ceiling. What had started out as a large patch of glistening damp had turned into a mess of wet and chunks of plaster.

'If you don' lemme do this now,' Ramon had warned direly before starting work, 'the whole ceilin's gonna cave in on you.'

It was hard, come Wednesday afternoon, to tell the difference.

She had just brewed fresh coffee for Ramon, Teddy and herself, and was fishing around in her own cup trying to remove a large paint flake, when the phone rang.

'How are things with you?' Sam asked.

'Don't ask.'

'Okay.' He paused. 'I have the information you asked for.'

Grace looked around for somewhere clean to set down her cup, but Ramon was drinking his coffee halfway up his ladder, and Teddy was picking plaster bits out of Harry's coat, so she decided to leave the kitchen and headed for the den instead.

'Okay,' she told Sam. 'I have a pen now.'

'I don't have many details,' he said, 'but what I do have

looks enough to be going on with, from your point-of-view.'

Grace felt a lick of foreboding. 'Go ahead.'

'Marie Robbins' first husband was a Dr John Broderick. He was a physician at Lafayette Hospital up in Tallahassee, which was where Cathy was born. The Brodericks were separated when he died in '89, though they had not divorced.' Sam paused. 'Seems the doctor was in quite a jam at the time, being investigated by the ethics committee at his hospital, which was why he took his own life.'

'Suicide?' Grace thought about Cathy aged five. *Oh, Christ.*

'He kept a sailboat at the Pensacola shore – it was hurricane season. He waited for the next big storm to hit, left a note for Marie, took off in his boat and got himself drowned.'

Grace said nothing. She didn't know what to say.

'Grace, are you okay?'

'Yes, I'm okay. It's like you said Monday night – it's not my pain, is it?' She paused. 'I guess it may begin to explain why her aunt doesn't like talking about the past.'

'A heavy load for a child to carry,' Sam said.

Grace knew what he was thinking. That the information represented more bad news for Cathy now. A severely traumatized young child, bearing Lord knew what kind of emotional scars into her adolescence, with a mother who had to have had her own burden to deal with … More grist to the State Attorney's mill if the intention was to suggest that they were looking at an out-of-control, perhaps even psychotic, teenager.

'It's not going to help her case, is it?' she said.

'Not so far as I can see.' Sam paused. 'I'm sorry, Grace.'

'I know you are.'

She hadn't seen or had a real conversation with Frances Dean for over a week – come to that, she'd never had much of a conversation with her. But after what Sam had just said, Grace was determined to try to put that right.

It was not easy to arrange. She called the same afternoon, asked Frances if she might drop by and see her, but she said she had an appointment, and next day, too, according to Frances, was too busy. Possibly, Grace thought afterwards, Frances hadn't been prepared for her persistence, which was why she ran out of excuses when Grace asked if she could come to Coral Gables on Friday morning.

'Cathy won't be here, you know,' Frances said. 'She's back in school.'

'I'm glad,' Grace said. 'That may help her a little.'

'Maybe,' Frances said. 'Nothing else has.'

Frances looked worse, Grace thought, each time she saw her. They sat in her living room as before, Frances sitting bolt upright, face pale and drawn, hands nervous in her lap. Grace regretted already that she was about to delve into an area that this intensely private woman undoubtedly considered no-go, but she also knew that if she was hoping to be of any significant use to Cathy, she needed to know as much as possible about her troubled early childhood.

Frances Dean did not want to talk about it. She wished, she said straight away, that Grace would leave her sister's past alone. That was what Marie had wanted more than anything when she'd left Tallahassee and brought Cathy to Miami. To start a new life, and to forget the old.

'She begged me not to talk about it to anyone,' Frances said.

'I understand that,' Grace said. 'but surely under the circumstances —'

'I made my sister a promise. No circumstances can or should change that.' She read the frustration in Grace's expression. 'I'm talking about guilt, Grace,' she explained. 'We're Catholics, you know, but my sister was far more devout than me, and far more burdened by guilt – much good it did her, God rest her poor soul.'

'Why did she feel guilty?' Grace asked, gently.

'She had nothing to feel guilty about,' Frances said, darkly, 'except perhaps, for choosing John Broderick as her husband.' She shook her head. 'But, being so devout, her vows meant everything to Marie, and she thought it at least partly her fault that their marriage turned bad.'

'I gather they were separated at the time of her husband's death?'

'Marie would never have divorced,' Frances said. 'And of course, when John died, she blamed herself for that too.'

Grace saw the other woman's lips purse tightly for a moment, observed the anger in her eyes, felt her almost straining against its power, and hoped she might let it go.

'I will tell you one thing, and no more,' Frances went on. 'John Broderick was a wicked, cruel man who used his position to abuse his wife and child.'

Awful, cold dismay lashed at Grace again. 'He abused Cathy?' Her voice was hushed.

'Not in the way you're thinking,' Frances said, 'though, Lord knows, what he did wasn't much better.'

'It might help if I knew.'

'Why? How? Cathy doesn't know about it. She was too young – she doesn't remember, which is at least one blessing.'

'She may not consciously remember, but —'

'Oh, *please.*' Frances rose from her armchair, propelled out of it by scorn, but then she brought herself visibly back under control, and sat down again. 'I'm sorry, Dr Lucca,' she said, reverting to formality, 'but I simply don't believe in these theories about forcing people to face dreadful things they've been fortunate enough to bury.'

'I don't necessarily disagree with you,' Grace said.

'My sister wasn't one of those women who use every opportunity to speak badly about their children's fathers. She was a good, kind, decent, God-fearing woman, Dr Lucca —' the anger was still there, still only just being held at bay '— and there are only two things left for me to do for her now, and one of those is to keep my word to her.'

'If you shared at least a little more with me, Frances,' Grace said, 'I promise you it would go no further.'

'That's not good enough. Marie wanted to leave all that shame behind her, and not be reminded of it ever again.' Frances' eyes filled suddenly with tears; she fished for her handkerchief in her pocket, found it, used it.

'And you don't think that my knowing about the past might help Cathy?'

'How could your knowing anything help her?' The scorn was evident again. 'Digging up the past isn't going to help find out who killed Marie and Arnold.' Frances took a breath, composed herself. 'If there is any justice beyond this world, John Broderick's burning in hell now, and Marie's surely in heaven. There's only *one* thing that's going to help that child now, and that's for the Miami Beach Police Department to do its job and catch the person who killed those good people, so that Cathy can go on with her life and put it behind her.'

Grace liked to think she knew when she was beaten.

'I didn't come here to pry, Frances,' she said. 'I hope you know that.'

'I'm not sure why you are here, Dr Lucca,' Frances said stiffly.

'I'm here as Cathy's psychologist and as her friend.'

'You're only here because the police asked you to come.'

'That's not true. I came in the first place because Dr Becket thought I might be able to help Cathy.'

'Because of what happened to her parents,' Frances said. 'Not what happened years ago.' She stood up again, this time with an air of finality. 'My sister and brother-in-law's bodies have been released for burial, doctor. The funeral is arranged for next Wednesday. That will be more than enough for Cathy to have to bear without making things even more terrible. I don't believe in dredging up every bad thing that's ever happened to a person.'

'Nor do I, Frances.' Grace stood up, too, knowing she was being dismissed. 'I never have believed in that.'

'Then let it rest.' Frances Dean paused. 'If you really want to help Cathy, then please just let it be. Otherwise, as her guardian, I may have to ask you to stop seeing her.'

Ramon was standing on the kitchen table when Grace got home, plastering the hole in the ceiling.

'How you doin', Gracie?'

She wondered where he'd got that from. She didn't think Teddy called her Gracie, but then again she supposed she didn't know what anyone called her behind her back. Not that it bothered her. If it was good enough for George Burns' wife, she figured, it was good enough for her.

She escaped back into her office and, with Harry up on her lap, debated getting back in touch with Sam. What Grace wanted now was to know what John Broderick had done to Cathy and her mother. Sam Becket was the obvious route to go, but she was concerned that all she'd achieved to date with her prodding was to give the police and the State Attorney more reason to suspect Cathy.

She decided to call David Becket instead, reached him at the medical centre in downtown Miami that he shared with two other physicians. He came to the phone directly, his voice warm and friendly.

'How's my favourite shrink?'

'Troubled.'

'I'm sorry to hear that. Nothing to do with that son of mine, I hope?'

Grace wasn't sure how she felt about that question, but it made her smile. David Becket usually made her smile, now she came to think about it.

'Cathy Robbins,' she said. 'I need some information about her background, and I'd prefer to get it off-the-record.'

'And you think I can help?'

'David, do you have contacts at Lafayette Hospital up in Tallahassee?'

'As a matter of fact, I do.'

'Are they the kind of contacts who might have access to nine- or ten-year-old information about a physician at the hospital?'

'Who are we talking about here?' David asked.

'A Dr John Broderick,' Grace answered. 'Cathy's natural father.'

He came back to her within the hour.

'Details I'm going to have to wait for,' he said, 'but I thought you'd probably want whatever I could get right away.'

'All tidbits welcome.' Grace grabbed a pen.

'What I have is very ugly,' he cautioned.

'Ugliness is what brings half the people I see to me,' she reminded him.

'Poor Grace,' the doctor said.

She called Sam just after nine a.m., having hardly slept all night.

'John Broderick,' she said.

'What about him?'

'Has anyone – have you – checked into his suicide?' She paused. 'You said he drowned, Sam, but I heard from someone else that he was just presumed drowned.'

'Who'd you hear that from?'

David had asked Grace not to tell his son about their conversation in case Sam thought they were meddling in police business.

'That's not important,' she said, hoping he wouldn't get heavy. 'I just want to know if there was an actual body.'

'Why would you doubt it, Grace?'

'I'm not sure. I'd just really appreciate knowing.'

Grace took an hour at lunchtime – she didn't really have the time to spare, but she needed to get out of the house, clear her head, be among people whose problems she didn't have to worry about. Nameless people.

She thought about getting in the car and driving up to the bustling Aventura Mall, but she really didn't have enough time for that, so she took a stroll across Kane Concourse and went to the Bal Harbour Shops with which she had a love-hate relationship; their lovely, if phoney, tropical garden setting made the stores amongst the most comfortable in which to wander, but their swankiness and, for the most part, sheer unaffordability, often put her hackles up. Still, Saks was still Saks, and Neiman Marcus was always worth a wander, and having to pass Chanel and Gucci and Hermès and Tiffany en route was, Grace had to admit, no great hardship.

It was what she needed today for a change of pace. Locals and wealthy tourists doing what they loved above almost anything: shopping. It all looked, on the surface at least, so gloriously uncomplicated. Grace knew better, of course, knew that if she chose to, she could sit in one of the cafés or restaurants and absorb an almost limitless psychologist's *Festspiel* – demonstrations of marital conflict, addiction, self-gratification and inferiority complexes – but today all she wanted was to gaze into some pretty windows, look at some tempting displays, get a decent cup of coffee and shut down.

It would have worked perfectly well, but for the curious feeling Grace had that someone was watching her.

It struck her the first time when she was wandering around the lingerie department in Saks and had a sudden, strong sense that someone's eyes were boring into her back. She turned around from the glorious, wildly priced racks of négligées, saw a small throng of people, but no one actually taking any notice of her whatsoever, shrugged off the feeling and turned back again.

Fifteen minutes later, sitting on what they called the side-walk outside Coco's, having a sandwich and espresso, the sensation hit her again. Grace turned around in her chair, moving more quickly this time, and saw – thought she saw – a young woman about fifteen feet or so away, stepping on to the down escalator and out of sight. Grace thought she was young from her contours and the swiftness of her movements. She had long blonde hair. She thought, though she knew it was more than unlikely, and she hadn't really seen her clearly, that it might have been Cathy Robbins.

Sam called back that afternoon.

'No body,' he said without preamble. 'But —'

'No body?' Grace's heart-rate sped up.

'Don't get excited. There are too many buts.'

'Such as?'

'One: a suicide note, which is still on file up in Pensacola.' Sam sounded matter-of-fact, like he was ticking items off a list. 'Two: three independent witnesses saw Broderick taking out his sailboat on a day when storm warnings were being broadcast non-stop. Three: he may not have been found, but his boat was. Capsized.'

'But no body,' Grace said quietly.

'Grace, what exactly is your angle on this?' Now he sounded distracted, almost impatient. 'You know enough about the ocean. You know it devours people, especially if they're crazy enough to go sailing in a major storm – or determined enough to die.'

Or if they want it to seem as if they want to die.

'You're right,' Grace said. She could tell there was no point in pushing him any farther, not today at least, with him in such an unreceptive mood. 'Are you okay, Sam?' she asked.

'Fine,' he said.

117

'Any progress with the investigations?'

'Nothing worth talking about.'

Time to go.

'I'll leave you to it then,' she said.

CHAPTER SEVENTEEN

SUNDAY, APRIL 19, 1998

On Sunday afternoon, Sam was in Sarasota.

It was the Florida city many people loved best, and up until nine years ago Sam had liked it a lot too, not least because it hosted so much fine opera. But it had become the place on earth he most dreaded visiting. It was the city that Althea had chosen to move to after their divorce.

It was also the place she had elected to bury their son.

Her mother lived there, and one of her sisters, and Sam had certainly heard Althea say, over and over again, that one day, when Sam had had his fill of Miami crime (she had always had that tendency – one that really pissed him off – when she was mad at him, to make it sound as if he got some sick fix from his work), she hoped they would move there too. But the cold-blooded immediacy and obstinacy of the decision Althea had made right after Sampson's death had shocked Sam way beyond words. He knew – oh, Christ, of *course* he knew – that the icy spikes of her cruelty had been fashioned out of unbearable grief and despair, but the savagery of her decision – from which she had absolutely refused to shift, and from which he could not have succeeded in shifting her without prolonging an agony that was already unendurable – to bury their son over two hundred miles away from him was something he would never be able to forgive.

He had tried, on the first and second anniversaries of the accident, to reopen some small channel of communication between them, and he'd tried it again, last year, on what should have been Sampson's eleventh birthday, but Althea hadn't wanted to know. Where Sam Becket was concerned,

119

she just wanted to hate. It was, Sam had grown to suppose, what kept her going.

Which was why he was there this afternoon, so late in the day and entirely alone. Because he had wanted to avoid seeing his ex-wife and her family. What he wanted, today, nine years exactly after that drunk had wiped out all his and Althea's hopes and dreams, was to be alone with his son.

He was safe. They had come and gone. The flowers testified to that. White roses for purity. Delphiniums and cornflowers, because Sampson's favourite colour was blue.

Sam never brought flowers. He brought seashells. Right from the start of his brief life, Sampson had loved water. Sam could still close his eyes and recall the feel of his baby son in his arms as he sat with him on the beach, right up close to the water, so that Sampson could feel the splashes and watch the rippling waves and hear the ocean's voice. Sampson had loved seashells, so from time to time during the year his father wandered the beaches looking out for shells of special beauty or colour, and collected them for the next time he could bring them here to his son's grave.

'Look what I brought for you today, son.' He fished around in his pockets. 'I got two nice tulips and a crown conch.' He squatted beside the grave and laid the shells down.

He had bought a book years ago to help him identify shells for Sampson, and the hollowness inside him that never entirely went away was a stark reminder that these tiny offerings were something he continued with for his own sake, not his little boy's. But still, it did no one any harm, and it gave him a bean or two of comfort now and again.

He put down a gleaming, brownish dappled Cowrie, followed it with a small moon shell, and then reached his right hand in his pocket for the final time. 'And here's the one I like the most. The book says it's common, but I never found one this pretty before.' He laid down a small, smooth, soft rose-coloured shell. 'It even has a pretty name, Sampson. Janthina – isn't that a neat name?'

He didn't know how long they remained on the grave after he'd gone, but there was never a trace of them from visit to visit. Maybe the oddness of the seashells offended whoever tended the cemetery, or maybe it was Althea herself who removed them, knowing they came from him. Whatever, Sam knew he was going to keep on bringing the tiny tributes to a beautiful child who had possessed an eye for the wonders of nature at such an early age.

The other thing Sam did, each time he came to the cemetery, was sing.

Sampson had liked his daddy's voice.

He always sang the same thing. A few verses from the 'Carousel' soliloquy about a father dreaming of his unborn child. He sat down on the grass beside the headstone and sang very softly, and he never made it very far because it choked him up, but that didn't matter because he knew Sampson couldn't hear him anyway. And it was okay for a father to get choked up over his son's grave.

If they'd buried him in Alaska, they couldn't have stopped Sam from doing that.

CHAPTER EIGHTEEN

On Sunday afternoon, Grace was home, going over and over the information David Becket had given her on Friday. Oh, she'd had plenty else to occupy her mind since Sam Becket had given her the brush-off on Saturday – a thirteen-year-old anorexic, a hyperactive third-grader and a juvenile pyromaniac-in-the-making, to name but three – but Cathy Robbins' childhood was still holding sway over the rest.

When Peter Hayman called, just after two o'clock, it was hard to stop herself from calling it fate. She knew, of course, it was just a coincidence that the doctor had decided to call her at exactly the moment she was feeling about to explode if she couldn't share her thought processes with someone else – but it didn't feel that way at the time.

He wanted to ask her how things were progressing.

Grace wanted to tell him.

'Want to drive down?' he asked.

'I don't know where you are.'

'About a mile from where we met,' Hayman said. 'On Key Largo.'

He lived at the ocean end of a small residential road that ran beside one of more than a dozen or so inlets in south Key Largo. Most of his neighbours lived in modern, expensive-looking, impeccably designed houses, many of them with handsome cruisers moored right in their backyards, but Hayman's house was an old timber three-storey affair, loaded with enough atmosphere to make the grade as a movie set. Huge old ceiling fans and local art on the walls, rattan furniture inside and out on the screened porches that ran all the way around the house, a small, semi-wild palm and orchid garden out back, and what Hayman said was a regular afternoon visitation from a bunch of herons and pelicans looking for hand-outs on the ocean side.

'How long have you lived here?' Grace asked, once they were settled on one of the porches, sipping homemade lemonade.

'A few years now.' Hayman leaned back comfortably in his rattan chair, his brown hair flopping over his forehead, the straw hat he'd been wearing on Grace's arrival laying on his right knee. 'Do you like it?'

'Very much.'

'The neighbours wanted to see it pulled down because it was too out of keeping with their houses, but I persuaded the zoning people to let me put the place right and keep some flavour in the road. I guess they're getting used to it – some of them even speak to me now and then.'

'Glad to hear it,' Grace said, looking around. 'I think you've done a wonderful job.'

Hayman shrugged. 'Once I'd decided to quit seeing patients on a daily basis and concentrate more on my studies and writing, there seemed no reason not to move to where I really wanted to be.' He adjusted the spectacles on his nose and smiled. 'I'm a bit of a sailor. I thought about heading all the way down to Key West, but then I figured that was less practical if I still wanted to see the occasional patient and mooch around bookstores and libraries on the mainland.'

'You remind me of my sister's husband,' Grace said. 'They live up in Fort Lauderdale half the time, and down on Islamorada the rest. Daniel's an architect, but his great passion is fishing, so now he can spend as much time as he likes doing what he loves where he wants.'

'Does your sister feel the same way?' Hayman asked.

'Claudia loves it. So do the kids – they have two boys.' Grace looked around, aware that she was already starting to be lulled into relaxation by the lush peace wrapping itself around her. She often found the Keys almost darkly seductive, tended to feel a little too removed from reality for her personal taste, so that returning to the jangling commer-

123

cialism of Miami felt almost as reviving as a welcome cool shower.

'This is a very pleasant surprise for me, Dr Lucca,' Hayman said.

'You don't mind my intruding then?'

'Far from it.' He paused. 'Though glad as I am to see you again, we both know you haven't driven down here to talk fishing or sailing.'

She took another sip of lemonade, then set her glass down on the wicker table. 'I've learned some things about Cathy Robbins' past – disturbing things – and they seem to have sparked off some wild ideas.' She looked directly at him. 'Some of which relate to the theory you and I were discussing last week.'

'So you thought another conversation might clarify things?'

'Or spark something new.' Grace hesitated. 'Even though none of this information has stemmed from my talks with Cathy, I don't need to tell you how confidential this has to be.'

'No, Dr Lucca,' the psychiatrist said, 'you don't.'

She shared with him what David Becket had told her about the late John Broderick. That Cathy had spent the first few years of her life with a father who had, according to the ethics committee at Lafayette Hospital, abused his wife and child with sedatives and other prescription drugs.

'He gave them both sedatives to keep them in order,' she told Hayman. 'He told Marie he was giving her monthly B12 injections when he was really injecting her with progestogen, and he gave Cathy longterm phenobarbitone for a non-existent condition.'

'Why?'

'I don't have the details,' Grace said, 'just the bare facts. Marie wanted more children, but the progestogen took care of that. It also screwed up her menstrual cycle, increased her weight and gave her headaches and nausea.'

'And depending on how much he was giving her, the phenobarbitone would have made Cathy sluggish or worse,' Hayman said.

'Exactly.'

'But we don't know why he did these things?'

'Not yet.' Grace paused. 'We do know that Broderick never allowed his wife to consult another physician. It was only after he walked out on them and Marie went for a check-up that a blood test showed up the progestogen.'

'And after that, they checked on Cathy?'

'That's right.'

'And you've been wondering about MSBP.' Hayman paused. 'Not only in relation to the drugs, but to the killings, too.'

'I know it's impossible.'

'With Broderick dead, yes, it is.'

'What if he isn't?' Grace asked.

They talked for a long time, about Münchhausen's and other factitious disorders, spilling over into various obsessional and control-related conditions that might or might not present clues in the Broderick-Robbins-Flager case. As afternoon drifted into evening, and her host threw some crayfish and snow crab legs into a wok on his barbecue for a casual stir-fry dinner, Grace found herself impressed by the depth of his interest. She watched the tall, slightly rumpled man focusing on his cooking, tossing in vegetables and spices, tasting as he went, and it occurred to her briefly that if it weren't for the undeniable fact that she was only just starting to acknowledge her attraction to Sam Becket, Grace might quite easily have found herself drawn to Peter Hayman.

'You know,' he said, suddenly, 'the more I think about what you're suggesting Broderick might have done, the more inconceivable I find it.'

'Because you believe he's dead?'

'Even leaving that tiny detail aside.' Hayman went on tossing ingredients in the big, fire-blackened wok. 'No, I'm talking about the bizarreness of that kind of crime.'

'Is it so much more bizarre than what that mother on the west coast did to her son?' Grace asked.

'I'd say so, yes.' He picked up the first of two clay plates warming by the side of the barbecue and spooned stir-fry on to it. 'The time factor and long-term planning turns it into something much more cunning, for one thing. For all I've seen and heard over the years, and even considering what we know

125

Broderick did to Marie and Cathy, I still find it difficult to imagine any father being so cold-hearted.'

'Or so evil,' Grace added.

Hayman looked up from spooning fish and vegetables on to the second plate. 'Do you regard sufferers of MSBP as evil?' His tone was even and friendly, yet there was an implicit rebuke in the question.

'I have, once or twice.' She wanted to be frank. 'I know I should be able to exercise greater tolerance than that, but I find it difficult – given that the victims, the real sufferers, are helpless children.'

Hayman carried the plates over to the wicker table, set them down and bade her have a seat. 'I'd say it's that old question rearing one of its ugliest heads – mad or bad? Sick or evil?'

Grace sat down. The appetizing aroma rose off her plate, blending with the barbecue smoke and the orchids from the backyard.

'If by the remotest chance,' she said, 'John Broderick did engineer these murders and the awful, unthinkable potential outcome for his own daughter, then I do have to say there's no doubt in my mind which category he comes under.'

They quit talking about death and evil and fell on their food. Hayman drank wine, but Grace stuck to water because of her drive back home – but then, just before leaving, she called Claudia and knew right away from her voice that something was wrong.

'Papa called,' her sister said.

'What's happened?' Grace had reached Frank midweek, had learned that Ellen had come through surgery well and was doing okay. She had wavered a little during that call, had told him that she and Claudia would certainly fly back to Chicago if Ellen wanted them to – not if *he* wanted them to, that much had not altered a damn in her heart or head – but Frank had gotten cold and nasty, had pointed out (not inaccurately) that if they'd really wanted to come, they'd be there. Now, in the half-second no-man's-land of waiting for her sister to answer her question, Grace wondered how she would feel if Claudia told her that Ellen had died.

'Nothing's happened' – the answer came – 'except Papa

says Mama's weak as a kitten, and I came off the phone feeling guilty as hell, which was exactly the way he wanted me to feel.'

'But knowing that doesn't make it less so,' Grace said.

She thanked Peter Hayman for his hospitality and kindness, made a call to Teddy Lopez to ask him to pick up poor neglected Harry, then headed south-west on Route 1 instead of north-east and was at the Brownley house before ten p.m. Daniel was up in Fort Lauderdale for the night, and the boys were tucked up in bed, and Claudia clung to Grace when she arrived in a way she hadn't done since they were scared, confused children in Chicago. Frank, Claudia now confessed, had said a whole lot more to her than she'd indicated on the phone. He had turned Ellen's cancer into a new kind of club to wield over his eldest daughter; her and her sister's leaving home, running out on their mama, had caused her years of unhappiness, he had said, and that was why Ellen was sick, because everyone said that now, didn't they? – that stress caused cancer – so Frank hoped that Claudia and Grace were real pleased with themselves.

The sisters sat up till late. They didn't say too much, just let some Phil Collins music play softly in the background, drifting over them, blending soothingly with the night voices of Florida Bay. Grace talked a little about her afternoon and evening with Peter Hayman, and Claudia had a few questions to ask about Grace's feelings for Sam Becket – there wasn't much of consequence in her sister's life that escaped Claudia's attention. But ever-present now, hovering above and around them, was the cloud of confusion and guilt that Frank Lucca had managed to plant over Claudia's head. Grace had hated their father for most of her life. She had never despised him more than she did tonight.

127

CHAPTER NINETEEN

Sam was in a bar about a mile from the cemetery.

He'd flown up before lunch, figuring on heading straight to the airport and catching a commuter flight back to Miami as soon as he'd finished at the graveside, but in the event he'd stayed there longer than he'd intended to, and by the time he'd gotten up off the ground he had been aching and one of his two old gunshot wounds – the one that had just missed shattering his left kneecap – had been growling at him, so he'd thought he might just find a bar first and have a drink.

It was a nice place, the right kind of bar for his mood. Dark and anonymous, with a ball game to watch and a consolingly extensive range of liquor lined up on the wall, and a good old bartender who knew when to leave a man to himself. Sam didn't especially like getting drunk and found the after-effects appalling, and he hadn't let it happen to him for a very long time, but today, once he'd downed the first whisky, it just seemed the right thing to do. So for what little was left of Sunday afternoon and the early part of the evening, he'd stayed in the gentle, undemanding bosom of that bar, drinking beer with whisky chasers, and when Joe the bartender knew he'd had enough, he'd extracted exactly the right number of bills from Sam's wallet, noted that the untroublesome drunk was a Miami Beach cop, and asked a friend of his named Hubie to drive Sam to the Turtle Motel and check him in.

Even now, in the motel room, drunk as he was, Sam remembered exactly why he'd gotten that way, but the whisky had served as a kind of anaesthetic, dulling, if not entirely annihilating the agony, and now the old images of a little boy lying fatally injured on the road were all jumbled up with other dark, bleak things ... A man and woman lying in their bed, throats cut ... a young girl with innocent blue eyes and golden hair who might just be a monster ... another victim, dead on a couch with a hole in her temple ...

And then there was Dr Grace Lucca, with her own golden hair, lovely, intelligent eyes and grave manner, gentling his messed-up mind, her image more warming than any shot of whisky.

Sam knew he'd been brusque with her last time they'd spoken, and he knew why he'd acted that way – it was the same way he always got with everyone around the time of the anniversary – but Grace hadn't known that, and he'd heard her back off, cut the conversation short, and he regretted it now, lying here all alone on the motel bed with the world spinning meanly around his head. But there wasn't a damn thing he could do about it. Not here. Not tonight.

He was too damned drunk to do a damned thing about anything.

CHAPTER TWENTY

MONDAY, APRIL 20, 1998

It was four-thirty in the morning, and David Becket was asleep on the couch in his office on West Flagler Street.

He had spent the evening and earliest part of the morning over at Miami General seeing Margie Fitzsimmons on her final journey, and when Margie had at last passed away a little after two a.m., David had just not felt like doing what he usually most wanted to do – namely going home and slipping between the covers with Judy. His wife was still the best possible person to be with at times like these – and there had been a lot of times like these in his nearly thirty years of practice. But on this occasion, going home and telling Judy (who always woke up when he came home late) that Margie Fitzsimmons was gone, would have meant acknowledging that she had died, and David just hadn't felt ready to do that quite yet. Maybe because Margie had been an old girlfriend – and the *only* woman David had slept with after meeting Judy, just a few weeks before he'd woken up to the realization that he'd now found the person with whom he wanted to spend the rest of his life. Maybe because he and Margie and Judy had stayed such good friends through the years, and he didn't want to admit yet that they'd lost her. Or maybe, David had thought, with a tired grin that was half shamefaced, half proud, because one of the last things Margie had said to him before she'd lapsed into her final unconsciousness, was that she'd never ceased getting horny whenever he was around her – and maybe that was how come she knew it was all over, because it was the very first time ever that seeing him hadn't gotten her all stirred up down below.

'That's probably it, you old son-of-a-gun,' he'd said out loud, wryly, at around three a.m., standing up from his desk and stretching his stiff limbs and thinking how welcome the couch looked. He'd been writing up some notes, and he'd called Judy to say he had to go on working a while longer and so she wasn't to worry about him. 'You're just not up to sharing that kind of flattery.'

That had been when he'd taken off his shoes and unbuttoned his shirt and loosened his belt and lain down on the couch for a nap.

Which was why he was sound asleep and the office was pitch dark when the door opened at four thirty-five.

It was the breeze that woke him. The breeze made by the arm as it came down hard through the still air on its way to his chest.

He wasn't awake for long.

Sam had just checked out of the Turtle Motel and was trying to crack his hangover with a cup of black coffee at a diner a half mile down the road, when he thought about checking for messages on his cellular phone and found out what had happened to his father. He didn't say a single prayer on the flight back to Miami – his brain was too locked down by dread, and anyway, he still hadn't forgiven the guy upstairs for snatching Sampson from him. He wasn't fool enough to think that if he'd been home last night instead of getting shit-faced in a bar near Sarasota, his father would have been any safer. But he was coldly, grimly aware that if David died before he got back to see him, he would never forgive himself for as long as he lived.

David was not dead when Sam got to Miami General, but his mother's and brother's faces and body language when he first glimpsed them, sitting waiting for news from the OR, spelled out a bad picture. Saul was crying openly. Judy Becket looked frozen. Sam knew that look – he'd seen it in the mirror on his own face in the hours during which Sampson had been in the ER. His mother had sat with him and Althea as they had waited, had been there when David had come into the waiting room, still wearing his green scrubs, to tell them that their son had died on the table.

Sam went to his mother, sat on the chair beside her, took both her hands in his, and looked her in the eye. 'It's not the same, Ma.' His voice shook with intensity. 'It's not going to happen.'

Judy looked right back at him. 'You can't know that, son.'

'Yes, I can.' He let go her hands and turned to Saul. 'How you holding up, kid?'

'I'm okay.' Saul's soft hazel eyes looked lost, terrified.

'He's going to make it, you know.'

'What if he doesn't?'

'He will,' Sam told him.

He felt a gentle touch on his right arm, turned back to his mother.

'Was it very bad for you up there?' Judy knew where he'd been. She'd asked him a few days ago if he wanted her company, and had been utterly unoffended when he'd told her he wanted to go alone. She understood about things like that, and Sam was doubly grateful for that now, for if she had been in Sarasota with him and unable to get directly to the hospital to be with her husband, that would have been something else for Sam to have hated himself for.

'It was okay,' he told her.

'No, it wasn't,' Judy said.

Sam stroked her cheek. 'No,' he agreed. 'It wasn't.' He checked his wristwatch. 'How long's he been in the OR?'

'For ever,' she said.

'He's going to be all right, Ma.'

Judy's mouth twisted a little.

'From your mouth to God's ear,' she said.

Sam caught up with Martinez and Beth Riley in the corridor, learned that Mike Rodriguez, the Miami Police Department sergeant investigating the Coconut Grove killing, was now taking charge of his father's attack, because the weapon appeared to have been another scalpel-type blade.

'Different MO, though,' Martinez told Sam. 'One of your dad's partners says that the instrument cabinet was open and one of the scalpels they use for minor surgery was missing.'

'Timing was about the same,' Detective Riley said. 'The paramedics who responded after the call came in from the cleaner said he'd probably been bleeding for about an hour, which means we're talking around four a.m. again.'

'We need to go talk to the Robbins girl,' Martinez said.

Sam was still stunned by the news of a possible connection with the other cases. 'I should be there.'

'I know. We waited for you.'

'We should go now,' Riley urged gently.

'I can't leave yet.' Sam looked at his watch. It was ten after ten.

'We need to find out if the girl went out last night,' Martinez said. 'Not that she or her aunt are going to tell us if she did.'

Sam took another moment to make up his mind. 'I'm not going to leave till my dad's out of surgery. You guys get over to Coral Gables and see what you can find out.' He paused, remembering Cathy's collapse during questioning less than a week ago. 'And be gentle. It's just routine, right?'

'Yeah, sure,' Martinez said.

'I mean it, Al.' Sam looked at his sceptical expression. 'And don't give them one more detail than you have to.'

'It doesn't make sense for it to be the girl,' Beth Riley said.

'I know it doesn't,' Sam said

'It doesn't need to make sense,' Martinez said. 'Not if she's a wacko.'

Riley put out a hand, touched Sam's right arm. 'We'll be thinking good thoughts for your dad, Sam,' she said.

Dr Helen Brodsky – a trauma surgeon and friend of his father's – came into the waiting room at ten forty-eight.

'He made it through.' She knew better than to make them wait another second. 'He's critical, but he's still with us.'

'Is he conscious?' Judy's voice was hoarse.

'Not yet, but his vital signs are good.' Brodsky nodded at Sam. 'It was touch and go – he lost a hell of a lot of blood.'

'I guess the old man's tough,' Sam said softly.

Brodsky smiled. 'As a Sherman tank.'

The Sherman tank lay in the ICU bed tethered by tubes and wires, very white and still apart from the rise and fall of his chest. Judy was in the bathroom and Saul was on a coffee and

133

soda run, and so, for just a very few moments – aside from the nurses moving back and forth between patients, equipment and records – Sam was alone with his father.

He looked for old familiar details to cling on to, trying to block out the tubes and ugly, frightening paraphernalia. The half-inch long scar on the suddenly fragile cheek, a vestige of a fight with a violent patient in an ER when David had been a young doctor, better able to fend for himself. The curved nose, one nostril slightly larger than the other. The receding grey hair. This was the man who had done more for Samuel Lincoln Becket than any other man on earth. Who'd taken a newly-bereaved, seven-year-old black boy into his heart and home and world, who'd given him a second chance at family, love, security, education. A future.

The monitors near the bed beeped erratically for a moment, then calmed down again, and Sam's pulse-rate reacted almost simultaneously. He looked at his father's hands, beautiful, capable hands that had helped so many children back to health, and his heart tore in his chest. He bent over him, his mouth right up against his ear, and spoke to his father softly and fiercely: private, intimate words about strength and recovery and coming back home to them all, words about finding the person who had done this to him.

A light touch fell on his left shoulder. Sam straightened up and saw his mother behind him, her face unfrozen now, but another, more unfamiliar expression in her eyes and on her mouth. Iron. The way he'd been told she'd looked when he'd been shot.

'Okay, son?'

'I'm okay, Ma.'

Her eyes, usually soft, like Saul's, were penetratingly sharp. 'You're going to find who did this?'

'It's not my jurisdiction, Ma.'

'But you're going to make it your business.'

'Yes, I am.'

'Could he have been wrong about that girl?'

'I don't know, Ma.'

The eyes didn't waver. 'You still hope it isn't her, don't you?'

'Yes, I do.'
'But it's not impossible, is it?'
Sam shook his head.
'Nothing's impossible, Ma.'

CHAPTER TWENTY-ONE

Al Martinez and Beth Riley sat in their car outside Frances Dean's house while Martinez reported back to Sam Becket at Miami General.

'Repeat performance, just like after the Flager killing. Both of them in their nightclothes, real bewildered, with the aunt saying they were both home all evening and all night and she never got to sleep, so she can swear to that —'

'She looked sleepy to me,' Riley inserted.

'Yeah, right.' Martinez nodded and repeated to Sam what she had said. 'And the aunt's saying how can we be so wicked as to imagine that Cathy might want to hurt a man who's been so kind to her?'

Sam, talking on his cellular outside the ICU, registered the sneer in the other detective's voice. 'She's not wrong, Al. She told Grace Lucca how much she liked my father.'

'Yeah, I know.'

'You think she was lying,' Sam said. He'd learned over the years to set great store by Al Martinez's gut feelings.

'Like I said in the hospital,' Martinez answered, 'I think she's a certified fruitcake and her aunt's lying to protect her.'

Inside her house, Frances Dean was standing outside Cathy's bedroom, trying to summon up her courage.

'Why don't you come in, Aunt Frances?'

Cathy's voice, through the closed door, made her jump.

She opened the door. Cathy, still wearing the oversized pink T-shirt she'd slept in, was sitting on her bed, crosslegged, the May issue of *Cosmopolitan* on the covers in front of her.

'I could hear you breathing out there,' she told her aunt.

Frances went into the room. 'Are you all right?'

'Not really.'

'Do you mind if I sit down?'

'Of course not.' Cathy picked up the magazine and dropped it on to the floor beside the bed. 'I wasn't reading, just staring at it.'

Frances sat down on the bed. 'I know what you mean. I lie awake at night with a book open in front of me, but I don't think I've actually read a word since ...'

Cathy said nothing.

'The thing is —' Frances stopped again.

'What?' Cathy looked into her aunt's face, saw the struggle in it.

'The thing is, I told the officers that I was awake all last night.'

'Yes.'

'I lied to them,' Frances said, suddenly speaking rapidly. 'I took a sleeping pill last night directly after dinner, because I just couldn't bear to go through another night without rest – that's why I took so long to hear them knocking on the door this morning.' She came to a halt and, cheeks flushed, looked away from her niece's eyes.

'What are you saying, Aunt Frances?'

'That I need —' She broke off.

'What do you need?' Cathy asked.

Frances faced her again. 'I need for you to swear to me that none of these terrible, evil things have anything to do with you.'

Cathy stared at her, speechlessly.

'I'm sorry, Cathy. It's just —'

'Just that you don't believe me.' Cathy got off the bed, went to the window, turned round and faced her. Her eyes were full of new horror. 'You actually think I could have killed these people —' Her voice pitched higher in distress. 'That I could have killed my *mom*? And Arnie? That I —'

'No!' Frances stood up, too, started to walk towards her.

'Don't come any closer.' Cathy sounded strangled. 'Don't come *near* me!'

'It isn't like that!' Frances was distraught. 'It isn't that I think you could have done it —'

137

'What is it then?'

'I guess I just need to hear you tell me once – just this one time – and then I'll stand by you forever.'

'How could you even *think* something like that?'

'I don't know, honey.' Frances shook her head miserably. 'I'm so confused, and it's all been so terrible, and the police keep coming by and I don't understand *why* – I don't understand how they can think you could have anything to do with the killings, yet they do seem to, and —'

Cathy turned away to the window. 'Go away, Aunt Frances.'

'Cathy, darling, please.'

'Just go away.' She paused. 'If there was anyplace I could go to, I'd leave right now, but there isn't anyplace, is there?' Her voice was still choked, but now it was harsh too.

'You don't have to go anywhere – you have a home here with me, always. You're my sister's little girl, and I love you.'

'You love me so much you think I could murder my mother.'

'No, I *don't*!' Frances made another move towards her, but stopped again, knowing she wouldn't get close. 'I'm sorry to have asked you that. I shouldn't have – I can see that now. Those people got me so mixed up.'

'Go away.' Cathy didn't turn around. 'Please.'

'Cathy, please —'

'Go *away*!'

Wringing her hands, Frances fled.

CHAPTER TWENTY-TWO

It was mid-afternoon when Grace got home, opened her mail and then played back her messages. There were five, but Sam Becket's and Frances Dean's were the real attention grabbers.

She cancelled the one remaining appointment she'd been hoping to keep – a routine update with a ten year old doing rather better than expected after her parents' bitter breakup – and headed directly over to Miami General.

Sam came out of the ICU when he heard she was there. He looked as Grace had expected him to look. Like hell.

'Thanks for coming.'

They hugged. It was the first time they'd done that, first time they'd been that physically close. Grace felt his heart beating fast and hard and found that she wanted to weep for him.

'How is he?' she asked softly when they drew apart.

'Too soon to say. He's still unconscious.'

'But the surgery went well?'

'That's what they say. It's still going to be touch and go.'

'David's strong, Sam,' Grace said, though she wasn't sure, suddenly, how strong he really was.

'He's going to need to be.' Sam glanced through the window of the ICU. David's bed, halfway into the room, was just visible. Judy Becket was sitting, very straight, her hand on her husband's.

'How's your mother doing?' Grace asked him.

'She's pretty tough, too.' Sam paused. 'Saul's on the move a lot of the time, getting cups of coffee, talking to nurses and staff in the commissary. It's hard for him, seeing Dad this way.'

'Do you know what happened?' Grace asked, finally getting to it.

'We don't know much,' Sam answered. 'We think he was probably catching a nap on the couch in his office – he sometimes does that if he has to work late.'

'Someone broke in?'

'Walked in. Dad may have left the door unlocked.'

'Would he do that?' Doctors' offices were such obvious targets for robberies that most of them turned into Fort Knoxes after closing hours.

'He might have,' Sam admitted. 'He'd spent half the night with a dying patient – an old friend.' He paused. 'Whoever walked in took a scalpel out of one of my father's instrument cabinets – one of his partners, Fred Delano, took inventory this morning, and there's an instrument missing.'

'A scalpel?' Grace was stunned and abruptly chilled to the bone. 'Are they sure?'

'Afraid so.'

She forced her mind to function. 'Anything else stolen? Drugs?'

Sam shook his head. 'Still locked up and accounted for – though Delano thinks some prescription pads may be gone.'

'They might still have been after drugs.' There was a sick sensation growing in Grace's stomach. She knew she was clutching at straws. 'Maybe they weren't expecting to find David in the office – maybe they stabbed him and ran.'

'The door was unlocked,' Sam said. 'They had to expect to find someone inside the office.'

She said it, finally.

'You're still looking at Cathy?'

His face was very sombre. 'At her and everyplace else.'

Through the ICU window, Grace saw Judy Becket stand up for a moment, stretch her legs and arms, rub her eyes. She saw a nurse come forward and check David Becket's IV drip feed. She saw the bank of monitors beside the bed and the bag of blood suspended above it.

She decided now was not the time to tell Sam about her trip to Key Largo to see Dr Peter Hayman.

She returned Frances' call from a public phone in the hospital.

140

Cathy answered, said her aunt was taking a bath. Grace asked her how she was coping. Cathy's answer was too light, too airy, troubling Grace more than if she'd wept or snapped at her. She asked if she might come out to Coral Gables.

'Sure,' Cathy said. 'Why not?'

It was just gone six o'clock when Grace got to Granada Boulevard. She rang the bell and waited. Cathy opened the door. She was dressed for running, her hair tied back in a ponytail.

'I thought we could go out again,' she said. 'If it's okay with you?'

'It's fine with me.' Grace was glad she'd worn a tracksuit and sneakers. 'Do you mind if I run with you this time?'

'Oh,' Cathy said. 'Okay.'

She was still standing in the doorway.

'How's your aunt?' Grace asked.

'Sleeping.'

'I guess she needs some rest.'

'I guess she does.' There was a tightness in Cathy's expression as she stepped out and pulled the door shut behind her.

'You want to run first and talk later?' Grace asked. 'Or we could just run.'

'You're the boss,' Cathy said.

'No, I'm not,' Grace told her firmly. 'I've imposed on you today, so you get to choose the game plan.'

Talking while they ran was out of the question, certainly for Grace, though she gave breathless thanks, as they sprinted along Anastasia Avenue towards the country club, to her gym and to Harry, who enjoyed accompanying her on fairly regular sandy jogs in Miami Beach. Grace was eighteen years older than Cathy, but in pretty good shape, and she knew more than Cathy did about pacing herself. Still, she also knew damned well that Cathy could, at any moment, have put on a burst of speed and easily left her behind, but she chose – whether out of kindness or because she wanted the company – to match and stay with Grace.

'Okay?' she asked somewhere around the ten-minute mark.

'Great,' Grace told her.

'Okay?' she asked again, about another ten minutes later,

141

and this time it was tough for Grace to manage more than a nod and a painful smile. Her heart was hammering, her calf and thigh muscles shrieking, she was wetter than she'd been from anything other than a shower for a long time and she suddenly realized that Cathy had been upping the pace for a while, steadily forcing her into a higher physical gear than she was used to.

Less than two minutes later, without warning, Cathy stopped, and as sometimes happened with exercise, it was the ceasing that almost felled Grace. She wasn't sure how long she stood, bent double, struggling to get her breath and quivering legs under control, but when she straightened up she saw they were standing in a small wooded area, and Cathy was watching her face.

'Want to sit for a while?'

Grace nodded, still not quite able to speak.

Cathy looked towards a tree stump, smoothed and rounded by time. 'I'll take the grass – you can have that.'

Grace mouthed thanks and sank on to the stump while Cathy got down on the ground a few feet away, bending her knees and circling her arms around them. Grace's muscles were still throbbing, but her heart was returning to something like its normal rate. She looked across at Cathy and saw that her eyes were closed. There had been things Grace had wanted to ask her: she'd wanted to ask if she'd been at the Bal Harbour Shops last Saturday lunchtime when she'd had that odd sensation of being watched; and more importantly she had intended to press Cathy at least a little harder about her memories of her father. But in the first place Grace was keenly aware that they were just two days away from the funeral, and in the second she suddenly felt certain that the teenager had her own agenda today, so she decided to keep silent. She didn't have long to wait.

'This morning,' Cathy said, her eyes still closed, 'after the cops had gone, Aunt Frances asked me to swear that I wasn't the killer.'

Grace felt a rush of pity, but said nothing.

Cathy opened her eyes. 'If my own aunt doesn't believe me, who else is going to?'

'I will,' Grace said.

Cathy shrugged. 'Maybe.' She paused. 'It's awful about Doc Becket.'

'Yes, it is.'

'Is he going to be okay?'

'I hope so.'

'But you're not sure.'

'Not yet. He came through surgery well, which means he's pretty strong.' Grace wasn't going to snow her. 'There's every reason to be hopeful, Cathy, but he's still unconscious.'

For several moments, neither of them spoke. Birds were calling from the trees, and the darkening sky and rising breeze warned that one of those short, sharp south Florida downpours might be imminent.

'Grace, how could anyone think I might want to hurt Dr Becket?'

There was bewilderment in that question and Grace knew, without a shadow of doubt, that it was genuine. 'I don't know,' she said. 'I think, maybe, it's because they feel they have no choice but to consider the possibility. Mostly because they haven't found anyone else to suspect.'

'It's crazy,' Cathy said.

Grace waited another moment. 'Is it any less crazy, do you think, to suspect you of hurting your mother and stepfather? Or Beatrice Flager?'

'In a way,' Cathy answered.

Grace sat very still.

'I mean, with my parents, I was there, wasn't I?' Her voice had become hazier, her eyes more distant. 'And no one knows what might have gone on with us. I can see that. I mean, some families hate each other, don't they?'

'Yes,' Grace said, quietly, 'they do.'

'And then, with Beatrice, I guess someone might think I hated her. If they already thought I'd killed my parents. If they thought *I* was crazy.' Cathy paused. 'Maybe they do think that – after all, I got sent to a therapist, didn't I?'

Gracc kept silent again.

'What are you thinking, Grace?' Cathy asked.

'About how logical you're trying to be.'

Cathy got off the ground. 'I've had a lot of time to think. About how it might be looking to the police.' She did some

143

muscle stretches. 'To people who don't know me.'

'But your aunt does know you,' Grace said.

'I thought she did.' She stopped stretching. The faraway look and tone were gone now, and suddenly all the logic was gone too and she was a bewildered teenager again. 'I couldn't believe she was *asking* me that.' Her fists were clenched and tears sprang to her eyes. 'I'm not crazy, Grace. How could she *think* that about me? She knew how Mom and I were together – how great Arnie was to me. How could she think I could ever hurt them?'

The rain began to fall, great warm drops that would turn into sheets of water any second, but Grace stayed put on the tree stump. 'I expect she doesn't really think that, Cathy.' She had to raise her voice against the sound of the shower. 'I expect she's just feeling very confused and mixed up.'

'That's what she said.'

'Then it's probably the truth.'

Wet as they both were, they walked slowly back to the house where Frances was awake and waiting for them. Having dispatched Cathy to dry herself and change her clothes, Frances offered Grace some tea. It was the first overture of something approaching friendship that she'd offered since she had virtually threatened to fire her as Cathy's psychologist on Friday. Grace was more than happy to accept.

'How do you think she is?' Frances poured out tea, passed a cup. Her voice was low, and it was obvious she didn't want Cathy to hear.

'Distressed,' Grace answered.

'Did she tell you I upset her this morning?'

'She told me you asked her to swear that she wasn't the killer.'

Frances sat back wearily, her eyes distraught. 'I shouldn't have asked her, I know that. But I —'

'You felt you needed to know,' Grace said, gently.

Frances stirred her tea. 'She's been going to the house, you know. She's been twice, on her own, not telling me till afterward.'

'Since she and I went together?' Grace was surprised. 'Have the police given her permission to do that?'

144

'No, I don't think so.' Frances put down the spoon, but made no attempt to pick up her cup. 'But if they know about it, no one seems to have stopped her.'

'I'd imagine they do know.' Grace was damned certain they knew, was pretty sure by now that the police were keeping a fairly close watch on Cathy. She hadn't been aware of any presence during their run this afternoon, but then again, psychologists weren't the world's greatest experts on checking for tails.

'She says she doesn't go inside,' Frances went on. 'She says she just likes being in the backyard.'

'That was where she seemed most comforted when I took her back.'

'So you don't think it's a problem?'

'Do you think it's a problem, Frances?'

'I seem to feel that everything's a problem these days, Grace.' She leaned forward, her whole manner fatigued, and picked up her teacup.

'I know about the drugs Broderick gave Marie and Cathy,' Grace said, softly, hoping to get some questions answered before Cathy came back down.

In the midst of raising the cup to her lips, Frances stopped, and her hand trembled, forcing her to put it down again. 'Who told you?'

'David Becket.' Grace saw the older woman's eyes widen at the mention of his name. 'He spoke to a contact at Lafayette Hospital in Tallahassee. I know that Broderick gave Marie and Cathy sedatives, and I know about the progestogen and phenobarbitone.' She paused. 'What I don't really know is why.'

'Does it matter?'

'I think so.' Grace lowered her voice even further. 'Frances, I know the funeral's on Wednesday – I know the timing couldn't be worse. But Cathy could be in terrible trouble. I wish you'd understand that if I'm to try and help her, I need to know everything you can tell me. I don't know what more I can say to convince you of that.'

'Jealousy,' Frances said, swiftly, abruptly. 'John was irrationally jealous of Marie, long before Cathy was born. He was always accusing her of having love affairs with other men. There were no other men. The very idea was anathema to my

145

sister.' She paused. 'Marie hoped the pregnancy might help matters, but they just got worse. You may find it hard to believe, Grace, but John Broderick even seemed jealous of his own child.'

'It happens,' Grace said quietly, willing her to go on.

'He was never a good father,' Frances said. 'I don't think he was ever really normal. He was clever, of course, or else I don't suppose he could have become a physician, but he was not a normal husband or father.'

'The records at Lafayette Hospital mentioned something about his having given them sedatives to keep them in order.'

Frances nodded. 'That sounds like John.' She leaned forward, picked up her teacup again and, though her hands were still trembling a little, she managed to drink some. 'He was the one having affairs, though Marie didn't suspect him back then, but by the time Cathy was two, he was rubbing her nose in his infidelity, saying it was all her fault.'

'I gather Marie wanted more children.'

'John put paid to that,' Frances said bitterly.

'The progestogen injections.'

She nodded again. 'Another way of controlling her. Maybe of punishing her.'

'What about the phenobarbitone?' Grace knew she was pushing hard, but she also knew that Frances would stop as soon as Cathy appeared.

'John told Marie one day – Cathy was about four, I think – that she'd had a seizure, and he was treating her with an anti-convulsant drug. Marie asked him if it was safe or necessary, and he said it was.' Clearly, Frances felt the same urgency. Now that she had begun, she wanted, needed, to get it all said. 'When Cathy's teachers at her kindergarten said they were concerned about the child's lack of concentration, Marie asked John if it might have something to do with the medication he was giving her. He said those symptoms just proved how much she needed the drug.'

'Didn't Marie suggest a second opinion?'

'John said that if she didn't trust him as a physician, then she was welcome to go elsewhere. Marie didn't dare go against him. She was too afraid of wrecking her marriage.' Frances shook her head. 'He walked out on her anyway. I

146

thought that was the best thing he'd ever done. Marie didn't agree with me, of course.'

'Not even when she found out what he'd been doing to her and Cathy?'

'Oh, yes,' Frances said. 'She agreed then. She hated him then. She got a court order to keep him away from the little one. John fought it, put all kinds of pressure on Cathy.' She paused. 'There was nothing he wouldn't stoop to, Grace. Even suicide attempts.'

Grace was startled. 'You mean he'd tried before?'

'Oh, yes,' Frances said again. 'Twice. Once, by slashing his wrists.' She stopped, hesitating.

'And the next time?'

'He cut his throat.'

Grace thought about Marie and Arnold Robbins. The possible implications of what Frances had just said made her feel ill.

Cathy came into the room. She'd showered and changed into a white sleeveless dress. 'Talking about me?' The question was posed lightly, but the resentment beneath was plain enough.

'Not really,' Frances said, nervously.

'You didn't tell me you'd been back to your house again,' Grace said.

'I didn't know I had to tell you,' Cathy said.

'You didn't,' Grace agreed easily.

'You were talking about my first father.' Cathy's voice became jerky and tense. 'I heard you.'

'I was asking your aunt some questions about your childhood.'

'We're not supposed to talk about that,' Cathy accused Frances. 'You know Mom didn't want us to talk about it.'

'I thought you didn't remember anything to talk about,' Grace said, gently.

'I don't,' she said.

'Why don't we all just have some tea?' Frances suggested.

'Why don't you just betray my mother some more?' Cathy was getting wilder, more bitter. 'Just tell Grace all our private stuff, and then maybe she'll understand why you think I killed Mom and Arnie and Beatrice —'

147

'I *don't* think that!'

'Yes, you *do* – you think I'm crazy or something – you think I'm like him, like my father —'

'Cathy, I don't think anything of the kind.' Frances was up on her feet, more wretched than ever. 'You're *nothing* like him – you're a sweet, good, normal girl —'

'So why do I have to keep seeing a shrink?' Cathy demanded.

'Because you've been through a terrible ordeal.' It was time to calm things down, Grace felt, before they got too far out of control – though in one sense she was glad to see the well-mannered, orderly, unnatural atmosphere of Frances Dean's house being tossed around a little. 'Because most people need a little help sorting through their emotions and reactions at a time like this.'

'Maybe I don't need help.'

'Maybe you don't,' Grace said.

'Maybe *I* do,' Frances said. There were tears in her eyes. 'I've lost my sister, Cathy, you seem to forget that. Your mother was my closest friend. I loved her very much – and I was very fond of Arnold, too.'

'What about me?' Cathy asked. 'Don't you love me any more?'

'Of course I do.' Frances took a step towards her niece, but Cathy backed away, moving towards the door. 'Cathy, of *course* I love you – you're all I have left.'

'Then why did you ask me to swear that I wasn't the killer?'

'Oh, Cathy.' Frances sank down onto the sofa. 'I shouldn't have asked you that. I know that now.'

'But why did you?' The girl couldn't seem to let it go.

'I made a mistake.' Frances looked up at her pleadingly. 'Haven't you ever made a mistake, Cathy?'

'It wasn't a mistake, Aunt Frances,' she said, softly.

'Of course it was.'

'No, it wasn't. You meant it.'

'I got muddled, that's all.'

'You weren't muddled,' Cathy said, still from the doorway. 'You told the cops you'd been awake all night so you knew I couldn't have gone out, but then you told me that was a lie because you'd taken a pill.'

148

'That's right,' Frances said despairingly. 'I'd taken a sleeping pill – they make my head foggy, which is why I wasn't thinking straight.'

'Sounds reasonable to me,' Grace said to Cathy.

'Not to me.' She was unbending.

'How are we going to get past this if you can't forgive me for one mistake?' Frances asked her beseechingly.

'I don't know,' Cathy said, and left the room.

CHAPTER TWENTY-THREE

TUESDAY, APRIL 21, 1998

Grace had left the Coral Gables house that afternoon right after Cathy had walked out on her aunt. Frances had been distressed and humiliated, and Grace had understood how badly she had wanted to be left alone.

She wished now that she had stayed.

It was another detective in Sam's office, a woman named Beth Riley, who gave Grace the news when she called next day at around two p.m. for the latest on Sam's father.

'No change there, I'm afraid, Dr Lucca.' Detective Riley was friendly. 'But I know Detective Becket was about to call you when he had to leave, to bring you up to speed on the latest with the Robbins case.'

Grace felt a tiny, needle-like chill pass down her spine.

'Something new?' She heard the wariness in her voice.

'Yes, ma'am.'

Detective Riley went on to tell Grace that Cathy Robbins had made a 911 call just after seven that morning, and that when the paramedics and officers on patrol had gotten to the house on Granada Boulevard, they had found Frances Dean dead in bed.

'Oh, my God. How?' Silently Grace prayed for natural causes.

'I don't know, doctor,' Riley said. 'The case is in the jurisdiction of the Coral Gables Police Department – though I know Detective Becket's over at the crime scene now, so I guess we'll probably learn more quite soon.'

Grace was shaky when she put down the phone. Part of her wanted to jump in the Mazda and drive over to be with Cathy, but another part wanted to crawl into bed, pull the covers over her head and quit answering the phone.

She did neither, because her temporarily forgotten two-thirty patient showed up fifteen minutes early, and for the next hour, shocked as she was, Grace was absorbed in trying to find out why a previously gentle six-year-old Chinese boy had begun picking fights with other children at school.

Sam called at three minutes past four, just after Teddy Lopez had brought Harry back home. The terrier was still careering around the house, the way he always did after time spent away, when the phone rang.

'I gather Beth Riley told you about Frances Dean,' Sam said.

'What happened, Sam?' The icy chill was back.

'Sure you want to know?'

'No, but I think I have to.'

'She was pierced through her forehead at around two a.m.' He paused. 'Cathy's in bad shape. The Coral Gables police have been trying to talk to her, but no one's getting through.'

'You want me to come?' Grace felt nauseous.

'I'd certainly appreciate it.'

Harry came hurtling into the living room.

'Could I bring Harry?' Grace asked. 'Cathy likes him.' Reality hit her sickeningly. She was going to a murder scene and all the horrors that had to entail. 'Am I going to be allowed time alone with Cathy?'

'If you're fast,' Sam said. 'They're through with her for the moment. She's been examined.' He was speaking quietly. 'No evidence has been found to link her with the crime.'

'But they're going to be looking, aren't they?'

'No doubt about it,' Sam answered. 'I'd understand, Grace, if you wanted to take some time to think about this.'

'I don't see much to think about,' Grace said.

'The extent of your involvement, for one thing,' he pointed out.

Grace knew perfectly well what he was saying. She was getting too personally bound up in Cathy Robbins; she was spending a disproportionate amount of time concerning herself with Cathy over and above her other patients. With Frances

151

Dean dead, there was no one else left to protect Cathy, which was going to make her even needier than previously. Grace was a psychologist, a therapist, not a relative or even a friend.

'Grace?'

Sam's voice jolted her from her thoughts.

'I'm on my way,' she said.

'Are you sure?'

'I'll see you there,' she told him.

She was back in Coral Gables by five o'clock. The area surrounding Frances Dean's home was the zoo she had imagined it would be, with marked and unmarked police cars, flashing lights, crime-scene tape, and, worst of all, reporters from newspapers, TV and radio news stations. Grace parked the Mazda more than a block away and, with Harry in her arms, his warm body snug and comforting against her, walked through the gathering crowd of rubberneckers; most people ignored her as she approached the house, but at the last minute, as she identified herself to a uniformed officer guarding the perimeter and he lifted the tape to let her through past the banyans and floss silk trees, she was conscious of eyes and even camera lenses turning towards her.

Inside the house, however, things were quieter than she'd imagined. A police sergeant escorted her into the living room, and less than a minute later Sam came into the room with Cathy. Grace held her for a few moments, felt the teenager let her body rest against hers, felt her give a brief shudder, but then Cathy drew away again, and there was no outward sign of what Grace knew she had to be going through.

'Mind if I stick around awhile?' Sam asked.

Grace didn't much like the idea. 'It's up to Cathy.'

'Cathy?' Sam said.

'I don't care,' she said.

'Are you sure, Cathy?' Grace said, concerned that she might be too closed down to be the best judge of her situation. 'We could be alone if you preferred it.'

Cathy threw a glance at the door, and the strangers just beyond it. 'I don't mind if Detective Becket stays,' she said. 'I don't have anything to hide.'

She was wearing a blue tracksuit and her hair, tied back,

152

was damp. Grace guessed that she'd showered after the forensics people had finished with her. Her eyes were red, but she seemed past weeping now. Grace hardly dared contemplate what she had been through, nor could she bring herself to think about the horrifically clear implications of the latest development.

'I brought Harry with me,' Grace said. 'I hope you don't mind?'

Cathy shook her head. She sat down on her aunt's white sofa, and Grace nodded at Harry, who knew the routine and liked it. He jumped up, sinking deep into the soft cushion, and Grace thought, for one pointless moment, that had she been here, Frances would probably have objected.

'He's so neat,' Cathy said, and began petting him. The motions seemed mechanical, but Harry wasn't fussy.

Out of the corner of Grace's left eye she noticed two people dressed in white coveralls talking quietly in the hallway. 'How about we go out for a walk?' she said.

Cathy didn't answer.

'I just think it might be good to get out of here,' Grace said, softly.

Cathy looked up from Harry into Grace's eyes. 'Could I go home?'

'To your place, you mean?'

'Would that be okay?'

Grace turned to look at Sam, who'd sat down in a deep armchair behind her. 'Would it?' she asked.

'I don't know,' he said. 'I'll need to check with the man in charge.'

He left the room and came back a few minutes later. 'It's okay, so long as I come along.'

'I don't know,' Grace said.

'It's me or one of the Coral Gable officers.'

'Cathy?' Grace looked at the teenager.

'Sure,' she said.

The drive to Miami Beach was dreadful for Grace, even if Harry did lighten the load a little by travelling on Cathy's lap. There was no doubt in Grace's mind that Sam's coming along was not what it might be seeming to Cathy. This was

153

not just a gentle, supportive gesture to help her get through the day. Sam might not be the man in charge of the Coral Gables case, but he was still the lead investigator on the first two killings, a police detective with what surely had to be ever-strengthening suspicion on his mind. With Frances' death, Grace knew without being told that Cathy had risen from top of the list of suspects to the absolute pinnacle – and she didn't think that the girl's outward calm was helping her case any. Maybe Sam could still see past that shell to the vulnerable, terrified child beneath, but Grace doubted if his colleagues or Coral Gables counterparts could understand why Cathy was not by now a broken down, hysterical wreck. In all honesty, Grace wasn't even one hundred per cent sure that *she* really understood either – except that she, of course, had seen this type of reaction before, in many shapes and forms. She and Sam had talked about it in one of their first conversations, when it had seemed that the killing of her parents was the worst thing that could ever happen to Cathy Robbins.

Deep shock. Blocking.

'How you doin'?' Sam asked Cathy, as Grace drove. He'd let Grace take her own car out of consideration to Cathy, knowing that the trip in a police car might be impossibly fraught for her.

'Okay,' she answered from the back seat.

Grace wondered suddenly if she should call a halt, encourage them to go back with her to Frances' house, or maybe take them to her own place – if she should try to find out which lawyer had attended Cathy's questioning at the police station the day she'd collapsed. She had a bad feeling, growing by the minute, about going back to Pine Tree Drive, though she couldn't say exactly what it was. She just felt it.

Yet still she kept on driving.

Cathy didn't want to go inside the house. Just as Frances had told Grace yesterday, all Cathy wanted was to go into the backyard.

It all looked and felt as it had the last time – except, of course, that this time they had Sam and Harry along for company.

154

'Could we talk alone, Grace?' Cathy asked, quietly, almost as soon as they got there.

Grace looked at Sam.

'Sure,' he said, and silently she thanked him.

They walked slowly, Harry trotting behind them, to the back section of the garden, past the swimming pool towards the pool-house. Close to, the structure was starting to show signs of inattention. The windows were dirty from rain showers and weeds were groping towards the walls from the edges of the lawn. There were a couple of canvas director's chairs beside a white table. They sat down, their backs to the swimming pool and main house. Harry sniffed around the outside of the pool-house, then trotted over to a palm tree and cocked his leg.

'I don't understand,' Cathy said, very softly. 'I don't understand why this is happening.' She looked into Grace's face. 'Is it real?'

'I'm afraid it is,' Grace said.

'It doesn't feel real.' Cathy shook her head helplessly. 'I can't even seem to cry properly.' She looked away again. 'I was awful to Aunt Frances. So mean. And now she's dead, too, and I can't even tell her I'm sorry.'

'She understood, Cathy.'

'I don't think she did. I think I just made her more unhappy.'

Attracted by something, Harry headed over to where Sam was sitting, waiting, on one of the swing seats. Grace didn't bother checking on the dog, safety-wise. Harry was too old and too smart to take a tumble into a swimming pool, and anyway, even if he did, he'd swum in rivers and oceans before now. He was a pro when it came to water.

'What's going to happen to me now Aunt Frances is dead?' Cathy asked. 'Will I have to go live in some home?'

'I don't know. Did your mother have any other relatives?'

'Just a couple of cousins someplace in California. No one close. No one I've even met or talked to.' Cathy paused. 'Maybe it won't matter. Maybe I'll be in jail.'

Grace leaned forward, felt one leg of her canvas chair wobble, touched Cathy's left arm. 'Of course you won't be in jail.'

155

'I will if they decide I killed them all.'

'They won't.' Grace sounded definite. 'They'll find out who did it.' She heard, from the top of the garden, the sounds of play. A ball being thrown. Sam's voice softly urging Harry to fetch. Harry wasn't big on fetching, unless it was edible.

Cathy looked at her again. 'You really don't think it was me, do you?'

'No. I've told you that.'

'You still feel that way? Even now?'

'Yes, I do.'

Grace heard Sam's voice again. He was calling Harry, but now he sounded like he was calling him away from something.

'What's Harry up to?' Grace asked Cathy, twisting around to try and see.

'I don't know,' she said.

'Hey, Harry!' Sam's voice, louder this time.

'Sam!' Grace called. 'What's up with him?'

'I'm not sure,' he called back. 'I think he's digging.'

Grace looked at Cathy. 'Shall we go see?'

'Sure.' She got to her feet, started back ahead of Grace. The white dog was over on the lefthand side of the garden, past the line of palms close to the Jacaranda tree, digging in a patch of dirt in true terrier fashion.

'Harry, what're you doing?' Grace called to him.

'Does he always do this?' Sam asked.

She shook her head. 'I've never seen him dig up so much as a buried bone in all the years we've been together.'

Harry was scrabbling crazily now, making small eager sounds.

'Well, he sure seems to think he's found something now,' Sam said.

Grace looked at Cathy, saw curiosity in her eyes. Then Grace looked at Sam, and saw that he, too, was watching Cathy.

Grace's bad feeling returned.

'There it is,' Cathy said, suddenly coming to life. 'Hey, boy, what've you got?' She got down on her knees beside Harry, delighted as a young child to see a dog digging up a find.

Grace felt sick. She looked up, and now Sam was looking at

156

her, and Grace realized at that moment that, cop or not, he felt as lousy as she did, like if he could have turned tail and got the hell out of there he would have.

But he couldn't.

Harry barked.

'What —?' The question died on Cathy's lips. What began as a simply quizzical, confused expression, turned almost instantly into sheerest horror. Grace watched her lips turn white, saw her sway, ran to stop her falling sideways.

'Harry, get away,' Sam said.

'Harry,' Grace urged from Cathy's side. 'Come here.'

Something in his mistress's tone warned Harry this was not a game, and he came away from the small hole he'd dug. Sam was already taking gloves out of his pocket. Swiftly, methodically, he pulled them on, then extracted a plastic evidence envelope – Grace hated seeing how prepared he'd been, as if he'd known he might strike lucky if he came along with her and Cathy. He crouched down, withdrew Harry's find, shook the excess dirt gently from it, then put it in the bag.

There was no doubting what it was.

CHAPTER TWENTY-FOUR

WEDNESDAY, APRIL 22, 1998

The funeral was hideous.

It was unclear, until the hour itself, whether or not Cathy was to be allowed to attend, but in the event the powers-that-were agreed that she could go to Our Lady of Mercy cemetery en route from the Juvenile Assessment Centre – where she had spent the last day and night undergoing basic evaluation and processing – to the Youth Facility up on NW 27th Street in Miami where she would remain at least until her case came before the grand jury.

Cathy, flanked by officers and handcuffed, looked to Grace as if she had lost several pounds in weight overnight and gained almost as many years. Her hair, lank and greasy, was tied back off her face, and she looked shockingly haggard. She was wearing a black skirt and blouse at least two sizes too large for her, and her eyes were bewildered and frightened. A man in a dark suit stood close by, giving her occasional reassuring glances, and Grace guessed that he might be the lawyer Frances Dean had retained for Cathy when she'd been taken in for questioning after Beatrice Flager's murder. He looked like a lawyer, aged about forty-five, sleek, sturdy and prosperous, with dark, curling hair cut framelike around his compact head, his nose small but curved, his eyes blue and piercing. Grace hoped, with all her might, that he was the best damned lawyer for the job.

'Hello, Grace,' Cathy said softly as she approached.

'Hello, Cathy.' Grace tried not to glance at her shackled wrists or at the officers to either side of the teenager, kept her eyes trained firmly on Cathy's mask of a face. 'Are you holding up?'

'I guess.' Cathy swallowed. 'I'm glad you're here.'

'Of course I'm here.' Grace put out a hand to touch her left arm. 'I'm going to be here for you as long as it takes to get this cleared up.'

Cathy didn't answer, seemed incapable of speaking again. Swiftly, apprehensively, she looked back at a dark-haired girl – her friend Jill, Grace thought, the one in the photograph in Cathy's room at home. Jill managed a brief, frozen smile, then, perhaps constrained by the woman beside her, looked away from her friend and down at the ground.

Out of the corner of her right eye, Grace glimpsed Sam, standing with another man; probably, she thought, another detective, or perhaps one of his superior officers. He saw her, nodded, gave the smallest of smiles, but made no move towards her. It occurred to Grace, not for the first time, that perhaps, no matter how Sam felt as a private individual, they were now on opposite sides of a great divide.

The service got underway. It was a hot, humid, wet afternoon, and as Grace allowed the words to float someplace over her head, she was hard put to decide which was the most dismal aspect of all. The pair of simple polished coffins being lowered into the ground. The chief mourner in handcuffs. Her utter isolation – the fact that if there were relatives or other friends present, they never approached her; a typhoid carrier, Grace thought, might have attracted more physical warmth from the other mourners than Cathy received. The knowledge that within a comparatively short time there would be another funeral to attend, probably in almost identical circumstances.

It got worse, briefly, after the burial, when the media, restrained till then by grudging respect, finally burst upon the scene like a maddened herd of cattle released from an abattoir, and suddenly Cathy, despite the best efforts of the dark-suited man and the police, was surrounded for several long moments by hungry press and television reporters and camera crews. Grace stepped back, escaping reflexively from the onslaught, but she caught one more glimpse of Cathy's face as she was hustled back to the black car she'd arrived in. There was sheerest terror in those blue eyes now, and Grace knew that that look in her eyes as a dozen microphones thrust into her face would be beamed into every home by nightfall and splashed on every front page in Florida, or perhaps even farther afield, by breakfast-time next day.

The thought made her feel sick to her stomach.

CHAPTER TWENTY-FIVE

FRIDAY, APRIL 24, 1998

It was another two days before Grace was allowed to see Cathy again, this time in a small locked room at the Youth Facility. Cathy had, to date, been charged with the first degree murders of Marie and Arnold Robbins and Frances Dean. There was little doubt in anyone's mind that there would be more to follow. Bail, Grace had learned, was out of the question.

The scalpel dug up by Harry had been confirmed as the missing one from the solid silver collection bequeathed to Cathy by John Broderick, her natural father. There were no identifiable prints on it, but Frances Dean's blood and brain matter were still on the blade. It was, Sam had grimly explained to Grace on the telephone after the funeral, what every police officer and State Attorney longed to get hold of these days: a smoking gun.

Grace had argued at great length over the discovery of the weapon. 'Cathy *wanted* to go to the house,' she had reminded him, more than once. 'She chose to go into the garden with us.'

'And we know – and you say her aunt knew it too – that Cathy's been back to the house more than once since you first took her there. Maybe she just felt compelled to go back.'

'But not with you,' Grace had maintained. 'Certainly not on the same day your people claim she buried a murder weapon there.'

'Cathy didn't know when she asked to go there that I was going to come along,' Sam had pointed out. 'And someone's bound to argue that maybe she wanted to be caught.' He had paused. 'Or that maybe she just wanted to be stopped.'

*

161

The scalpel had not been the only find for the prosecution that Tuesday. Within a half-hour of Sam's bagging, photographing and documenting the new evidence and notifying the county medical examiners' and State Attorney's offices, as well as the Coral Gables and City of Miami Police Departments, the real pros had taken over from Harry, and in less than two hours a pair of rubber kitchen gloves had been unearthed just eight or nine feet from the first hole. Same brand as the ones used in Frances Dean's kitchen. Both gloves loaded with blood, dirt and smudged prints – Frances' and Cathy's among them. Whoever had buried them had, it was being hazarded, probably washed their hands in the Robbins' swimming pool. The water had been drained and all the filters carefully checked, but thus far nothing conclusive had been discovered.

Cathy said, in questioning, that she had used rubber gloves any number of times in her aunt's kitchen for washing up, so of course if they'd come from Frances' house then her prints would be on them, inside and out – that didn't mean she'd taken them from Coral Gables to Miami Beach in the middle of the night to use them to bury a murder weapon. Anyway, Cathy said, when was she supposed to have *done* all this and how was she supposed to have gotten from her aunt's place to her old home when she didn't even drive a car, and when none of the buses ran at night?

Grace knew about those questions of Cathy's because she'd raised the same points during one of her conversations with Sam.

'She made the 911 call just after seven a.m.,' Sam had told her, 'and the ME has the time of death down for sometime around two, which means she could have gotten to Pine Tree Drive and back in time to pretend she'd just woken up, and to make the call.'

'And how exactly is she supposed to have made this journey?' Grace had asked, fighting the knot in her stomach. 'I'm sure if she'd called a cab company, you'd know about it – or are you suggesting she's a secret driver?'

'I'm not suggesting anything,' Sam had said. 'There's no record of a call to a cab company or any booking. It's not impossible that Cathy has learned to drive – some kids do –

but if she'd taken her aunt's car during the night, the local patrol officers would have noticed it gone.'

He'd paused. 'One line of thinking is that she might have used a bicycle and sneaked out quietly. She says she brought her bike over from home two weeks ago.'

'A *bicycle*?' Grace might have laughed if she hadn't been so furious. 'Over the MacArthur Causeway in the middle of the night?'

'It's possible,' Sam had said, quietly, taking no pleasure in his argument. 'Cathy could have ridden the distance in about an hour, maybe a little more, which means she could have left Granada Boulevard at around two-thirty, gotten home by three-forty-five, buried the weapon and gloves, left Pine Tree Drive again at around four-fifteen, and been home by five-thirty.'

Grace had asked if anyone had reported seeing a blonde fourteen-year-old female riding a bicycle along that route that morning. No one had – but then, no one was looking. She asked if physical evidence had been found that Cathy had undertaken such a long and arduous bike ride that morning.

'Cathy's a strong kid,' Sam had reminded Grace. 'We both saw the trophies for running in her room. Anyway, if she got back at five-thirty, that would have given her plenty of time to shower and recover before making the 911 call at seven a.m.'

It Cathy had seemed bewildered and scared before, now, to Grace's eyes, she seemed totally lost. When Grace arrived, the girl fell into her arms and wept for several moments, but there was still nothing approaching hysteria, though the psychologist knew by now that that was simply not the way Cathy Broderick Robbins functioned. Truth to tell, Grace didn't claim to begin to understand how she *was* functioning, let alone surviving. They were keeping her away from her fellow inmates much of the time, and nights were being spent under lock and key in solitary confinement.

'Take me home,' Cathy said, just once, in the small, secure room that had been provided for Grace's visit. And then she remembered that she no longer had any place to go, and stopped begging. Grace thought that it was like watching someone being punched in the solar plexus. Once realization struck her that there was nothing more Grace could do for her at that moment other than offer comfort and promise to do her best for her, Cathy withdrew, both physically and emotionally.

'It's the goldfish all over again,' she said, softly, harshly. 'No one believed me then either.'

And after that, she wouldn't say a word.

Grace went to Miami General to get the latest on David's condition. She knew he was out of the ICU, and that he was, thank God, no longer deeply unconscious but running a high fever and making no sense at all. Neither Sam nor young Saul was in his room, but Judy Becket was at her husband's side.

She jumped to her feet the instant Grace entered the room.

'Dr Lucca.' There was not a trace of a smile on the small, elegant woman's mouth. Her eyes were darkly shadowed, and her ill-fitting beige blouse betrayed the abrupt and unhealthy weight loss that so often accompanies shock and ongoing fear.

'How's he doing?' Grace asked.

'What do you want?' Judy Becket stood between Grace and the bed, so that Grace could not see her husband's face without moving sideways, though she could hear that his breathing was laboured.

'To see Dr Becket,' Grace answered. 'I thought maybe, if you didn't mind, I could sit with him for a while.'

'I do mind very much.'

'I know he needs to be quiet.' Grace felt thrown by the other woman's hostility. 'I promise I'd just sit, nothing else.'

Judy Becket didn't answer. Instead, she raised her right arm, indicating the door, giving Grace no choice but to go back through it. She came outside with her and closed the door very softly.

'It's very clear to me,' she said, 'that your main concern for my husband now must be for him to recover sufficiently to clear that evil child you're so fond of.' Her eyes glinted with anger. 'Or maybe you're hoping he never recovers in case he confirms to the police that it was she who stabbed him?'

'You're wrong,' Grace said, stunned by her attack. 'You must know that you couldn't be more wrong, Mrs Becket.'

164

She was loth to fight back more vociferously. Lord knew she could understand the other woman's anguish.

'I don't know that, Dr Lucca.' There was a slight tremor in her voice now, and she had to compress her lips for an instant before continuing. 'Frankly, I don't know what to believe any more. I do know that I would like you to leave.'

'Then of course I will,' Grace told her. 'But I hope you will believe that my coming here has nothing whatever to do with Cathy Robbins. I've known your husband for a long time, Mrs Becket. I have the greatest admiration and respect for him.'

'If you have any respect for me,' Judy Becket said, 'please go now.'

Grace left fast, cheeks burning, eyes stinging. She felt as if she'd been slapped. At the far end of the corridor she saw a tall, dark figure just coming around the corner, and for an instant thought it was Sam. Half of her hoped it was, because she badly wanted to see him, talk to him, make sure he didn't feel the way his mother did. The other half was intensely relieved when she saw that it was not him. Grace supposed that she was just loth to find out that Sam, too, might by now have come bitterly to resent her wanting to continue in support of the girl suspected of stabbing his father.

Jerry Wagner, the dark-suited man at the Robbins' funeral, was the defence lawyer who had been retained by Frances Dean before her death. The issue of whether he would, or would not, choose to continue in that role had been a complex one in some respects. First, there was the problem that Wagner had in theory been Frances Dean's attorney, one of Cathy's alleged victims, but he was satisfied there was no conflict of interests because as a criminal lawyer he had never actually dealt personally with the late Mrs Dean, had merely been recommended by Michael Doughty, the attorney she used for personal affairs, another partner in the same law firm. Second, and more crucially so far as Jerry Wagner was concerned, was the matter of his fees. He'd received a retainer from Cathy's aunt, but when that ran out – as, in a case of such enormity, it certainly would before long – there was a risk that there might be no funds available to pay him. It was not yet clear whether Frances' will had been made in favour of

165

her niece, but even if it had been – and it *was* known that Marie Robbins' estate had been left to Cathy – then if the girl was found guilty of murdering her mother and aunt, it was highly improbable that she would be allowed to benefit from their untimely deaths.

Jerry Wagner appreciated money as much as the next lawyer, but he also appreciated good publicity, and the Cathy Robbins case was going to be *big* publicity. The days following the teenager's arrest had already seen more than their fair share of headlines: **Nightmare on Millionaire's Row ... Restaurant Heiress 'slashed' Mom, Dad and Aunt ... Teen Monster in Miami Beach**. With media attention like that, law firms were lining up to take the case *pro bono*. It was already in Jerry Wagner's lap, and he had no intention of handing it over to anyone else.

Five days after Cathy's arraignment, Grace Lucca was granted an interview in Wagner's office, a dark wood power base in a sleek tower on Brickell Avenue. The attorney's desk was huge, highly polished and immaculately tidy, and the whole room was a bastion of good taste; but from the moment Grace entered, was offered a comfortable leather chair and a cup of excellent coffee, she found herself wishing, curiously, that she'd walked into a shabbier, more chaotic, perhaps even frenetic scene, one that might have spelled passion and the kind of blazing commitment she knew Cathy was going to need behind her.

'So, Dr Lucca, I gather you want to help us?' Wagner was friendly and dignified.

'In any way I can,' Grace told him.

'You're aware, of course, that a psychologist will probably be appointed for Cathy under the guardian *ad litem* system,' Wagner said. 'With her aunt gone, she's in custody of the state now, so they'll be taking care of Cathy's welfare for the foreseeable future.'

'I am aware of that,' Grace said. 'I'm hoping that because Cathy and I have built up a pretty good relationship, I'll be allowed to go on working with her. I think Cathy's come to trust me, Mr Wagner, and the feeling's mutual.' She paused. 'Which is why, if you're going to be looking for an expert

166

psychological witness to testify on Cathy's behalf, I hope you'll think of me.'

'I appreciate the offer, Dr Lucca,' Wagner said, 'and closer to the time, we may be more than grateful to you for your assistance, but it's still very early days. The case hasn't yet gone before the grand jury. If they do bring in an indictment, and if and when we have to prepare for a trial, both sides will be hiring at least two forensic psychologists to evaluate Cathy.'

'I've worked as a forensic psychologist before,' Grace pointed out, 'for defence attorneys and for the state.'

'But not, I understand, in a homicide case.' His sharp eyes were watchful.

'That's true,' she had to admit.

Wagner leaned forward slightly, his manner confidential. 'Just as a point of interest, doctor, what kind of testimony would you hope to give on Miss Robbins' behalf?'

Grace had no problem with that question. 'I would tell the court that I don't believe that Cathy is a killer, or that she is unbalanced, let alone psychotic.'

Wagner steepled his beautifully manicured fingers thoughtfully under his chin. 'And you would be basing your opinions on what exactly, doctor?'

'On the meetings I had with Cathy prior to her arrest,' Grace answered steadily. 'And, hopefully, on those sessions yet to come.'

The steepled fingers parted, and the lawyer leaned back again. 'I'm sorry to say that, as things look right now, that might not be nearly enough to help get Cathy out from under these charges, Dr Lucca. I'd be a liar if I didn't tell you that the situation is pretty bleak.'

Disquiet surged inside Grace. 'Cathy is pleading not guilty, isn't she?'

'Yes, she is.'

'And you do believe she's not guilty, don't you, Mr Wagner?'

'My client has told me she didn't commit the crimes.'

Grace wasn't letting him get away with that. 'Do you *believe* her?'

'I'm Cathy's defence attorney, Dr Lucca.' Wagner was

167

unperturbed. 'I have a sworn duty to defend her, and I can assure you that I'm going to do everything – use every possible means at my disposal – to do just that.'

'So you're not rejecting my testimony?' Grace said.

'I am most definitely not rejecting anything, doctor,' Wagner said. 'It's just too early to do anything except examine all our options. As I said, the case hasn't even reached the grand jury stage yet.'

'But looking at a worst-case scenario' – Grace felt the need to persist, unsure of when or even *if* she might get to see the attorney again – 'if they do indict Cathy —'

'Then, looking at a worst-case scenario' – Wagner took up her line of thought – 'in the absence of any good, strong evidence in my client's favour, it's not inconceivable that we might find ourselves hard pressed to do much better than an insanity plea.'

Grace was horrified. 'But Cathy isn't insane.'

'That might not necessarily be the good news you seem to feel it is, doctor,' Wagner said. 'If we don't find a way to clear Cathy of all charges – and believe me, everyone on my team is going to do their damnedest to do just that – but if we don't, then an insanity plea may just prove our only means of keeping her out of jail.'

Peter Hayman telephoned that evening while Grace was making an omelette.

'I heard the news,' he said. 'How are you coping?'

'I'm not the one incarcerated.'

'I guess I don't need to ask how Cathy's doing.'

'As you'd expect.' Grace paused. 'I'm hoping to get authority to keep on seeing her.'

'Professionally, you mean?'

'Preferably, yes – though I'll settle for plain visitation if I have to.'

'You sound frustrated,' Hayman remarked.

'I am.' She tucked the cordless phone between her chin and right shoulder, and used both hands to flip the omelette. 'Peter, I don't seem to have helped that poor child at all, and now she's so tied up in bureaucratic tape I can't see how I'm ever going to.'

168

'But doesn't this happen all the time, Grace, in our profession?' Hayman said. 'Don't we always feel we're getting nowhere for the longest time? Wouldn't we always prefer to make a positive difference more quickly than we do?'

'My patients aren't usually locked up in a youth facility accused of three counts of murder one.' Grace bent down to take a warmed plate out of her lower oven, and tipped the omelette out of its pan. As if by magic, Harry-the-food-magnet appeared at her side. This was his kind of omelette, one wrapped around slices of *prosciutto*.

'Are you still pondering the father's possible role in all this?' Hayman asked.

'I haven't stopped pondering,' Grace answered. 'But I don't have any more good reason to ponder than I did when I saw you.'

'Poor Grace,' Hayman said.

'Poor Cathy.'

He offered what little help he could before they ended the call. Any time she wanted to use him to test a new theory, he said, or simply to unload, he'd try to make himself available to listen. And if, he added, Grace ever found herself able to take a few days' real vacation, then he wanted her to keep in mind that his sailboat was ready and waiting off Key Largo.

'I'm sure you know there's no better form of relaxation,' he said, 'than time spent out there on the ocean.'

It was the best offer Grace had had in a long while.

CHAPTER TWENTY-SIX

Sam showed up at six-ten Tuesday evening. Up until the moment when Grace opened her front door and saw that tall, hard frame again, that keen-boned mocha face and those warm, tired eyes, she thought she simply hadn't understood – maybe she hadn't *allowed* herself to understand – just how much the man blew her away. The whole package.

'Hello,' he said, still on the doorstep.

'Hi.'

'Can I come in?'

'Sure.'

Grace stepped back to let him through. He was wearing jeans, white T-shirt, sport coat and loafers, and his cologne had a faint, pleasing forest smell. She closed the door just as Harry came swaggering through from the deck into the hallway, stubby tail wagging. Sam got down to his level.

'We're both glad to see you,' Grace said. 'How's your father doing?'

Sam was raking Harry's curly white coat with his fingers exactly the way he liked. 'The doctors seem hopeful enough that they can beat this fever, but until he comes to properly, talks and walks, no one's taking bets.'

'I went to see him.' She wasn't certain she ought to have said that.

'I know.' Sam got up. 'I'm sorry about what Ma said to you.'

'I understood.'

'More than I did.'

'She thinks Cathy's guilty, and I'm still standing by her. I

170

can't blame her for being bitter about that.'

'I saw the flowers you sent,' Sam said. 'They were lovely.'

Grace looked up at him. 'Can you stay for dinner?'

'Sure you want me?'

'Never surer.'

They hung out in the kitchen while Grace fed Harry, then cheat-baked high-speed potatoes in her microwave oven, tossed a salad, grilled a couple of steaks and crisped a loaf of bread. They ate hungrily – Sam, she noticed, always seemed to be hungry – batting small talk around, grateful for some respite before they got around to what they both had on their minds.

Grace started first, knowing it was high time for her to share with Sam what his father had told her two days before he'd been attacked in his office. Sam listened attentively, not speaking at all until she was through telling him about the evils of John Broderick.

'That's what you wanted to talk to me about Saturday morning, wasn't it?'

'It was,' she said. 'But you weren't in the mood to listen.'

'No, I wasn't.' Sam paused. 'It was the anniversary of my son's death on Sunday. No excuses, but I always get a little crazy when it gets close.'

'Oh, God,' Grace said, softly. 'I'm sorry, Sam.'

He shrugged. 'It's over now.'

'Now you have your dad to worry about.'

'Yeah,' he said. 'But I should have listened to you.'

'Do you see now why I wanted to know if you'd checked out Broderick's death? Why it troubles me that his body was never found?'

'We can't be sure it was never found,' Sam pointed out. 'He could have washed up a John Doe somewhere, maybe even out of state.'

'But don't computers link up about missing persons these days?'

'Mistakes happen. People get buried in the wrong places.' Sam looked at her sharply. 'Suicide scams happen, too, Grace – you're right about that, of course. But there's usually a solid reason – mostly financial. I've checked Broderick's death out

171

pretty thoroughly. He left a note, so there was no question of Marie or anyone else claiming life insurance, and he left almost everything he had to his mother in Fort Lauderdale —'

'Is she still alive?'

'Died three years ago,' Sam said.

'Doesn't it strike you as odd that he left everything to his mother, but left some surgical instruments to his five-year-old daughter?'

'Not exactly the most charming of keepsakes,' Sam agreed.

Grace's mind was still moving. 'Suicide scams aren't always about money, are they? Broderick was being investigated – he was going to get in a lot of trouble, lose his job, maybe even go to jail.'

'So you're thinking flight,' Sam said.

'Why not? If he couldn't face it.'

'Sounds like a perfect motive for suicide to me.'

'Maybe,' Grace said. 'Maybe not.'

Sam waited until she was ready to pour the coffee before hitting his own big one. He wanted to stay in the kitchen rather than go out on the deck, he said, because he had something he thought Grace ought to see.

'We found Cathy's journal on her computer.'

Grace felt her stomach jolt.

'She had one of those notebook models. She took it with her to her aunt's place.' Sam paused. 'The journal was password-protected, but our guys opened it up.'

Grace had just picked up her coffee cup. Now she had to put it down.

'The password was H-A-T-E,' Sam said.

'Shit,' Grace said.

'Yeah,' he agreed.

'So?' She looked across the table at him. 'Do I take it the journal was another gift for the State Attorney?' Her tone was bitter.

'Right first time.'

'Go ahead,' she said.

'Sure you want to know?'

Grace thought, suddenly, about his position, rather than her own. 'Is it all right for you to be sharing this with me?'

172

'Probably not,' Sam said. 'But I won't tell if you won't.'

'Okay,' she said.

He had taken off his sport coat before sitting down to eat. Now he retrieved some folded sheets of copy paper from an inside pocket and smoothed them out on Grace's kitchen table. There were three relevant entries.

The first, logged on the last day of March, two days before Marie and Arnold Robbins' killings, read:

I see their faces, see them smile, know their betrayal, and I hate them more than I can say.
I don't think I can wait much longer.

The second, dated April 9, the day after Beatrice Flager's stabbing, said:

She shouldn't have done it to me. She ought to have minded her own business.
She was always a bitch, anyway.

'There's one more,' Sam said. 'It was the last entry in the journal.' Grace's head was spinning. She hardly trusted herself to speak. Sam laid the last piece of paper on top of the others.

I feel like I'm about to explode. No one believes me.
No one *ever* believes me.
I know I'm on my own now.
Maybe I always have been.

'That was dated April 18.' Sam confirmed Grace's worst fear.

'And nothing after that?' Her voice was very quiet and a little shaky.

'*Nada.*'

'I guess there couldn't have been.'

'I guess not.'

Grace took a few moments. She felt desolate. A new thought struck her. 'No entry that might relate to your father?'

173

Sam shook his head.

'Isn't that a little strange?'

'Could be.' He paused. 'But then, the whole thing's a little off.'

'How so?'

'It's not exactly subtle, is it?'

'She's fourteen years old, Sam. How subtle do you want her to be?'

'I don't know.' He was looking troubled. 'But when it comes to charging Cathy with Beatrice Flager's killing – and that's going to happen any moment now – and when it comes before the grand jury, the police and the prosecution are going to try and persuade them that she was smart enough – *cunning* enough – to get up in the middle of the night without rousing her aunt, get herself over to Coconut Grove, stab Flager through the neck without waking her first – and maybe even to have done more or less the same thing at my dad's office ...' His voice trailed away. He was shaking his head.

'What's your point, Sam?'

'My point ...' He rubbed the side of his head. 'My point is that if she did have what it took to do all that, then she sure as hell knew better than to write what amounts to a confession in her journal for all the world to read.'

'The entries were password-protected,' Grace said.

'She'd know better than to think that meant anything if any kind of an expert got a hold of her computer. Kids these days all know better than that.'

'Have you questioned Cathy about the journal?' Grace remembered that Cathy had volunteered the information to her about keeping a computer journal, had even told her that it was a notebook model she'd taken to her aunt's house.

'She admits to keeping a journal, but she denies writing those entries. She also denies having created that password.' Sam shrugged. 'Majority opinion in the department is that her denial means zip.' ('*Jack shit*' was actually the way Al Martinez had put it, and both Sergeant Kovac and Chief Hernandez agreed with him.)

'Am I right in thinking you have another opinion?' Grace asked with a swift rush of hope. 'I mean, what are the options here? Is there a chance that Cathy didn't write those entries herself?'

'If she didn't write them – *if* – then I guess someone else did.'

'But how could they get into her computer memory?' Grace thought for a moment. 'Aren't all entries automatically timed and dated by the computer?'

'Yes, they are,' Sam said, 'and we removed Cathy's notebook computer from her bedroom at her aunt's house.' He read her unspoken question. 'Which means whoever made the last entry almost certainly had to be in the house at that time.'

'Could it have been sent by modem?' Grace suggested.

'I'm no expert,' Sam said, 'but our guys said no to that when I raised it.'

Grace didn't know exactly what she was feeling. She didn't know whether to be optimistic or not about his doubts. 'More coffee?' she asked.

'Sure. Please.'

She stood up, went to pour them both some more. She was taking her time, moving slowly, trying to get her head wholly around Sam's position.

'What is it you're really saying, Sam?'

'I don't know.'

'Yes, you do.' She brought the cups back to the table, bent down to give Harry a quick ruffle, then straightened up and sat back down. 'I think you're saying that you still don't believe that Cathy killed anyone.'

Sam's eyes were still deeply troubled. He took in a long breath, let it out slowly. 'You have to appreciate this is me talking, Grace. Not the department. Certainly not the State Attorney.'

'I do appreciate that.'

'So this is strictly off-the-record.'

'Of course,' she said.

'Then yes, I am saying that I still have doubts.' He saw the spark in her eyes. 'But that's no reason to get your hopes up. You were right when you called the journal entries another gift to the State Attorney. That's exactly what they are.'

Grace nodded, then poured a little half-and-half in her coffee. It was an effort to maintain her composure, but she was managing it. 'Any other developments?'

'Off the record?'

'For now, definitely.'

'What does that mean, Grace?'

She met his eyes calmly. 'That I won't mention a word of what you tell me without discussing it with you first.'

'Okay.' Sam stirred sugar into his black coffee. 'I might not have thought this worth talking about if you hadn't told me what my dad got out of Lafayette.'

Grace's spine was starting to prickle.

'According to the toxicology reports,' Sam began, 'all the victims except my father had tranquillizers or sedative drugs in their systems, which is why, we're guessing, there was no sign of struggle in any of the attacks.' He paused. 'The State Attorney doesn't seem to think that's a big deal because the drugs were definitely prescribed for them, and a big percentage of adult Floridians take that kind of medication daily, so the presence of drugs is coincidental and has no bearing on the case against Cathy Robbins.'

'And you?' Grace asked. 'What do you think?'

'Going on the hard evidence, I think they could be right.'

'But now that you know about John Broderick's history of drug abuse' – Grace was unable to contain herself any longer – 'you're starting to wonder.'

'Don't get excited, Grace.' Sam's smile was brief and tense. 'I'm not sure I trust myself around this case. Al Martinez said something to me a week or so back that implied I might be letting Cathy's vulnerable façade influence me. He may have been right.'

'I know how you feel,' Grace said quietly. 'I've had the same concerns about my own attitude.'

'And bringing Broderick into the question is still plain crazy, you know that too, don't you?' Sam shook his head. 'I've found nothing to suggest he might not have drowned nine years ago.'

'But you have been checking into it.' The knowledge warmed Grace. 'Even before you knew about the drugs and Lafayette's inquiry into him, you were concerned enough to wonder about his death.'

'I don't like loose ends,' Sam said, simply. 'I didn't like the fact there was no body.' He paused. 'Now I like it even less.'

The two of them went out on to Grace's deck, while she ran almost impossibly wild theories past Sam. First, going back more than a year, she brought up the cannabis and goldfish accusations, which even now, in the face of infinitely vaster charges, still exercised Cathy's mind. If Broderick was by any chance still alive, given his track record, Grace suggested, it might not have been beyond the bounds of possibility for him to have found a way to get dope into his daughter, then mutilate the fish and watch Arnold's and Marie's horrified reaction.

'Physician turns housebreaker,' Sam said sceptically.

'He was already an abuser,' Grace reminded him. 'And cunning. I don't see him breaking in – I picture him finding a way to get hold of the house keys and walking through the door at night.' She was becoming galvanized. 'And once he had the keys, he could have just walked in again on April 2.'

'And doped and killed Marie and Arnold?'

'I can believe in him as a killer more easily than I can Cathy.' Grace stood up, began to pace the deck. Harry, who'd been lying down peaceably, raised his head and followed her with his eyes. 'He could have broken the window from the inside,' she went on. 'And made an entry in her journal.'

'Why?' Sam asked.

Grace stopped pacing and looked down at him. 'Why what?'

'Why would he kill them?'

'Who knows? Revenge – at least on Marie – for blowing the whistle after he walked out on her. On Arnold, too, perhaps, for taking his place.' Grace paused. 'We know he was a very jealous man. Frances said he was jealous of Cathy, even before she was born.'

'Jealousy's one thing,' Sam said. 'This kind of warped cruelty's something else.' He looked at Grace, seeking an answer. 'Why would a man want to punish his own daughter so brutally?'

'I don't know, Sam,' Grace told him, 'except that maybe before she came along he thought his life was okay, and afterwards it all went downhill.'

'And why wait nine years to take this so-called revenge?' Sam asked.

'Best eaten cold, they say, don't they?' Grace said. 'Or maybe the planning was the part he liked best.'

'A guy would have to be seriously sick, Grace,' Sam said. 'Not to mention *alive*.'

She wasn't ready to let up. 'If it is Broderick, I imagine they don't come much sicker.' She sat down beside Sam again. 'And I've never been a gambling woman, but I'd bet my boots he's very much alive, too.'

They both fell silent.

'What about Beatrice Flager?' Sam asked after a while.

'I don't know.' Grace paused. 'He may have thought she and her records posed a potential threat if Cathy, or even Arnold, had talked about him and the past to her.'

'So what? Your theory is that Broderick's been watching their every move for all these years?' Sam said. 'I mean, Cathy only went to Flager one time.'

'But the very fact that she refused to go back again slides right into the notion that Broderick's prime aim was – is – to frame her. If she didn't get along with her therapist, resented her even, then that makes her a more plausible suspect in Ms Flager's killing.'

'If Broderick's been keeping tabs on them for nine years, how come no one ever recognized him?'

'I guess he'd have been careful around the Robbinses,' Grace said. 'And don't forget, he lived and worked in Tallahassee before the suicide, so chances are no one would remember him. And maybe he's changed his appearance.'

'You've been watching too many movies, Grace.'

'Maybe I have,' she admitted. 'It does get more complicated with Frances,' she went on, thoughtfully. 'We know she hated Broderick, probably counselled her sister against him – and we also know that Cathy got upset because her aunt doubted her. Though it's unlikely Broderick could have known that, of course.'

'You mean, you don't have a theory about his bugging the house?'

Grace smiled, then quickly grew sombre again. 'It seems to me that if what we're looking at is an elaborate revenge on

Cathy, Frances' killing was the obvious final act to have pinned on her.'

'And where does my father fit into this scenario?' Sam said.

'He tried to help Cathy,' Grace said, softly. 'That might have been enough motive.' She saw something change in Sam's expression. 'What?'

'Did you tell Cathy what my father told you about Broderick?' he asked.

'No, of course not.' Grace hesitated. 'But I did tell Frances.'

'Was Cathy around? Might she have heard what you said?'

'I know she heard some of it. I don't know how much.' *Strike another one for the State Attorney*, Grace realized with a pang, watching Sam's face for anger or, at least, renewed scepticism for her unsubstantiated theorizing. He didn't look sceptical, though. He looked faraway and even grimmer than before.

'What are you thinking, Sam?' she asked.

'Nothing.'

'That's not true.'

'Okay.' He took a moment. 'I was thinking about what you just said about my father getting hurt because he wanted to help Cathy.'

'That makes some sense, doesn't it?'

'As much sense as any of this, given that we're still talking about a dead man.' He paused again. 'But my father isn't the only person who's been trying to help Cathy.'

Grace saw where he was heading. 'You're talking about me.'

'It springs to mind.'

'Broderick won't hurt me,' she said confidently.

'Because Cathy's been charged?'

'Absolutely. He's got what he wanted. Touching me or anyone else now would blow the case against her out of the water.'

'So long as —' Sam stopped.

'What?'

'Some killers get addicted,' he said, quietly. 'They don't plan on it, but it happens.'

'If it's Broderick, though,' Grace said, holding fast to her

179

confidence, 'he's highly organized, isn't he?' She had read a
little about the basics profilers used in the hunt for multiple
murderers; enough at least, to know that one of the things they
did was to divide types into 'organized' and 'disorganized'
categories. 'If the accusations against Cathy are what he's
been working towards for so long, then surely he'll probably
be more than satisfied for a good long while, waiting for the
grand jury to indict and then hoping for more.' She paused.
'Don't you agree?'

Sam was looking at her intently.

'Now what?' she asked him.

'Truth?'

'Of course.'

'I was just thinking that up until just a minute or so ago,
there was nothing I wanted – as a private individual, not as a
cop – quite so much as for you to be right about Broderick, so
that Cathy could be proven innocent.' He paused. 'But
suddenly I find myself almost hoping you're wrong – that
John Broderick *did* drown off Pensacola nine years ago.'

A rush of emotion shot through Grace. Part of her wanted
to get angry at Sam for shying away from her theories. Part of
her wanted to stand up and yell that proving a fourteen-year-
old girl innocent was more important than anything else. But
she had seen the look in Sam Becket's eyes as he'd considered
the possibility of her being at risk. In one way, of course, it
had scared her, forced her to think about dangers that had not
previously occurred to her.

Mostly, though, she had to admit silently, it thrilled her.

CHAPTER TWENTY-SEVEN

WEDNESDAY, APRIL 29, 1998

Tuesday had ended on a kind of a high for Grace. Wednesday started out with the same kind of promise, but then went downhill fast.

Sam called from Miami General just after nine a.m. 'My father's fever broke last night,' he told her. 'Looks like he's going to make a full recovery.'

'Sam, that's wonderful news.' Grace stopped herself from asking the question she wanted to. Judy Becket's hostility and suspicion still troubled her, and she didn't want Sam thinking even for a second that her only concern for David was in connection with Cathy.

He saved her the awkwardness.

'Grace, I asked Dad if he remembered what had happened.'

'And does he?' Her mouth was dry.

'Not enough,' Sam said. 'The good news, I guess, is that he can't ID Cathy as his attacker. The bad news is that he can't say it wasn't her either. It was dark, and he was asleep almost right up until the blade hit him.' He paused. 'Dad remembers waking up and feeling a breeze which he thinks was probably the weapon arcing down over him, but that's all. He didn't even see a shape.'

'So he can't even say if it was a man or woman?'

'Uh-uh.' Sam paused again. 'Grace, if it makes you feel any better, he got mad as a wet hen when I told him she'd been charged with the murders. Dad doesn't feel any differently with a hole in his chest about Cathy Robbins than he did before.'

'May I tell her that when I see her?' Grace asked.

'I don't see why not,' Sam answered. 'Though you'll obviously be wrecking any hopes she might have had of Dad clearing her name.'

'What's the alternative? I don't see much point in nurturing false hopes – and there's always a chance she might hear it from someone else and figure me for a liar.' It was an effort to sound anything other than despondent, but Grace was doing her best. 'I'm so very glad your father's going to make it, Sam.'

'I know you are,' he said.

Grace was just writing up case notes after an appointment before leaving for her visit to the youth facility, when Dora Rabinovitch (the woman Grace sometimes called her 'angel of mercy' because she came over whenever Grace was really snowed under to take care of overdue correspondence and to let the psychologist know when she'd forgotten to pay something vaguely significant, like her power bill) stuck in her two cents' worth.

'Isn't this girl dangerous?' Dora asked. She was a round, warm, efficient and, on the whole, generous-hearted woman, but like many people in Miami, she'd read all about Cathy Robbins and couldn't conceive of someone like Grace spending any more time with her than was absolutely essential.

'I don't think she's in the least bit dangerous,' Grace told her.

'But they won't leave you alone together?' Dora wanted to know. 'You'll have a guard with you.'

'I hope not,' Grace said.

There was no guard, Grace thanked the Lord for small mercies, at least not with them in the small locked visitors' room made available again for their session. There was just herself and a young person who had visibly declined since Grace had last seen her.

'I didn't do it,' Cathy said almost as soon as they'd sat down.

'I know you didn't. I've told you that before.'

'Last time I saw those goldfish, they were alive and swimming around. I always hated the way they were trapped in that tank, like they were in a prison.' She paused. 'I guess I know now how they felt.'

Still those damned fish, as if homicide was too great a horror to absorb. Grace's heart sank at the deterioration in her. Cathy was now clearly not so much denying as *in* denial.

'Is there anything special you wanted to talk to me about?' Grace asked, putting off the evil moment when she was going to have to tell Cathy about David Becket. 'Or shall we just spend some time together?'

'I think Mr Wagner wants me to say I'm crazy,' she said, coming right to it. 'But I'm not crazy, am I, Grace?'

'No, you're not.'

'So why does he think I am?' Cathy's blue eyes were antagonistic. 'You're the shrink – I know he talked to you. You must have said something that made Mr Wagner think that about me.'

'On the contrary,' Grace said firmly. 'I told him that I was certain you were entirely sane, and that you were also not guilty.'

'So why didn't he believe you?' Her tone was still accusatory.

'I don't know why. I only know what I said to him, which is what I believe, and what I'm going to go on saying to anyone who'll listen.'

Grace reached out across the table, wanting to take Cathy's hand, but the teenager pulled away so violently that the table rocked.

'Take it easy, Cathy.'

She flushed. 'I'm sorry. I guess I'm getting jumpy.'

'Are you sleeping okay?' There were dark circles under her eyes.

'Not really.'

'Is your bed very uncomfortable?'

'It's awful,' Cathy confided. 'And it smells bad.' She lowered her voice. 'The whole place stinks, Grace.' Her eyes filled with tears. 'I don't want to stay here – can't you make them let me out?'

'I wish I could.'

'I could come and stay with you,' Cathy pleaded. 'You know I didn't do anything – you could tell them again, and maybe they'd listen to you.'

'I can try.' The sense of frustration caused by her inability

183

to help her patient made Grace feel almost physically sick, but she fought it, aware that showing weakness was only going to make matters worse. 'I will try, Cathy,' she said very gently. 'But I have to be honest with you. It's too early for me to make any difference – no one's going to listen to me, not just yet.'

'So why did you bother to *come*?'

Cathy stood up so abruptly that her chair tipped back and hit the ground with a loud bang. Behind her, through the small window in the door, Grace saw the female guard standing outside the door checking through the glass pane. She nodded to the guard, raised her right hand, palm towards her, wanting to pass the message that there was no problem. The guard stayed outside, but went on watching through the glass.

'I came because I wanted to see you,' Grace said.

'I wish you hadn't.'

Grace remained seated, in the hope that Cathy would calm down. 'Why don't you pick up the chair and come and sit down again?'

'What's the point?' she asked, belligerently. 'What's the point in *anything*?'

Grace had seen Cathy resentful and angry before, but never that rude or hostile. If a single week inside the youth facility could have this much of a damaging effect on her, the prospect of what was almost certain now to follow filled Grace with trepidation for her. With more time, more space, more *freedom* to talk to her, it was possible that Grace might have been able to get through to her, at least try to pull the poor child back on some sort of track.

But there was too little time to achieve anything worthwhile.

In any event, this was most definitely not, Grace now realized, the right moment to dash her hopes any further by giving her the news about David Becket.

184

CHAPTER TWENTY-EIGHT

THURSDAY, APRIL 30, 1998

'Hey, Becket, get with it, man!'

'Hey, Sam, you're on!'

'Hey, detective-sir, quit goofing off!'

'Yo, Count di-fucking-Luna, get your black ass up on this stage and sing!'

Sam snapped out of his fantasy and got ready to work.

S-BOP had come through for him again, and this time they were letting an undependable – and now, it was beginning to seem to him, lovestruck – black cop play the part of a Spanish count. The plot of *Il Trovatore* stank – an implausible, wildly politically incorrect tale of gypsies and witches – and the Count di Luna was a vengeful son-of-a-bitch but also a doozy of a role, and the music was heaven and demanding and exactly what Sam needed to help him escape from the sickness of the real world that left its stench on his doorstep every day of the week.

It had not been that sickness he'd been thinking about just now when he was supposed to be getting ready to burn Azucena at the stake. It hadn't been bloodsoaked bodies or a possibly psychotic teenager. It hadn't, for once, even been his father, now truly on the mend and already starting to hassle the doctors and nurses about letting him go home.

It was Grace Lucca.

When he thought about her, he thought about a smart, warm, caring, tenacious, beautiful woman. Oh, yes, she was certainly that. Willowy but strong, long-legged and golden, with blue eyes that he'd already seen spark with intensity, crease up with fatigue and frustration, warm with humour. If his mother hadn't been so dead set against her because of Cathy Robbins, Sam was certain the two women would have gotten along. *And she can even cook*, he could imagine Judy saying.

He was thinking about Grace more every day. It was the first time he'd thought about the possibility of getting involved – really involved – with a woman since Althea. He'd met a few nice women since their divorce – hell, he'd met a few *great* women – but there'd been no one who'd really pierced his hard shell until Grace.

He wondered now, suddenly, as he picked up his copy of the libretto and slipped silently on sneakered feet through the semi-dark of the S-BOP theatre towards the stage, if race and religion were finally, almost for the first time in his adult life, going to raise their uglier heads.

Black man, white woman was tough enough.

Black Episcopalian-Jew, white Catholic-Italian woman was bound to toss up all kinds of predicaments along the way to wherever they might, or might not, be heading.

'Hey, Count-di-Becket, you ready to try burning me yet?'

Sam took the steps at the side of the stage in two strides and grinned at Linda Morrison, *mezzo-soprano*, whose imminent torture he was all set to start bragging about.

'You bet your sweet life,' he said.

Grace flew back into his mind. Tanned legs, bare feet dangling in the river. And the look in her eyes the other night when she'd understood he was concerned for her safety.

He would be concerned, all right, if John Broderick turned out to be one of the undead.

And unlikely as that whole scenario still seemed, it was one more thing he couldn't seem to get out of his mind.

The other preoccupation close to Sam's heart this week was Saul's barmitzvah on Saturday. While David had still been in his worryingly feverish limbo state, Judy had wanted to postpone the event, but Sam had changed her mind. It had been tough for Saul, as it was for most kids, getting himself to this stage of readiness, and postponing would mean that he would either stay nerve-frayed for the foreseeable future, or go off the boil and maybe even lose the plot – it wasn't as if they could pinpoint another date, after all.

'What you're saying,' Judy had said to him, voice strained but low, so that Saul wouldn't hear her, 'is if your father doesn't make it, Saul might never be barmitzvah?'

'No, Ma,' Sam had said, 'that isn't what I'm saying.'

They'd settled on going ahead with the service, sharing a kiddush glass of wine with the rest of the congregation at temple, then a quiet lunch for the three of them.

'No party till Dad can be with us,' Sam had said, 'but we can get the whole thing on video for when he's better —'

'Or I could maybe do it again for him,' Saul jumped in.

Now, of course, the whole mood had radically changed. There was every likelihood that David might talk his way into being in temple with them – even if it did mean his giving in to staying in a wheelchair and going back to Miami General afterward – and suddenly Judy was a whirlwind of activity, throwing herself body and soul into making sure that what was left of the weekend's plans went smoothly.

Sam knew that he'd mentioned the barmitzvah to Grace the first time he'd gone to her place – the night she'd shared her *Cacciucco* with him and they'd both talked a little about their backgrounds. He'd thought a number of times in the past week or two about how much he would have enjoyed having her there, but with the way things had been it hadn't seemed possible.

And then, this morning, a package had arrived on his desk.

He'd opened it, intrigued, found a sealed envelope addressed to Saul, and a note for himself.

Dear Sam,
I came upon this and thought of Saul and his big day. I hope it's the right thing – and I hope that I'm offending no one by sending it. If you think it might cause more upset to your mother, then don't worry about hurting my feelings.
I'm so happy your father's going to be there.
Grace.

The gift itself was packed in tissue paper. Sam opened it up carefully, found a leatherbound book on the history of the State of Israel. *I came upon this*, Grace had written. Sam smiled at the obvious understatement. It was a wonderful gift, painstakingly chosen and generously given. And as for the line about not upsetting his mother ...

CHAPTER TWENTY-NINE

FRIDAY, MAY 1, 1998

Jerry Wagner agreed to see Grace again just before lunch on Friday. (His lunch, not hers, since Grace knew she'd be lucky to find time to grab more than cheese and crackers until nightfall at the earliest.)

Top of her anxieties about Cathy was the option open to the State of Florida to try the fourteen year old as an adult rather than a minor. They could do that, Grace had discovered, if the grand jury came to an indictment, because of the grievous nature of the crimes. It happened quite often, she had learned, when kids killed, and one of the worst aspects from Grace's point-of-view was that it would mean Cathy's being transferred to an adult prison facility for the long wait until the trial.

'I need to know,' she told Wagner, 'if there's anything I can do or say that might make a difference to the judge's decision about that.'

'Unfortunately, I don't think there is.' He shook his head. 'In our state, in a case like this – four brutal deaths – it's almost a foregone conclusion that Cathy's going to be bound into the adult court.'

'But surely we can try and fight it?' Grace was trying hard to keep calm again in the face of this man's depressing response. 'Maybe if I go before the court and tell them what I think this might do to Cathy?'

'Compared to what she's accused of doing to the victims, I'm afraid that any traumatizing effect on Cathy you could come up with just wouldn't balance the books.' Wagner leaned forward, his short curly hair, piercingly blue eyes and

189

curved nose giving him the look of a Roman in a dark suit rather than a toga. 'Dr Lucca, I know this is tough to take, but—'

'What this is is guilty till proven innocent,' Grace cut in passionately. 'I mean, it's so appallingly *unjust*.'

'It does seem that way.'

'It doesn't just seem that way, Mr Wagner – it *is* that way. I can just about begin to contemplate the rationale that a juvenile found guilty of a terrible crime like homicide should be treated as an adult, though I find even that hard to accept – but we're talking here about taking an innocent child and doing our best to destroy her before she's even come to trial.'

Wagner sat back again. 'I didn't say I agreed with the system, doctor,' he said gently. 'Don't you think I want to help my client every step of the way? I'd like nothing more than to keep her out of the adult facility – no, that's not true. What I'd really like is to get her out on bail and into some kind of safe, state-approved home until the trial.'

'That would be wonderful.' Grace jumped hungrily on his words.

'I said that's what I'd really *like*,' Wagner pointed out, 'but it's wholly and absolutely out of the question.' He paused. 'This is a long haul case, Dr Lucca. We all need to keep clearly focused on our ultimate goals.'

'My goal's to keep Cathy sane,' Grace said.

'And mine's to make sure she walks free when all this is over,' Wagner added. 'And I have no doubt that you can do a whole lot to keep Cathy sane, no matter where she has to spend the next few months.'

Grace nodded, bit her lip, then took a deep breath.

'I do have something else I think you should know about,' she said.

Wagner checked his Cartier wristwatch. 'I have a lunch meeting in twenty minutes.'

'It's very important,' Grace told him. 'Possibly crucial to the case.'

His mouth pursed and he nodded. 'Shoot,' he said.

She told him, as concisely as possible, about her still-hypothetical, still-off-the-planet, theory about John Broderick.

190

'It's certainly a fascinating notion,' he said, once he'd finished writing notes on his yellow legal pad.

Grace's heart began to sink.

'I take it there's no hard evidence to support your theory that Broderick didn't die in that storm?'

'None except that his body was never found,' she replied. 'I was hoping you might ask one of your investigators to check into his last weeks, maybe even hours.'

'We might do that,' Wagner said. 'I'll certainly be raising it with my colleagues.' He paused. 'You have to admit your suggestion that he's waited almost ten years to resurrect himself in order to murder a bunch of people and frame his own daughter is pretty far-fetched?'

Grace gritted her teeth and ploughed on. 'It may sound far-fetched at first hearing, Mr Wagner,' she told him. 'But we're talking about a man *proven* to be possessive, obsessive, jealous and cruel.'

'Unfortunately, the case against him never came to a hearing stage.'

'It did up to a point,' Grace pointed out. 'Marie Broderick did get a court order to stop him seeing Cathy.' She continued as if he hadn't interrupted. 'We know Broderick was an unethical physician and an immoral man who forced medication on his family in order to punish, control and manipulate them. Now just supposing he didn't die nine years ago, don't you have to consider him the most likely suspect?'

Wagner scribbled a few more notes on his pad. 'You know, even if we don't manage to find anything to support your theory, this information may help Cathy,' he said, thoughtfully, 'though perhaps not in the way you're hoping.'

Grace's heart sank further, to someplace below her stomach.

'If nothing else,' Wagner went on, 'this should at least strengthen our chance of pulling off an insanity plea. We can argue that all she'd been through in her young life just drove her right over the edge.'

'But that's the *last* thing I'm saying.'

Wagner glanced at his watch again, and began to stack the three neat piles of paperwork on his desk into one pile – the clearest message yet that their meeting was drawing to an end.

'I'm grateful to you, Dr Lucca, for what you've told me. We'll certainly be checking into Broderick's death. If we find even a scrap of something useful, I can assure you we'll jump on it with everything we've got.'

'Thank you for that,' Grace said, despondently.

'Will you do something for me, doctor? If we don't come up with an alternative suspect?'

'If I can.'

'Think about – just *consider* – helping us, down the road, to persuade Cathy to go with an insanity plea.' Wagner paused, his eyes serious. 'I know it sounds like a negative approach, and I can see how it would go against the grain for you – and, I promise you, it would only be a last resort. But just keep in mind that at the end of the day, it may make all the difference to getting Cathy out of jail.'

Grace felt like crying as she walked out of that perfect office. The worst of it, she decided, getting into the elevator, was that with Cathy in such poor shape, and with the evidence so heavily weighted against her, she thought she could almost see Jerry Wagner's point-of-view.

Almost.

Sam's call that morning had been the high spot of Grace's day. She had found the book for Saul a week earlier in Barnes & Noble in Coral Gables and had held back for a few moments, worrying about Judy Becket's feelings – but the book had been particularly handsome, and Grace liked the idea of giving some kind of keepsake, so she'd gone ahead, sent it to Sam and left the final decision to him.

'It's a wonderful gift,' he'd told her on the phone. 'Much too generous, but very, very kind.'

'I liked it,' Grace had said, 'though it did cross my mind afterwards that Saul would probably have preferred something a little cooler.'

'No way,' Sam had put her straight. 'He's going to love it.'

'You don't think it's inappropriate for me to send a gift?'

'The only thing that's inappropriate, Grace, is that you should have been put in a position where you have to think twice about it.'

That was when he'd told her about the quiet way they'd

decided to organize the barmitzvah, and when he'd asked if she would like to come to Golden Beach Temple on Saturday morning and to stay for kiddush afterward.

'I don't know, Sam,' Grace had said, uncertainly.

'You don't know if you can come, or if you want to come, or you don't know because of what my mother said last time she saw you?'

'Not guilty on the first two,' she'd said, grinning into the phone.

'My mother will be too busy being scared in case Saul screws up and being proud when he doesn't, and being happy because Dad's there to share it with her, even to notice who else is there.'

'I just don't want to spoil the day for her, Sam.'

'What about my day?' he'd asked.

'I don't want to spoil your day either.'

'So you'll come?'

Grace had still been smiling when she'd put down the phone.

CHAPTER THIRTY

SATURDAY, MAY 2, 1998

She had been to temple a few times in her life, all of them since she and Claudia had moved to Florida. Friends' weddings, a patient's batmitzvah – and Grace had attended a Passover seder that still ranked with her as a warm and happy memory. But Saul Becket's *bar*mitzvah was her first, and from the moment Sam's young brother got up there and Grace heard his halting, semi-broken voice singing those ancient, to her incomprehensible, words, she felt transported. The notion that with this rite of passage a boy moved into manhood had always struck her as fanciful, mostly because it was, from her standpoint, impossible. Not that she hadn't seen children flung headlong into maturity almost overnight, but that had always been because some terrible adversity or trauma had catapulted them out of childhood. A ritual in a place of worship, followed most often by a party of some kind, was not, thank God, in the same league.

And yet, as she saw David and Judy Becket's younger son standing up there between the rabbi and the cantor, his prayer shawl over his narrow shoulders, his face so earnest, his whole bearing probably eight million miles away from how Saul Becket usually comported himself, Grace was intensely struck by the solemnity of the event. Even if this so-called man turned back into a regular thirteen-year-old kid within an hour or so, she found herself suddenly understanding that this experience would remain with him, within him, rounding the angular youthful features that lived inside the boy, and forming a strong spiritual springboard for the rest of his life.

It was a reform temple, with men and women sitting

194

together, which Grace found warmer and more natural from her perspective. To her left, an old lady sucked peppermints and followed every Hebrew word in her prayerbook, her frail right index finger tracing the letters, her mouth moving silently as she read.To her right, a girl of about eight shifted restlessly in her seat and did her best to involve her sister – a year or two older and determined at least to *seem* as if she was following the service – in some sort of a game to pass the time. Grace understood how she felt. She remembered interminable hours spent in church back in her early Chicago childhood, while the old Latin prayers and rituals had flowed over her head. She remembered being chastised for daydreaming by her parents, for in those early days Frank Lucca had still found his way into church on a regular basis – and Grace supposed he might have spent many hours in the confessional for years after that, probably seeking absolution for his crimes against her sister. Except, of course, that absolution could only be given if the confessor was determined not to sin again, and if Grace knew Frank better than that, she was pretty sure that God did, in which case it was only a matter of time before hell-fire got around to consuming him.

She had taken a seat about a third from the rear, well away from the Becket family. Under other circumstances, Grace would have enjoyed nothing more than walking right up to David – who had, being the stubborn man he was, insisted on leaving his wheelchair at the entrance – and letting him know how very glad she was to see him again, but she had resolved not to cause Judy Becket even a moment's discomfort during the service. Despite her good intentions, however, about a half-minute after Sam had been called up to read from the Torah, Judy swivelled around and met her eyes, and Grace felt almost as if the other woman was piercing what she had hoped was an impenetrable mask of calm, uninvolved pleasure. Maybe, Grace thought, Judy could sense the effect that Sam's remarkable voice, so deep and rich and effortlessly melodic, was having upon her. Maybe Judy Becket knew, in that brief moment, that Grace's involvement with him was deepening way beyond merely professional, and maybe, too, that troubled her.

*

195

'Mazeltov, Saul,' Grace said to him afterward at the kiddush in the hall attached to the temple, shaking his hand. 'I thought you were great, though I'm afraid I didn't understand much.'

'That's okay,' he told her, then grinned. 'Neither did I.'

'You don't have a drink, Grace,' Sam said, coming up behind them. 'Let me get you something.'

'I can't stay,' she told him quickly.

'You have to take a drink with us for luck,' Sam said.

He brought her a glass of kosher wine, and she drank a toast to Saul.

'I loved it,' she said to Sam. 'I mean, I really enjoyed it.'

'How'd I do?'

'Very impressive, I thought.' She smiled up at him. 'Not that I'm exactly an expert.'

'I'm glad you came, Grace.'

'Me, too.'

She saw Judy Becket coming their way. David, back in his chair, was still at the far end of the hall. Grace tensed, wanting to avoid the slightest unpleasantness.

'I really do have to go, Sam.'

Judy was upon them. She was wearing navy blue, a dress and jacket, with white piping around the borders of the jacket, repeated in her wide-brimmed hat.

'Dr Lucca,' she said, looking elegant and at ease. 'How kind of you to come.'

Grace put out her hand, wished her mazeltov and told her how fine she thought Saul had been. Judy's grip was firm and calm, and her eyes met Grace's evenly as she thanked her. Grace felt more than a touch of admiration, together with regret for the bad start their relationship had been dealt.

'I was just telling Sam that I have to leave.'

'What a pity,' Judy said, quietly. 'Don't let me keep you.'

She turned away and moved back into the crowd. Grace looked at Sam, saw the anger in his eyes, reached out and briefly squeezed his hand. 'It's okay,' she said, softly. 'Don't get upset.'

'She keeps this up for too long,' he said, 'I'll be telling her what I think.'

Grace smiled. 'Give her some time.'

'You have to stay and see Dad before you leave, Grace.'

She glanced across to where Sam's father sat surrounded by a cluster of affectionate-looking well-wishers, and saw that Judy was back by his side.

'Not today, Sam. Just give him my love – I'll see him soon.'

She gave him no more chance to argue, just kissed his cheek, told him again how glad she had been to be there, and slipped quietly out of the hall. Back in the Mazda, she took a few moments to calm down, turning on the air-conditioning, switching her cellular phone back on, trying not to dwell too long on all the increasingly complicated feelings that Sam Becket was stirring up in her.

The message icon was on display. Glad for the distraction, Grace pushed the buttons for retrieval and, a few seconds later, heard Claudia's voice.

'Grace, it's me. I'm sorry to have to leave a message this way, but I don't know what else to do.' Pause. 'Papa called me,' she said. 'Mama's gone.'

Grace – having gone home to pick up Harry – was jumpy on the drive down to Islamorada. She knew it was the news affecting her, probably combined with the potent mix of emotion that the barmitzvah and kiddush had stirred up in her, but two or three times on the journey she had the uneasy sense of being watched again – the same kind of feeling she'd experienced in Saks two weeks ago when she'd thought, for just a moment, that it had been Cathy watching her. It had been nothing then, and there was no one tailing her today, either. She checked a few times in her rear-view mirror, and the car behind her for a long while was a small VW being driven by an old man, and then there was a blue truck with a youngish woman at the wheel. Grace shook herself out of it, told Harry that she was getting paranoid, and he wasn't to worry about her because they said that was one of the things that happened to psychologists over time.

They were at the Brownley house by mid-afternoon. Daniel had just gotten back, too, from some business in Tampa, and Mike and Robbie were on their way home, being brought by a friend's mother.

197

Claudia was putting on a brave face, keeping busy in the kitchen, telling Daniel she didn't need help, telling him to go upstairs, take a shower and relax a while and leave her to put together a snack, but inside Grace knew she was a mess.

'He's called three times,' Claudia said as she sliced cheese, while Harry and Sadie, the dachshund, hung around waiting for pieces of food to fall down. 'He wants us to come home for the funeral – he keeps saying we have to make things right between us.'

'Words,' Grace said.

'He sounds as if he means it, Grace.'

'Sure he does. He was always able to do that when it suited him.' Grace took a kitchen knife and stabbed at a large red pepper. 'He's pushing your buttons, Claudia.'

'Don't you want to go back for the funeral?' Claudia asked softly.

'Want to?' Grace put down the knife. 'Of course I don't *want* to. I don't want to go back to Chicago, I don't want to see Frank, and I certainly don't want to watch my mother being put into the ground and have to deal with all those emotions.' She sighed. 'But I guess I'm going to do it just the same.'

'Thank God,' Claudia said and slumped on to one of her stools. 'I was so scared you were going to say no, and I might have to go back alone.'

'I'd never let you do that.'

A shadow of a smile tugged at her sister's mouth. 'I guess I knew that.'

Grace took Claudia's hand, drew her off the stool and over to the kitchen table. They both sat down, still holding hands.

'Poor Ellen,' Grace said. Suddenly, she realized that she didn't even know exactly what had killed her. 'Did Frank say what happened? I mean, was it the cancer? I thought he said they'd caught it all.'

'Heart attack,' Claudia told her. 'He said it was very sudden. There was no warning. One minute she was there, the next she was gone.'

'Better for her,' Grace said, softly.

'It must have been a big shock for Papa,' Claudia said.

The bigger the better, Grace thought.

198

'I wish it had been him,' she said.

'Don't say that, Grace.'

'Why not? You know how I feel.' Grace paused. 'At least she doesn't have to live with him anymore. That's something.'

Claudia's dark eyes filled. 'I guess it is.'

'Oh, sweetheart.' Grace got up and put her arms around Claudia's shoulders. 'You cry – you let it out.'

For a moment, Claudia drew back a little and looked up into Grace's face. 'What about you? Don't you want to cry too?'

'No,' Grace said, and pulled her closer again. 'Not yet anyway.'

'How do you feel?' Claudia asked against her shoulder.

'I don't know, Claudia.'

It was the truth. Grace didn't know how she felt. She couldn't seem to feel anything much. Oh, she understood the reasons behind that all too well. Denial. Blocking. All the usual stuff she'd spouted for so many years to and about patients. That didn't help her now.

Not for the first time, Grace was aware that her situation was far more complex than Claudia's. Her sister was the victim – the more obvious victim, at least – of both their parents. Of Frank, physically, and of Ellen, his accomplice through her silence. Claudia was entitled to hold on to her hate and fear, Grace felt strongly. Claudia ought, by rights, to have been the one not wanting to go back for the funeral – and she sure as hell didn't have to consider going for Frank's sake. But it was different for Grace. She had never actually been abused. Her personal suffering had come from seeing what Claudia had gone through, from the guilt she herself had felt about being spared, from the atmosphere of misery, rage and fear that permeated their childhood home. That was all Grace had had to get over after they'd left Chicago, while Claudia had needed to get past years of terror, shame and betrayal. And that was why Grace still felt thrust now, after all those years, into the position of having to make all the decisions about their level of participation in Ellen Lucca's funeral arrangements and their father's future.

'There are a lot of things happening now,' Grace said later

199

after dinner, once the boys had taken Harry and Sadie up to bed and the three adults could finally talk in peace, 'that I never thought would happen.'

'Such as?' Daniel asked. They were out on the deck, citronella candles flickering all around to ward off the mosquitoes. Daniel had opened a good bottle of Chianti, and all three of them had by now drunk more than they were accustomed to.

'Frank, the bully, begging us to come back when he first told us Ellen was sick.' Grace paused for a second, conscious that it was probably the wine loosening her tongue. 'The way my feelings haven't changed at all, about him, especially – but about Ellen, too.'

No one else said anything.

'I'd never really thought about either of them dying, or about how that might make me feel,' she went on.

'I had.' Claudia's voice sounded harsh in the soft night air. 'After we left Chicago – before I met you, Dan' – she smiled gently, briefly, at her husband – 'I often used to imagine Papa dying.' She turned her head away from them both, so they couldn't see her face. 'It was always a painful death I pictured for him. He was always pleading for our forgiveness.' She paused. 'And when I imagined Mama's dying, she was always begging, too – begging me to forgive her for not taking my side against Papa.'

She turned back, and in the flickering light her face looked full of pain. Daniel put out his left hand, touched her arm, let his hand stay there, just touching, nothing more. Grace knew that Claudia would be all right so long as she had Daniel.

She woke up early, while everyone else was still asleep – Claudia and Daniel probably sleeping off the effects of the Chianti. Her head ached a little, but otherwise her worst symptom was nervousness because of the call she knew she had to make – the one she'd put off the previous night.

Frank answered groggily. Grace had known he would be out of it. She supposed she'd chosen early morning because he'd always been a slow starter, would be less able to fight back.

'Oh, it's you,' he said. 'Took your time.'

'Yes,' she said. 'I drove down to be with Claudia when I heard. It got pretty late, so I thought I'd wait till morning.' She paused. 'Claudia said it happened suddenly. I'm sorry.'

'So when are you coming?'

'When's the funeral?' Grace couldn't believe how detached she felt. She'd experienced greater emotion talking to absolute strangers about funeral arrangements than she did now with her own father.

'I don't know,' Frank said. 'That's what I need the two of you to fix up. The funeral, and your mother's will, and that kind of thing.'

'That won't be possible,' Grace said.

'Why not?'

'We both have commitments,' she told him. 'If you let us know when the date's set, we'll do our best to be there.' Her pause was very brief, her voice quite hard. 'If anything comes up that you really need our help with – and I mean really need – then please call me, not Claudia.'

'Now you're telling me I can't call my own daughter?'

If the memory of his ugliness had ever gone away, the meanness in his voice would have brought it all flooding back.

'I'm your daughter, too,' Grace said. 'I mean it, Frank. You call me. Leave Claudia alone, for once in your lousy life.'

She put down the receiver. Her detachment had gone, and her hands were trembling. But at least the decisions had been made.

Even at that emotionally charged time, Cathy was still looming large in Grace's mind. Perhaps remembering their own past was highlighting the poignancy of Cathy's predicament – another abused, traumatized child in need of all the friends she could get. Grace left Islamorada after breakfast and then, on the spur of the moment, took a chance on Peter Hayman being at his house on Key Largo, and being both willing and able to see her.

He was there, seeming delighted to find Grace and Harry on his doorstep, and within minutes they were all sitting out on the screened porch overlooking his palm and orchid garden. The air was too heavily perfumed, and if Grace had known

201

him better she would have requested a move to the ocean-facing side of the house, but she was an uninvited guest and so she said nothing, while Harry, uncomfortable, too, stayed low and almost glued to her right foot.

She drank some of the coffee he brought for her and, careful not to divulge any information that Sam had given her in confidence, brought Hayman up-to-date on their John Broderick-related theorizing.

He sat quietly, listening until Grace had come to a halt.

'Have you also considered that you may be entirely wrong?' he asked at last, gently. 'That Cathy may, after all, be guilty?'

'Of course I've considered it,' Grace answered. 'But I don't believe she is.' She could hear Harry panting. She reached down and fondled his ears for a moment, and resolved not to stay too much longer for his sake.

Hayman stood up, wandered over to the screen, gazed out into the semi-tropical garden. 'I'm troubled, Grace,' he said without looking back at her. 'It concerns me that maybe I was wrong to have found even the most tenuous of similarities with that old case of mine.' He turned to face her. 'Maybe I planted utterly fallacious notions in your mind.'

'Maybe you did,' she conceded calmly, 'but with the life of a fourteen-year-old girl at stake, I'm not prepared to take the chance that you were not wrong.' She paused. 'Anyway, I've moved some distance from the Münchhausen's notion, so that needn't trouble you.'

'Okay.' He paused, apparently taking a moment to accept her point-of-view. 'Simple question. Do you know what John Broderick looked like? Do you have a photograph of him?'

'No, I don't.' Grace told him about Cathy's bedroom in the Robbins home, about the family photographs she'd seen which had excluded the man Cathy always referred to as her first father.

'Mightn't it be an idea,' Hayman suggested, 'to get hold of one? If you're staying with this theory that he might still be alive?' He smiled. 'I mean, Grace, you wouldn't know the guy if you fell over him.'

'That's true.' She considered the best way to obtain such a photograph. Lafayette Hospital were bound to have a snapshot on file, but they were unlikely to release it to her, which meant she'd probably have to ask Sam to deal with it. She saw no reason for him to object – for all she knew, he already had one. 'I'll get one,' she said to Hayman. 'I can't imagine why I didn't think of it myself.'

'Maybe because you know he's dead,' he said, gently. 'You just aren't ready to admit it yet.'

He remarked as Grace was leaving, about a half-hour later, that she was looking rather tired. She told him she'd had some bad news, but did not elaborate. He said he was sorry to hear that, but asked for no details, for which Grace was grateful. He did, however, mention once more, that his invitation was still open for her to join him for a day or two's R and R aboard his boat.

'Don't forget, Grace, will you?'

'I won't,' she said.

'You mustn't make yourself sick. You won't be any use to anyone then.'

'I know.'

They shook hands. Grace noticed that he held on just a little longer than he needed to. She wondered, for a brief moment, if she might have sent out some misleading signal by just showing up unannounced, but there was nothing else, no intense look in his brown eyes. Just simple care and concern.

'See?' she said to Harry as they headed back on the Overseas Highway towards the mainland. 'That's another thing that comes from being a psychologist.' She reached across and ruffled the top of his head. 'You start reading ten times as much as there really is into a simple handshake.'

The terrier gave one of his grunts, settling contentedly down on the seat beside her. Grace knew they were both looking forward to going home.

CHAPTER THIRTY-ONE

WEDNESDAY, MAY 6, 1998

Grace and Claudia flew out of Miami International on Wednesday morning, arrived at O'Hare in Chicago early afternoon and took a cab to their hotel. Daniel had wanted to come, but Claudia had told him that he'd be helping her more if he stayed home with the boys, and Daniel knew she meant it. Claudia had left the travel arrangements to Grace, who had decided to follow her own instincts. The Lucca family had lived in Melrose Park all their lives, had moved into a pleasant row-house in the days when Frank had made a better-than-decent living from his suburban grocery store – before he'd begun substituting quality for profit, gradually falling out with and losing all his and Ellen's best customers. They'd managed to stay in the house after **Lucca's** had closed down, and Grace knew that their mother had worked hard to keep things together. She wished now with all her heart that she could have loved and admired Ellen for that, but all the sweated labour in the world could not, would never, make up for the fact that she had stood by and done nothing while her husband had abused Claudia.

Which was why, Grace supposed, she had made up her mind that if she and Claudia were going to pay their respects to Ellen Lucca, they were not going to stay anywhere near the Melrose Park house. They were going to a fine hotel, to the Mayfair Regent, to an elegant, intimate place with views over Lake Michigan, where the rooms were packed with indulgences and the bar had a fireplace. Claudia had balked at it when Grace had told her, had suffered an instant attack of the guilts, but Grace had stood firm.

204

'I'm not going to analyse the way I'm dealing with this,' she told her sister. 'I'm not a psychologist where this is concerned – I'm just a woman who happens to be able to afford a decent place to stay, and what I want when we get back from the wake and the cemetery and from anyplace near Frank Lucca, is to have the most comfortable room, the best-smelling bath I can get, and the biggest, straightest Scotch to go along with it.'

The last couple of days prior to their departure had been hard on Grace because she had learned that the date of the funeral was to clash with the State Attorney's presentation of the case against Cathy to the grand jury. Jerry Wagner maintained – and Sam Becket said that, in his experience, Wagner was right – that there wasn't a damned thing Grace could do at this stage to help her patient. That didn't stop Grace from wanting at least to be around for Cathy. But in the event, all she'd been able to do was speak to her on the phone. It had been an unsatisfactory, even distressing conversation, largely one-way. Cathy who now knew that David Becket's recovery had done nothing to improve her own situation, said she understood about Grace having to leave town for her mother's funeral, and that she was sorry for her loss. But she had sounded so listless, so *flattened*, that Grace's fears for her had grown.

'I'll call,' Grace had promised, 'to find out what happens.'

'We know what's going to happen,' Cathy said.

'Perhaps,' Grace said, forcing a positive note into her voice, 'but whatever goes on this week, Cathy, you have to remember that this is just the beginning. It's early days – Mr Wagner and his team – all of us – we haven't been able to really start fighting for you yet.'

'Sure,' Cathy had said. 'I know.'

And she had put the phone down.

Grace and Claudia, with Frank Lucca and a handful of friends, said their farewells to Ellen on Thursday morning, participated in the rituals. Grace couldn't really know what was going on in her sister's mind, but she did know there was both too much and too little going on in her own. Too many still-vivid bad memories and unresolved recriminations. Too

205

little love and no genuine forgiveness. It was, she guessed, simply too late to make peace with their mother, and she thought Claudia knew that as well as she did.

Frank had altered physically, was ageing badly. He had, Grace allowed, been quite a good-looking man when he was younger, thrusting and vigorous, but now his hair was almost gone, his skull unbeautifully shaped, his nose seemed larger, and the sourness, the meanness, of his spirit seemed to have been sucked out of his brain right into his dark eyes and weak mouth.

He wept when they lowered his wife's coffin into the ground. *Crocodile tears*, Grace thought, uncharitably, seeing them trickling down his cheeks; but later, when she was safely away from him again, she thought that perhaps they might have been genuine. Ellen had been a good wife to him, after all, had stood by him, even against her own daughters.

'You're the shrink or the mother?' one of Frank's neighbours asked Grace after the burial, back at the house in Melrose Park. She was thin, wearing black satin, and she smelled of salami.

'I'm the shrink,' Grace answered. 'Grace Lucca.'

'Your father was very sad that you and your sister didn't come to see your mother while she was still with us, God rest her soul.'

Grace resisted an astonishingly violent urge to spit in her eye. 'It was impossible for us to come, unfortunately.'

'Your mother was a wonderful human being,' the woman told her.

'I'm glad you thought so,' Grace said, and turned away.

'I behaved badly today,' she said to Claudia, later, back in their suite at the hotel. 'I didn't mean to – I intended going along with it all, no matter what, but I just couldn't stand it.'

'You didn't do anything so terrible,' Claudia said.

'Didn't I?' Grace asked, vaguely. 'Then maybe I just wanted to.'

They had both taken hot showers, wrapped themselves in hotel robes and ordered dinner from room service – fillet steaks, which they'd eaten ravenously, and Bordeaux, which they were still drinking now, slumped in front of the TV, drained but immeasurably relieved that it was over. There was a kind of a fog over the whole, awful day; detachment had now returned to Grace. There had been no surprises. No acts of contrition from their father; on the contrary, he had made it abundantly clear to anyone who would listen – not that there'd been many there – that he felt Claudia and Grace had let both him and Ellen down badly.

'Is it very sinful,' Claudia asked now from the depths of her armchair, 'for me to be enjoying myself this evening?'

'Is that a serious question?' Grace asked from the sofa.

'Afraid so.'

'You know my answer,' Grace said. 'You're an honest person, Claudia, not a hypocrite. You're not capable of faking grief, and I don't think either of us is feeling it, are we?'

'I can't grieve for Mama,' she admitted. 'But I do feel very sad.'

'So do I.' Grace was holding a coffee cup, comforted by its smooth, snug feel in her hands. 'But I think that's about the past, isn't it? I think maybe we're mourning what might have been.'

'I suppose we lost her years ago,' Claudia said, softly.

'Ellen lost us,' Grace said. 'She threw us away.'

They sat up talking for a long while, the way they usually did when they were alone together, but by morning, as they boarded their flight back to Miami, Grace had the sense of something fundamental having shifted between them. 'Closure' was a fashionable word these days. Men and women sought it after a love affair had ended, or a marriage had gone sour; victims were told they would feel better if they found a way to achieve it for themselves.

Closure.

Grace was the sister who had talked about her lack of emotion with regard to their mother's death. Claudia, historically, was the more easily upset, the more needy sister. And yet, as they parted in Miami that Friday afternoon, Grace was aware that Claudia was the one who had achieved closure, who had somehow come of age during the last twenty-four hours. So far as she was concerned, from now on, all the family she needed – would ever need – was in Florida. As for Grace – supposedly the stronger sister, the leader – she just felt empty. There was a cold void inside her now that had, she guessed, previously been filled with the slow-burning heat of old anger. Ellen was gone forever, and Frank had assuredly lost the power to so much as disturb her.

But she would have been a liar if she'd said she felt peaceful about that.

As anticipated, the grand jury had indicted Cathy and the prosecutor had filed papers to have her bound into the adult court for trial. In addition to which, she had now been formally charged with the Flager killing and the attack on David Becket. The next time Grace could see her, Jerry Wagner's assistant, Veronica Blaustein, said, Cathy would be in the Female House of Detention a few blocks from the Flagler Dog Track in the City of Miami.

On the Monday following Ellen's funeral, when Grace called to try to arrange a visit, she was informed that Cathy was unwell and refusing visitors. Probably, Grace figured, she was meant to take that on the chin and melt away, but she hung in until finally they let her talk to Dr Parés, one of the facility's physicians. His voice was soft and lightly accented, and Grace was relieved to find him clearly concerned about Cathy's welfare.

'She is very depressed, Dr Lucca,' he told her. 'She has been weeping a great deal.' Parés paused. 'I'm afraid she feels both abandoned and betrayed.'

'What are you doing for her?' The idea that prison policy might be to pump troublesome inmates full of state-approved medication to keep them in line alarmed Grace, especially in view of what Cathy's own father had done to her as a young child.

'There isn't much I can do,' Dr Parés answered. 'It's early days. I have tried my best to reassure her – not an easy task, as you can well imagine.'

'Have you prescribed medication?' Grace couldn't resist asking.

'She will be offered two milligrams of diazepam before lights-out to help her rest,' the doctor answered, a touch stiffly.

'Can you try to persuade her to see me, Dr Parés?'

His hesitation was brief but unmistakable. 'It could be difficult.' He paused. 'You are, after all, one of the people Cathy feels most betrayed by.'

Grace was dismayed, but not surprised. Her own sense of guilt, irrational as she knew it was, had been intense since Harry had dug up the murder weapon, and had worsened considerably during the last week.

'I just want to help her,' she told the prison physician. 'I believe that Cathy's innocent – I want to be her friend. If there's anything at all you can do to get that across to her, I'd be very grateful.'

'I'll do what I can,' he said, more gently. 'It's hard for me to believe her guilty, too. Though appearances, as we know, can lie.'

Grace knew, of course, that he was right about that. She knew, too, that she was sinking ever deeper into the trap she had sensed from her first meeting with Cathy a little over five weeks before. The girl was a patient and victim, but she was also a multiple murder suspect. Of all her numerous patients, Cathy was the one Grace knew she needed to be most vigilant about keeping in emotional perspective – keeping her thoughts about her as clearly labelled as the notes in the buff-coloured folder in her cabinet – ROBBINS, C. – and considering those thoughts only immediately before, during and after a session. But the truth was that Cathy was now on Grace's mind day and night, even creeping into her dreams as she slept; and, even more unpardonably, she was, from time to time, starting to impinge on Grace's sessions with other patients.

What she ought to do, Grace was beginning to realize, was to consult with another Miami psychologist, perhaps even consider handing over Cathy's case to a more detached third party.

Cathy would feel even more betrayed if Grace passed her on – but then, according to Dr Parés, that was how she already felt. And what if – however much Grace hated contemplating the possibility – but what if she *was* guilty? Mightn't she then be far better off with a psychologist who was willing to accept that truth, someone who would start right out tracking the best way to help Cathy from that perspective? As a potential psychotic. As a multiple killer, not to mention a matricide.

209

'Maybe it's time,' Grace said to Harry, her faithful confidant, just before lunch, 'I started really taking those possibilities on board.'

He sat very still, his bright, dark eyes fixed on hers.

He had nothing to say. He knew she was only casting around. Snowing herself. Grace knew that too.

There was no way she was going to give up on Cathy.

CHAPTER THIRTY-TWO

TUESDAY, MAY 12, 1998

On Tuesday morning, David Becket called Grace. Sam had told her that his father was now back home full-time and getting cantankerous. His familiar voice sounded as warm as it had ever been to her ears.

'Last time you and I had a real chance to talk,' he said, 'it was about that son-of-a-bitch, so-called physician father of Cathy Robbins.'

'I guess it was,' she said.

'Next thing I knew – well, you know what happened then.' David paused. 'Sam told me about your mother, Grace. I'm sorry.'

She hadn't seen Sam since the barmitzvah, but they'd talked on the phone, and she'd told him about the visit to Chicago. He had asked what she needed, or if she wanted to be left alone, and she'd answered that there was nothing she needed, but that she didn't especially want to be left alone either. One of these days, Grace had thought, she might even tell Sam the whole miserable story of her childhood – if, that was, they ever found the time and space.

'Thank you, David,' she said now, into the phone. 'How are you feeling?'

'Getting fitter every day. Driving Judy crazy, wanting to do more than she thinks I should.' He paused again. 'I gather she cold-shouldered you because she knew you were backing Cathy?'

'I understood why.'

'Well, I didn't understand, and I've told her so.'

'That wasn't necessary, David.'

He came to the point. 'We need to do something more about that girl. I don't like what I'm hearing – sounds to me like she might be in danger of being sold down the river.'

'In what sense?' Grace asked, though she thought she knew.

'This garbage about considering an insanity plea.'

'I take it you've been talking to Wagner?'

'Yesterday,' David said. 'I was trying to find out what he's doing for Cathy, trying to see how I could help, and I got nowhere fast. I told him since I'm supposed to be one of her so-called victims, surely having me as a character witness ought to be useful?'

'And what did he say?'

'He said he wants to wait and see how the case shapes up overall. He said they were going to need a lot more than a character witness – he said that since I couldn't testify that it definitely wasn't Cathy who stabbed me, anything I did say might not make enough difference. I said surely anything would help, and he didn't disagree with me, but he didn't exactly catch fire either.'

'You don't rate Wagner too highly then,' Grace said, quietly.

'I don't know – I'm *hoping* he's not an asshole.' David paused. 'He said you'd told him about Broderick, and that he'd had his people do some checking, and that to date it hadn't yielded anything worthwhile – I just hope they're trying hard enough.'

'I suppose it's a pretty tall order,' she said.

'Playing devil's advocate doesn't become you, Grace,' David rebuked. 'You know as well as I do that Cathy needs someone who's going to move heaven and earth to find a way to help her – I mean, for Christ's sake, this guy must know the media's going to go crazy if he manages to dig up a dead, murderous father.'

'I'm sure Wagner does know that,' Grace said. 'I just don't think he believes the father's still alive.' She took a breath. 'Has Sam talked to you about Broderick?'

'Sam tells me most things I want to know.' David sounded smug. 'He thinks he's so close-mouthed, a real hard-case cop, but I get stuff out of him when I really want.'

'Do you think it's possible that Broderick might be behind all this, or do you think I'm whistling in the wind?'

212

'I know someone's behind it, and I know it isn't Cathy.'

'Why are you so sure, David? Is it still just instinct?'

'You can call it that,' he said. 'I held that child in my arms the morning after she climbed into her dead parents' bed. If she killed them then I'm a KGB spy, and if I'm wrong about her, they can lock *me* up and throw away the key.'

'Wagner says he wants to choose the best route to keep her out of jail.'

'And put her in an institution instead,' David said scornfully. 'That's supposed to be better? That's supposed to be justice?'

'You don't have to convince me,' Grace said.

She tried that afternoon and again the following morning to organize a visit to Cathy, but both applications drew the same response: Cathy didn't want to see her. Becoming ever more concerned, Grace put in another call to the prison doctor.

Dr Parés sounded tired, but did his best to be courteous. He'd visited Cathy that morning, he said, and was glad to report that her emotional condition seemed no worse than previously.

'But no better?' Grace asked.

'Under the circumstances,' the doctor told her, quite kindly, 'Cathy is quite composed.'

Those words, Grace knew, were intended to reassure her, but instead they struck dread into her heart. '*Composed*' smacked of resignation, which led her to fear that Cathy might be giving up.

She waited until afternoon to make another call. She felt in need of comfort, and it seemed to her, suddenly, that the person most likely to console or at least calm her was Sam. Trying his direct line at the department, she got his voice mail, then called the cellular number he'd given her. He answered almost instantly, his voice clipped.

'Sam, it's Grace. If you're too busy to talk, just hang up.'

'I'm busy, but I have a couple of seconds.'

'Any chance of seeing you?' She felt oddly nervous.

'When? Now?' The clipped tone was gone.

'I don't know. This evening? If you can make it.'

'Will you cook for me again? I love the way you cook.'

'I love the way you eat.'

213

'Seven? Eight?'

'Eight.'

'Deal,' Sam said.

When Grace put the phone down, her cheeks were hot.

'Oh, boy,' she said.

She knew she had it bad.

'What's this called in Italian?' Sam asked her that evening.

Grace had gone out to the meat market right after their brief call and had bought duck, then come back and found a jar of damsons marinated with wine, cinnamon and coriander that she'd put away last fall, and even now, as they came to the last morsels of the roasted combination with wild rice and fresh, light salad, the mouth-watering aroma still lingered in the kitchen.

'It isn't, so far as I know,' she said, mopping up juices with a slice of bread. 'The only specifically Italian thing on this table is the *ciabatta*.' She noticed Harry doing his best to coax tidbits from their guest. 'Don't give him any duck – it's too rich, and he's getting fat.'

'I don't know about the dog, but a guy could get seriously fat knowing you.' Sam eyed her. 'Why aren't you fat, Grace?'

'Tension, maybe.'

'Cathy?'

She looked at him. He seemed so calm, sitting at her table. Grace thought of the horrors he had to have seen in his career. She had told David Becket once that she was used to hearing about ugliness, but it was unlikely to compare to the living daily nightmares of Sam's working environment.

'Talk to me, Grace,' he said.

'About what?'

'About what's on your mind.'

She stood up. 'Dessert first.'

'How can I say no?'

A little time passed while Grace grilled fresh peaches with honey and cinnamon and Sam loaded some dishes into the dishwasher and then fooled around on the floor with Harry. The peaches were done in minutes, and Grace served them with vanilla ice cream.

'Jeez,' Sam said, sitting down again.

'Call it therapy,' Grace said.

'Eating or cooking?'

'Both. It works for me almost every time.'

A few more missing pieces of their respective puzzles slotted into place over dessert. Grace talked some more about life with the Luccas in Chicago in the bad old days, and then Sam told her about his great-grandfather's great-grandfather, the slave who'd run away from Georgia in the 1830s and escaped via Key Biscayne to the Bahamas.

'I got all my information from my father and his journals,' Sam said. 'My mother's side of the family never wanted to talk about the past, but I guess my daddy's background's enough to play with.'

'What happened in the Bahamas?' Grace asked.

'He worked as a farm labourer on Eleuthera, and his wife went into service, and the family stayed put for about fifty years until my great-great grandfather moved them to the Florida Keys. According to my father, he tried his hand at fishing but he was sick all the time, so he worked on a pine-apple plantation on Key Largo. When the soil gave out, they moved on to the mainland and settled in the Black Grove.'

'Which is where you were all still living back in 1971,' Grace said, softly.

'Except that my grandfather moved the family to Liberty City when my daddy was a baby. They owned a restaurant there, and my grandmother took in dressmaking. My father went to Dorsey High School, spent as much time as he could get away with in Overtown, sneaking into jazz clubs – and then they built the expressway and as good as finished the place, which as good as finished Liberty City, so the family went back to the Grove and my father became a cop and had yours truly.' Sam paused. 'And the rest you more or less know.'

Grace was very still. 'So you joined the force because of your father.'

'It was partly that,' Sam said, softly. 'Staying connected with him.'

'And was it also something to do with the way your parents and sister died?' Grace remembered what he'd told her about the shooting by the white police officer that had sparked the

215

riots up in Opa-Locka, thought again about the long-term effects that might have had on a seven-year-old boy.

'I think it was a lot to do with that, too,' Sam said. 'Keeping the faith with my father and the things he'd hoped for.'

'How did David and Judy feel about it?'

'Troubled. They'd sent me to a private school and then on to Spellman College.' Sam's smile was gentle, hazy. 'They never put pressure on me to follow in David's footsteps or anything like that, but I guess Judy could have lived without the fear factor.'

'David's certainly very proud of you,' Grace said.

'And Ma, too.' Sam grinned. 'And at least Saul's talking about going the doctor route, so there's still hope for the next generation.'

They went outside again after they'd finished eating, to the spot on the edge of the deck where they always seemed to end up with their coffee cups.

'If you don't want to talk about Cathy,' Sam said, 'that's cool. But if you're bottling it up for my benefit, don't bother.'

'It's nothing new.' Grace sighed. 'Except I seem to be getting more scared for her with every passing day.'

'You're right to be scared,' Sam said.

She smiled wryly. 'That makes me feel better.'

He waited another second. 'I've had a pal in the FBI field office in North Miami Beach run a kind of upside-down profile on what Broderick might be up to if he were still with us.' He paused. 'It supports your thinking.'

A new thought struck Grace. 'Did someone profile the scalpel killer?'

'Not officially, no,' Sam answered quietly.

'Why not?' She knew the answer. 'Because most people figured they had their suspect right from the start.' Sam kept silent, and she didn't blame him one bit. 'You said not officially.'

'Because I had a profile run by the same pal, off the record.'

Grace shook her head. 'Why does it seem as if every decent idea in this case has had to be kept off the record?' She paused. 'Did the profile fit Cathy?'

'Not really,' Sam said. 'But it was too inconclusive to help

216

clear her.' He drank some coffee and stared out over the river. 'My pal certainly thinks that if Broderick didn't die, you could be right about him.'

'How could the same profile begin to match a grown man *and* a teenage girl?'

'It couldn't. But there were no clues as to the killer's gender, for one thing. And as you know, the victims were all sleeping, so no special strength was needed for the stabbings.'

'What about the force of the stabbings?' Grace was starting to think about things that had never occurred to her previously. 'Can't they measure things like that these days – how fast and hard the scalpel hit?'

'It's the kind of thing the ME considers,' Sam said. 'The killer in all these cases struck hard and with precision, but in theory there was nothing a physically fit fourteen-year-old girl couldn't have managed.'

They both fell silent. Harry got up from his place between them and wandered back into the house, probably heading for the kitchen in search of any scraps of duck that might inadvertently have been dropped.

Grace remembered, suddenly, Peter Hayman's suggestion the last time she'd seen him. She couldn't believe she'd forgotten about it till now. Maybe her mother's death and the funeral had taxed her more than she liked to admit.

'Could you get a photograph of Broderick for me, Sam?'

'I already have one,' he said.

'Why haven't you shown it to me?'

'Last time I looked, you were a psychologist, not a cop,' he said.

'That hasn't stopped you from telling me things you're not supposed to.' She paused. 'I need to see the photograph, Sam. I might recognize him.'

He smiled into the dark.

'What?' Grace said.

'The photo only arrived yesterday. I requested it a week or so ago from Lafayette Hospital, but the fax they sent was lousy, and the one they mailed took its sweet time.'

'So do you have it here?' she asked impatiently.

'Would I dare eat your duck and peaches and keep it from you?'

They went inside and Sam retrieved the photograph from his inside jacket pocket. He laid it on the kitchen table and Grace sat down and gazed at it.

Her first sight of John Broderick.

He was fair, like his daughter. Hair several shades less golden. Blue eyes. Nose large, lips narrow, but the whole face was roundish and suntanned. No special distinguishing features. No obvious scars or pock marks.

The snapshot was mounted on a sheet of white paper, and a few statistics were handwritten beneath in black ink. *9/8/85.* (The date the photograph had been taken – four years or so before his disappearance.) *Height: 6'1". Weight: 210lbs.*

'Big man,' Sam commented. 'Overweight.'

Grace nodded.

'Maybe he drank too much.' Sam paused. 'I wonder if he took steroids.'

Still, Grace said nothing.

'What is it?' Sam asked.

She shook her head. 'It's nothing – nothing real.'

'You think you've seen this man?'

'No, nothing like that. I don't think I've ever seen him.' She hesitated. 'It's just – there's this familiarity about him.'

'He's Cathy's father.'

'No, that's not it.' Grace continued to stare at the photograph. 'Or maybe it is just that – I'm not sure.'

'Take your time,' Sam said, gently. 'Remember this was taken over twelve years ago. If he's alive, he'd be that much older and he might have changed his appearance.'

'If he is the killer,' Grace said, 'he'll *certainly* have changed his appearance. I would have, if I were him.'

'He could have gone all out,' Sam conjectured, 'had surgery. At the very least, he could have coloured his hair, or maybe shaved it, or bought a wig – he could have grown a beard, maybe dropped some weight or put on some more – he could use tinted contacts in his eyes.'

'In other words' – Grace looked away from the picture up at Sam – 'there's almost no point in trying to place this John Broderick.'

'There's always a point,' Sam said. 'Still look familiar to you?'

She looked back down again. 'I don't know. Maybe it is because Cathy's in there somewhere. Or maybe it was just wishful thinking.' She paused. 'May I keep this?'

Sam nodded. 'It's a copy. Keep it if you like, but it's for your eyes only, Grace. You can't start showing it around places, playing detective, okay?'

'I understand.'

He sat down. 'Word of advice?'

'Sure.'

'Don't think about it too much. So far as we know, it's an out-of-date picture of a dead man.'

'I know it is,' Grace said, 'but —'

Sam's hand laid over hers was tentative but firm. It silenced her just the way he'd intended it to. 'But nothing, Grace. Don't let Broderick obsess you.' He glanced down at the snapshot. 'Frankly, if you were going to recognize him it would probably have happened the moment you saw that.'

'Is that the way it usually works?' She made no effort to remove her hand. She liked the feeling of his skin on her own. She liked the slight pressure.

'Most times, yes.'

'I suppose afterward your imagination can start to play tricks on you.'

'It can happen,' Sam agreed.

'So I'll just put it away.' Grace still wasn't moving, and neither was he.

'And if - and it's a very unlikely if - you ever see anyone you think just might be the same guy a dozen years on, you call me right away.' Sam's eyes and tone were serious. 'You've got that, Grace, haven't you? Even if you're only a quarter sure, you call me, and you keep your distance from him.'

'You make it sound like you think it really could happen.'

'If we're not both crazy - if there is anything in the Broderick suspicion - then yes, I guess it could.' The grimness was still there. 'And if it does, that means he's a very dangerous man.'

This was not, Grace decided, a romantic conversation. She took her hand away. 'More coffee?'

'Why not?'

219

She stood up, started making a fresh pot.

'You remember when we talked about opera?' he asked.

'Yes, I do.' She paused. 'I said I liked listening, and you said there was no such word as *like* when it came to opera, and I said perhaps I needed to be taught how to listen.'

'You don't forget much, do you?' he remarked.

'Listening and remembering are both part of my job.'

'Mine too.' He waited a moment. 'I have a rehearsal scheduled for tomorrow evening.'

'Rehearsal?'

'You ever hear of S-BOP? As in South Beach Opera.'

'No, I haven't.' She felt apologetic. 'I'm sure I should have.'

'Not unless you're crazy about opera, which we know you're not,' Sam said. 'Only people crazy enough about it to make do with third-rate, or with close friends or relatives in the group, come to our performances.' He grinned. 'I'm not even offering you a performance, just a rehearsal.'

'It sounds like fun.'

'You haven't asked which opera we're rehearsing.'

'Does it matter for a philistine like me?'

'I guess not.'

CHAPTER THIRTY-THREE

THURSDAY, MAY 14, 1998

Grace's phone rang early next morning while she was toasting an English muffin.

'Grace?'

It was Cathy from a payphone. For a split second, Grace experienced relief at hearing from her. Then she realized that the teenager was crying.

'Cathy, what's wrong?'

'Grace, you have to help me!'

'What's happened?' All kinds of alarm bells were going off in Grace's mind. Images of beatings or rape or Christ-knew-what. She fought to ensure her voice stayed even, knowing that Cathy was unlikely to be able to stay on the line for long. 'Cathy, calm down and tell me what you need.'

'Why weren't you there?' The question was plaintive.

'Where?' Grace's mind raced.

'Why didn't you talk to the grand jury or the judge?'

'You know why.' Grace was dismayed. 'Cathy, I told you I couldn't be there – that I had to go to Chicago. And even if I had been there, Mr Wagner told us both I couldn't have done anything.'

'You could have written something down – you could have made them keep me in the youth facility.' For the very first time, there was real hysteria in Cathy's voice. 'They're going to give me the chair, Grace – they're going to strap me down and *kill* me!'

'Of course they're not.' Grace was very firm in spite of the chills spiking through her veins. 'Who's been filling your head

221

with nonsense, Cathy? Tell me who it is, and I'll see if I can have them stopped.'

'You can't have anything stopped.' Cathy's voice was suddenly harder. 'You said that yourself – you can't do anything for me.'

'I said I couldn't do anything about what's already happened,' Grace said, cut to the quick. 'Cathy, you have to know that we're still working for you out here. You haven't let me come in to see you, but I've written to you telling you we're not giving up on you.'

'Who's we?' she asked.

'You have been getting my letters, haven't you?'

'Who's we?' Cathy asked again.

'Dr Becket, for one,' Grace answered.

'He can't help me either,' Cathy said. 'Mr Wagner said he didn't see who stabbed him, so he couldn't testify for me.'

'But he still believes you're innocent, and if a man you're accused of injuring believes in you, that means it's only a matter of time before we convince everyone else who counts.'

'What if you can't?'

'We will, Cathy.'

'But if you can't, they're going to kill me, aren't they?'

'That's never going to happen.'

'But it could, now they've said I'm an adult!' The hysteria was returning, pitching Cathy's voice higher again. 'I could end up on Death Row, and even if I don't, I can't take much more of this place! They're all against me – they all *hate* me —' She stopped suddenly.

'Cathy?' Grace could hear something going on at the other end, voices and other sounds, but they were distorted by the connection and she couldn't distinguish what they were. She gripped the phone tighter. 'Cathy, what's going on? Are you okay?'

She came back on the line. 'I have to go.' She was weeping again.

'Cathy, who was that? What are they doing to you?'

'Grace, I have to go now.'

'Are you being ill-treated?'

The line went dead.

Grace didn't know what to do. She had appointments scheduled for every hour that day until six o'clock, and there wasn't one single patient among them who could legitimately be postponed. Even if she could have dropped everything and driven to the detention centre, it was unlikely she'd have been allowed to see Cathy without a prior arrangement – and Grace was afraid that a suggestion of ill-treatment, without evidence, might make life even tougher for Cathy. For all she knew, the call might just have been a hysterical delayed response to the trauma of the decision to try her as an adult. Worse than that, Cathy might be right. The stakes had unquestionably risen with that decision, and the ultimate outcome might just be a nightmare too horrific to contemplate.

At eleven a.m., Grace tried reaching Dr Parés, who was unavailable. At five minutes to one – her next free moment – she tried Jerry Wagner who was, predictably, out to lunch. At three p.m. she left another message for Parés. An hour later, she called Sam.

'I hate bothering you at work ...'

'Problem with tonight?'

'No, nothing like that.'

She told Sam about the call. To his credit, his voice betrayed the fact that Cathy's terrors about the death penalty had pierced him every bit as deeply as they had Grace, but that didn't mean he had anything to offer.

'I told her it was nonsense,' Grace said, 'but it isn't, really, is it?'

'Not entirely,' Sam said grimly.

'I told her that your father still believed in her. That seemed to get through to her for a moment.' She paused. 'How well is David doing?'

'You mean, is he well enough to visit Cathy?'

'It did cross my mind. I'm sorry – it's probably too much to ask.'

'I don't think Dad would think so, but I know someone who might have different ideas.'

'Your mother. Does she still think Cathy stabbed him?'

'I'm not sure.' Sam paused. 'I think Dad's starting to wear her down.'

'Could you please mention the idea to him? It might make a big difference to Cathy.'

'Consider it done.'

Grace threw herself back into work, commanded her brain to focus sharply and completely on her other patients. Next time she came up for air, Dora Rabinovitch, who'd come by to deliver a batch of typing, had left two messages: the first to say that Wagner had returned her call, the second that Dr Parés had left word that he was due to visit with Cathy Robbins later that day.

Grace had made up her mind before Sam picked her up just after seven that evening, that she was not going either to mention or even *think* about Cathy once, at least until she went to bed. As it turned out, there was no room for Cathy or any other baggage from the real world; Grace's mind, from seven-thirty until a little after ten-thirty, was filled to the rafters with opera.

The S-BOP theatre was small but intimate, decorated and furnished in warm reds and stark black and without a sharp line or corner anywhere to be seen – everything gently curved or rounded. It appeared and felt like a building upon which great love, care and infinite patience had been expended. It might have been in Italy or Spain or England or some exotic place. It didn't look or feel like anywhere Grace had ever been in Florida or Chicago. And that was *before* the lights went down, and the action started ...

She loved theatre, always had. In her college days, she'd taken part in amateur plays whenever time and their producers allowed. She liked the way tired, often jaded students became energized the instant they hit the stage or rehearsal hall. She supposed she had expected tonight to feel much the same way, just noisier – she'd thought the S-BOP singers might even be painful on the senses. How little she had known.

Lord, what talent was cradled in the midst of a city, hidden in those crazy streets and buildings, straining to explode out of the men and women who waited on tables or stared into computers or nursed patients or sold newspapers or performed surgery or carried bags in hotel lobbies. Or investigated sickening homicides.

Grace had never dreamed.

*

224

'When it's going right,' Sam said much later, up on his roof, where they'd gone with pizzas and beers, 'it seems to wrap me up, like I'm wearing this great, warm, magic cloak, and the whole world, the real world, is gone, and I'm someone else, someplace else, and I'm filled with music, and it's the greatest feeling I know.' He looked at her, sideways. 'Make any sense to you?'

'Perfect sense,' Grace said, very softly.

'You really liked it, didn't you?' he asked.

'Oh, no,' she said. 'No such word as like in opera, remember?'

'Oh, yeah.'

Without looking at him, she could hear the smile in his voice.

They both let a few moments pass. They were sitting close to the edge of the roof, munching on pizza with extra Jalapeno peppers and pepperoni, gazing up at the stars and listening to the late-evening buzz down on the South Beach streets.

'I understand why you love it up here,' Grace said, after a while.

'I'm glad,' Sam said.

'It's a little like the music, isn't it?'

'That it is,' he agreed.

It was only a matter of time now. They both knew it. Up until this evening, Grace had known how she felt, what *she* wanted, but she hadn't been sure if Sam felt the same way. Now she knew. Not because he'd said a word about it, or because they'd come closer physically in any tangible way. But they had, unquestionably, *come* closer. Their minds had been drawn tantalizingly close, and that was the key, Grace thought, for both of them.

Sam had apologized for the presence of his beach lounger, the air-filled makeshift bed he said he often chose to sleep on in preference to his real bed. Grace had told him it didn't bother her, and she'd meant it, of course, at the time.

It was bothering the hell out of her now.

They finished the pizza and the beer. They talked a little more about opera and theatre. Sam told Grace that Althea had never much encouraged his singing; it wasn't that she didn't think he could sing, more that she was the kind of woman who leaned toward the best of everything. Althea loved opera, so long as it was being performed at the Dade County Auditorium, or in the Sarasota Opera House, or, preferably, at the Met in New York City. She was, at heart, a snob, who ought never to have gotten herself married to a cop.

'And that' – Sam's voice was so low it was almost gravel – 'might have saved a whole lot of pain all around.'

'Except,' Grace said, 'that then you'd never have known Sampson.'

They leaned in toward each other then. Their shoulders touched first, cotton covered. Then their arms. Bare skin. It felt wonderful. Grace looked down, saw the differences between them, so clearly defined, brown against white, and felt nothing but rightness.

'Grace,' he said, softly.

She turned to face him, looked right into his eyes, said nothing.

'Oh, man,' he said.

And kissed her.

Oh, man.

The beach lounger was too small for what they were getting up to, but they didn't care. They rolled off on to the concrete any number of times, scraped their backs and knees and heels but hardly noticed. They were hot, they knew that, they were so *hot* and together, and so *right* together, so wrapped up in each other, body and soul, physically and emotionally, and Grace wasn't sure they would have or *could* have stopped if a hurricane had ripped right across South Beach. Feeling rolled over them, swept them away, like the stormiest, the most amazing of torrents, like all the grand operas soaring around them, lifting them up in a great collective embrace. It was the finest lovemaking that Grace, for one, had ever known, and it was most certainly the best, mind-and-body-blowing sex ...

Until they heard Sam's pager.

'No,' he said.

Grace was beyond words, almost beyond breathing.

'Go 'way,' Sam said.

226

'It won't,' she managed to say.

He rolled them both over so they were face to face. 'I'm sorry, Grace.'

'It's okay.'

'No, I mean I'm really sorry.'

'I know you are.' She smiled into his eyes. 'Shouldn't you answer it?'

'Yeah.' He started kissing her mouth again.

'Sam.'

'Mm?'

'Your pager.'

It wasn't the pager that got to Grace in the end – there was something semi-comical about being interrupted in the middle of lovemaking by a beeper, and next time she knew it might well be her own cellular phone that got in the way of things. But the sad and awful truth about Sam's job, even more than her own, was that a call in the night was likely to mean nothing less than more violence and pain, and that was the salutary thought Grace went home with to her house on the water, and the one that kept her awake for most of the rest of the night, with Harry lying across her feet, the way he usually did. She wanted to think about Sam, about the broadness and leanness and strength of him, about his gentleness and passion and humour. But flashes kept coming into her mind instead of somebody traumatized or even injured, of a body lying on some street or on some floor or across some bed, maybe bloody, maybe strangled, maybe cut, maybe . . .

'Stop it now, Grace,' she told herself out loud in the dark.

Harry grumbled and turned around.

Grace wondered if it was a man, woman or child, waiting for Sam, dead or injured or merely in shock. *Merely.* She thought about the tenderness of the man, of the bereaved father, the disappointed husband, the kind and grateful son. She thought about his talent, about his glorious, vibrant voice and the way he'd talked about wrapping himself in a magic cloak when he sang. It was hard reconciling those things with the man who right now might be kneeling over a dead civilian, checking for clues, maybe even already making an arrest . . . maybe in danger . . .

227

'Cut it *out*, Grace,' she told herself.

She was a very disciplined woman when she really set her mind to it.

She cut it out, and went to sleep.

CHAPTER THIRTY-FOUR

FRIDAY, MAY 15, 1998

It had been on the wall when Cathy had come back into her cell after dinner. There was no way of knowing when it had been done, or by whom. It might have happened while she was still on kitchen duty, scrubbing vegetables and floors, scraping her fingers and her knees – or it might have been done at dinner time.

It was dark now. The lights had been turned off hours before, and though that first, terrifying blindness had long since passed, it was still much too dim to see anything more than vague shapes and shades of grey.

Cathy didn't need light to see what was on her cell wall.

It was etched into her brain, right behind her eyes.

The hideous parody, carved into the stone.

CATHY ROBBINS TOOK A KNIFE AND SLICED AWAY HER MOMMY'S LIFE AND WHEN SHE SAW WHAT SHE HAD DONE, SHE FIGURED IT WAS SO MUCH FUN, SHE DID IT TO HER DADDY TOO ... AND HER SHRINK ... AND HER DOC ... AND HER AUNTIE ...

Cathy had screamed when she'd first seen it, and a guard had come running, but when she'd looked at the writing, she'd just shrugged and given a mean kind of smile.

You deserve everything you get, that smile had said.

And she'd locked Cathy's door and, not long after, the lights had gone out.

And now Cathy was still sitting all hunched up on her bed,

trying to keep warm, trying not to feel the walls closing in on her, trying not to see those ugly words, trying not to hear them going around and around in her mind.

Trying not to scream.

CHAPTER THIRTY-FIVE

It had been a rape case that had taken him away from her the previous night, Sam told Grace when he called her just before ten o'clock.

'How's the victim?' she asked.

'Battered. Shocked.' Sam paused. 'As you'd expect.'

'Do you know who did it?'

'Maybe. It's too soon to say much.' He paused again. 'I'm going to be pretty tied up all day and probably most of tonight. I'm sorry, Grace.'

'What for?'

'I'd like to have seen you is what for.'

'Me too,' Grace said. 'But you don't have to give me a thought, Sam. Just do what you have to do.'

'I'll be doing that,' Sam told her, 'but don't expect me not to think about you at least once.'

Just after two-thirty p.m., Dr Parés telephoned.

'Did you get to see Cathy yesterday?' Grace was swift to ask.

'Yes, I did, but that's not why I'm calling,' he said.

Something in his tone set Grace's antennae on alert. 'Has something happened to her?'

'In a sense, yes, I'm afraid it has.' The doctor went on swiftly but gently. 'There was an incident this morning – another young woman was discovered in her cell with lacerations to her back and shoulders. According to her, she was attacked some time before lockdown last night.' Parés paused. 'She says she didn't see who it was, but when Cathy's cell was searched, a weapon was found.'

Grace's stomach was in knots. 'What kind of a weapon?'

'A potato peeler. Apparently, Cathy was on kitchen duty yesterday.'

'I don't believe it.'

'I understand, Dr Lucca,' Parés said, sympathetically. 'But I gather there were traces of blood still on the implement.'

Grace's mind reeled. 'I have to see her.'

'That won't be possible,' Parés told her. 'She's in solitary confinement. The only people they'll allow in are her lawyer and myself.'

'But surely, as her psychologist—'

'By all means, you can always ask, doctor,' Parés said. 'I think you should ask, but I would imagine it will be some days before you're admitted.' He paused again. 'I'm very sorry to give you bad news.'

Grace put down the telephone and called Jerry Wagner whose assistant, Veronica Blaustein, informed Grace that her boss had been out on business when the call had come in from the house of detention, but that he would be calling there before the end of the day.

'Would you please ask him to call me when he gets back?' Grace asked.

'I'll certainly ask him,' Ms Blaustein said, 'but he may not come back to the office until Monday.'

'I'm sure you'll be talking to him,' Grace pushed.

'That depends on his schedule, Dr Lucca.'

Grace thought about calling Sam, but then she remembered the rape victim, and she knew without being told that the Female House of Detention was out of the Miami Beach Police Department's jurisdiction, which meant that there would be nothing Sam could do for Cathy. On the contrary, his involvement in this latest development would probably just end up adding more weight to the case he'd already handed over to the State Attorney's office.

'I don't know what to do,' she said to Dora later, over a cup of tea.

'There's nothing you can do.' Dora was to-the-point, as usual. 'There are some people even you just can't help, Dr Lucca.' She never balked at giving Grace a dose of her opinion, but she drew the line at calling her by her first name – something, she'd once explained, to do with the pleasure she took in working for a woman doctor. 'Anyway,' she went on, 'you have a patient coming in ten minutes – now *her* you may be able to do something for. So just drink your tea and try to relax a little.'

Grace managed, as she always did, to focus on her patient, but she did not relax. Nor did Jerry Wagner get back to her. Sam did, nearing the end of his own twenty-four-hour working day. He was too bushed to have much in the way of comfort to offer her regarding Cathy, but he promised to keep his ear to the ground and let her know the minute he heard anything.

'That's if I do hear anything,' he added. 'It's out of—'

'Your jurisdiction,' Grace finished for him. 'I know, Sam. I'm just letting off steam. I feel so cut off from her – I mean, if ever there was a time when a patient needed me, it has to be Cathy right now, and all I'm supposed to do is wait till Monday morning and make an application to visit her.'

'It's rough,' Sam said. 'I'm sorry, Grace.'

She heard the exhaustion in his voice, and felt guilty. 'No, I'm sorry. You've got more than enough to deal with, and what you need now is some wind-down time and sleep.'

'I gotta admit, sleep sounds pretty tempting.'

'Any time off for good behaviour tomorrow or Sunday?'

'Depends how soon we get this bad guy nailed down.'

'I hope it's real soon,' Grace said, 'for everyone's sake.'

Sam called twice next morning before eleven, but each time Grace was engaged with a patient and both times, when she tried getting back to him, he was unavailable.

At five minutes past eleven, Peter Hayman called.

'In case you hadn't noticed, it is now officially the weekend,' he said, 'which is when some folk get it into their heads to quit work and relax. Now I just happen to be planning to put in a few hours' sailing with some friends this afternoon and tomorrow. How about you come down and join us?'

'I can't, Peter,' Grace said.

'Wall-to-wall patients?'

233

'A few,' she told him. 'And some other commitments.'

'Pity.' He seemed easy about it. 'It might have been fun, and just the break you needed.' He paused. 'You don't mind my calling to ask, do you, Grace? It's just a gorgeous morning down this way, and when my friends called, I thought of you.'

'I'm glad you called,' she said.

She called the house of detention, tried and failed to speak to Cathy or to get any useful information, and was told yet again that if she wanted to arrange a visit, she would need to call again on Monday.

Two hours later, while she was making a sandwich, Sam got third time lucky, though it was a short and gruesome conversation because there had been another rape down on South Beach, which meant that he and all his colleagues were going to be on heavy duty all weekend.

'I'm sorry, Grace,' he said. 'And not just because of the case. Being paged the other night was a real bitch.'

'For me too,' she told him.

'I'm not sure when I'll even be able to call,' he went on. 'Cases like this, everyone tends to get pretty steamed up.'

'I can imagine,' Grace said.

'I guess you probably can.'

Across the telephone line, Grace heard voices in the background.

'Don't worry about me, Sam,' she said, gently.

The voices got raised.

'Gotta go,' he said.

Grace put down the phone. Her mind went, unbidden, to the night before last, up on Sam's roof. Her body was still sore, grazed in parts from its rough and tumble brushes with concrete, but the tenderness just brought back the other memories. Hot, spicy and damn near overpowering.

And she wasn't remembering the pizza.

She ate her sandwich, cleared away that and breakfast, took Harry for a stroll around the island, came back and scanned her notes for her two-thirty patient. When the phone rang again, she found herself hoping it might be Sam, but it was the mother of her four p.m. patient, explaining that her daughter had suddenly become extremely upset about coming to see Grace, and so, if she didn't mind too much, she felt it better to postpone. Grace told her that she didn't mind, that it was important her daughter felt at least reasonably comfortable about coming, and perhaps they could try rescheduling in a few days' time.

She put down the phone and checked her calendar. The cancellation meant that her next patient was her last for the day – and she knew without looking that Sunday was appointment-free, since she'd been planning to bring her records and paperwork up to date.

That had been before the night on Sam's roof and the news about Cathy.

Suddenly, Grace felt terribly restless. Aimless.

If she sat at home all weekend, Grace began to think she might be in danger of regressing to adolescence, hoping each time the phone rang it would be Sam telling her that they'd caught the rapist and that he was free to see her. She thought she'd learned a little more than that about the complexities of violent crime and police work during the past several weeks; unless the rapist turned himself in or *was* turned in by a relative, she knew a speedy resolution was probably unlikely.

If she sat around the house for another day and a half, thinking about Cathy Robbins and potato peelers and attacks on other inmates, she'd be in need of therapy herself by Monday.

With five minutes to go before her two-thirty was due, she made up her mind and made the call to Peter Hayman.

'Is the invitation still open?'

'Sure is,' he said.

'I could leave town a little after four,' she told him. 'I guess it's a bit late in the day to plan much sailing, but at least I could check into a hotel and be ready for an early start, if that's what you and your friends have in mind.'

'Sounds great,' Hayman said. 'You sure you want to go to a hotel? I mean, if you don't want to stay at your sister's, you'd be welcome to use my guest room.'

'My sister's up in Fort Lauderdale,' Grace told him. 'And frankly I think I'm just in the mood for a hotel. Maybe Pelican

Lodge – I've been wanting to try it for a while. But thank you for the invitation,' she added.

Her doorbell rang.

'I heard that,' Hayman said. 'Is it a patient?'

'It is.'

'How about I call the hotel for you, get you booked in?'

The bell rang again.

'That would very kind. I don't like to impose—'

'Grace, go let them in. I'll call you in an hour, let you know about the reservation.'

She hesitated for about another half-second en route to her front door, but then after that she was too busy focusing on her young patient to think of anything else; and then later, after Hayman phoned back to tell her that things were all set at the lodge, Grace was busy packing a bag and asking Teddy if he could come by and get Harry and leaving the number of the hotel on her machine for anyone who might need her urgently.

Sometimes, she remembered herself telling Claudia more than once or twice, one just had to go with the flow, to do something when the urge struck, to just *do* it, grab the moment.

So she grabbed it.

CHAPTER THIRTY-SIX

SATURDAY, MAY 16 1998

At three-ten, Sam was just leaving Metro-Dade headquarters where he'd been checking criminal records on their number one suspect in the rape cases – for which Sergeant Kovac had made Martinez lead investigator – when a thought unrelated to the current case slipped into his mind for the third time that day, making him reach for his personal cellular phone (Miami Beach PD didn't run to that kind of expense) as he climbed into his car.

Angie Carlino was an old pal, an outsize, sexy, kind-hearted Italian who'd worked in a series of clerical jobs down on Washington Street before falling in love with a Tampa-based cop and moving to the west coast where she now worked for the Pinellas County Sheriff's office. Sam had gone to Angie's wedding, sent her gifts when her babies were born, and she always sent him a caring note around the time of the anniversary of Sampson's death. From time to time, when one or the other needed a little coast-to-coast help, they used each other to short-cut the system. Her home number was one of about twenty that Sam had logged on his cellular phone's memory.

'*Angela, bellissima, come sta?*'

'Hey, handsome, what's doing?' Angie always recognized Sam's voice, complained his Italian was lousy unless he was singing it.

'Usual stuff, babe how's the family?'

'Gorgeous and healthy, thank God.' Angie paused. 'So what's up, Sam? What do you need?'

'Anything you can find on a double shooting in St Pete a few years back.'

'How many years is a few?'

'Can't tell you that exactly – any place between three and six.'

'That's a big help. Do we have a name?'

'Uh-uh.'

'Well, do we have *anything* to make this halfway possible?'

'We have a mother and father in St Pete shot by their teenaged son. Both parents survived and sounds like Dad twisted some arms to get the case dropped – but there has to be something on record.'

'Depends how many arms he twisted,' Angie said wryly. 'When do you need this, Sam? I mean, this is Saturday afternoon and I'm about to go out and buy me a new négligée.'

'Special occasion?'

'Do I need a special occasion to get my husband excited?'

'I'll bet Tony's in a permanent state of excitement, Angie.'

'Damn right, Sam. So can this wait till Monday, or is it urgent?'

Sam's face twisted a little. 'Tell the truth, Angie, I don't know what to tell you. No, it's not legitimately urgent – it's not even official business – but something's bugging me, and I'm not sure what. I just have this feeling I should have checked it out a while back.'

'Okay, kiddo, I'll see what I can do – ' there was a smile in her voice – 'soon as I've gotten over to *Victoria's Secret.*'

'I owe you one,' Sam said.

She called him back on his cellular two hours later.

'Nothing,' she told him.

'Nothing at all?'

'*Niente. Nada.* Nothing that even vaguely approximated the scenario.' Angie paused. 'I can run it by some of the local guys on Monday, see if it rings any bells off the record.'

'That would be good,' Sam said.

'So do I get to go home now?' Angie asked. 'I waited here at the office in case you wanted me to check anything else.'

'Did you get your négligée?'

'You bet I did. My Tony's going to be a happy guy tonight.'

'Lucky Tony.'

'So, nothing else?' Angie nudged.

Sam took a moment, trying to understand why he felt so disturbed. 'Yeah, maybe, one little thing.'

'Shoot.'

'Check out any references to a psychiatrist name of Hayman – Dr Peter Hayman – now resident down in Key Largo, used to work over your way, possibly in St Pete.'

'How urgent is this one?'

Sam's mind worked on. 'Not urgent.'

'I'll take a quick run at him anyway,' Angie said, 'and if I don't come up with anything fast, I'll get back to it Monday. Okay?'

'I double owe you,' Sam said.

CHAPTER THIRTY-SEVEN

Grace arrived at Pelican Lodge a little after six to find there was no reservation in her name. The place was pretty as a picture – especially spectacular, in fact, after the strip-mall-dullness of the Key Largo main drag – and the couple at the front desk were charmingly distraught about her predicament, but they were also insistent that no one had made a booking for her.

'Do you know who your friend spoke to, Dr Lucca?' The woman, with short grey hair, efficient eyes and a name tag identifying her as Jane, looked to Grace like the kind of person not only unlikely to make a major error, but equally likely to own up if she had.

'I'm afraid I don't,' Grace said. 'All I know is that Dr Hayman must have called you between two-thirty and three-forty-five.'

'If he did,' Jane said, 'he didn't talk to me.'

'Nor me,' her dark-suited colleague named Carl added, dolefully.

Grace considered getting angry, and decided against. She thought about calling Hayman, and decided against that too, since he was bound to get mad at the hotel, and then presumably reiterate his invitation for her to stay in his guest room, and she didn't feel quite comfortable with that notion. So instead, she just stood at the reception desk and waited for Jane and Carl to sort things out. It was, she figured, one of those situations where if she stood there long enough, a solution was bound to be found. After all, didn't they always say that all hotels had spare rooms for emergencies?

'You must have a room somewhere,' she said after another moment. 'I'm really not very fussy. So long as it's clean and—'

'There's nothing,' Carl told her. 'It's just *awful* for you, Dr Lucca, and I wish we could just magic up a room, but there's not so much as a broom closet.'

'I cannot begin to imagine,' Jane said, 'who Dr Hayman talked to—'

'Or thought he was talking to,' Carl suggested, darkly. 'Maybe he got a wrong number and someone hoaxed him. Maybe some kid with a lousy sense of humour.'

'That doesn't seem terribly likely,' Grace said dryly.

'The problem is, Dr Lucca,' Jane said, 'this weekend's been fully booked for a long while. There's a fishing tournament on – people tend to book from year to year.'

Grace began shifting impatiently. 'Can you call another hotel for me?'

'Well, of course we can,' Carl answered, 'and we'll do our very best, but frankly, unless they've had a last-minute cancellation or no-show, I'm afraid we're going to find the same story all over.'

He was right. They sat Grace in a palm-shaded rattan chair on a beautiful porch and brought her complimentary iced tea while they pulled out all the stops – and failed; and then they offered her a free weekend in their best suite for another time – if, Carl said, effusively, she could ever forgive them. But the bottom line was there were no rooms to be had on Key Largo, Tavernier or Islamorada.

Grace had three choices. One, she could drive on down to Claudia's and open up the house, but that meant playing games with the sophisticated alarm system which Daniel always switched on when they were up in Fort Lauderdale. Two, she could go back home. Or three, she could simply accept Hayman's offer – and since it was him she was supposed to be sailing with first thing Sunday morning, nothing else made much sense. Yet still, even as she was digging her address book out of her canvas tote bag to find his number, Grace was less than perfectly happy about what she was doing. She found herself remembering the last time she'd seen Hayman, a couple of weeks back, that moment when she'd thought he'd held on to her hand for that second or two longer than necessary. Grace had wondered then if perhaps she'd misled him in some unintentional way, and she wondered now if choosing to stay with him might lead to awkwardness.

She found his number.

What if he hadn't made the reservation at all?

Up until that very instant, Grace had been sure that some other hotel staff member – someone less irreproachable than either Jane or Carl – had created the error here. Could it have been a deliberate – possibly predatory – male ploy?

'Don't flatter yourself, Lucca,' she muttered, pulling her cellular phone out of her bag. Dr Peter Hayman was a respectable psychiatrist, researcher and writer – besides which, Grace had already visited him at his place twice, and he'd been a perfect gentleman both times.

Leaping to absurd conclusions, Lucca.

She made the call.

It was only after they'd finished talking and she'd persuaded him there was no need for him to come and give the Pelican Lodge a piece of his mind, that it suddenly occurred to Grace that what might really be troubling her was how Sam might read her staying with another man for the weekend, just because he was too overloaded to see her.

That, too, of course, was patently nonsense. Sam knew that her relationship with Hayman was a professional one, that it had been Cathy Robbins who had, inadvertently, brought them together.

Though if it hadn't been for Cathy, Grace reminded herself, she and Sam might not have met either.

And, if she was entirely honest with herself, she wasn't one hundred per cent sure if going sailing on a Sunday was exactly the standard mark of a professional relationship.

CHAPTER THIRTY-EIGHT

Sam came out of the interview room where he and Al
Martinez had been questioning their number one suspect for
over an hour. If they did have the right guy, it was only a
matter of waiting for blood and DNA tests to come through
before they nailed him, since the rapist had done them the
favour of leaving half a textbook of damning physical
evidence – semen, saliva and even blood – under one of the
victim's fingernails, more than probably corresponding to the
rake marks they'd now found on their suspect's buttocks. All
of which meant that with luck and a lighter-than-usual case-
load at the ME's office, Sam and Martinez might get their bad
guy charged and locked up before the entire weekend was
screwed.

'Sam, you got a call from Angie Carlino in Tampa.' Mary
Cutter, another detective in Person Crimes, strode along the
corridor towards them.

'When?' Sam glanced at his watch, saw it was after seven
p.m., two hours since they'd spoken the last time.

'Just a few minutes back – said can you call her at home?'

The door to the interview room opened and Martinez came
out just as Cutter was swinging around and heading back
where she'd come from. Sam noted Martinez's eyes following
her, watched as the colour in his cheeks rose a notch. Al
Martinez had the reputation of being a confirmed bachelor
who seldom dated or partied, but there was no doubt in Sam's
mind that since the dark-haired, petite but curvaceous detective's arrival on the Beach, a big hole had been blown in the
bachelor's composure.

243

'Our guy's about to cave in, Sam,' Martinez said as Cutter vanished.

Sam thought about taking time out to call Angie Carlino back.

'Hey, Becket,' Martinez urged, and opened the door again.

They went back in.

The guy spilled his guts, but it was after eight-thirty before Sam had a chance to return the call to Tampa. Tony, Angie's husband, didn't sound disgruntled when he heard Sam ask for Angie, so Sam figured they probably hadn't gotten to the new négligée part of the evening yet.

'Whatcha got for me, babe?'

'More of the same, mostly,' Angie told him.

'You didn't need to waste your Saturday night on this, Angie. I told you it wasn't urgent.'

'You know me, Sam. I'm like you – something bugs me, I'm like a dog with a bone. I ran the usual checks on this Hayman guy – nothing jumped out at me, which was fine – no felonies or misdemeanours. But then I thought I'd just look him up, get his credentials, you know.' Angie paused. 'I found his listings for Key Largo, like you said, going back to '92, but nothing in St Petersburg – nothing before '92 any place I looked.'

Sam frowned. 'Nothing at all?'

'Not so far. Being the weekend, I couldn't call any of the shrink-type associations, but we got listings going back ten years for St Pete and Clearwater, and there's no Dr Peter Hayman, psychiatrist, in any of them.'

Sam thought back to what little Grace had told him about the guy she'd met at a seminar down in the Keys. 'I only said it might have been St Pete – I guess I could be wrong.'

'So do I get to go back to Tony now?' Angie asked, amiably.

Sam grinned. 'He seen your purchase yet?'

'Not yet. I got two steaks ready to go first.'

'Have a good night, Angie – and thanks.'

'You going home now, kiddo?' she asked.

'Not yet. Al and I got a case to finish up on, and then I've got a stack of paperwork to take care of.' Sam made a mental note to ask Grace for more details on Hayman next time they spoke.

'Talk to you next week, Sam.'

'Go strut your stuff for Tony, Angie babe.'

CHAPTER THIRTY-NINE

Grace had to admit the guest suite at Peter Hayman's house made her glad that Pelican Lodge had been full. She'd liked the look and feel of the house the first time she'd been there, but if he'd taken a hand with the decor of this room, then Hayman really had excelled himself. It was homey and laidback, with its very own piece of porch, railed off from the rest for privacy; yet the things that needed to feel crisp and clean looked and felt and smelt as if some old-fashioned personal maid had just been through the place with fresh flowers and an iron.

'I hope you don't mind,' Hayman had said as he'd helped carry Grace's bag into the room when she'd arrived, 'but I've arranged to meet some people at my sailing club for a drink.'

'Of course I don't mind.'

'You're welcome to join us,' he'd gone on, 'but I figure after all the aggravation at Pelican Lodge you probably could use some time by yourself.'

He'd shown her around, told her to make the house her own, to take or use whatever she needed: the phone, the kitchen and the big old timber chest that put her in mind of the one in which the old ladies had stashed their victims in *Arsenic and Old Lace*, but which in this case was Hayman's drinks cabinet, handsomely stocked with choice malt whiskies.

'If you're up for it later,' he told Grace before he left, 'I've taken the liberty of reserving a window at Atlantic's Edge at Cheeca Lodge.'

Grace had eaten there a couple of times over the years with Claudia and Daniel, and knew it to be perhaps the most elegant place in the Keys.

246

'I hardly think that qualifies as a liberty,' she said.

She made three calls on her cellular while Hayman was out. First, she called her sister to let her know where she was in case Claudia needed her for any reason. Second, she called her own home phone to check her messages. Grace told herself she was checking in case one of her patients had had an emergency, but she knew damned well it was chiefly to find out if Sam had called again. He hadn't, which Grace also knew damned well was because he was trying to find out who'd raped two poor women in Miami Beach, but that knowledge didn't prevent a brief, painful flaring of the kind of disappointment that hadn't troubled her for very many years.

The third call was made after she'd had a long and wonderful shower, brewed a pot of excellent coffee and was sitting on her little private porch drinking it and letting the early-evening air, sweet and heavy with perfume and bird calls, wash over her. Her little mobile phone lay in her lap. Grace waited a few more minutes, then dialled Sam's home number.

His machine picked up and his voice directed her to leave her name, number and any message. Grace had never been psyched out by answering machines, but that particular voice had been making love to her less than forty-eight hours before, and she guessed that might have been why the sound of it threw her.

She put down the phone without saying a word.

'Jesus, Lucca,' she said out loud, 'you really are regressing.'

The evening at Cheeca Lodge was more than pleasant: crab cakes and baby snapper as good as Grace had remembered in lovely surroundings, and intelligent conversation with an attractive man. An elusive man, in some ways, she was beginning to realize. They'd reached an agreement, before sitting down at their table, not to talk about Cathy or the homicides – unless, Hayman had added, unloading some more was going to help Grace relax more fully – so the conversation tonight was on an entirely different footing than in their previous encounters. Maybe it was the fault of their profession; maybe Hayman, like Grace, was simply more accustomed to listening than speaking, but by the end of the meal she felt she barely

247

knew more about the man than she had at the outset. She knew just a little about his psychiatric philosophy and about his long-term writing plans, and she knew that he was happier living in the Keys than he had been living any place before. But aside from the loosest of references to his years on the Gulf coast, Hayman had scarcely alluded to his past. Each time Grace had asked him a direct question, he had answered it clearly and without prevarication, but also without the slightest elaboration; thus she knew, for example, that he'd never married, but not if he'd either ever come close or had any desire to do so; she knew that he considered himself a contented man now because he felt in almost absolute control of his daily life, but she had no idea if, or why, he had felt *out* of control before.

Then again, Grace told herself, none of these things were remotely her business. She was neither Peter Hayman's psychologist nor his lover, nor was she even, strictly speaking, his friend. She was merely a colleague to whom he had been kind enough to extend an invitation that she had accepted. There was no reason for them to become close. And anyway, with every passing hour, Grace was becoming increasingly aware that the only man she wanted to get closer to was Sam Becket. Too many times during dinner, her mind skipped back to Miami and to Sam. She wondered how he was making out with his new investigation, wondered how much care he took of himself at work. Grace found that the very idea of Sam's being in danger made her go cold. She had an urge, several times between her snapper and coffee, to go outside and try calling him again. She wanted to know he was okay, she wanted him to know that even if she was away with Peter Hayman, *he* was the one on her mind.

She wanted to hear his voice.

'Who's the lucky man?'

Hayman's voice jarred Grace's thoughts as they headed back to his house in a cab. They'd decided, before dinner, to enjoy a few glasses of wine without running the risks of driving.

'I'm sorry?' She looked sideways at him. She could see, in the dim light of the taxi, that his brown eyes were amused.

'Is it the policeman?' he asked.

That startled her. 'Which policeman?' she asked defensively.

'Detective Becket,' Hayman said, still looking amused. 'The man you keep mentioning.'

'I do?' Grace was still surprised. She had thought, as a matter of fact, that she had been particularly careful – especially because of the confidential nature of the discussions she and Sam had shared regarding the Robbins-Flager-Dean homicides – *not* to talk too much about Sam.

'Oh, yes, you do,' Hayman said. 'And I don't think I'd be too far off the mark if I said I thought you'd been thinking about him a good deal of this evening.'

Now Grace was embarrassed. 'Peter, I'm sorry if it's seemed that way. I can assure you I've had the loveliest time – if my mind's been straying a little, it's probably just because I'm not as good as I ought to be at leaving work behind.'

'Uh-uh.' He raised his right index finger in mock admonishment. 'No work talk – we agreed.'

'Yes, we did. But I'm not the one who brought up the subject.'

'But Samuel Becket doesn't exactly qualify as work, surely?' The brown eyes grew even merrier. 'Come now, Grace, don't be coy.'

That irritated her. 'Peter, can we please change the subject?'

'By all means.' He looked straight ahead. 'We're almost home.'

She felt awkward from that moment on. Hayman paid the driver and they went inside, and though the subject of Sam Becket had been dropped and her host did not appear to have been offended by her reluctance to discuss her private life, the easy mood of the evening, certainly from Grace's point-of-view, had vanished.

'How about a nightcap?' Hayman asked.

She hesitated. 'I think maybe I've had enough.'

'I have a particularly fine cognac that I've been reluctant to open just for myself. If you had just a taste with me, you'd be doing me a favour.'

Grace didn't want to be rude. 'Just a very small one.'

They took their glasses outside on to the porch on the ocean side of the house and sat in the same comfortable rattan chairs in which they'd shared the stir-fry dinner Hayman had cooked for Grace a few weeks back.

'Cognac to your liking?' he asked after a few minutes.

'Mm. Very smooth.'

They were quiet again for a while.

'I didn't mean to offend you, Grace,' he said.

It was out of nowhere, but she knew he was talking about Sam again.

'You didn't.' She tried to sound sincere. 'I'm sorry if I was brusque.'

'You were entitled.'

She didn't argue.

'He's a lucky man,' Hayman said, softly.

Grace did her best to suppress a sigh. Clearly, he had no intention of dropping the subject.

'I have to say,' he went on, 'that if I were in his shoes, I'd let you out of my sight as seldom as possible – and I'd certainly do anything I could to talk you out of spending weekends with another man.'

Grace gritted her teeth. 'I don't think Sam Becket's the jealous type,' she said, as lightly as she could. 'Especially when there's nothing to be jealous of.'

'Don't you believe it,' Hayman said. 'Every man's the jealous type – if he cares enough and has enough pride.'

She wished, abruptly, that she had stayed home with Harry.

She asked him, a few minutes later, if he'd mind if she borrowed a book for the night, and he told her, easily and pleasantly, to help herself.

'Anything you want from the shelves in my study.' Hayman paused. 'There's some fiction near the window – and quite a few decent biographies if that's your poison.'

Grace took a glass of water from the kitchen first, then went in search of the study. She thought, when he'd shown her around on her arrival, it had been the room nearest to the staircase, but the door, when she tried it, seemed to be locked.

'Can I help?'

His voice, right behind her, startled Grace. She turned around. 'I thought this was the study.'

'No, it's not,' Hayman said. 'Study's next door along.'

She apologized, went on to the next room, took down a book without much ado, and came back out into the narrow corridor.

Hayman was still standing by the locked door.

He smiled at her. 'Got what you need?'

Grace nodded and held up *Tom Sawyer*. 'I expect I'll be asleep before I've reached page two.' She passed Hayman on her way to the staircase.

'Good night, Grace,' he said. 'Sleep well.'

'Thank you, Peter.' She started up. 'See you in the morning.'

'Looking forward to it,' he said.

When she glanced down from the top of the staircase, he was still in the same place, looking up at her.

CHAPTER FORTY

SUNDAY, MAY 17, 1998

The South Beach rapist, self-confessed and, temporarily at least, glorying in his infamy, was now safely off the streets and in the system, where Martinez and Sam could only hope and pray he would remain for as long as the law allowed. Not that that did much to help the women he'd attacked and violated.

It did mean, however, that Sam got to go home for what was left of the night. Not enough, by the time they'd gotten the paperwork squared away. It was half-past two when he got there. Much too late to call a hardworking psychologist, who was more than likely in bed and fast asleep.

He checked his machine in case Grace had tried to reach him, knowing, of course, that there would have been no reason for her to do so, since he'd told her at lunchtime that he was going to be tied up for the whole weekend.

The only message was from Judy, wanting to know when he was going to find time to come over and see his father. That was his mother's new trick – she no longer had to demand that he came to visit her; all she had to do was remind him – as if he was likely to forget – about what his dad had been through and how lucky they were to still have him.

Sam remembered telling Grace that he would try to get David over to the house of detention to visit with Cathy. He felt bad about not having gotten around to doing that yet. He didn't like the idea of letting Grace down in any way at all.

'*Don't worry about me,*' she'd said when he'd told her he probably wouldn't even find a spare second to make a phone call. Her voice had been so filled with warmth that he'd had an urge to drop everything and get over to her place to see her again. He still felt that way now, though the fact was that if he were able to be with her right this minute, he'd be too dog-tired to do anything more than go to sleep.

The thought of sleeping next to Grace Lucca was pretty damned wonderful.

The thought of waking up beside her, of course, was even better.

CHAPTER FORTY-ONE

At two-thirty-three, Grace was still awake and reading *Tom Sawyer* in Hayman's guest bedroom when she heard a step outside the door. Quickly, reflexively, she put out her right hand, switched out the bedside lamp and lay down on her side.

She heard the door open, quietly, slowly, heard the tread on the carpet. She closed her eyes, forced herself to bring her breathing under control, wanting it to sound even and calm so that Hayman would think she was sleeping.

What the hell was he *doing*, coming into her room in the middle of the goddamned night? Had he seen the light from under the door? Did he know she was shamming sleep?

It's okay, Lucca, Grace told herself behind closed eyelids, *if he does turn out to be a major creep, you're a big girl, you know how to handle yourself.*

'Grace?'

His voice was very low and close. He sounded unsure of whether she was asleep or not. He sounded, thank God, she thought, as if he didn't mean to wake her if she really was out of it. She considered stirring and answering him, then decided against. If he had a good reason for wanting her up at this time of night, he'd hardly be tiptoeing around the room like a goddamned burglar.

She went on with the act.

'Okay, Grace,' he said, just as softly.

She felt the air fan a little close to her face as he moved again – it was desperately hard not to hold her breath, not to squeeze her eyelids more tightly shut or open them to see what he was doing.

A floorboard creaked beneath the carpet. He was moving away, Grace thought, back towards the door, which meant he was probably somewhere behind her now, and no longer able to see her face. She tried to remember the positioning of the two mirrors in the room – the one on the dressing table, the other a freestanding cheval glass – in case he could still see her reflection.

She heard the door close.

And waited. Was he gone, or was he still in the room with her?

Nothing.

She went on waiting.

Still nothing.

From somewhere else in the house, some distance away this time, she heard another door closing, and knew he really was gone.

Thank you, Jesus.

Slowly, Grace opened her eyes, stared into the darkness and let out a long exhalation of relief.

She wanted to turn the light on. She wanted to find her clothes and leave. But that didn't seem like the best thing to do.

"*Okay, Grace.*" She couldn't figure out what that had meant. She couldn't decide if it had meant, "*Okay, Grace, if you're sound asleep I don't want to disturb you*", or if it had meant, "*Okay, Grace, have it your way – play your little games*". If it was the first, she could just about contemplate staying, at least until morning. If it was the latter, there was something implicitly unpleasant behind the words that made her want to get the hell out of Peter Hayman's house sometime within the next five minutes.

Her eyes grew more accustomed to the dark. Slowly, carefully, she climbed out of bed, went over to one of the windows, and opened the blinds a little. There was enough of a moon to light her way, enough for her to be able to check that she had slid the bolt on the porch door. *Why would he need to come that way, Lucca, when he can use the regular door?*

She couldn't recall a lock on the door to the hallway, but she tiptoed across to double check. There was a lock, but no

255

key. She looked around. She could have pushed a chair under the handle, which would not only delay anyone entering but make a noise, too – but that seemed a little heavy-handed, especially as she felt it was now somewhat unlikely that Hayman would put in a repeat appearance that night.

In the end she chose a slightly subtler approach, one that might allow her to get at least *some* sleep, and that – if her host decided to bring her a cup of coffee in the morning – could be politely explained away. The old travel bag left in front of the door in error. A simple piece of carelessness that Hayman could hardly argue with by saying that it hadn't been there when he'd come into the room in the middle of the night.

Grace went to the bathroom, peed without flushing the john in case he heard her, then washed her hands, splashed her face and went back to bed. For about another hour, she lay awake, becoming more and more sure by the minute that she would get no rest at all. But slowly, gradually, her mind and body let go their grip, sheer fatigue took over, and she drifted away.

CHAPTER FORTY-TWO

At a little after four-thirty Sunday morning, Sam was still awake. He'd wanted to sleep, he *needed* to sleep, dammit, but something was going around and around in his overtired brain, and he couldn't seem to focus on it precisely. It was like watching out for an individual on one of those high-speed fairground rides – now you saw them, then they were whipped away and gone.

He'd just about given up on sleep *and* on working out what was bugging him, had just got up to drink some juice and switch on an old movie on cable, when he suddenly understood what the problem was.

It had gotten submerged beneath the mixed-up satisfaction and sense of despair that the rapist's confession had brought him, and then it had been all but forgotten in the paperwork frenzy that had followed.

Dr Peter Hayman.

The fact that Angie Carlino had found no record for the psychiatrist until he'd arrived on Key Largo in 1992.

There could, Sam knew, be any number of explanations for that. Most likely, come Monday, he or Angie would contact the American Psychiatric Association in Washington DC and resurrect the whole of the rest of Hayman's professional life from college to the move to the Keys, and the blip could be wiped out. Sam knew he had no choice but to wait for that to happen.

But meanwhile, he couldn't help dabbling with some disturbing possible connections.

John Broderick had disappeared off Pensacola in the fall of

1989. As of this moment, Peter Hayman seemed to have *appeared* out of nowhere less than three years later. More than enough time for a man to have had extensive plastic surgery heal completely, and to have created a new, safe, living situation for himself under a new identity.

Broderick had been a physician. Dr Hayman was a psychiatrist with – as of tonight – dubious credentials. Broderick had been an abuser. Peter Hayman had a self-professed interest in a particular branch of mental illness considered by many to be a grievous form of abuse.

And then there was the double shooting: the reason Hayman had given Grace for his particular interest in the Robbins case. Except that Angie Carlino had found no record of that either.

Sam sat up in an armchair in front of his TV, the sound muted, the black and white picture blurring in front of his weary eyes.

'You're being crazy, man,' he told himself.

Of course it was a crazy connection to be making. A few words from the song 'Jealous Guy' played in his mind. Could that be all it was? Had the fact that Grace had been spending time talking to Hayman, shrink-to-shrink, about the Robbins case, been bugging him? He frowned at the possibility. He preferred to think he had a greater respect for both Grace Lucca's professionalism and personal choice than that; he hoped he was better than that.

Grace had looked at Lafayette Hospital's photograph of Broderick and had said there was something familiar about the man. They'd both concluded it was simply because he was Cathy's father, but what if it *hadn't* been a heredity thing?

'Damn,' Sam said.

He got up out of the chair, stalked across to the window, rubbed the back of his neck with his right hand, rotated his shoulders to try and relax himself. He didn't have a clue what Hayman looked like. Obviously, he didn't look anything like Broderick, or Grace would have placed him the instant she'd seen the photograph.

'C'mon, Becket.'

He turned away from the glass. Grace was a trained observer with years of practice in seeing past exteriors to the stuff inside that really counted. If Hayman was Broderick –

even if she had no cause to contemplate their being one and the same – she would have sensed enough to mistrust the man.

Wouldn't she?

He wanted to talk to her, but it was five in the morning, and in any case he wasn't sure what the hell he could or should have said to her. What he was going to have to do instead was contain himself and go on trying to check out Hayman. He thought that Grace had said he was concentrating on writing these days rather than practising as a psychiatrist. If the guy had anything in print, his publishers were the obvious route to go – and maybe those missing years would emerge on Monday.

Except it wasn't just years that seemed to be missing.

It was most of a life.

CHAPTER FORTY-THREE

'Boy, have we lucked out with the weather today,' Hayman said as he set a dish of pancakes on the white-painted rattan table on his ocean-facing porch. 'Best sailing weather I've seen in a while.'

'It does look tempting,' Grace admitted.

She *was* tempted. In the light of the gorgeous morning, with a serious breakfast all laid out before her, she also had to admit that her nighttime fears seemed groundless – especially in view of the fact that Hayman had asked her almost as soon as she'd appeared in the kitchen a half-hour ago if something had disturbed her in the night.

'I thought I heard a sound from your room,' he'd told her.

'What kind of a sound?' Grace had asked him, giving nothing away.

'I thought it was you, crying out,' he'd answered. 'I went to check on you, but you were sleeping, so I didn't wake you.' He shrugged. 'I guess it was a night bird or maybe it was just in my head – or maybe you were dreaming.'

'I don't remember any bad dreams,' Grace had said. 'Though that doesn't mean I didn't have any.'

'Strange bed, strange place,' he'd said lightly, closing the subject, and Grace had decided she was happy to close it, too.

Sitting on the porch now, eating pancakes with pure maple syrup, drinking good coffee and gazing out to sea through palm trees and mangroves, she also decided that it would be plain foolish to go back to Miami without getting in at least a few hours' sailing with Hayman and his friends.

They'd just about finished clearing away the dishes and

Hayman was insisting on doing the washing up when the door-bell – an old ship's bell – clanged, heralding the arrival of two of those friends.

'Betty and Miles Flanagan' – Hayman brought them into the kitchen and made the introductions – 'Dr Grace Lucca.'

'Glad to know you, Grace,' Miles said. 'May I call you Grace?'

They all settled down around the kitchen table while Hayman put on more coffee. The Flanagans were both small and slim, a trim, agile, pink-cheeked pair who looked more like brother and sister than husband and wife, which she knew them to be.

'Peter tells us you have a sister with a place close by,' Betty said.

'On Islamorada,' Grace told her. 'She loves it.'

'How about you?' Miles asked. 'Wouldn't you like to escape too?'

'Not really,' she answered. 'I'm pretty much set where I am.'

It turned out that the Flanagans had their own boat, and were impatient to be on the ocean, but Hayman said he had a few things he needed to see to around the house before going out, so they made a tentative arrangement to meet for a picnic lunch on El Radabob Key and the Flanagans left.

'I'd assumed we were all sailing together,' Grace said as they drove away.

'Uh-uh.' Hayman shook his head. 'Miles is nuts about his own boat and can't stand having anyone tell him what to do. You wouldn't want to actually sail *with* him, believe me. We'll probably meet up with Jack and Tina Weintraub – they keep their boat at the same marina as mine. They're a lot more easy going than the Flanagans.'

'How come you don't moor your boat here?'

'She's pretty big, and she's been getting a spruce-up.' Hayman smiled. 'The *Snowbird's* the apple of my eye. I hope you're going to like her.'

'I'm sure I shall.'

He took his coffee cup over to the sink, and started washing up. Grace glanced around for a cloth to help with the drying.

'No work for you,' Hayman said. 'You have one whole

day's vacation. That is, assuming you'll be wanting to get back in time for business as usual tomorrow – or am I wrong about that?'

'Afraid not,' Grace said.

'Then you just sit and let me work.'

She smiled at him. 'You don't need to tell me twice.'

He took a sponge cloth and wiped over one of the counters. 'Mind if I ask a work-related question, Grace?'

'Not really,' she said. 'It's not as if I can pretend to forget or even wind down in a single day.'

'Do you still think Cathy's father's alive and the killer?'

'I'm more certain than ever,' she answered.

'We haven't really talked since her transfer to the adult jail.' Hayman rinsed out the coffee pot. 'How's she coping?'

'She's a mess, Peter,' Grace said, 'which is why I'm so determined not to rest until I've found a way to prove Broderick faked his death. The more I think about it – the more I look at everything that's happened – the more I feel that nothing else seems to make sense.'

'Nothing except the possibility that Cathy Robbins is a very sick young woman,' Hayman said, turning off the water and wiping his hands with paper towel.

'No, Peter,' Grace said firmly. 'That's the other thing I've grown increasingly convinced of over the weeks. Cathy is *not* mentally ill – which is not to say that she isn't terribly disturbed by all that's happened to her, but that's a normal, a wholly sane reaction.' She paused. 'I've seen her angry a couple of times now, but that anger's been rational.'

Hayman came back across and joined her at the table. 'What degree of anger are we talking about here?'

'Nothing really violent, if that's what you're asking,' Grace said. 'It's frustration and fear. And Cathy's grown very suspicious of adults, but there's good reason for that – it doesn't mean she's paranoid.' She paused again. 'You know, Peter, I've observed her closely when she's talked about the old incident with her mother's goldfish.'

'You said she's always denied that.'

'She not only denies it, but her revulsion over those ugly little killings is very real and her distress over that accusation is just as acutely painful as it ever was – even now.' She read

262

Hayman's expression. 'And no, I don't think she was obsessed enough by that to kill.'

'And you don't believe she killed the fish either,' Hayman said.

'No, I don't,' Grace said. 'Her blood may have tested positive for cannabis at the time, but I wouldn't be too surprised if Broderick didn't find a way to get that into her, the same way he gave Marie progestogen instead of B12.'

'I hate to put a damper on all this, Grace,' Hayman said, 'but I did tell you last time we met that I was concerned about it.'

'I know you did,' Grace said. 'Just before you suggested I get hold of a photograph of Broderick.'

'Did you do that?'

'Yes.'

'And?' He paused. 'Did you recognize him?'

'No,' she said.

Hayman shook his head and stood up. 'Grace, isn't this starting to sound like the old get-out for the wife-and-child-beater abused in his own childhood? I mean, I don't know – maybe Broderick did survive that storm – maybe you're right, and he did slip cannabis into Cathy's vitamin capsules, and maybe he did even get her high and wild enough to cut the heads off those fish – or maybe, as you're suggesting, he did do even *that* himself—'

'If he did survive,' Grace interrupted, 'then I'm almost certain he did all those things and more.'

'I still don't think you can entirely ignore the possibility that all that old trauma really may have helped turn Cathy into exactly what the State Attorney thinks she is.'

'A multiple murderess?'

'Maybe.' Hayman sat down again. 'And maybe she's also become a damned accomplished liar.'

Grace felt almost too disappointed to speak.

'I'm sorry, Grace.' Hayman was gentle. 'You know that up to a point, I'm just playing devil's advocate.'

'But only up to a point,' she said.

'I'm afraid so,' he agreed. 'I just think it's important you get some balance back into your thinking about this case.'

'Is that why you asked me down here?'

'Only partly.' He paused. 'Mostly, I asked you because I figured you needed a break.' He stood up again. 'How about I squeeze a few oranges and make us some juice before we get ready to hit the water?'

Grace nodded. 'That sounds good.'

Hayman picked up their cups, put them into the sink, then went to the refrigerator and pulled out a half-dozen oranges.

'Can I help?' Grace asked.

'I'm fine. You just sit there and take it easy.'

'Okay,' she said.

Something had just struck her. Something Hayman had said. His reference to the possibility of Broderick's having slipped cannabis into Cathy's vitamin capsules. Such a clear, precise image. The thing was, Grace didn't know if Cathy had taken vitamins.

Surely, if it was true, only one person could know about that.

'All done.' Hayman poured juice into two glasses and brought them over to the table. 'Are you all right, Grace?'

'Yes, of course,' she said.

'I've upset you, haven't I?'

She shook her head. 'Not really.'

'It's the last thing I wanted to do.' He smiled at her. 'Have some juice.'

Grace reached out for her glass, but it was slippery, oily, and fell out of her grasp on to the stone tiled floor, smashing into fragments. 'Damn,' she said. 'I'm sorry, Peter.'

'Don't worry about it.'

She was already off the chair and down on her knees, starting to pick up the broken pieces.

'Grace, leave it.' Hayman got down beside her. 'There's no need for you to do this – let me get a brush, and I'll—'

He covered Grace's right hand with his own to stop her picking up the glass, but her fingers had just closed on a jagged piece and as Hayman squeezed her hand to pull it away, the shard cut into her palm.

'*Damn,*' she said again.

Hayman let go her hand and the fragment fell back to the floor.

'God, Grace, I'm so sorry. Let me see.' He took her fingers

in his, very carefully, and examined the cut. 'That looks nasty – it's quite deep.'

'It's not so bad,' she said, quickly. 'Not deep enough to need suturing.'

'Maybe not' he said, still examining it. 'But it needs cleaning and dressing.'

Grace drew her hand away, got off her knees and slid sideways back on to the kitchen chair. 'Give me just a second,' she said, 'and then I'll go take care of it.'

'Please,' Hayman said. 'It was my fault – least I can do is clean it up.'

'I dropped the glass,' Grace said.

'I hardly think a broken glass compares with a damaged hand.' He left the kitchen and was back in moments with a first-aid kit. 'May I?'

'Sure.' Grace held out the hand. 'Thank you.'

He was gentle, thorough and skilful, cleaning the cut carefully, covering the palm with antiseptic-impregnated gauze and then sealing it with a length of sticking plaster. By the time he was through, Grace was starting to feel deeply ashamed. Maybe Hayman was right – maybe she had been running her imagination about Cathy in overdrive, to the extent where now she was in real danger of seeing dead men around every other corner. For heaven's sake, the thing he'd said about the vitamin capsules had *obviously* been no more than a reasonable supposition – a plausible guess as to how Broderick might have fed Cathy cannabis without her knowing – given that they both knew about Broderick's previous use of B12. And it wasn't as if Peter Hayman even *slightly* resembled the old snapshot of John Broderick that Grace had seen.

'How's that feel?' he asked her.

'Fine,' she said.

'Sure? Not too tight?'

'No, it's great.' She flexed her hand, showing him.

'I'd keep it still for a little while,' he told her, 'or the bleeding might start up again.' He looked down at the floor. 'And better watch your feet while I clean that up.'

'Peter, I should be doing that.'

'You just sit still, Grace,' he said, firmly. 'And please don't start making a big deal about one cheap glass again.'

She smiled at him. 'I won't.'

He brushed up the glass, folded it safely in old newspaper, then relegated it to the trash before washing the floor. It was all done in minutes.

'Are you going to be up to sailing, Grace?'

'Oh, I think so.'

'Are you really sure about that?' He looked at her quizzically. 'You look a little pale.'

'It's only a cut, Peter.' She was, in fact, feeling a little shaky, but she didn't want to admit to it after all his efforts.

'Why don't you go sit out on the porch for a while? I still have a few errands that could use taking care of before we leave – I can give you some more juice and you just take it easy.'

'I hate to hold you up,' she said. It was true, especially after all his kindness – and the more Grace thought about it, the more sure she became that neither the night-time visit to her room nor the capsule remark had been remotely sinister. She was tired, that was all – exhausted and frustrated over Cathy – and jumpy as a cat because of it all.

'You're not holding me up,' he said.

She stopped arguing.

CHAPTER FORTY-FOUR

Martinez had called four hours ago, at six-thirty a.m., about forty-five minutes after Sam had managed to doze off. Sometimes Sam wondered if Martinez ever slept; he certainly appeared not to *need* more than an hour a night. He'd called this time with news dropped clean off the grapevine of a new homicide in the City of Miami jurisdiction: an office cleaner named Anna Valdez had been stabbed to death in a downtown doctor's office.

'Looks like they used one of the doc's instruments on her,' Martinez had said, then waited for Sam to react.

'A scalpel?' It had felt like an instant cold shower.

'In one.'

Sam's mind had raced back over the MO at his father's office. 'Any drugs missing?'

'Only scrip pads.' Martinez had been ready with his answer.

'Was she sleeping?' Sam had asked.

'She was certainly sitting down on the job – they found her in the doc's chair. Seems she should have finished work and been out of the place a good half-hour before she was killed.'

The ME on the case was Marina Garmisch. As physically imposing as her name suggested, with the body and head of a Wagnerian heroine, she was rumoured to have terrorized more than one six-foot cop, yet where the dead were concerned, Garmisch was as tender, delicate and caring as a lover. Like the other medical examiners in the county, she knew all about the other scalpel attacks.

267

'Could be the same perp as in your father's case,' she told Sam on the phone after Anna Valdez's body bag had been taken to the morgue to await her further attention. 'Though without the weapon or any usable prints, it's going to be hard to prove.'

'Do you know if she was asleep when she was stabbed?' he asked.

'She may have been dozing, but the blade definitely roused her. She put up quite a fight.' The ME paused. 'My under-standing is that Dr Becket never knew much about his attack.'

'Which could have been down to the angle the blade hit,' Sam said. 'I mean, my dad was sleeping on the couch in his office, so the perp had a clearer target.' He paused. 'You know that all the other scalpel victims had sedatives in their bloodstreams? My father was the odd one out.'

'I'll let you see the results soon as we have them,' Garmisch told him. 'But I'd say it's unlikely that Anna Valdez either took or was given anything. Like I said, she put up a good fight – I think she was a hundred per cent alert in the last few minutes of her life.'

'Even if it is the same sleaze who whacked your dad,' Martinez said over a cup of fourth-rate coffee, 'it won't be enough to get the Robbins kid off the hook.'

Sam knew that only too well. Ever since some asshole had leaked the news that the weapon in the other cases had been a scalpel, they'd been waiting for some other SOB to try a copycat.

Martinez was still thinking aloud. 'Unless the same guy offed her family and the therapist,' he said, 'and now he wants us to think this is someone else because he wants to keep the girl in jail, but he's gotten a taste for killing, the way they do.'

'I thought you were dead-set on Cathy Robbins being the one,' Sam said.

Martinez shrugged. 'You know I never like it when things get messy. I like my ends all tied up, nice and neat.'

Sam didn't say anything.

Broderick had come back into his mind.

And so had Peter Hayman.

*

He called Grace five minutes later, listened to her message giving the number of the hotel where she was staying. She hadn't said anything to him about plans for going anywhere this weekend – but then again, he hadn't given her much of a chance to tell him anything much last time they'd spoken.

She'd left the number, but no name. It was a 305 area code, which meant she was staying somewhere in south-east Florida, any place between Miami and Key West. Sam couldn't imagine why she'd be staying in a hotel on the Keys when her sister lived on Islamorada.

Peter Hayman lived on Key Largo.

He was just about to pick up his phone again when it rang and Maria Mitchell, the captain's personal assistant, told him he was wanted right away.

'Maria, can you tell the cap I just have a—'

'He said right away, detective.'

The only time Maria called him anything other than Sam was when her boss was in the room with her, and the strident tone in her voice was a clear warning that the captain was on the warpath about something. Captain Hector Hernandez pissed off was not a man to be kept waiting – especially not on a Sunday.

Whichever hotel Grace was staying at in whichever part of south-east Florida would just have to wait a while longer.

'Detective Becket?' Maria's tone was holding steady.

'On my way,' he said into the phone.

CHAPTER FORTY-FIVE

Grace wasn't feeling too good. It had started suddenly, just a little while ago, sitting out on Hayman's porch. Nothing too specific, mostly a dull headache and some queasiness, and now a great wave of exhaustion seemed to be taking her over, making her just want to flop where she was.

She'd used her cellular phone to check her messages and had found only one demanding an immediate response, from Cathy, but now her phone had died. She went in search of Hayman, passing the locked door of the previous evening – still closed – and found her host at his desk in the study, reading some papers.

'Peter?'

He twisted around, saw her in the doorway. 'Come in.'

'I'm afraid I need to call Miami, but my phone battery's all used up, and the only way I can recharge is while I'm driving.'

'You don't need to ask to use the phone. I told you when you first got here – help yourself to whatever you need.' He took a longer look at her. 'You don't look so hot.'

'I don't feel so hot,' Grace admitted.

Hayman stood up. 'What's up?'

'I don't know.' She was leaning against the door frame, glad of its support. 'It started just a little while back.'

'Do you think it's a reaction to the cut?'

'No way.' She managed a smile. 'I hope I'm not that feeble.'

'I don't think you're feeble at all.'

'Anyway,' she said, 'where would you like me to call from? I don't want to disturb you.'

'Anywhere you like,' Hayman said. 'You won't disturb me.'

Grace headed back into the kitchen and used the phone mounted on the wall, glad the cord was long enough to allow her to sit at the table. Cathy hadn't left the number, but Grace knew she'd written it down in her address book. The problem was that the book was in her tote bag in her room, and she didn't think she could summon up the energy to go fetch it, not when she could dial 411 instead.

Maybe, she thought while she was waiting for the operator, Cathy calling was a fragment of good news. Perhaps, if she was being allowed to make calls, they'd let her out of solitary.

She'd just written the number on Hayman's grocery list pad, when Grace remembered what else she'd put in her address book. Broderick's photograph. Hayman had asked only an hour or so ago if she'd obtained one, and she hadn't thought to show it to him.

Her head ached. Grace closed her eyes for a moment and rubbed her right temple with the back of her hand. *Stop procrastinating*, she told herself. *One problem at a time.*

She made the call to the Female House of Detention, and within a surprisingly short time Cathy was on the line. She sounded lousy, but at least she wasn't weeping this time.

'Did you hear what happened?'

'I heard they thought you attacked someone,' Grace said.

'I didn't do it, Grace.'

'Dr Parés told me they found a peeler from the kitchen in your cell.'

'I didn't put it there. Someone planted it.' Cathy paused. 'Do you believe me, Grace?'

'Yes, of course.'

'Why haven't you come to see me?'

'They said I couldn't come,' Grace told her. 'They told me I'd have to wait till tomorrow and call again.'

'It's because I was so awful to you on the phone, isn't it?'

Hysteria was obviously lurking just below the surface. Grace trod carefully. 'Cathy, we only spoke on Thursday, and the reason I didn't get in my car and drive straight over to see you was because I had appointments I couldn't break – and then Friday, the doctor called me, and after that it was impossible.'

271

'I'm sorry,' Cathy said.

'You don't have to be sorry, Cathy. I just need you to understand.'

'I do.'

Now she sounded flat and dull, like a stone.

'Listen to me, Cathy,' Grace said. 'I'm out of town today, but I'm going to do my best to get over there to see you either tomorrow or Tuesday.'

'Can't you ask if they'll let you come later today?' Now her voice was small, pathetic.

Grace's heart felt like it was twisting inside her chest, but the fact was that even if she'd thought there was any chance of being allowed into the facility on a Sunday without prior arrangement, she felt too ill to contemplate driving back to Miami.

'There's no way I can get there today, Cathy,' she said, trying to sound gentle and calming, 'but I promise you I'll do what I can to get there by Tuesday at the latest.'

'Where are you, Grace?' Cathy asked, suddenly.

'I'm on Key Largo,' Grace said, then bit her lip.

'Oh.'

That was all she said, but Grace heard the resentment and knew she'd probably just added about a hundred pounds or so to Cathy's burden of isolation. There she was, innocent and locked up with real offenders, and here Grace was – the shrink who was always making promises about helping her – too busy vacationing in the Keys to come see her.

'I'm thinking of you all the time, Cathy.'

'Yeah,' she said.

'You just have to be patient, I'm afraid.'

'I don't have much choice, do I?'

272

CHAPTER FORTY-SIX

Sam was holed up with the captain going through overdue monthly statistics. He wanted to get the hell out of there and talk to Grace, and then he wanted to get on with checking out Hayman – not to mention the fact that he was more than a little eager to find out how Miami PD were doing with the Valdez killing and whether or not the perp was the same piece of shit who'd stuck a scalpel in his father. But Hernandez said he'd had the chief on his phone at home first thing this morning, and his ulcer was playing up, and what Sam *really* wanted to do was tell him to go find someone else to hold his hand, but a voice in his head kept reminding him that he was getting worked up for all the wrong reasons, and none of them was Captain Hernandez's fault. And so far as Anna Valdez and even his father's case went, Sergeant Rodriguez and his team were on the job and Al Martinez was almost certainly keeping his ear to the ground.

He finally got back to his own desk at twelve-fifty-three, picked up the phone and punched the number of Grace's hotel.

'Good afternoon, this is the Pelican Lodge, how may we help you?'

'Dr Grace Lucca, please.'

'One moment, please.'

He was on hold for several moments, drumming the battered sole of his right Nike sneaker on the base of his desk.

'Sir?'

'Yes.'

'What was the name of the guest you were asking for?'

Sam repeated it. The woman at the other end told him that

they had no guest of that name. He told her that Dr Lucca had left a message for him the previous day, stating that she was staying there. She went away again, and came back with the information that Dr Lucca had indeed arrived yesterday, but had left again almost immediately. No, she did not know where she had gone to.

Sam tried Grace's house again. Still the same message. He didn't know if her machine was the type that would allow her to change an outgoing message from an outside phone.

Where the hell was she?

'With her sister,' he told himself, and started to dial information, only slamming the phone back into the cradle again as he realized he didn't know Claudia's second name.

Didn't know or couldn't remember.

He closed his eyes and leaned back in his chair. He thought about Grace talking about her sister – Claudia, that much he was rock sure of – and her brother-in-law, the architect ... Daniel – that was his name ... Claudia and Daniel what? Damn it, he didn't know, never *had* known.

He opened his eyes again and dialled his parents' home, hoped his father would pick up instead of his mother.

'Dad?'

'Sam? You okay?' David knew Sam was on duty.

'I'm fine.' Sam wasted no time. 'Listen, Dad, you probably can't help me with this, but I wondered if you happened to know Grace Lucca's sister's surname?'

'Has something happened to Grace?' Now David was anxious.

'No, nothing like that. Do you know her sister's name?'

'No, son,' David said. 'I don't think I've ever heard it.'

'Okay, Dad, sorry to have—'

'Why can't you ask Grace?'

'She's away – I think she's at her sister's.'

'Oh.' David paused. 'You could call the father in Chicago.'

'I guess I could,' Sam said.

'Or Grace must have people who work for her – a secretary, maybe?' David chuckled. 'Hey, are you the cop or am I?' He paused. 'Or are you just a cop who's fallen in love?'

Sam barely hesitated. He and his father seldom kept secrets

from one another. 'As a matter of fact, Dad, I think that about sums it up.'

'You couldn't find better, Sam,' David Becket said.

Sam smiled into the phone. 'I know.'

CHAPTER FORTY-SEVEN

'What you probably need,' Hayman said at around one o'clock, 'is a gentle hour or two out on the boat, get away from your worries.'

Grace looked at him dubiously. She'd urged him several times in the past hour and a half to head out without her, just to leave her behind to rest, but he'd refused to entertain the idea, had told her there was no way he was going to abandon her when she wasn't feeling well, and anyway, he could sail any day.

He was right, of course, about the possible benefits of getting away from her anxieties. Grace's conversation with Cathy had unsettled her even further, pushing her to leave messages for both Dr Parés and the deputy governor at the house of detention, asking them to keep a watchful eye on their young charge.

'You don't have a fever,' Hayman said, 'and you say the queasiness is about gone.'

'I still have a headache,' Grace reminded him.

'No better headache remedy than the ocean. All that fresh air and tranquillity ...' He slipped his grey tinted eyeglasses partway down his nose and looked at her over the tops of the frames.

'It does sound good.' She was starting to think he might be right.

'It is good,' he said.

'I guess if I sit around here, I will just brood over problems.'

'I guess you will.'

Grace took a deep breath, nodded and stood up. 'Maybe I

should take a couple more Anacin before we go.'

Hayman shook his head. 'The ocean will take care of your head. I always carry basic medication on board anyway, so there'll be something if you really need it.'

'Great,' she said, doing her best to shake off the fatigue that was still hovering around her brain like a raincloud. 'Let's go sailing.'

Sam was inside Grace's house. He'd lucked out, driving by just at the moment when Teddy Lopez had been going in through the front door to water the plants and clean up. Having checked Sam's credentials with the utmost suspicion, Teddy had let him inside and given him Claudia Brownley's telephone number in Fort Lauderdale.

Sam made the call from the kitchen, where Teddy could keep an eye on him. A child's voice answered.

'This is Robbie, who is it, please?'

'Robbie, this is Samuel Becket, calling for Mrs Brownley. Is she there?'

'Just a minute.'

Sam heard a clanking noise as the phone was apparently dropped on a hard surface. In the background, he heard Robbie calling his mother, then the high-pitched sound of a small dog barking.

'Detective Becket?' Claudia sounded wary.

'Mrs Brownley, I'm sorry to bother you.'

'Is something wrong?'

'No, not at all.' Sam regretted the way people assumed trouble the instant they heard a cop's voice on the phone. 'I was just wondering if you knew where your sister is staying?'

'Yes, I do.' Claudia's voice relaxed. 'She's down in the Keys, staying on Key Largo.'

'She left me a number for the Pelican Lodge.'

'Oh, no, she isn't there,' Claudia said quickly. 'There was a mix-up with the reservation, so she had to go and stay with a colleague.'

She paused, and Sam's pulse rate sped up.

'Do you know Dr Hayman?' she asked.

'Not personally,' Sam answered, 'though Grace has talked about him.' He kept his voice even, not wanting Claudia to sense his anxiety. 'Did she happen to give you his address or number?'

'Yes, she did.' There was a gentle smile in Claudia Brownley's voice. 'Grace almost always lets me know where she's going to be if she leaves town for more than a day at a time.'

Sam wrote down the information, got off the line with indecent haste and called the Key Largo number. He could feel Teddy Lopez's suspicious eyes on him, and was glad that Grace had such a good support system.

A man answered after three rings.

'Peter Hayman.' The voice was pleasant.

'Dr Hayman, this is Sam Becket.'

A tiny hesitation. 'Grace's friend.'

'That's right. Is she there?'

'Yes, she is, but she can't come to the phone this minute.'

'Why not?'

'She's taking a shower.' Hayman hesitated. 'She was feeling a little under the weather, but she's okay now, so we're going to try and get in a couple of hours' sailing.'

Alarm spread through Sam like a brushfire. 'What was wrong with her?'

'Nothing major.' Hayman was reassuring. 'She had a minor accident – nothing to get concerned about.'

'What kind of an accident?'

'She cut herself on some glass. I took care of it.'

'So why was she feeling under the weather?'

'I don't think the two things were really connected,' Hayman said, still patiently. 'As I said, she's okay now, which is why she's getting set for us to go out.'

'I'd like to talk to her,' Sam said.

'I told you, she's in the shower, but I'll tell her you called.'

'Why don't I hold till she's through?'

'Because I need to use my phone.' A touch of irritation was starting to show through Hayman's courtesy. 'I assure you, Detective Becket, I'll let Grace know you wanted to speak to her.'

'Tell her I'm at her house, please.'

'Really?' Now Hayman sounded surprised. 'Has something happened at her house? Is there a problem?'

'Nothing like that,' Sam said.

'You're sure there's nothing wrong?'

'Nothing at all,' Sam said.

'I'll tell her you called,' Hayman said. 'Goodbye, detective.'

Sam put the phone down, looked over at Teddy Lopez and smiled. 'Mind if I wait for Dr Lucca to call back?'

Teddy looked doubtful. 'I have work to do.'

'Go right ahead,' Sam said. 'I promise not to steal anything.'

'We can't stay here too long,' Teddy said. 'I need to get back to Harry – you know Harry?'

'Harry-the-Hoover.' Sam grinned. 'Sure I know Harry.'

'He doesn't like to stay alone when Dr Lucca's away,' Teddy told him.

'We won't be long,' Sam assured him.

'You want some coffee?' Teddy asked, grudgingly.

Sam shook his head. 'Not for me, thanks.'

He looked at the phone, then at his watch. It was one-seventeen. He wondered how long Grace took to have a shower. He wondered how she had cut herself, and how badly. He didn't like the idea of her feeling *"under the weather"*, as Hayman had described it. He didn't like the fact that he hadn't been able to talk to her.

He checked his watch again.

One-eighteen.

On the other side of Grace's kitchen, Teddy Lopez began to polish the top of the stove. It didn't need polishing.

Sam waited.

CHAPTER FORTY-EIGHT

At one-thirty-eight on Sunday afternoon, Cathy was in the infirmary with Dr Parés and a nurse. The doctor, a tall, slim man with dark eyes, receding hair and a neat beard, was less formally dressed than the last couple of times Cathy had seen him, wearing jeans and a white cotton shirt. It was unpleasantly warm, despite the ceiling fan, but Parés appeared cool and calm as always. He sat on the edge of the desk, a couple of feet away from where Cathy, in her short-sleeved blue uniform dress, slouched in a straight-backed chair.

'Your friend Dr Lucca called me a little while back,' he told her in his softly accented voice. 'She has been worrying about you again. She worries about you a lot, you know. You should be grateful to have such a caring friend.'

'She's not my friend,' Cathy said. 'She's my shrink.'

'Believe me,' Parés said, dryly, 'Dr Lucca is probably the best friend you have right now.'

'So why did she call you?'

'Because you sounded so upset when she talked to you, so afraid.' The doctor opened the bag on the desk and took out a small bottle. 'So I will give you something to calm you again.'

'I don't want a pill.'

'Just a little tranquillizer, same as before – nothing to worry about.'

'I told you, I don't *want* a pill!' Cathy was close to tears, almost shouting at the doctor. 'I want to get out of here – I want this all to be *over* – I want my mom and Arnie back again and Aunt Frances!' She covered her face with both her hands.

'Which is why you should take the pills I give you.' Parés shook his head at the nurse to let her know there was no need for her to intervene. 'And then I will try to teach you some relaxation techniques.'

'That'll be a waste of time,' Cathy told him, still through her hands.

'I don't think so.' The doctor uncapped the small bottle and shook out one pill. 'For one thing, if you can master these techniques, you won't have any need of pills.'

'I told you I don't want your dumb pill.' Cathy took her hands away from her face. Her cheeks were red, her eyes wet.

'Come on, Cathy,' the nurse said from over by the drugs cabinet.

'Well, I *don't*.'

Parés went over to the sink and half filled a glass with water. 'I also think that you would be wise to stop fighting those who wish to help you.'

'Like who? You?'

'Like me, yes.' He came back with the water and held it out to Cathy. 'Just take this one small pill to make you a little calmer, and then we can maybe start to see how you can stay calm without medication.'

Cathy took the pill and glass from him. 'There's nothing that's going to make me calm,' she said, but swallowed the pill anyway.

'I think Dr Lucca would like to help you more than you have allowed her to, Cathy. She understands what dark times these are for you, and she believes in you.'

'That's what she says,' Cathy said, sullenly.

'Don't you trust her?' Parés asked, quietly.

'I don't trust anyone any more.'

'I suppose I can't blame you for that,' the doctor said. 'But it's wise in this harsh world to learn to differentiate your enemies from your friends.'

'Are you my enemy or my friend?'

'Mind your manners, Robbins,' the nurse said sharply.

'It's all right, nurse,' Parés said, and kept his eyes on Cathy's face. 'Which do you think I am, Cathy?'

'I don't know,' she said.

'Oh, I think you do,' he said, gently.

CHAPTER FORTY-NINE

The marina was no sparkling power parking lot for glitzy millionaire toys. It looked to Grace more like what it was: a rather grubby, workmanlike service station for boats that represented, for many of their owners, their most regular mode of transport and, in some cases, their livelihood. It smelled of diesel and seagull crap and hot dogs – emanating from a stand at one end of the marina – and the combined effect on Grace was to make her feel queasy all over again. Yet, in spite of all that, she had to admit that just the sight of the *Snowbird*, Hayman's sailboat, a two-masted white mono-hull with lovely sleek lines, moored beyond the main working area, apparently fit and ready to move out, was enough to lift her spirits.

'What do you think?' Hayman asked, watching her face.

'I think she's perfect,' Grace said.

'Do you know much about sailboats?'

'I know I like being on them, and I've heard enough sail-speak, back home on Lake Michigan and since I got to Florida, but I still don't really know a cleat from a clew – it all just tends to fly straight over my head.'

'No problem,' Hayman said. 'You know the basics: raise the sails, tension them off and go with the breeze.' He smiled at her. 'And since the *Snowbird* has auxiliary power, we don't even have to wait for the wind to get out of here.' He paused. 'Sure you're up for this, Grace?'

'I'm up for it,' she said, 'but worst-case scenario, if I turn into a liability, you can always toss me overboard.'

'Oh, I doubt it'll come to that.'

Over on the far side of the marina, a middle-aged bald guy straightened up from a job of work and waved at them. Hayman set down the box of supplies he was carrying, raised his right arm in acknowledgment, then glanced around.

'I guess the Weintraubs gave up on us.'

'That's my fault,' Grace said. 'I'm sorry to have held everyone up.'

'Will you please stop apologizing?' Hayman said. 'Everyone feels lousy now and then – and if you do feel bad again, there's a small bunk down below.'

'I won't need that,' she said confidently.

She meant it. Now that they'd moved away from some of the unpleasant trapped smells on the working side of the marina, the ocean was already beginning to exert its power over her, the way it often did. It was one thing living and working by water, but the prospect of getting out *on* it was entirely another. Even back in Chicago, Grace had always grabbed any opportunity she could to catch a ride on someone's boat, however humble, on the lake, but the ocean was another beast entirely, and one of which she was in awe. She might have talked, sometimes, about getting her own boat sometime down the road, but even if that did come to pass she was only talking small potatoes compared to the *Snowbird*, some little craft like a Sunfish, just big enough for a woman and her dog, a minnow compared with a shark.

'You are looking better,' Hayman said.

'I'm feeling it.' Grace shrugged. 'I think maybe this has all been down to overstretching myself for too long without a break.'

'I'm not surprised you're exhausted.' Hayman reached out and gently touched her right arm.

Grace didn't pull away. For one thing, his words acted as an instant reminder of how tired she still was. And for another, she seemed, she realized with relief, to have stopped feeling so edgy around him.

'Ready to board her?' Hayman bent down to pick up their supplies.

'You bet,' Grace said.

Sam had stopped waiting for Grace to call a while back. He

had tried Hayman's number again just before two o'clock, and gotten no reply, and by then Teddy Lopez, who'd gone on keeping him under close surveillance, had became infected by Sam's growing anxiety.

'Is something wrong with Dr Lucca?' he'd asked finally, watching Sam pace the kitchen floor.

'No, I don't think so,' Sam had said.

'Then why are you so upset?' Teddy had nailed him.

'I'm not upset. I just really need to talk to her.'

'She's a very good lady,' Teddy had said.

'I know she is.'

'I like taking care of her.'

'I'm glad she has someone as conscientious as you *to* take care of her.'

He'd left less than five minutes later, chosen the Miami Beach route, going south on Collins as far as the MacArthur Causeway and then continuing in the same direction on US1, heading out of Miami towards the Keys. Sam was fully aware of what he was doing, knew he was on duty and how much hell he was going to catch from Hernandez if and when he got to find out about it. But he was also suddenly cold-as-Jack-Frost-*certain* that he needed to hightail it down to Key Largo as fast as he could.

However innocent Grace's reasons for not returning his call, Sam was unhappy as hell about her being down there, probably alone, with a guy who had, so far as he could tell, deliberately insinuated himself into her life with a case history that might be invented, and who, at the very least, was right now far too much of an unknown quantity for his liking.

Hayman had told Sam that Grace had been feeling unwell and that she'd cut herself on some glass. He'd said that he'd taken care of her, and that she was in the shower, which was why she'd been unable to talk to him. He'd also said that he would tell Grace that Sam had called and wanted her to get back to him.

And she hadn't.

There was no real doubt in Sam's mind that she *would* have called if she had been given his message. *If* she'd been given the message.

If she'd been able to call.

All of which had left him with four choices. One, he could do his job, go back to Hernandez's goddamned statistics and try to put Grace to the back of his mind – *impossible*. Two, he could tell Captain Hernandez what was on his mind – which would, he was pretty certain, be a waste of time and effort. Three, he could call in a favour with one of the guys down in the Keys – not a great idea, since if by the remotest chance Hayman *did* turn out to be Broderick, they would probably just be waving a great big warning flag right in his face.

Or four, he could do exactly what he was doing.

Dropping everything and going to find Grace himself.

CHAPTER FIFTY

Grace watched Hayman cast off, winch up the anchor, check a bewildering array of cables, ropes and winches from bow to stern, taking time out to plump up the cushions for her on a bench in the part of the boat even she – sailboat philistine that she was – knew was known as the 'aft' section, before starting the engine to take the *Snowbird* out to sea. She felt comparatively relaxed as they left the harbour, glad to be on board at last, appreciating the fact that Hayman appeared a calm, efficient sailor, well used to his boat, his long frame at ease with the rocking motion, his rubber-soled feet firm and agile on the polished teak deck.

'I should be helping,' she called to him a few minutes out.

'You should definitely not be helping,' he called back.

'I feel guilty.'

'How do you feel otherwise?'

'Fine.'

That wasn't exactly true, but it wasn't exactly a lie either. The air was helping in one sense, but that curious fatigue – to which Grace was entirely unaccustomed – still seemed to be wrapping itself tighter about her head, like an overly effusive hug from a fat maiden aunt.

She leaned back against the cushions, tilted her head and watched Key Largo drift slowly away as they moved out into the ocean. Less than a month ago, the water would have been crowded with boats of every kind, but the fishing contingent aside, the really busy season was over for the time being, and though they certainly didn't have the wind's sweet, warm breath to themselves, if Grace half closed her eyes, it did almost feel that way.

'I'm going to cut the power now and get the sails up,' Hayman told her.

'Lovely,' she called back lazily. 'Want some help yet?'

'No need. I'm used to coping alone.'

'Just yell if you change your mind.'

She watched him put on sailing gloves, the kind that left his fingertips exposed but would protect his palms and fingerpads from getting burned by the lines as he heaved and worked to get the mainsail up. Hayman had shown her where the PFDs – life jackets – were stored, but neither of them had put one on, Grace because frankly she couldn't face the added weight or bulk, just when she was trying to shed her headache, and Hayman because he said he never did unless conditions indicated it advisable. As it was, while she was wearing denim cut-offs and a cotton T-shirt, he had on a long-sleeved sweatshirt and was sporting a blue bandanna around his neck, and Grace figured that a PFD would probably have made him boil.

'We have to make sure the boat's pointed into the wind,' Hayman called out to her, explaining as he went, 'so the sails don't fill when we raise them.'

'Otherwise we'll take off before you want us to,' Grace said. 'Sure you don't want me to lend a hand?'

He shook his head. 'I told you, I'm used to sailing solo and I could use the exercise.'

'You look pretty fit to me.'

'You don't look so bad yourself.'

Grace was already feeling the first signs of what she and Claudia called vacationitis – the careless, floating, limitless sensation that Grace sometimes found glorious, other times irritating – pushing its way through the fatigue clouds and injecting its own cottonwool layers into her brain.

'Sorry I can't concentrate on you for a while,' Hayman called.

'I'm happy as I am,' Grace assured him.

'Soon as we're on course, I'll fix us both a drink.'

'Take your time,' she said. 'I'm not going anywhere.'

Sam was still on the South Dixie Highway when he made the decision to call Martinez. Cellular to cellular, just in case.

287

He answered after one ring.

'Where the hell are you?'

'Al, are you home or in the office? If you're in the office, don't let on that it's me.'

'It's okay, I'm home alone. What's up? The cap and Maria have called me twice. Why aren't you answering your pager?'

Sam tucked the phone under his chin and kept his eyes on the road.

'I need you to do something for me, Al.'

'What's going on?' Martinez demanded. 'What's the big secret? You in some kind of trouble, Sam?'

'Not yet. Will you do this for me? It's nothing heavy – I just need you to chase down some people who think Sundays are rest-days and persuade them to open up their computer records for you.'

'Unofficially, I take it?'

'For now,' Sam said, and got right to the point. 'I need someone – anyone – who can check a shrink's background. Try the American Psychiatric Association in DC, or maybe someone at Miami General or one of the private hospitals—'

'What shrink?' Martinez sounded startled. 'Not Doc Lucca?'

'Name of Peter Hayman, lives on Key Largo,' Sam said. 'Used to work over St Petersburg way or thereabouts.' He paused. 'And I need you to call Angie Carlino at home in Tampa, tell her that the stuff I told her could wait till Monday suddenly got real urgent.'

'She's gonna understand that, is she?'

'She'll understand. Tell her especially the no-show shootings, okay?'

'What shootings?'

'Just tell her, Al, okay?' The old guy moseying along at around twenty mph ahead of him was starting to drive Sam nuts, and he hit his horn hard.

'What car you driving?' Martinez asked. 'Where you going, man?'

'No place you need to know about,' Sam evaded.

'I'm not going to tell Hernandez,' Martinez said.

'I don't want to put you in a bad place, Al,' Sam told him. 'Just do what you can and get whatever you find to me in the next hour or so – even if there's nothing, Al – *especially* if there's nothing.'

The air-conditioner in the unmarked white Chevrolet Lumina – the car that Sam had no business driving on unofficial business – was working at full blast along with his mind and heart-beat as he drove through Goulds, passing the turn-off to the Monkey Jungle. He had Pavarotti singing *La donna è mobile* on the radio, and he'd tried doing what he usually did, namely singing along with him, his baritone underpinning the great man's tenor, but this afternoon it just wasn't working for him.

He'd turned off both his pager and radio after the call to Martinez – knew he'd done the unpardonable, but Sam was running on pure, high-octane intuition now, and he was pretty sure he was going to live to regret it, but there wasn't a damned thing he was prepared to do about it. His cell-phone had rung twice in the past ten minutes, and both times Sam had glanced down to check the caller ID in case it was either Grace or Martinez, but once he'd recognized it as a departmental number – probably Hernandez trying to catch him off-guard – and the next time it had been his mother. He'd answered neither call, and the automated message service had cut in for him.

He'd worry about the flak when today was over – when he'd quit worrying about Grace's safety.

That was quite an admission, if he paused to think about it. Sam Becket had always known where his priorities lay till now: David's, Judy's and Saul's health and safety aside – and in the old days, of course, Althea's and Sampson's – work had always come first.

Grace Lucca was not family. They had liked and respected each other, Sam reflected, almost from the get-go, their mutual concern over Cathy Robbins bringing them closer. They'd become comfortable with each other – *real* comfortable and easy. And then they'd made amazing love up on his roof – just that one time – and even *that* had been interrupted by his damned pager. On the surface, their relationship was hardly established enough to make Sam take the kind of risks with his career that he was running this afternoon. If Hernandez or the chief found out what he was up to, they'd probably have his head first, then his badge, and ask questions later.

Questions.

There were a whole lot of questions Sam might well be asking himself. Like what were the exact ingredients for this giant mess he was cooking up in his brain, and on what grounds was he breaching regulations and going off half cocked into who knew what situation?

Peter Hayman's old records hadn't jumped right into Angie Carlino's lap on a Saturday afternoon – which might or might not mean that the man had materialized out of nowhere on Key Largo just a handful of years ago, just the right kind of decent time lapse after John Broderick had disappeared.

A double shooting that Hayman had talked about happening in St Petersburg had also failed to show up – which might or might not mean that it had never happened. And if it had *not*, that might or might not mean that Hayman had invented it, maybe just to open up a channel of communication with Grace.

Anna Valdez had been stabbed to death with a scalpel in a doctor's office, which might mean zip in this context, or might mean a whole lot, or might even, at a pinch, mean the whole damn schmear.

Grace had arrived at a hotel on Key Largo to find she had no reservation, and had apparently therefore gone to stay with Hayman. She was, according to her host, feeling unwell, and had, also according to him, previously injured herself, albeit in a minor way. She had, since then, failed to respond to a message left with Hayman, and they had both now, if the unanswered telephone was anything to go by, apparently left Hayman's home.

It wasn't much to go on, Sam reminded himself as he reached the Overseas Highway and drove through a lovely cluster of white butterflies as fast as he could without tearing them apart or getting stopped for speeding by the highway patrol. For one thing, Grace had given him no indication of what Hayman looked like – for all Sam knew, he could be Chinese or eight feet tall – and as he'd already reminded himself, surely if he bore a resemblance to John Broderick's photograph, Grace would have noticed.

Or maybe she had noticed by now.
And maybe that was why she had not called him back.
Maybe she couldn't.

CHAPTER FIFTY-ONE

The queasiness was back, and the headache, too. They were out on the open sea now and the wind was rising and some bad-looking clouds were gathering, and suddenly Grace wasn't so sure after all if this was the right afternoon to be out on the ocean, especially feeling the way she was.

She said as much to Hayman.

'Weather looks okay to me,' he said.

'It's getting bumpy.'

'There's maybe a little more movement than before, but it's nothing to worry about.'

He looked the opposite of how she felt, his cheeks warmed by sun, wind and exertion, facial muscles relaxed, body movements easy. Just looking at him made her feel envious. Worse.

'I'm sorry,' she said. 'You should have left me on dry land.'

'You know there was no way I would have done that.' He glanced at her face, checking her over again. 'Just give it a little more time, Grace, and I guarantee you'll be feeling better.'

'What if I'm not?' Her optimism seemed to have vanished along with the temporary cottonwool euphoria that had set in when they'd started out.

'You will.'

There was a tinge of hearty authority – almost of gently couched dictatorship – in those words that made Grace wonder if she was maybe dealing with a control figure. She felt her hackles rising, but suppressed the urge to snap back. She did not, after all, want to fall out with Peter Hayman, especially not when he was all that was standing between her and an increasingly rocky Atlantic.

'I'll give it another half-hour or so,' she compromised, 'but if I still feel lousy, or if the weather gets worse, I'm going to want to go back.'

'No problem.'

Hayman's smile was beginning to have a patronizing tilt to it.

'Peter, I mean it.'

'Grace, so do I,' he said.

He was still smiling.

Sam located Hayman's house easily enough, heard the ship's bell clang several times, then stepped up on to the porch and began to follow it around the house, climbing over rails where they got in his way.

'Watcha doin', mister?'

He turned around slowly, saw a craggily handsome man of about sixty, dressed in a short-sleeved Polo shirt and slacks, staring accusingly up at him from the road.

'Looking for Dr Hayman,' Sam said.

'He's not in.' The man had steel grey hair and piercing eyes to match.

'Do you know where he's gone?'

'Depends who wants to know,' the man said.

Sam was beginning to feel he'd landed in the deep South. Any second now, he half expected the man to pull a shotgun on him and order him off the doctor's land. He thought about showing his badge, but he wanted to avoid that if he possibly could.

'My name's Sam Becket, and I'm actually looking for Dr Lucca, the woman who's been staying with Hayman.'

The man nodded. 'Pretty woman.'

'Do you happen to know where they went?'

'Sailing.'

Broderick flashed through Sam's mind again.

'Sailing where?' he asked.

'I don't know.'

'Then how do you know they went sailing?'

'It's what he does most weekends.' The cold eyes narrowed again. 'You ask a lot of questions.'

293

Sam turned towards the closest steps back down to the road. 'Does Hayman have his own boat?'

'He does.'

'Do you know where he keeps it?'

'I might.'

Sam wasted no more time. He showed the man his badge. 'Do you know where Dr Hayman keeps his boat, sir?'

'Dooley's Marina.' The change in attitude was half-hearted.

'Where might I find that?'

The guy gave directions, his voice clipped.

'Do you know the name of the boat, sir?'

'No, I don't.'

'Do you know anyone around here who might know?' Sam asked.

'People around here mind their own business,' the man said.

Sam's cellular rang just as the marina came into view – the caller ID displayed Martinez's home phone. Sam answered.

'What do you have, Al?'

'Zilch so far,' Martinez answered. 'You said you wanted to know even if nothing was showing up, and so far I got nothing on Hayman except what you already know, like he's listed in Key Largo with fancy letters after his name.'

'Did you reach Angie?' Sam asked.

'Yeah, I reached her, and she called me back five minutes ago. She says she needs more time, and she can't do much before tomorrow, but everyplace she's looked she still can't find anything about those shootings.'

'Okay, Al,' Sam said. 'Thanks.'

'So what now?' Martinez asked. 'You coming home or what?'

'I don't know.'

'Where are you, man? What's going on?'

Sam heard the anxiety in his partner's voice, and the temptation to share the situation with him was intense, but he knew he'd be doing Martinez more favours by keeping quiet.

'Better you don't know, Al,' he said. 'Like I said before, I don't want to put you in a bad place. Okay?'

He cut off the call before the other man answered.

CHAPTER FIFTY-TWO

'It's no good, Peter – I'm feeling worse, not better, and this swell isn't helping one little bit.'

Grace was standing a couple of feet away from where Hayman still appeared to be having a great time steering the boat through the rising waves, while she hung on to a guardrail on the gunwale and told herself she was *not* going to throw up under any circumstances.

'Peter, I'd like us to turn back.'

'Not much sense in that,' he said, looking right ahead.

'There's *perfect* sense in it,' she said, getting ready for a fight she wasn't at all sure she had the strength left for.

'I mean there's no sense going back when we're not that far out from Long Key,' Hayman pointed out. 'We could put in there for a while if you like – give you a break till the weather passes. Or I can give you something for seasickness – I have something that works pretty fast.'

'But I don't think this is seasickness,' Grace said. 'I've hardly ever suffered from it – and anyway, this started on dry land, didn't it?'

'The medication I have works on nausea in general,' he said.

Grace didn't answer. She was too busy remembering exactly when the queasiness and headache had started. Soon after she had cut herself on the glass – the glass that had felt oily when she'd taken it, which was why she'd dropped it and broken it. Soon after Hayman had gone to stop her picking up a jagged fragment and had inadvertently closed her hand on the shard.

Inadvertently?

And then he'd fixed the wound for her.

He'd covered it with antiseptic-impregnated gauze.

At least that was what he'd *said* it was.

The boat rocked, and Grace shut her eyes and held on harder to the guardrail. It was getting more difficult to think straight, to keep her thought processes going along cleanly, sensibly.

Where exactly were these processes heading? What precisely was she thinking *about*?

She was thinking about the brief, but shocking, bout of suspicion she had experienced that morning after Hayman had talked about Broderick slipping cannabis into Cathy's vitamin capsules. She'd told herself that she'd been imagining things, over-reacting, but suddenly she wondered if that was true. Which was making her think back again to the fact that he'd come into the guest bedroom – *her* bedroom – in the middle of the night and stood right up close to the bed, and then, next morning, he'd told her that odd little lie about hearing her crying out. That *had* been a lie – she was suddenly certain that it had been.

'Grace, I'm going below.'

She opened her eyes.

'We're all steady.' Hayman's expression was concerned. 'I'm just going to get that stuff to help you feel better. Okay?'

Grace didn't answer. She was still thinking.

The photograph.

She had remembered the photograph tucked inside the address book in her tote bag. She wanted to look at it. She needed to look at it, just to reassure herself that there was no way on God's earth or ocean that Peter Hayman could be John Broderick.

'Grace?' His voice jolted her.

'I'm sorry,' she said.

'It's okay,' he said, gently. 'I just wanted to check you heard me. I'm going below to fetch some of the medication I told you about – I'm going to take care of you.'

'Okay,' she said, sounding vague. 'Thank you.'

It was an effort to speak normally, but then again if she sounded strange Hayman was only going to think it was because she felt so bad – and maybe, Grace hoped, that *was* part of it. Maybe all these wild thoughts were crowding in on her because she was sick.

Except what if she *wasn't* just sick in a normal, natural sense? What if it hadn't been antiseptic in that gauze, soaking into the gash on her hand?

A new thought struck. What if Hayman had found the photograph in her bag? What if he thought she'd recognized or at least suspected him?

But it had been Hayman who had first asked her if she'd ever seen a picture of Broderick, he who'd suggested she get one.

Or had he just been on a fishing expedition, checking to be sure she hadn't made a connection.

I'm going to take care of you.

Grace watched his back, watched him open the hatch that led below and disappear through it.

He's great with boats, really at home.

Broderick had kept a boat. Had died on a boat.

Or not.

Grace ripped the sticking plaster off her palm, took off the gauze, held it up to her nose and sniffed at it. She could smell something, but she didn't know what it was – it might have been antiseptic, it might have been some chemical, poison even, something that could have entered her bloodstream, triggered a reaction, made her feel this way ...

Wasn't that just the kind of thing Broderick would have done?

'Oh, Christ,' she said, out loud.

She moved as fast as her unwieldy limbs would let her – not as fast as she wanted to move, not *nearly* as fast – it was the way one sometimes felt in bad dreams, the common dreams that some of her young patients had, in which they wanted to run but their legs felt leaden.

Still, she made it, over to the side, and if Hayman came up and saw her, Grace thought he'd probably assume she was about to throw up, but that wasn't what she was doing. She stuffed the gauze into the right-hand pocket of her jeans, waited for the next wave to rock the boat so that she could lean closer to the water—

297

There ...

The boat heeled about seventy-five degrees, enough for her to dunk her injured hand into the salt water.

It hurt.

Better than being poisoned.

Grace felt the small but fiery pain burn through her palm.

One thought, now, was going through her mind, repeating itself over and over again. It was short and to the point.

Why the *hell* had she agreed to come on Hayman's damned boat?

How the hell could she – a supposedly intelligent woman – have been so utterly and completely *stupid*?

CHAPTER FIFTY-THREE

Sam was still ignoring the small – not *so* small – warning voice that kept reminding him he was way out of his jurisdiction and that he ought, by rights, to be handing this over to the Monroe County Sheriff's department. To begin with, he told the voice, he didn't know what the hell he was supposed to *be* handing over to them, and to end with, rational men and women as he presumed they were, they were hardly likely to raise their blood pressure over what was little more than a probably ill-founded hunch.

He'd found Dooley's Marina, found a middle-aged bald guy cleaning a boat who'd said he knew Peter Hayman and his boat, the *Snowbird*.

'Took her out a while back.' Stripped to the waist and well-muscled, the guy had gone on scrubbing the deck.

'Was he with anyone?'

'A woman.'

'What'd she look like?'

'Didn't much notice. Blonde.'

Good enough.

'Is this your boat?' Sam had taken a better look at the runabout – name of *Delia* – with its Yamaha outboard motor and back-to-back seats.

The man had looked up for the first time, with pale eyes. 'Why?'

'I need you to take me out.'

'I'm not for rent.'

'I'm not renting,' Sam had said.

'Take a hike.' The man had gone back to work.

299

Which was when Sam had dumped every rule in the book, gotten on board the *Delia* and pulled out his badge for the second time.

'Police business, sir,' he'd said. 'I really need your help.'

The man had dropped his scrubbing brush and given Sam his attention. 'I thought you guys had your own boats?'

'No time,' Sam had told him. 'This is an emergency.'

The pale eyes had started calculating. 'It's going to cost me.'

'You'll be reimbursed.'

'You're a Miami Beach cop – you sure they'll pick up the tab down here?'

'Same state.' *Not exactly a lie.* 'You'll get your money.'

'You want to go after the *Snowbird*?'

'You got it.'

'It's a big ocean, man.'

'You saw which way Hayman was headed, didn't you?'

'Only so many ways out of here – they could have gone anyplace after that.' The boat-owner looked up at the sky. 'Mind you, there's weather coming in, so he'll probably be sticking close to land.'

Unwilling to waste another second, Sam had stopped to pull the runabout closer to the dock and stepped on board. The bald man had opened his mouth to protest, then remembered either the badge or what he might possibly get out of the situation.

'Suppose it won't hurt to help the law.'

'The law'll be very grateful.'

The man had stowed his scrubbing brush and bucket, then turned back to Sam and held out his hand. 'Name's Kuntz. Phil Kuntz.'

Sam had gripped the hand firmly. 'Sam Becket.'

'Detective, huh?' Kuntz had moved towards the controls.

'We need to get going, skipper.' Sam was no sailor, but he knew enough to untie the lines tethering the boat to dry land.

'Just make yourself at home, why don't you?' Kuntz was ironic.

'Just trying to help.'

'How grateful is grateful exactly?'

'More grateful if you get us moving fast.'

Kuntz had looked up at the sky again. 'I don't like the look of this weather.'

300

'All the more reason to move fast,' Sam said.

The pale eyes had veered back to Sam's face. 'This isn't going to turn into a heavy situation, is it, detective?'

'No way,' Sam had assured him. 'All I need is to find *Snowbird* and speak to the woman with Hayman. Okay with you, skipper?'

'I guess.'

They were out on open water now, bouncing over increasingly choppy waves, and Sam was grateful that the occasional queasiness that had made him the butt of certain medical examiners' jokes had never extended to seasickness.

'This gets much worse,' Kuntz told him, 'I'm going to take her in.'

'Not until we have to,' Sam said.

'Can you see any other boats this size, detective?'

Sam looked around. 'No.'

'That's because most people got more sense than to stay out with a storm blowing in.'

John Broderick's actions of nine years ago came back into Sam's mind.

'We could use the radio,' Kuntz suggested, 'to track the *Snowbird*. I got a handheld VHF, got a range about five miles. We could ask other boats to look out for her?'

'Not a good idea,' Sam said.

'Why not?'

'Because Hayman might hear us.'

The pale eyes grew suspicious. 'Thought you said this wasn't going to turn heavy?'

'It isn't,' Sam said, easily. 'I just think Hayman might not want me to find him, that's all.'

'Who's the woman?'

'A friend.'

Another wary glance, not exactly condemning but definitely an arched eyebrow kind of disapproval. If he and Grace had any kind of a future together, Sam knew they were going to have to get used to looks like that.

'Can you take the wheel a second?' Kuntz asked.

'If you trust me,' Sam said.

'Just hold her steady.' Kuntz got up, reached into a small

storage compartment, pulled on a T-shirt and white baseball cap, then took the wheel back. 'It's getting cool.'

'A little,' Sam said.

'Hayman been treading on your toes?' Kuntz asked.

'Nothing like that,' Sam said.

'Over to the east,' the other man said, suddenly.

Sam turned his head and saw white sails on the horizon. 'Think that's her?' His heartbeat quickened.

'Could be – too far to tell.' The boat turned, and a big wave rocked them. 'Hold on, man.'

Sam didn't need telling – he was grabbing on to the side and trying to keep his eyes fixed on the sailboat. 'Do you have binoculars?'

'In the cubbyhole aft.'

Sam got off his seat and moved carefully to the back of the boat, found the cubbyhole and binoculars and lurched back.

'See anything?' Kuntz asked.

'Not yet.' He could see the boat more clearly now, enough to see its blue trim and a distant figure on deck, fighting with the sails, but he couldn't see the name on the boat and he couldn't see anyone who might be Grace, and he still didn't know what Hayman looked like.

He felt and heard the engine note change.

'Why're we slowing down?'

'It's not the *Snowbird*.'

'Are you sure?' Sam kept looking through the binoculars.

'Sure.' Kuntz slowed them right down. 'Listen, man, I don't like being out in this weather, and I don't like that you won't let me use the VHF.'

'I didn't say you shouldn't use it,' Sam said, 'just that I don't particularly want to alert Hayman to the fact that we're looking for him.'

'I don't like the sound of that either.'

'You want to help or not?' Sam asked.

'Not as much as I did.'

Through the glasses, Sam saw that the boat they'd been chasing was called *Lady Blue*. He bit down on his disappointment, and turned his head slowly, checking for more possible sightings.

'I'm going to switch on Weather One,' Kuntz said. 'Okay?'

302

'Sure,' Sam said.

'I still think the working channels are our best bet for finding *Snowbird*.'

Sam thought for a moment. 'If we haven't spotted them in ten to fifteen, we'll try it your way.'

'If the weather warnings tell us to take *Delia* in, we may not have another fifteen minutes,' Kuntz told him.

'Just keep us moving, skipper,' Sam said.

'So long as you remember this is going to cost you, man.'

'I'll remember,' Sam said. 'Especially if you find them.'

CHAPTER FIFTY-FOUR

Grace didn't know what he'd been doing down below, but by the time Hayman came back up, she'd had time to get a good minute's worth of salty ocean water into the cut on her palm, had dried it off and stuck back the plaster as well as she could manage.

'How're you doing?' he asked.

'Not bad,' she said. It was almost the truth – the sting of the sea water had cleared away a little of the fuzziness in her head.

'You got more colour in your cheeks.' He came up to Grace, put his right hand up to her forehead, and she flinched. 'It's okay,' he said. 'Just making sure you're not running a fever.'

'I think maybe I am.' She moved out of his reach, trying not to be too obvious about wanting to keep her distance from him. 'I really think I need to get on shore as soon as possible – Long Key sounds good – anyplace I can rest for a while, maybe find a doctor.'

'I don't know if finding a doctor's going to be all that easy,' Hayman said. 'But since you have one right here, that's not such a predicament.'

The boat rocked and rolled and Grace grabbed on to the rail closest to her, but Hayman stayed almost steady on his feet.

'Forget the doctor,' she told him, shakily, 'but if you don't get me back on dry land soon, I'm going to get real sick.'

'You're going to be fine, Grace.'

He held up his left hand, and she saw that he was holding a hypodermic syringe. Her heart began to race. 'If that's what you have in mind for my nausea' – she struggled to keep sounding at least reasonably light – 'I'll do without.'

'Don't tell me you have a thing about needles,' he said.

'I'm not crazy about them – especially when I don't know exactly what's in them.' She wanted to move away, but the waves were hitting the boat so hard that she didn't dare let go of the rail. 'Do you always keep a loaded hypodermic around, Peter?'

'I'm a psychiatrist, remember?' He was gentle, calm. 'Fully qualified to administer medication – and this is hardly the first time I've had a seasick passenger on board.'

'I told you, I'm not seasick.'

'It doesn't matter what's causing the nausea, Grace,' Hayman told her. 'This stuff is fabulous – one little shot and you'll be feeling better in next to no time.'

The boat pitched hard, and even Hayman stumbled backwards. The wind was starting to whistle in a way that would probably, under other circumstances, have unnerved Grace, and the sky was growing meanly black, yet right there and then she was grateful for the diversion.

'Forget my nausea, Peter, and do something about the sails.' She had to raise her voice over the strengthening wind. 'And I really think we should be heading into shore.'

The *Snowbird* rolled again, badly, but Hayman was back upright, leaning on the rail close to Grace. He transferred the hypodermic to his right hand and raised it in front of his face.

'Peter, what are you doing?'

'I'm just going to give you your shot, and then I can concentrate on riding out this wind.' He sprayed a little into the air.

'Peter, you're not *listening* – I don't want a shot.'

'Come on, Grace, don't be a baby.'

He reached for her arm, but Grace snatched it away and backed further up the side of the boat, still holding the rail for support, knowing she couldn't afford to fall. The wooziness was coming back again, and she was finding it harder to focus, physically and mentally. All she could see was Hayman coming closer and closer with the syringe in his hand, and the only thing she was sure of now was that she had to stop him sticking it in her.

'Is this what you did to Marie?'

The words were blurted before she had time to think about them. She didn't know which of them froze the fastest. Grace could hardly believe she'd *said* that. If he was Broderick, it was the craziest thing she could have asked him.

As for Hayman, his face seemed to go almost blank with confusion.

'What did you say?'

Grace's head was swimming, but there seemed to be no way back.

'I asked you if this is the way you gave Marie her injections.'

CHAPTER FIFTY-FIVE

'We're in luck,' Phil Kuntz yelled over the noise of the wind and ocean less than five minutes after Sam had given him the go-ahead to put out a radio call. 'There's been a sighting about two miles south of Long Key.'

'How far away is that?' Sam yelled back.

'About six, seven miles – but you're going to have to tell someone else to find the *Snowbird*.'

'What does *that* mean?'

'It means it's too far, which is why I'm going to take us into shore right now.'

'Six miles is *nothing*.'

'Six miles is more than enough to turn us over and drown our asses.' Kuntz was fighting with the wheel to keep the boat straight in the increasingly turbulent water. 'I'm sorry, man, but I don't want to lose my boat, never mind my own skin.'

'You're not going to lose your boat, Kuntz.'

'Can you guarantee that?'

'No, but I can give you five hundred bucks *and* take full responsibility for replacing the boat if the worst does happen.'

Kuntz stared at him. 'Is this you talking, or the Miami Beach Police Department or the Florida Marine Patrol or who?'

'This is me, Sam Becket.'

'You got that kind of money?'

'I can get it if I have to.'

The pale eyes looked suddenly amused. 'That blonde must be quite something, Becket.'

'Yes, she is,' Sam yelled, 'so can you just get this boat the fuck *moving* again so we can find her?'

Driving the *Delia* through the rising Atlantic was getting more and more like forcing a blunt knife through a gigantic, super-toughened pumpkin and getting buffeted and half-drowned into the bargain – but whether it was the promise of five hundred dollars and a new boat if this one foundered, or whether some sense of challenge was now filling Phil Kuntz's veins with fortitude, he seemed just as hellbent on reaching the *Snowbird* as Sam.

'There she is!' he bawled, a few minutes after he'd put on a life vest and thrown a second one to Sam.

'Where?' Sam followed the line of Kuntz's pointing hand. 'Is that it?'

'Has to be,' Kuntz told him. 'I don't see any other damnfool sailboats hanging around, do you?'

Sam dragged the binoculars hanging around his neck up to his eyes and tried frantically to focus. Pure white, dipping up and down wildly like a swan on speed, half disappearing every couple of minutes beneath the swell. Sam adjusted the focus so that details came more sharply into view – for the first time since coming on board Kuntz's boat, his stomach started to heave from the unnerving sensation of keeping the lenses trained on the right spot.

He saw the name.

'It's the *Snowbird*,' he shouted.

'Told you.' Kuntz glanced at him. 'What now?'

'Get closer so I can see what's going on.'

'What should be going on?'

Sam was too busy looking to answer. He could see a figure – it was a man – had to be Hayman ... He scanned around for Grace – there she was, looking tiny and fragile from this perspective ...

'Shit!' he cried out.

'What?' Kuntz stared at him. '*What*?'

'She's too close to the side!' Sam yelled.

'Probably just looks that way from this angle – she's probably just hanging on to the guardrail.'

Sam had the binoculars jammed so tightly against his face that the pressure was hurting his nose. 'I don't know – I can't tell—'

'Want to get closer?'

'I want to get close enough to get on *board*,' Sam said. He had Hayman in his sights again, trying to see if he looked like Broderick, but it was almost impossible to tell from this distance. He looked to be around the right height, but a lot lighter - which meant zip - but none of that mattered right now. What mattered was that it looked as if Hayman was almost on top of Grace.

Sam's heart had started pounding again, felt like it was hitting his ribcage as roughly as the waves were blasting against the sides of the *Delia*. 'Do you have a gun, Kuntz?'

'What?'

'Do you have a *gun*?'

Kuntz slowed the runaround right down. 'No, I do not have a gun.'

'How about one of those fishing harpoons?' Sam persisted. 'Anything that would do for a weapon?'

'Jesus Christ, man,' Kuntz protested. 'You promised this wasn't going to get heavy, and suddenly you want a goddamned *gun* - I don't have any fucking weapons on my boat, and if I did, I wouldn't let you have them—'

'I'm a police officer,' Sam shouted over the wind. 'If you have any kind of weapon on board you have to let me have it.'

'How about I turn us around and to hell with the *Snowbird*?'

'How about I make sure you lose this boat after all?' Sam bluffed.

'You told me you'd replace the boat if something happened to it!'

'Do you see any witnesses to that?'

'You're a lying bastard, Becket,' Kuntz shrieked, getting distraught.

'The woman on that boat is in big trouble - can't you *see* that?'

'Oh, for fuck's sake' - the skipper dragged the cap from his bald, perspiring head and flung it into the wind where it was whipped away in an instant - 'there's a goddamned flare gun in the other locker in the stern. But I don't know if it's in working order.'

'Where's the key to the locker?' Sam yelled, on his way.

'It's open, damn you!'

CHAPTER FIFTY-SIX

'I don't know what the hell you're talking about, Grace,' Hayman shouted as he came closer again, 'but you're really beginning to worry me.'

'I don't mean to worry you, Peter.' Her vision was blurring, but Grace could see enough to be sure the hypodermic was still in his right hand, and there was no way on God's earth that she was going to let him stick that in her without a fight. 'I just want you to get back to steering the boat so I can get on to dry land.'

'I'll get back to steering the boat,' he said, 'as soon as you've calmed down.'

'I'm calm,' Grace said, backing away. The wind whipped her hair across her face, lashing her cheeks.

'I don't understand what you said about Marie.' His glasses were wet, and he put up his left hand to wipe them. 'Marie who?'

'It doesn't matter.'

Hayman came at her suddenly, took hold of her right arm.

'No!' she yelled, trying to pull away.

'Come on, Grace.' Close up, his face looked concerned, his brown eyes perplexed, but he still held on to her arm. 'I have to do this – I have to calm you down. You're presenting a risk—'

'To *whom*?' She yanked her arm free. 'To you?'

'To us both – to this boat,' Hayman yelled. 'I have an obligation to keep my passengers under control.'

'Broderick was always big on control,' Grace yelled back.

'What does *Broderick* have to do with anything?' Hayman shouted.

'I think he has *everything* to do with it!'

She started to back away again, glancing around wildly. The boat was heaving back and forth, and she was still feeling dizzy and sick, but her need for self-preservation seemed to be keeping her upright.

'Grace, what are you talking about?'

She could see the hatch, thought about getting through that and maybe locking herself in below, but then she truly *would* be trapped, and maybe, if push came to shove, she'd sooner take her chances in the ocean – it had certainly worked for Broderick, if she was right about Hayman.

'Grace, what is *wrong* with you?'

'There was nothing wrong with me until I cut my hand this morning.'

'What does that mean?'

Now she knew for sure there was no going back. 'There was nothing wrong with me until you put that stuff on the cut.' Her back was up against the side of the boat again – she could feel the guardrail pressing into her spine.

Hayman still had that same confused expression on his face. 'Grace, what are you getting at? You sound like you think I did something to you.'

'Didn't you?' she demanded. The sickness had receded again – she thought maybe anger was keeping it at bay.

'I put antiseptic on your cut and covered it.' He shook his head. 'Is it throbbing, is that it? Maybe you are running a fever. Let me take another look at that hand.' He came towards her again.

'You stay away from me,' Grace said, sharply enough for him to stop dead in his tracks.

The boat heeled to the portside and for a moment or two they were both clinging to the rail. Hayman threw a look up at the sky.

'Looks like a thunderhead coming. I need to get the mainsail down.'

'Don't let me stop you – just keep the hell away from me.'

Grace knew she was talking wildly, maybe crazily – she knew she wasn't thinking straight – she *certainly* wasn't thinking the way a trained, practised psychologist was supposed to think, and for all she knew – all she could be *sure* of –

311

Hayman might even be right and the thing that had gotten into her system that morning – maybe it *was* an illness, some virus, she didn't know – maybe it was muddling her thoughts. And yet, how could she take the chance? The guy had a hypodermic syringe he wanted to plunge into her, and if he *was* Broderick, then that was likely to mean he was going to *kill* her ...

'I am going to keep away from you,' Hayman told her, keeping half an eye trained on the mainsail and jib. 'Why don't you go below, Grace?' Now he was talking like a psych nurse speaking to a deranged, dangerous patient. 'There's a bunk down there. Why don't you just try and rest until I get us ashore?'

'No, thank you.'

'Then at least sit over there.' He gestured to the cushioned seats.

'I prefer it here,' she told him. 'It's closer to the exit.'

'Grace, this is nuts,' Hayman protested. 'Even if we weren't in the middle of a gale, this is no place to go swimming.'

'I'm not going swimming – I'm just not taking orders.'

'I need to get the engine started and get those sails down.'

'I'm not stopping you doing anything, except giving me a shot.'

'Is this all because of the hypodermic?' he asked. 'Because if that's what's freaking you out, I'll throw the damned thing overboard.' He held it out carefully in front of him at thigh level, needle end facing the deck.

'Sure you will,' Grace said. 'It's evidence, isn't it?'

'Oh, God.' Realization hit Hayman at last. 'Oh, my *God*, you think I'm John Broderick, come back from the dead.'

'Except Broderick never died.'

Very carefully, Hayman slid the hypodermic into his right jeans pocket.

'I don't know what's put this nonsense into your head, Grace,' he said 'but as a colleague, I have to warn you that you're in danger of sounding seriously paranoid.'

'That's one of Broderick's specialities, isn't it?' she said. 'Making people look crazy.' She took a deep gulp of Atlantic air. 'How come you knew about Cathy getting the cannabis in vitamin capsules?'

'I didn't know,' Hayman said. 'I was just guessing.'

'I don't believe you.'

'Why not? You said the cannabis was ingested, and we knew how Marie was given the progestogen—' He stared at her. '*That's* what you meant before, wasn't it? You really think I'm Broderick.'

'Give me one good reason not to.'

'I could probably give you a thousand, given time.'

'Give me one piece of proof now,' she said.

The boat heeled again.

'I *have* to get those sails down, Grace, or we're going to get pushed right over on our side.'

'I told you,' she said, coldly, 'go right ahead.'

Hayman took a sideways step, then stopped as the boat steadied again. He took off his glasses, wiped his eyes – the expression in them was half amused, half angry. 'Grace, you have to know none of this makes any sense—'

'So prove you're not Broderick.'

'That's a little hard right now, wouldn't you agree?' He put the glasses back on. 'The photograph. You said you had a photo of him – do you have it here?'

'Don't you know the answer to that?' Grace asked. 'Didn't you take a look while you were creeping around my room last night?'

'I told you what happened last night!'

'You lied about hearing me cry out – I wasn't dreaming, and I didn't make a sound.'

'Okay,' Hayman said. 'So maybe I imagined hearing you – I just came in to see if you were okay.'

'I was perfectly okay, until I heard you come in.'

'Jesus,' Hayman said. 'Oh, Jesus, so *this* is really where all this has come from. Because I walked in on you while you were sleeping—'

'Let's say it didn't add to my trust.'

'Did you have doubts *before*?' Hayman looked incredulous. 'Not exactly.'

'Not exactly,' he repeated. 'What does *that* mean?'

'Let's say maybe I wasn't as comfortable with you as I might have been.'

'Not as comfortable.' He was angry now. 'So you – Dr

313

Grace Lucca, a so-called *psychologist* – made the leap from being less than perfectly comfortable with me to concluding I'm a killer come back from the dead!' He clapped a hand to his forehead. 'You think I murdered Cathy Robbins' parents and the therapist, and the aunt, too.' His face was contorted. 'And your boyfriend's father – you think I stabbed him too! *Jesus*!'

The wind, which had calmed for a few minutes, shrieked again, lashed at the *Snowbird*, making her pitch and groan.

'Why don't you deal with those sails?' Grace's fear was growing by the second – it was hard to know if she was more afraid of Hayman now or the maddened ocean.

'I am not going to deal with anything until you move away from the side of the boat.' He seemed to be struggling to hold on to his temper. 'I am not going to let *anything* happen to you.' He paused. 'I *swear* I'll prove I'm not Broderick, Grace, but you have to get away from the side so nothing will happen to you.'

Grace stared into his face, trying to see beyond the glasses covering his eyes again, trying to remember Broderick's features in the photograph and to superimpose them on to Hayman's.

'Why did you make it your business to find me at that convention?' she asked suddenly.

'I *told* you why!'

'Because you thought it might be Münchhausen's related?'

'That's right,' Hayman said.

'Except that weeks later, when I'd come to see that the only *truly* feasible suspect had to be Broderick, you said you'd changed your mind about a parent being responsible – that maybe it was Cathy herself who was guilty after all.'

'Because I could see you were in danger of becoming obsessed with proving her innocence. Because I was concerned you might have taken the wrong route through my suggestions. My *God*, Grace, if you only knew how far off the beam you are with this whole—'

'Or maybe you were just playing games with me.' Grace was breathing hard, hanging on tighter than ever.

'Get away from the side,' Hayman ordered, suddenly.

'Don't play your power games with me – I told you, I'm not moving.'

314

'This is bizarre, Grace. I want you away from the *side*.' His face dark with anger, he came at her again.

'Don't you lay a *hand* on me—'

The sound and sight of the flare stunned them both. They looked up and saw it curving neatly over their heads like the trail of a small red comet.

'What the *hell* was that?' Hayman had let go of Grace.

They both saw the runaround plunging towards them at the same time, and Grace knew instantly, almost before she saw him, that Sam was in that boat.

A second flare shot up from the *Delia*, skimmed their heads even more closely than the first.

'Jesus!' Hayman yelled. 'Who *is* that maniac?'

'It's Sam!' Grace yelled back, jubilantly.

Hayman took a step back, and suddenly she saw his right hand snaking into his jeans pocket, and she knew that he was going for the hypodermic again, knew that he was either going to stab it into her or throw it overboard.

'No *way!*' she yelled and grabbed at his hand.

'Grace, *stop* it!' He wrenched his hand away, then lunged at her – his left arm around her waist was strong. Grace heard chugging, and out of the corner of her eye she saw that the runaround was almost alongside the sailboat.

'*Grace!*' she heard Sam yell.

'Jesus, Becket' – another man shouted – 'you're out of your fucking *mind!*'

Both men were bawling over the noise of the storm – but Hayman was still holding Grace, and she couldn't turn around to see what was going on. The *Snowbird* heeled again, throwing them off their feet on to the deck, and for a moment or two Grace was winded, and she saw Hayman getting up again, but she couldn't seem to move. A loud thump jarred her, and when she started to sit up the *Delia* was banging into the side of the sailboat – and suddenly there was Sam, clambering over the guardrail, coming towards her.

'Grace, hang *on!*'

She heard the cracking first, as the mainsail ripped, and the mast split and wrenched, and then an awful groaning as the *Snowbird* reacted. She sounded like a great, living, wounded creature as she rolled and pitched.

'Oh, dear *God*!' Hayman yelled. 'She's going over!'

Everything broke loose, went wild. Grace knew she was in the water, knew she was under, and it was so black, and she was swallowing the ocean, and she knew she was going to drown, and the only things that went through her mind then were Sam, and then Claudia, and then Harry, in that order ...

And that was all.

CHAPTER FIFTY-SEVEN

'Oh, no, you don't.'

Grace came to to the sound of a strange voice and someone's hands pumping at her back to get the ocean out of her lungs – and then she was too busy retching and coughing to think about anything else.

'You're all right now,' the voice said.

The hands rolled her over. Grace stared up into pale, frightened eyes below a bald, domed head, and suddenly reality came back.

'Sam!'

'It's okay, Grace,' the bald man said, holding her down. 'I'm Phil Kuntz, and you're going to be all right.'

'Let me *go*,' she said as violently as she could, her voice still half choked.

He let her go and Grace sat up, saw she was on the deck of a small boat – the runaround that had rammed the *Snowbird*. 'Where's Sam?'

'He's in the water,' the man called Kuntz told her.

'What?' She struggled to her feet, and he helped her. '*Sam!*'

'He's trying to find the other guy,' Kuntz said.

Grace tore herself away from his hands and got to the side of the boat, and there was Sam, in the ocean, over to the left, treading water and gulping air.

'Sam!'

The *Delia* rocked wildly – for the first time, Grace noticed the *Snowbird* on her side a distance away over to the right.

'*Sam!*' she yelled at him. 'Get up here!'

He raised a hand, took another big gulp of air, and dived underwater.

'Oh, my God, what's he *doing*!' Grace turned to stare at Kuntz, saw that he was wearing a life vest, saw another on the seat behind him. 'Why don't you *do* something – *help* him? Why isn't Sam wearing a life vest?'

'Because your crazy boyfriend took the damned thing off so he could dive for Hayman.' Kuntz shook his head. 'Best way I can help now is stay on the *Delia* with you – if he finds the other guy, we can get the PFD back to him.' His pale eyes were fixed on the water. 'I've put out a Mayday – the Coast Guard should be here any time.'

Grace stared back at the water. There was no sign of Sam.

'Give me the vest.' She tried to grab at the second PFD. 'Give it to me – if you won't help him, I will!'

'No way, lady.' Kuntz took hold of the life vest with one hand and grabbed Grace around the waist with his spare arm. 'Not after your man went to so much trouble to save your hide.'

Sam came up, gasping for air.

'Sam, for God's sake,' Grace screamed at him over the wind, 'give it up!'

'She's right, man!' Kuntz yelled beside her. 'Get on the boat!'

Sam shook his head, and Grace saw him take another great gulp of air, and then he was arcing back into the water like a strong, dark seal, gone again, down into the depths.

'He's crazy,' Kuntz said. 'He's not going to find him now.'

'You have to *do* something!' Grace was crying.

'I told you, lady, there's help on the way.'

He was still gripping her around the waist, but Grace could feel her legs starting to give way, and she'd forgotten for those few minutes how bad she'd been feeling before, and what scraps of sense remained in her warned her that if she got back into the water she'd probably just end up needing to be rescued all over again ...

Sam reappeared. It was obvious from the way he was gasping, from the way every sinew on his neck was standing out, that it was getting harder.

'Sam, please give it up!' Grace begged, her voice cracking.

'I *can't*!' His own voice was hoarse and weak – it was a struggle to hear him. 'I can't just let the bastard drown!'

He was gulping air again – it was obvious he was getting ready to take another dive—

From somewhere, Grace heard the wail of a siren and a motor. She and Kuntz whirled around and saw the Coast Guard launch and a cluster of smaller boats all heading towards the *Delia* from one of the Keys.

'Sam, *look*!' Grace screamed. 'They're coming to help!'

'You can quit now, man,' Kuntz yelled.

'Not until I find him!' Sam took a final breath and dived again.

'*Sam!*'

'Come on, you guys!' Kuntz was yelling at the Coast Guard officers.

'You have to *help* him!' Grace screamed at them. 'He's down there!'

'Two overboard!' Kuntz shouted. 'One black, one white!'

The officers on board were getting their equipment on – Grace wondered why the hell they hadn't put it on before.

'The black guy's a cop!' Kuntz told them. 'Get him out first!'

Grace looked sideways at his ugly, bald head, and wanted to kiss him, and then she looked back at the Coast Guard launch, and the divers were already sitting on the edge, backs to the water, and then they did that back flip thing that professional divers always did and were gone from sight . . .

She didn't know if she held her breath or simply stopped breathing.

She thought later that if it had taken another few seconds, she might have passed out again from lack of oxygen if nothing else.

She saw one of the divers' heads emerge first.

'Oh, dear God,' Grace cried out and grabbed at Kuntz, dug her fingers into his right arm. 'Where's Sam? Where's *Sam*?'

'There!' Kuntz yelled.

'*Where*?'

'Over there – to the right!'

Grace whipped her head around so fast she felt dizzy enough to fall down – but there he was, looking exhausted, but there he *was*, and he was alive, and one of the divers had him around the chest and was towing him back to the big launch.

'Is he okay?' she shouted across the water.

No one answered her.

'Is he *okay*?' she screamed.

Sam raised a hand, gave a limp kind of a waving salute, and Grace knew it was for her and started crying again.

'I don't mean to be a killjoy, lady,' Kuntz said, on her left, and his voice was pretty shaky, too, 'but do you think you could get your nails out of my arm while I still have some skin left?'

The search for Hayman went on for several hours, they told Grace, long after she, Sam and Kuntz were back on dry land, getting taken care of and answering a few preliminary questions. But they didn't find him.

Sam came to see Grace in her room at Mariners Hospital on Plantation Key. She was too out of it to say anything much, and she wasn't sure that what she did manage to say made any sense. Sam didn't say too much either. Grace could tell, just by looking at him, that he felt the same about her being alive and in one piece as she did about him. But neither of them was in the mood for celebration.

A man was, in all likelihood, dead. Even if he was Broderick, escape-artist-supreme, there could, on this occasion, have been no escape, not with so many there on the scene, searching for him.

So he was, almost certainly, dead.

Because of Grace and Sam.

If he did turn out to be John Broderick, they probably would, in the fullness of time, remember that his death, second time around, was a good thing.

The other possibility was almost too unthinkable to endure.

Grace asked the question first, before Sam. She thought he might not have asked it, not that night, anyway, because of the effect he feared it would have on her.

But she did ask it. She had to.

'What if it wasn't him? What if he was just Peter Hayman?'

Sam said nothing, just held her hand tighter, but his eyes were tortured.

There was no answer to the question.

Or if there was, they were much too afraid to hear it.

320

CHAPTER FIFTY-EIGHT

THURSDAY, MAY 21, 1998

In the days following the capsizing of the *Snowbird*, nothing good had happened except, from Grace's standpoint, for having had Claudia by her side just about morning, noon and night. Hayman's body still had not been found; Sam was in considerable pain from having jarred his back during his rescue bid on the boat and was, additionally, in twenty-eight different kinds of trouble with the Miami Beach Police Department; and Grace had undergone every kind of test in the book – under David Becket's supervision – to try to ascertain what had started making her feel so bad halfway through Sunday morning, but nothing had showed up.

'Probably a virus,' they'd told her at Mariners Hospital.

'One of those things,' they'd said at Miami General after running the tests. Medical tests were something Grace generally did her level best to steer clear of, but in this instance she was so desperate to have her instincts proven at least *halfway* sound that she was prepared to put up with almost anything.

'Could have been a touch of the 'flu,' even David Becket had been forced to admit on one of his visits, 'probably compounded by the tension you were going through.'

'You mean I was imagining it,' she had said flatly.

'Nothing imaginary about the 'flu.'

'Then I was imagining being poisoned.'

'I wish I could argue with you there, Grace,' he'd said.

She knew no other doctor in the world could have meant that more than David Becket, knowing, as she did, what his son was currently up against.

*

Captain Hernandez and the chief *and*, worst of all, Internal Affairs had all gotten in on the act from day one, and Sam had been suspended, pending investigation, from day three. It was, according to him, hardly surprising, given the cumulative weight of his misdemeanours.

One: abandonment of his duty in Miami and going AWOL.

Two: use of his badge out of jurisdiction to involve a civilian, one Philip Kuntz, in a potentially dangerous situation.

Three: failure to report the situation to the Monroe County Sheriff.

Four: probable aggravation of an already lethally tense scenario on board the *Snowbird*. Result: the capsizing of the craft and, ultimately, the probable drowning of Dr Peter Hayman, a resident of Key Largo.

'And there could be more,' Sam told Grace over supper at her house on day four, the Thursday after the incident, 'depending on how badly Phil Kuntz feels towards me as time goes by.'

'Kuntz thought you were a hero,' Grace said. 'He told me he figured you were brave enough when you rescued me, but he thought you were borderline crazy when you went down for Hayman for the fourth time.'

'He may change his mind,' Sam said, grimly realistic. 'I bullied him into taking his boat out in bad weather. I offered him inducements. I threatened him when he didn't want me to use his flare gun.'

'You were afraid for me,' Grace pointed out miserably. 'The whole fiasco was my fault, Sam. I should never have let myself get into a situation I had doubts about from the start. I'm supposed to be a trained psychologist – I'm supposed to have a *brain* – but all I did was underreact before I got on the *Snowbird* and then overreact once I was on board.'

'The guy was coming at you with a hypodermic, Grace.'

'I know he was.' She shook her head. 'I know. And you thought I was in danger – which I guess I was—'

'Don't misunderstand me,' Sam said. 'Given it all to do again, I have a feeling I'd do most of it the same way.' He shook his head. 'Doesn't make it right in the eyes of my superiors.'

'Makes it right for me,' she said.

322

'That doesn't count,' he said.

The really crazy part of it was that no one was doing what seemed to Grace the most obvious thing to do: searching Peter Hayman's house. Sam shared her frustration, but understood better than she did the protocol governing the situation. Hayman's body had not been found. Nor had any family members been located. He had, as it turned out, written two published volumes on Münchhausen's Syndrome by proxy, and his Tampa-based publishers had cooperated fully, making Hayman's author questionnaire available to the Monroe County Sheriff. The psychiatrist's answers, succinctly given in black ink, indicated his single, childless status, and gave University of Washington in Seattle as his *alma mater*. Relatives were still being sought by the sheriff in all the accustomed ways. Everything else was, for the time being, on hold.

Grace and Sam had only come into possession of those few sparse facts courtesy of Al Martinez (who'd undertaken, off the record, to run his own check on Hayman's credentials in Seattle) and it was through Martinez also that they had received confirmation of what Sam had already anticipated: that until Hayman was officially recorded as dead or presumed dead, there was absolutely no good reason for the authorities to invade his privacy.

'Forget my suspicions,' Grace said to Sam, 'but what about yours? You're not just some cranky civilian – you're a *police* officer.'

'I'm on suspension, Grace,' Sam answered matter-of-factly. 'I broke the rules without a scrap of hard evidence to back me up.'

Under the surface, he was just as frustrated as Grace was – and *she* hadn't heard the words that Martinez had actually used. That the combined bullshit-rat-smellings of a neurotic head-shrinker and her screw up cop-lover were not grounds for a warrant to search a fucking paper *bag*, let alone an upstanding citizen's home.

They'd been over the events of the previous Sunday more than a dozen times and it always came out the same way for both Grace and Sam. Sam's job meant almost everything to him, but he still could not bring himself to regret having gone to help Grace out of what he'd felt certain had been a dangerous situation. Seeing her apparently struggling with a man he thought might be a killer, Sam had not felt he had any choice.

And there, of course, was the rub.

They didn't *know* if Hayman had been a killer.

They didn't know if he'd been anything more or less than he had claimed to be. A psychiatrist whose only *proven* misdemeanour to date was that he'd spooked Grace by coming into her bedroom in the early hours of Sunday morning.

The illness that had struck her so abruptly had passed almost as swiftly as it had come, and there was no way of accurately checking what might have been on the gauze Hayman had put on her cut, because it had been as soaked as the rest of her when Grace had taken her tumble into the ocean – and whatever might have been in the hypodermic syringe had been lost along with Hayman.

Grace had gone back and forth, with and without Sam, trawling her memory for worthwhile clues. Sam had reminded her that Broderick had made two botched suicide attempts before the supposed drowning by slitting his wrists and throat, and she'd struggled to recall seeing any signs of scarring on Hayman's neck or arms. She'd come to realize then that each time she'd seen him, Hayman had worn long-sleeved garments and had his neck covered, but even if that added a tad more weight to their personal suspicions of the man, as evidence it was probably *less* than circumstantial. In other words, unless Peter Hayman's body washed up comparatively soon, they wouldn't know if it bore any traces of scars that might correlate to Broderick's.

And Hayman – like Broderick before him – was still missing.

That was what could happen when a man got swept overboard in the ocean. That was what all kinds of people had pointed out to Grace when she had raised the question of Broderick's survival – and now, it seemed to her, she'd handed them their proof of that on a plate.

Any confusion Grace had been left with immediately following the capsizing of the *Snowbird* had now turned into a vast sense of guilt. If she had not reacted in that hysterical, unprofessional way ... if Sam had not seen her struggling with Hayman ...

All her suspicions – every *one* of them, it seemed to Grace now that she had time to reflect on them – had been purely circumstantial or even less. They might even have been entirely in her mind.

And the bottom line was that an innocent man – a decent man – might be dead because of her.

CHAPTER FIFTY-NINE

WEDNESDAY, MAY 27, 1998

Hayman had still not been found, dead or alive. Sam was still on suspension, able for the first time to give too damned much of his attention to S-BOP and his role in *Il Trovatore*.

Cathy was still in the Female House of Detention.

Grace had gone to see her just once. She'd found her listless and depressed, and had come away anguished at not having had one single crumb of comfort to offer her. The only fragment of halfway decent news was that David Becket had come good and had visited her twice since Sam had remembered to ask him to – and since the murder of Anna Valdez, Judy Becket had withdrawn her opposition to the visits.

Grace wished to high heaven that anyone had said that the Valdez case strengthened Cathy's position in any way, but they had not said that.

She wasn't sure if she could face seeing her again.

With Sam unable to get to his case files and loth to ask too much of Al Martinez, he had requested his father to ask his contact at Lafayette Hospital for another photograph of John Broderick. It arrived three days later on the last Wednesday in May, and Sam brought it directly to Grace's house together with the author photograph from the back flap of one of Peter Hayman's books.

Grace stared at them both for a long time.

'Anything?' Sam asked at last.

Her eyes were sore from staring. 'Not really.'

'We know the height's a match,' Sam said.

'But that's all that is,' Grace said.

They were so utterly different. Broderick was fair-haired, blue-eyed, round-faced – overweight – with a large nose and narrow lips. Hayman was a slim-built man with brown hair and eyes and a regular kind of nose and mouth. He could, of course, as they'd already discussed, have coloured his hair and worn tinted contacts. He could have radically altered his diet and the shape of his nose, mouth and face, but chances were they would only find out if Hayman had ever undergone plastic surgery if his body washed up – and if the ocean's greed held on to him long enough for his flesh to decompose or even fall away, the only thing the ME would be able to judge was whether or not any facial bones had been surgically interfered with.

'When you first saw Broderick's picture,' Sam reminded Grace, 'you thought there was something familiar about him.'

'I remember.'

'But you don't think now it was because of Hayman?'

'I don't know.' Grace felt frustrated enough to weep. 'I don't *know*.'

Sam reached out and stroked her cheek. 'Take it easy, Grace.'

For a moment, she didn't trust herself to speak.

'I started wondering,' Sam said, slowly, 'if we could maybe show Hayman's photograph to Cathy – but in the first place, I think it might be too heavy for her, and anyway, I don't think there's much point at this stage.'

'She was so young,' Grace said, 'when she last saw her father. If I thought there was some real hope of her recognizing Hayman, I think I'd consider taking the chance, but to be honest, it would take something close to a miracle for her to link that face with one she's done her best to forget.'

'Even if she did,' Sam said, 'in order for it to be admissible as an ID, I guess it would have to be organized in front of witnesses acceptable to the State Attorney, and that could be a no-win situation, If Cathy didn't recognize Hayman, she'd be back to square one, and if she did, the prosecution would claim she was just trying to save herself.'

Sam and Grace had previously played out one game, just between themselves, with a modicum of success. Sam had

327

brought Grace a gruesomely accurate timetable of when and where the scalpel killer had struck each time, and she had done what she could to see if what little she knew of Peter Hayman's movements might rule him out as a suspect.

It was, of course, much too little.

They knew that Marie and Arnold Robbins had been murdered in the early hours of Friday, April 3, and they knew that Beatrice Flager had been killed at around four a.m. on Wednesday, April 8 – all three deaths coming before Grace's first encounter with Hayman at the seminar at the Westin in Key Largo on Monday, April 13. They knew that Sam's father had been stabbed at his downtown Miami office one week later on April 20 – a matter of some eight hours or so after Grace had shared dinner with Hayman at his house. They were, of course, because of the killing of Anna Valdez, no longer certain if the same person had attacked David Becket as the other victims, but there was no question that Hayman could, theoretically, have driven to Miami in time to stab the doctor.

Frances Dean's death had occurred early on Tuesday, April 21, and Anna Valdez had died early on Sunday, May 17.

'While you were *with* Hayman at his house,' Sam had reminded Grace.

'But I wasn't with him all night,' she had pointed out. 'I know he came into my room just after two-thirty and was there for a few minutes. After that, I heard a door close somewhere—'

'But not the front door,' Sam had said.

'I don't know – just a door.'

'Did you hear a car?'

'I don't think I heard a car,' Grace had answered, 'but that doesn't mean Peter stayed home the rest of the night. Next time I saw him, he was making breakfast at around nine a.m.'

There were Cathy's journal entries to consider, too, those which Sam had found unconvincing from the moment he'd seen them. The first two entries had been created on Cathy's computer on March 31 and April 9 – both dates falling before Grace's first meeting with Hayman – and the final damning entry had been logged on Saturday, April 18, one day before Hayman had called to invite Grace down to Key Largo. Once again, there was nothing to rule him out, but neither was there anything clearly supporting the notion that he might have found a way to tamper with Cathy's computer.

The night after Grace and Sam had tried comparing the photographs, Martinez called Sam at home.

'Absolutely no record of any Peter Hayman at the University of Washington.'

Sam fought not to raise his hopes prematurely. 'Did you try births?'

'Births and marriages and high school records,' Martinez told him.

'And?'

'*Nada.*' Martinez paused. 'Nothing from any hospital in Seattle either. And Angie Carlino says no one by that name and description ever worked as a shrink in St Pete or any other city on the Florida west coast.'

'Ok*ay*,' Sam said.

'What does that mean?' Grace asked him later, after he'd told her the news. 'I mean, what can we really *do* with this non-information?'

'Not much, yet,' Sam answered. 'Except I think we can at least allow ourselves to believe that Hayman may not have been what he claimed to be – which maybe means we're not quite as guilty as we've been afraid we were.'

'It isn't very much, is it?' Grace said.

'Better than nothing,' Sam said.

Grace was back at work. She'd had a long telephone conversation with Dr Magda Shrike, the woman who had been her mentor at the University of Miami, but who had relocated to San Francisco a few years back. Grace was beginning to sense that she was on the brink of some kind of crisis of confidence, and what she needed was someone she trusted and respected to reassure her that it was reasonable and safe for her to go on looking after patients while struggling to come to terms with her own problems.

'Do *you* think it's safe?' Magda had asked.

Grace had known, of course, that was how it would go.

She'd toss her the ball, and Magda would toss it straight back, which was, no doubt about it, the right thing to do since it was Grace's damned ball.

'I think it is,' she had answered. 'Or maybe I just hope it is.'

'Isn't that all we ever do?' Magda had reminded her. 'We're not cardiac surgeons, Grace – our errors aren't as swift to rebound on us – or as lethal, thank God. Do we ever really know for sure how effectively we're doing our jobs?'

Grace had smiled into the phone. 'Is that your way of telling me it's all right for me to go back to work, Magda?'

'It's as close to that as you're going to get from me.'

Dora Rabinovitch had begun scheduling appointments again, and Grace had promised herself that if she developed any post-traumatic symptoms that might affect her judgment in the line of duty, she would think again, maybe even seek some counselling.

Dora was being supportive, and Claudia was calling daily to check that Grace was getting by. She and Sam were having quiet meals together regularly, but somehow neither of them seemed to feel it was right to continue where they'd left off that night after the S-BOP rehearsal, when his pager had snatched him away from her side.

Harry was Grace's most constant companion.

He didn't seem to care that it was still possible she might have caused the death of an innocent man.

CHAPTER SIXTY

MONDAY, JUNE 1, 1998

Things got worse before they got better.

On Monday afternoon, Al Martinez told Sam that there'd been another scalpel attack in a doctor's surgery up in Dania, and the familiar MO had got people thinking that maybe Dr Becket's attack needed a little fresh scrutiny. However, no one investigating the Dania attack or the Valdez killing in Miami had anywhere close to enough new evidence to lead to the charges against Cathy being dropped in the Becket stabbing. And even if that evidence were forthcoming, Martinez said, since the growing consensus of opinion was that all the surgery attacks were probably unconnected to the other scalpel killings, it wouldn't really help Cathy at all.

On Tuesday afternoon, they buried Frances Dean close to her sister and brother-in-law's recently filled graves in the Our Lady of Mercy cemetery in SW Miami. When Cathy had stood at the graveside on that other wet, humid afternoon, a newly charged juvenile, she had been in handcuffs. This time, she was in shackles. At her parents' funeral, there had, at least, been one friend present. This time, there was no sign of Jill or any other young friend of Cathy's.

Grace was there for her, standing some distance away from Sam and Martinez, and her heart warmed just a scrap to see both David *and* Judy Becket in the small gathering. Grace wanted to get close to the grieving, haunted looking teenager, but was not permitted, and the only one allowed in touching distance was Jerry Wagner who, Grace noted gratefully, was gripping his client's arm in support and murmuring to her every now and again, presumably to help her get through.

331

Try as they all might, Grace and Sam and even Martinez agreed later over a Jack Daniel's or three – Martinez being off-duty – it had been impossible to give proper attention to the service, or the memory of Frances Dean, or even to Cathy's feelings.

The only real point of focus for all of them, from start to finish, had been those bands of iron chaining her ankles together.

On Thursday afternoon, Cathy told a guard in the laundry room that she had bad menstrual pains and needed to go lie down. She was asked if she needed to go to the infirmary, but she said that all she thought she needed was fifteen to twenty minutes' rest. They let her go.

Thirty-five minutes later Cathy was declared missing. Ten minutes after that, two other guards found her in the shower block hanging by her twisted up and knotted uniform jumpsuit from a shower head. She was alive and semi-conscious. Aside from some localized bruising to her neck and throat, no significant damage appeared to have been done.

It was Eric Parés, the facility's physician, who telephoned Grace on Thursday evening to notify her.

'Cathy's at Miami General, Dr Lucca. Physically she's okay, but they're keeping her in for a seventy-two-hour hold.'

'Will they let me see her?' Grace's heart was pounding.

'Do you know Dr Rajiv Khan, the psychiatrist?' Parés asked.

'Only slightly.' Grace thought she remembered Khan, a short, slim man with warm, sad eyes and a kind smile. 'Is he taking care of Cathy?'

'I told him about your relationship with the girl. Dr Khan says he'll be glad to speak to you with a view to your going to visit Cathy tomorrow – if you have the time.'

'Have you seen her?' Grace asked Parés.

'Very briefly,' he said. 'She was quiet, depressed ... much as I'd expected.' He paused. 'I didn't feel she regretted too much having been saved.'

'Thank you, doctor,' Grace said.

'I've done nothing,' Parés said.

'It was kind of you to tell me that.'

332

'I think I know a little of how you must be feeling, Dr Lucca. I, too, feel I've let Cathy down badly.'

Grace met with Rajiv Khan outside Cathy's locked ward on Friday afternoon. He was just the way she'd remembered him. His eyes were as sad as ever.

'It doesn't take a genius,' he said, 'to imagine why she wanted to die.'

'Do you think she really meant to?' Grace was feeling nauseous again, but on this occasion she knew it was down to the almost paralysing dread of the moment when she was going to have to face Cathy.

'I'm afraid so,' Dr Khan said. 'Cathy told me that she decided on Tuesday evening, after her aunt's funeral, that she couldn't endure any more pain, and that no jury was ever going to believe she was innocent.'

'Dr Parés thought she wasn't too angry about having been saved.'

'I think that's a fair analysis,' Khan agreed. 'I had the impression that Cathy knew there was a chance it might not work out first time.'

Grace felt the proverbial goose creeping over her grave. 'First time.'

'Indeed,' Khan said. 'I have to say that on the surface at least, Cathy seems to be thinking quite clearly and logically. She said this morning that she thought maybe the fact that she hadn't died, might mean it was worth holding on a while longer.'

'Until the next time she decides she can't bear it,' Grace said, softly.

'Indeed,' Khan said again. 'Eric Parés seems a caring man.'

'Thank God he is,' Grace paused. 'Do you believe Cathy?'

'With regard to not trying another suicide bid for the time being?'

'Yes.'

'She seemed sincere at the time.' Khan knew better than to commit himself.

'Any feelings about her general mental state?' Grace asked.

He gave the kind, sweet smile she'd remembered. 'I've known her for less than twenty-four hours, Dr Lucca, but

Cathy certainly strikes me as perfectly sane.' He shook his head. 'My greatest concern is that she waited this long before screaming for help.'

'Cathy's a remarkably strong person,' Grace said.

'No one's strong enough to completely withstand what she's been going through.'

'You feel she's innocent, too, don't you, Dr Khan?'

Rajiv Khan's smile turned as sad as his eyes. 'I'm not on the jury, Dr Lucca,' he reminded her.

The bruises on Cathy's neck were vivid and shocking against the terrible whiteness of her skin, and her hair was greasy and fastened away from her face with kirby grips. Grace realized something else that was shocking as she walked towards the bed, steadying herself for the encounter. She didn't feel like Cathy's psychologist as she approached. She didn't feel at all the way she was *supposed* to be feeling. She felt like someone who cared far more deeply than that about her. Too deeply. Like an intimate friend or relative. Maybe even like a mother.

Bad news, Lucca.

Grace resisted the impulse to kiss Cathy, or even smooth her hair.

'Hello, Cathy.'

The blue eyes filled with tears.

'I'm sorry, Grace.' Her voice was husky.

'Me, too.'

Grace sat down on the hard plastic chair beside the bed and watched Cathy's mouth work for a moment or two as she fought to bring herself under control. Grace wanted to tell her to let it go, but instead, for now, she let her do it her way.

'I know I let you down,' Cathy said when she was ready.

'Me, too,' Grace said for the second time.

'I really am sorry, Grace.'

There was a glucose drip into Cathy's left arm, so Grace guessed she hadn't eaten, perhaps because of her bruised throat – or maybe she just didn't *want* to eat. She wanted to hold Cathy's right hand, but for an instant or two she wavered, as if contemplating an impropriety, and then Grace realized she had, of course, held the hands of countless chil-

334

dren and young people during sessions.

She reached for Cathy's hand now. It felt very cold.

'I'm just glad you're alive,' she told her. Her voice sounded shaky, but there was nothing she could do about that.

'Why are you glad?' Cathy asked.

'Why would you ask me that?' *That's more like it, Lucca – get back into your role, hide behind the shrink's mask.*

'Because I've been nothing but trouble for you.'

'You've been no trouble, Cathy.' Grace still held those cold fingers.

'Yes, I have,' she said, and now tears were rolling down her cheeks and she was making no effort to wipe them away. 'I've been difficult, and I've blamed you for things that weren't your fault.' Her nose was running. 'And now I've even screwed up dying, so here you are – you've had to come see me again, and if I'd done it better you could've just maybe come to my funeral – just one more funeral – and then at least you'd never have had to see me again.'

'And that's supposed to have been better?'

Cathy shrugged, still weeping. 'It would have been better for me.'

Grace said nothing for a moment or two, just went on holding her hand. She was working hard now under the surface, knowing how crucial it was for her to say the right words from now on, or else keep silent.

Her next question was fundamental.

'Why have you given up, Cathy?'

'Haven't you?'

'No,' Grace said. 'Not at all.'

'Why not?' Cathy asked.

'Same reasons as before. I believe in you. And I'm still not the only one who does – in fact, that list is growing, slowly but surely.'

'How's Detective Becket doing?' Cathy asked suddenly.

'He's doing fine.' Grace didn't know if the prison grapevine had yielded any information about what had gone on down in the Keys, but if Cathy didn't know about that fiasco, she was happy for it to stay that way.

'His dad came to see me, you know.'

'Yes, I know.'

'He told me to stay strong. He told me that truth would prevail.'

'He's right.'

Cathy drew her hand away. 'I wanted to believe him.'

'I know it's hard, Cathy.'

'I asked Dr Becket about that woman who got stabbed with a scalpel in the doctor's office a couple of weeks ago. He didn't want to talk about it at first, but I bugged him until he did.'

Cathy's voice was getting hoarser the more she talked, but Grace didn't want to stop her – her need to talk was more important than a sore throat.

'Dr Becket said it proved he was right about me not having stabbed him – and if the cops and the State Attorney accepted that was true, then they'd have to stop thinking I'd killed anyone.' Her mouth was working again, and her nose was leaking. 'But Mr Wagner told me that it wouldn't necessarily make any difference to the other charges, because the scalpels that Dr Becket and Anna Valdez got stabbed with were stolen from the doctors' offices, which made it a different MO.' Cathy swallowed hard, closed her eyes for a second, then opened them again. 'Mr Wagner was nice – he's okay, I guess, now I know him better – he just says he doesn't like raising my hopes falsely.'

She stopped. Grace remained silent, waiting.

'I guess maybe that's why I gave up on what Dr Becket said – about the truth prevailing.'

'Oh, Cathy,' Grace said. 'I am so sorry for what you're going through.'

'I know you are.' She paused again. 'I don't blame Harry, you know, for digging up that horrible thing.'

'I'll tell him.' Grace smiled. 'He'll be relieved to hear it.'

'Tell him I still think he's a cool dog.'

'I hope you'll be able to tell him yourself one of these days.'

'They don't allow dogs in jail, Grace.'

'You know I'm not talking about jail.'

'I know you're not,' she said, very softly, almost on a sigh.

Grace sat forward, her eyes intent. 'Do I have to be scared for you all the time from now on, Cathy?'

It was hard for Cathy, but she met the gaze squarely. 'You're asking me if I'm going to try and kill myself again.'

'That's what I'm asking you.'

Cathy caught at her upper lip with her teeth for a moment and chewed at it, as if making up her mind how to answer. Whatever she was going to say, Grace hoped to heaven it would be honest, so that she could try dealing with it.

'I won't do it again, Grace,' she said, finally. 'At least, not until after the trial.' She looked away again. 'I can't tell you what I'll do after that.'

CHAPTER SIXTY-ONE

MONDAY, JUNE 8, 1998

Sam was home, cleaning the small kitchen in his Art Deco
South Beach bargain apartment – at least the place was getting
some long overdue attention these days – when Captain
Hernandez called at eleven a.m. Since the cap had personally
bawled Sam out four times since the disaster in the Keys, calling
him a fucking idiot and a disgrace to the department and worse,
Sam was learning not to enjoy the sound of his master's voice.

'Thought you'd want to know that the Monroe County
Sheriff has applied for a warrant to search Hayman's house.'

Sam's brain did a three-hundred-and-sixty-degree spin-
around. *Hernandez had come through for him.*

'How come, captain?'

'We had a coupla conversations. Things being as they still are,
with no body and no family, seemed like the only thing to do.'

Yo, cap.

'I don't suppose there's any chance ...?'

'Not a Chinaman's, Becket.'

Sam called Grace, caught her between patients.

'Tell them about the locked room,' she said.

'What locked room?' he asked.

'Didn't I tell you about that?'

'Not that I recall.'

'I can't believe I forgot about that.'

'What locked room, Grace?'

'It's probably nothing at all,' she said.

'Grace, just tell me.'

*

338

Tuesday afternoon, Sam was hosing down his roof when Sergeant Kovac phoned.

'They want you down in the Keys.'

Say what?

'They got the warrant already?'

'I don't have details, Becket.' Though fair as he had to be, Kovac had never been warmly disposed to Sam, and since the suspension, Martinez had given Sam the impression that their sergeant seemed to consider him someplace lower than Benedict Arnold.

'Does it have something to do with Hayman's locked room?'

'I already told you,' Kovac said, 'I don't have details. They want your ass down at the house is all I know.'

It was the room, all right.

Grace's instincts had been right on the money about that. Of course, if she'd only *listened* to herself the night she'd first come upon that goddamned locked door, and gotten the hell out of Hayman's house, that whole particular drama, at least, would never have come about.

The Monroe County Sheriff had said as much, as had Hector Hernandez, but no one knew better than Sam that Grace Lucca would be harder on herself than any of them.

All that aside ...

For one thing, it was a borderline temple to Münchhausen's Syndrome by proxy. Perhaps as many books, they all surmised, as had been written on the subject – and no one believed that Hayman had been using them purely as research material for his own books.

They might have believed that if it hadn't been for the photographs.

Dozens of them, on the walls and in drawers. Of child victims. With handwritten accounts of their sufferings at the hands of their parent torturers. More ways to create awful physical symptoms in little boys and girls than any of the police officers at the scene cared to know about.

That was for sure.

And then there was the wall of photographs that had driven the

339

local police and Hernandez to summon Sam Becket in spite of themselves. Photographs of Grace Lucca, and of Cathy Robbins, and of Arnold and Marie, and Frances Dean.

'None of Beatrice Flager,' Sam noticed right off.

'Nor of your father,' Hernandez added.

The excitement pumping through Sam was heating him so high he wouldn't have been surprised if smoke had poured out of his ears.

'There's more,' the captain said, quietly, pointing to a purple folder on the desk on one side of the room.

Both men were wearing surgical gloves. Sam bent to flip open the folder. His eyes widened.

'Holy *shit*,' he swore, softly.

'Sure looks that way,' Hernandez agreed.

There were at least ten sheets of paper, photocopies mostly, in the purple folder. Each and every one of them on the same subject.

The life and works of John Broderick.

CHAPTER SIXTY-TWO

WEDNESDAY, JUNE 10, 1998

Other than a rushed phone call to tell her that he had no time to talk to her, Grace heard nothing from Sam until he showed up on her doorstep just after seven a.m. on Wednesday.

'You look like hell,' she said.

'You look wonderful.' Sam looked at Grace, wearing a big white T-shirt, hair tied back, face and feet bare. 'You look about sixteen. Hey, Harry, what's new?' He got down to greet the dog, whose tail was beating like a metronome gone crazy.

'I was about to make breakfast.' Grace shut the front door.

'I could certainly use some coffee.' Sam straightened up, wincing.

'Back still lousy?'

'Too much driving.'

They walked into the kitchen.

'Part of me wants to offer you a hot bath, back rub and a few hours' sleep,' Grace told him, 'but that would mean I'd have to wait to hear whatever you have to tell me, so I'm going to make you pancakes instead.'

Sam's tired eyes perked up. 'You have syrup?'

'Of course.' Grace opened the fridge door and took out eggs. 'Bacon?'

'Sounds like heaven.'

'Why don't you sit down before you fall down, Sam?' She nodded at a rocker in the corner of the kitchen. 'Take the comfy one.'

'If I sit in that,' Sam said, 'I'll be zeeing in three seconds.' He lowered himself carefully on to one of the chairs at the table. 'Need some help?'

'All I need,' Grace told him, 'is your news.' She glanced at him. 'I take it you do have news?'

'That I do,' Sam said.

It had been as much as she could manage actually to get their breakfasts *cooked* while listening to him talk, but once it was on the dish in front of her, Grace found she couldn't eat a thing.

'So what now?' she asked.

Sam's dish – no big surprise – was clean as a whistle. 'Now we have one big question to get answered. Who is – or was – Peter Hayman?'

Grace's mind was still reeling. 'Are we assuming that he's not John Broderick, given that he was keeping a folder of data on him?'

'I'd say the good news is that I don't think anyone's assuming *anything* from here on in, but' – Sam paused to take a mouthful of coffee – 'it would be real strange if the guy was keeping a file on himself.'

'Except that we are talking about a seriously strange man.'

'Yes, we are,' Sam agreed, 'and the data was in a locked room. I just think that a man who's switched identities is not likely to have kept that kind of material on his property.'

'Unless he was still angry about having to leave his life as Broderick behind?' Grace suggested. 'Maybe he was proud of what he did to Marie and Cathy?'

'You mean the way some psychopaths keep press clippings about themselves and their crimes?' Sam shook his head. 'This didn't feel that way, Grace. It was really just a series of details on the subject of John Broderick. A record of his life and deeds – mistakes, too.'

'So who the hell is – was – Peter Hayman?' she asked quietly.

'And do these photographs on his walls of you and Cathy, and the Robbinses and Frances Dean, mean that he still may be the killer?' Sam's eyes were no less tired, but his expression was alive with grim curiosity.

'And doesn't it also mean . . . ?' Grace stopped.

'What?'

She shook her head. 'Just a selfish thought.'

342

'Can I guess?' Sam's smile was wry. 'Doesn't it also mean that maybe our instincts about Hayman weren't quite as many miles off-base as we were scared they were?'

'That's about it.'

'I guess that's part of the reason Hernandez let me see it.'

Grace stood up to dump her uneaten breakfast down the waste disposal in the sink, then picked up Sam's empty plate. 'More coffee?'

'Why not? I'm buzzing anyway.'

She threw away the old grounds and made a fresh pot. 'Do I take it that we don't have enough yet to get Cathy out of jail?'

'Not enough,' Sam said, gently. 'But it's a hell of a start.'

'And you?' Grace turned around to look at him. 'Is the fact that you were at least half right about Hayman enough to get your suspension lifted?'

'It doesn't change what I did,' he said. 'I still broke the rules.'

'Is that what Hernandez says?'

'Not exactly. I asked him if I could help with the investigation. He reminded me that anything I might achieve while suspended would be inadmissible and worse than useless.' Sam paused. 'But Hernandez did admit that before Hayman came into the picture, our idea about Broderick's not being dead sounded like garbage. Now, suddenly, we have two possible bad guys to look at – Broderick *and/or* whoever Hayman was before he came to Key Largo.'

Grace brought the fresh pot of coffee to the table.

'Do you think Hernandez might be relenting about you?'

'It's not all up to him. It's mostly up to the chief, and Internal Affairs.' Sam smiled. 'Don't worry about me so much, Grace. Think about what it might ultimately mean to Cathy.'

'I think I can manage to worry about you both.'

'Now you sound like my mother,' he said.

343

CHAPTER SIXTY-THREE

FRIDAY, JUNE 12, 1998

Grace had, with Dora's help, juggled enough appointments to make it possible for her to make the trip south on Friday morning. She hadn't realized, until she reached the Overseas Highway, how tense she was, but passing Lake Surprise, the memories of that Sunday in May had suddenly crowded in on her with almost suffocating clarity, and her hands had gripped the wheel of the Mazda tightly as she fought to push them away.

She made it to Dooley's Marina by ten past ten. Philip Kuntz was there, a few yards from the closed-up hot-dog stand, holding a plastic cup of coffee, waiting for her. The sight of his bald, suntanned head and pale eyes sparked it all off again for her. She took a deep breath.

'Mr Kuntz, thank you so much for agreeing to see me.'

He shook her hand. 'No problem.'

Grace looked around. 'Is there any place we could sit for a while?'

He shrugged. 'There's a bench around the other side of the marina. It's not real pretty, and I guess it smells bad, but if you don't mind ...'

'I don't mind at all.'

She told him what she'd come for. She didn't know how much Kuntz knew, how much exactly Sam had shared with him before he'd hooked him into taking him out in the *Delia*, or how much, if anything, the local police had told him after the event.

Not much, as it happened.

344

'There are all kinds of things I don't think I'm allowed to tell you either,' Grace said. 'About Dr Hayman, I mean.'

'They haven't found him yet, I gather,' Kuntz said.

'Not yet, no.' Grace paused. 'As I told you, so much of what went on that afternoon was my fault, not Sam's – but the way things are now, he's been suspended. He could even lose his job.' She waited another moment. 'He's a very good detective, Mr Kuntz.'

'Do me a favour,' he said. 'Call me Phil. I figure we got kind of close that day on the *Delia*, don't you?'

Grace smiled. 'We certainly did.'

Two men drove up in a pick-up, got out, nodded at Kuntz and made their way over to a small cabin boat on the far side.

'So you reckon it was all your fault,' he said to Grace.

'A lot of it was,' she told him. 'The fact that I was foolish enough to get on the *Snowbird* in the first place. And then, that I panicked, lost my head. You were there, Phil – you know that Sam believed I was in danger when he saw what was going on.'

'That's true enough,' Kuntz agreed.

'You said to me that afternoon that you thought Sam was crazy – I think it was when he was trying to save Hayman.'

Kuntz nodded. 'I thought he was a damned fool the way he kept diving.'

Grace waited a second. 'You also said you thought he was a hero.'

Kuntz nodded again. 'I'm not sure if I said he was an actual hero – he certainly showed a lot of guts.' The pale eyes narrowed. 'Do I have this right? You want me to tell Detective Becket's boss that your boyfriend was a hero?'

'They won't listen to me,' Grace said, quietly. 'I'm the idiot-woman who got herself into trouble. You're one of the two civilians they say he endangered. They'd have to listen to you, Phil.'

'I don't know how much danger I was in.' Kuntz grinned. 'I guess I could have drowned out there – but that was nothing compared to what I figured Becket might have done to me if I hadn't agreed to help you.'

'But you don't really blame him for wanting to help me, do you?'

Kuntz's eyes warmed a little as he looked at her. 'I guess I'd like to think I'd do the same if my girlfriend was in a jam.'

Grace felt as if she was holding her breath.

'Will you at least consider speaking up for him, Phil?'

'I'll think about it,' he said.

CHAPTER SIXTY-FOUR

A whole new investigation was underway, and though Sam was still on the sidelines, frustrated as hell, he was being informed whenever, and *how*ever, possible by Al Martinez.

Hayman's prints had been lifted from all over his house and been sent for checking against the millions of others stored in the massive fingerprint data base now being used States-wide. No match, to date, had leapt out from the computer, but that only meant that Hayman had not been arrested or been in the armed forces or employed in any of the occupations that required printing.

So far as checking his prints against Broderick's, that, too, remained an unresolved problem, since despite his troubles John Broderick had never been arrested and had been exempted from the Vietnam draft and had, therefore, never been printed either.

The Monroe County Sheriff's department had been conducting its own localized enquiry into the Key Largo-based alleged psychiatrist, including trying to discover if Hayman had cast-iron alibis for any of the murder dates and times. Friends and colleagues – including Betty and Miles Flanagan and the Weintraubs, the two couples Hayman had told Grace they were going to sail with that Sunday – had been asked if they could vouch for the doctor's whereabouts on any of the murder nights. No alibis had presented themselves, and when it came down to talking about what they knew of their acquaintance, no one seemed actually to know too much. One of the things Miles Flanagan said he had liked most about Hayman, now he came to think of it, was that he never spent time bragging about himself. Regarding his roots, Hayman had told his Key Largo friends the same as he'd told his publishers: that he hailed from Seattle and had gone to the University of Washington. The FBI had now verified what Martinez had already checked, off the record, after the accident. No such student at that university.

The most intensive and intriguing part of the fresh investigation, however, centred on another two photographs that Monroe County officers had found inside Hayman's house towards the tail-end of the search.

Both photographs had been taped to the underside of his bed.

One was of a child, a boy aged about five, wearing dungarees, a red and white striped T-shirt and a gentle smile. He had brown hair and eyes, and he was, everyone agreed, too thin for his age.

The second photograph was of a grave, recently dug and filled. Smaller than average. There was no stone yet, just a tiny marker plaque. The angle from which it had been shot made it impossible – even magnified several times over – to read the name on the marker. The closest grave with a stone and legible name was that of a woman named Agnes Brown, and three stones in the row behind all bore the name of Tully. The epitaphs on all those stones offered no clues as to their location, other than that they were written in English. What could be seen of the sky was cloudy, and the grass appeared green and well-watered. A man, some distance away, walking along a path, was wearing a dark, formal-style winter overcoat, so they knew they were probably looking at a cemetery close to, or perhaps within, a city, where they experienced some cold weather. The only trees in sight were firs. No flowers or shrubs to help pin it down. The photograph had been focused on the grave itself, which was why the white, blurry mass on the horizon, cut off by the top of the picture, was not even noticed for some time – and certainly not recognized as a mountain.

If only the summit of the mountain had been included in the photograph, they could probably have pinpointed the location of the cemetery within a day or two. But all they could say for sure was that there appeared to be snow even on its lower reaches at the time the snap had been taken.

Both photographs were copies, so there was no chance of tracing them as there might have been if they had been original prints with telltale numbers on their backs.

Still, at least they now had something to go on.

And at least, as Sam said to Grace, everyone now seemed to give a shit.

The quest was on, nationwide, to identify the boy in the picture taped to the underside of Peter Hayman's bed. There were a few, wholly unsubstantiated, conclusions being drawn – the way that tended to happen when investigators became deeply motivated, even passionate, about a mystery – and one of them was that the boy might be, or more likely have *been*, a victim of Münchhausen's Syndrome by proxy. Another possible conclusion was that he might have been a relative of Hayman's. The grimmest of all, of course, was that the five-year-old boy might also be the occupant of that grave.

They were busy contacting every association, organization or institution that treated or counselled sufferers or victims of MSBP, and the boy's picture had been sent to every medical examiner's office in every county in the United States that sported mountains as part of their landscape.

They were also doing their damnedest to locate a cemetery in a part of the United States where it got cool enough in winter to warrant an overcoat; where there were at least a handful of fir trees; and where some people with the names of Brown and Tully were buried. And from which, even on a cloudy day, it was possible to see a mountain on the horizon.

That narrowed the search down quite a bit.

But it was still going to take time.

CHAPTER SIXTY-FIVE

MONDAY, JUNE 22, 1998

Grace had never been so glad to have a jam-packed calendar. If it hadn't been for her patients, she thought she might have exploded with impatience. As it was, she was doing the only three things she seemed able to do, work aside. One, doing whatever she could – in conjunction with Dr Parés' relaxation therapies – to try and keep Cathy's spirits up. Two, doing much the same for Sam, while the powers-that-be continued to hold his badge hostage. And three, making sure that Jerry Wagner – about whose whole-hearted commitment she was no longer in any doubt – was kept as thoroughly in the picture as possible so far as the investigation was concerned.

'She does seem to be coping better,' Wagner told Grace at a quick meeting in his office after one of his visits to the house of detention. 'But it's getting to be a real tightrope dance trying to keep Cathy positive without giving her false hope.'

'At least there is real hope now,' Grace pointed out.

'Tell me the latest,' Wagner urged.

'Nothing on the cemetery yet,' Grace said, reporting what she'd just *happened* to hear Martinez telling Sam. 'The climate and the mountain, in particular, seemed to point to Seattle again – you know, the Olympics or maybe the Cascades – but so far everything's drawn a blank.'

'It'll come,' Wagner said.

'Do you really think so?'

'Yes, I do. One way or another. Either Hayman's body will wash up and then they'll have dental records and blood to help them along, or the boy's photo's going to stir someone's memory.'

Grace was getting ready to ask the $64,000 question again.

'All these people are working now, all over the country, law enforcement agencies getting involved in Seattle and up in Maine and wherever – the State Attorney must *know* that Hayman keeping those photographs of Marie and Arnold and Frances has to mean that Cathy shouldn't have been charged with the killings.'

'It's still all completely inconclusive, Grace,' Wagner said.

'But enough for reasonable doubt, surely? Enough at least to let her out of jail while they carry on investigating, maybe on bail?'

'There was no bail at the start of all this,' he reminded her, 'and it's not going to be allowed now. The judge would have to drop the charges in order for Cathy to get out.' He paused. 'My people and I are working on that possibility all the time, Grace.'

'So you do think it's worth pursuing?' she persisted.

'I think there's a chance,' he said. 'Just don't tell Cathy that.'

Grace smiled at him. 'Who's the psychologist here?'

'He really seemed to mean it,' she told Sam that evening.

'You seem surprised.'

'I was a little surprised,' Grace said, 'at how committed he seems now to getting Cathy out of that place.'

'Why should that surprise you?' Sam wanted to know.

'Because if the charges against her are dropped, there'll be no trial and Wagner's hype's going to get cut by about seven-eighths – not to mention his fee.'

'But all the hype he *will* get's going to be great hype.'

'I thought the theory was that all publicity's worth having,' Grace said.

Sam shrugged. 'Believe me, if Jerry Wagner manages to play a significant part in getting those charges dropped, he'll find a way to capitalize on that.'

Grace smiled. 'I didn't know you were such a cynic.'

'I'm a cop,' Sam said simply. 'How can I not be a cynic?' He paused. 'Or, at least, I hope I'm still a cop.'

351

CHAPTER SIXTY-SIX

THURSDAY, JUNE 25, 1998

Wagner caught Grace just as she was about to begin a session late on Thursday morning.

'I don't want to get anyone's hopes up,' he said, 'but I think there's a real chance that if we prepare this thing solidly enough, the judge might react well.'

'You mean, let her out?' Grace had almost stopped breathing.

'I'm talking about a chance, Grace. No guarantees.'

Grace's eyes moved to her wristwatch. There was a child waiting for her.

'You said we need to prepare. Anything I can do?'

'There might be,' he said.

'Tell me.'

'The judge is going to be concerned about Cathy's well-being. He's going to want to take a number of elements under consideration. Even if the charges are dropped, until another person stands accused, there's always a possibility that Cathy could be re-arrested.'

'So that's going to be hanging over her.' The prospect was awful, but even that had to be better than staying in jail. 'What else?'

'The case has attracted a lot of publicity,' Wagner said. 'You think Cathy's going to be left in peace if she's released?'

Grace thought she knew now where he was going. 'Are you saying that the judge is going to want to know she has somewhere secure to live? A place of safety, that kind of thing?'

'Let's just say I think it might affect the judge's decision-making.'

Grace left a couple of moments' silence before she spoke again.

'Do you think my house would get approval?'

'I don't know,' Wagner answered, 'but it's got to be worth, a shot.'

Grace knew that at least a dozen thoughts *ought* to have scudded through her mind, raising their heads to be considered, but if they were hoping to get her to glance their way, they were hoping in vain. Only one thought, one *word*, was coming through, loud and clear.

Yes.

'Go for it,' she said. 'By all means, go for it.'

'Are you certain, Grace?'

She remembered the way Cathy had looked in the hospital after she'd tried to hang herself.

'Absolutely,' she said.

The doubts began creeping in about a half-hour after her patient had departed. This was, Grace knew, not a problem to be dealt with in total isolation; she ought, she was well aware, to be discussing it with someone.

She started with Harry, but he was in a mood for eating, walking or having his belly scratched, and not in the mood for listening. Grace knew she had no alternative but to speak to an intelligent, at least slightly detached, *human.*

She began with the person most likely to agree with her.

She called David Becket.

'No one knows better than you,' he said, 'that we're dealing with a terribly traumatized teenager. Have you considered the disruption that Cathy would bring into your home – into your life?'

Grace told him that she had, and David said that aside from that, he thought it the best possible idea he'd heard in a very long time.

Bolstered, Grace called David's son. Sam said that he felt much as he guessed she did; he was much too glad at the prospect of Cathy getting out of the house of detention to allow practical issues to cloud the pleasure.

'They couldn't find a better person to take care of her, that's for sure.'

'I hope that's true,' Grace said.

'You know it is,' Sam told her. 'Come on, Grace, you spend your whole life taking care of kids with problems, and you've believed in Cathy from the start every way you could.'

'Yes, I have,' she agreed, quietly.

'I do have a couple of questions,' Sam said.

'Shoot.'

'How long would you envisage her staying?' He paused. 'Or are you thinking about a permanent kind of arrangement?'

'I don't know, Sam. I haven't had time to think about anything too much.'

'And what if it all goes wrong for Cathy? What if nothing sticks against Hayman and they re-arrest her? That's a lot of potential heartache down the road for you, Grace.'

'Wouldn't I feel the same heartache wherever Cathy was staying in the meantime?'

'I think it would be worse if you'd been living together.'

Grace thought about it for all of two seconds.

'Isn't that a chance I have to take, Sam?'

'That's up to you,' he said. 'You'll have my support whatever you decide. For what that's worth.'

'A lot,' Grace said.

After Sam, she called Magda Shrike. As always, she was swift to ask all the right questions. She wanted to know what the other options might be for Cathy, asked Grace what effect she thought swapping prison for another institution might have on Cathy if Grace refused. And then she asked the big one: did Grace really trust Cathy enough to have her in her home?

'Yes, I do,' Grace said, unhesitatingly.

'Then I'm just going to tell you what you already know,' Magda said. 'That if you say no, you're likely to find it tough to live with yourself – but that may not be a good enough reason to say yes.' She paused. 'And it certainly doesn't mean you shouldn't take as much time as you can over making the decision.'

'I don't even know if the judge is going to accept the offer,' Grace said.

'Not to mention Cathy herself,' Magda added, dryly.

*

354

The only strongly dissenting voice was Claudia's.

'You're not really considering this, Grace?'

'Of course I am.'

'You mustn't. It's a terrible idea.'

'Why is it?' Grace was startled by her sister's vehemence.

'Because she's a *murder* suspect.'

'She's innocent, Claudia. And if this happens, it'll be because a judge believes that too.'

'Maybe she is, maybe not. Either way, you can't take the chance.'

'I can,' Grace said.

'You mustn't,' Claudia told her again.

All her life Grace had reacted badly when people had tried to tell her what she could or could not do. She tried not to get mad at Claudia now, because she knew that her sister was only trying to be protective.

'It's a done deal,' she told her, 'or as good as.'

'You said you were just thinking about it,' Claudia said. 'You said the judge might not even accept it.'

'That part's true,' Grace said. 'But I'm not just *thinking* about it any more. I've made up my mind.'

'Grace, you *can't.*'

'Claudia, I can, and given half a chance, I'm going to.'

That night, Grace dreamt that a powerful, fair-haired man was beating a small girl with long, blonde hair. He was yelling at her, though in the dream his voice was so muffled that Grace couldn't hear his words, yet she could hear the girl's crying with strident and painful clarity.

The dream switched, like a bad edit in a movie, to another man – Frank Lucca – standing over Claudia, aged about seven. She was not crying and he was not yelling at her. He was bending over her, and the dream was silent except for the sound of Grace's own breathing and heartbeat as she hid and watched her father lowering himself over her sister.

Grace woke up, her lashes and cheeks wet. She couldn't remember when she had last wept in her sleep.

She switched on her bedside lamp. It was almost three a.m. Harry was at the end of the bed, watching her with his sharp, warm eyes.

355

'Hey,' Grace said softly, and he got up and padded his way across the duvet until he got to just below her right shoulder, and then he lay down again and gave one of his grunts.

Ordinarily, Harry was all the company Grace needed.

Not tonight.

She telephoned Sam.

'Becket.' He sounded too alert for that time of night.

'Why aren't you asleep?' Grace asked.

'Ask my body.'

'I'd love to.' She swore she could hear his smile through the phone. 'At least this is one advantage of you being on suspension,' she said. 'It's the middle of the night and you're home when I need you.'

'Do you?'

'Do I what?'

'Do you need me?'

Grace thought for about half a second.

'Yes, I do.'

'Give me fifteen to twenty,' Sam said and put down the phone.

She told him about her dreams over a cup of hot chocolate in the kitchen.

'At least you don't need to bother analysing them,' he said.

'I'm not sure why they got to me as strongly as they did.'

'They were awful dreams,' he said simply. 'Ugly and scary.'

'I guess they were.'

'You want to talk about them some more? Or you want to put them away? What's better for you?'

Grace smiled at him. 'I want to go back to bed.'

'Okay.'

'I don't want to go back alone.'

Sam smiled back at her. 'Good,' he said, softly.

It was the first time they had made love, fully and completely, since that other first time, up on Sam's roof, six weeks before. They had both agreed that they were holding off, mostly because of all the bad stuff happening, partly because of the pain in his back – for which Sam was now having to take anti-inflammatory medication – but suddenly they both realized that if Wagner got lucky and Cathy moved out of jail into Grace's place, their intimate life might have to get put back on hold.

Enough was enough.

'Wonder stuff,' Sam said against her ear, a little while after they'd finished making love.

That close up, his baritone voice sounded almost like a big cat's purr.

'I don't think,' Grace said, 'I've ever felt so relaxed in my whole life.'

'Me neither.'

She drew her face away from his shoulder just far enough to see his profile. 'I feel safe, too, Sam.'

She saw a muscle tensing in his jaw.

'I hope you go on feeling that way,' he said, softly.

'Any reason I shouldn't?' Insecurity hit Grace harder than she'd anticipated.

'Many reasons.'

She drew another inch further away. 'Am I coming on too strong?'

'No way.' He turned towards her, wrapped her close. 'Don't think that, whatever you do.'

She allowed herself to relax into his body again.

'We haven't talked about the problems, Grace,' Sam said.

She understood, instantly, what he meant.

'You're talking black and white,' she said.

'You must have thought about it.'

'Not really. Not in a problematic sense, anyway.' Grace paused. 'I knew it was something that was going to figure sometime, but then again, I think I've always had a tendency to ignore headaches until they hit.' She could feel Sam watching her. 'What?'

'You remind me of my father.'

'David? I'm flattered.'

'You should be.' Sam paused. 'He's never really seen me as any different to himself or Judy. Even to Saul.' He shrugged. 'It's natural with Dad. I sometimes think he's like a blind man – he sees right past the surface. And it's not just a colour thing – he's just the same with everyone.'

'I think you're right,' Grace said softly, then thought about that some more. 'I can't say the same thing is true for me though. I can't say that I don't see your brown skin' – she kissed his chest – 'or feel the different texture of your hair.' She rubbed her cheek against him. 'It's all you, Sam. I love the way you look – I would hate, more than I can say, being blind to any part of it.' She smiled. 'Anyway, we both know I'm nowhere close to being as fine a person as David.'

'Shit, woman,' Sam said. 'You mean you're not a saint, after all?'

She chuckled into the dark and wriggled further down the bed. 'Would a saint want to do this?'

They both stopped talking for quite a time, then slept for an hour or so, and it was daylight before they were ready to return to the subject that they both knew wasn't going to get forgotten.

'I'm not about to insult your intelligence,' Grace told Sam after they'd carried two cups of coffee back to her bed, 'by making out that I don't know we're going to encounter prejudice if we stay together any length of time.' She shrugged. 'I guess I've always been lucky that way till now.'

She shared her limited experiences with him. She had seen enough of the ugliness, of course, on the streets of both Miami and Chicago – she'd heard the ignorant *salt-and-pepper* jibes and much worse – but she'd never actually met racism in person. Grace had grown up with an Italian name inside a largely Italian community. She had dated an African-American law student at university and she'd spent three months in the frequent company of a doctor from Hong Kong soon after graduation. No one had ever openly hassled either Grace or the men, but she was prepared to accept that she had, probably, been fortunate in that.

'That is Florida,' Sam said, simply, when she'd finished. 'No matter how we dress it up or how many laws get fixed, it's still the South. You hang around with me long enough, Grace, and you'll get proof of that.'

'It goes both ways,' she pointed out.

'But I'm bigger and uglier and tougher than you are,' Sam said, 'and I've had a hell of a lot more years to get used to it.'

'I've always been good at learning.'

'It could be a hard lesson, is all I'm saying.'

Grace switched angles. 'How does Judy feel about me these days?'

'Ma wants you to come to dinner one Friday night. She said she'll even cook fish for my nice Catholic girlfriend.'

'I'm lapsed, Sam,' Grace reminded him.

'Are you ever,' he said.

CHAPTER SIXTY-SEVEN

MONDAY, JUNE 29, 1998

'I can't believe this really might happen,' Cathy said to Grace during her visit on Monday afternoon. 'I can't believe I might really be getting out of here.'

Grace did her best to hide her dismay. 'Who told you that?'

'Mr Wagner,' Cathy said.

'He shouldn't have done that.'

'Why not?' Fear flashed in Cathy's eyes. 'Isn't it true?'

They were in the big visiting hall since Grace was there as Cathy's friend today rather than her psychologist, surrounded on all sides, sitting on two hard plastic chairs talking across a Formica-topped table. Grace hated it with a passion. All those women, separated from their loved ones by those damned tables and the vigilant guards – no real privacy, not a *chance* of the slightest, often clearly desperately yearned for, intimacy.

'Grace' – Cathy's voice nudged her – 'isn't it true what Mr Wagner said?'

Grace took another moment to answer, painfully aware of the need to be cautious. 'It's true that there's a chance, Cathy, but a lot could still go wrong.'

'But there really is a chance?'

'Yes, there is,' Grace allowed. 'I just don't want you getting your hopes up in case it falls apart.'

'Oh, Grace, you can be such a downer.' The fear was gone again. 'This is the first time anything's gone *halfway* right for me in months – I know it could all turn bad again, but right now I just don't want to think about that. Can't you understand that?'

360

'Yes, of course I can.' There was such optimism in Cathy's expression, the last thing Grace wanted to do was take it away. 'I have to say, you're looking much better.'

'I guess that's down to the doc,' Cathy said warmly. 'He stopped giving me tranks because we both figured they were bringing me down, and he's been giving me vitamins instead because he knows I hate the food in here.'

'I'm glad you're off tranquillizers.' Not for the first time, Grace felt real gratitude and appreciation for Eric Parés.

'And I think I'm getting better at doing those relaxation exercises he's been teaching me,' Cathy went on. 'The doc says nothing feels quite so bad if you can get right down *inside* yourself, take yourself away from the stuff that scares you.'

'Sounds like he's been teaching you meditation.' Grace was impressed.

'"*Meditation, not medication*" – that's what the doc says, and that's cool, because I don't really like taking all that junk, not even the vitamins.' Cathy's blue eyes, so dulled since she'd been in this place, were almost shining. 'Lucille says I'm feeling better because I know there's a chance I could get out of here.' Lucille Calder was another inmate, an older woman who'd lately taken Cathy under her wing. 'I'm feeling so much *stronger*, you know?' She hardly paused for breath. 'I've never been able to sleep well in this dump, Grace, which was why I was so tired all the time, but suddenly I just seem to have all this energy and hope—'

'Are you sleeping better?' Interrupting seemed the only way for Grace to get a word in, and she was conscious of time slipping past.

'Not really, but I don't seem to care so much. That's the whole *point*, Grace. Nothing's getting me down the way it was.'

'I wasn't entirely happy about the cloud she was on,' Grace told Sam late that night, 'but on the other hand, it was a hundred per cent better than the way she has been feeling – and I *do* like the sound of Dr Parés' relaxation therapy.'

They were lying naked in each other's arms in her bed after making love, and Sam was gently stroking the inside of her

361

left arm with his fingertips, letting Grace talk, knowing by now how much those visits to the prison always got to her.

'I'm glad Wagner didn't tell her about wanting her to come stay here,' Grace went on. 'I'm so afraid of letting Cathy down.'

'Have you been having second thoughts?' Sam asked.

'No, not at all. But the judge might decide I'm not a suitable guardian.'

'Why would anyone do that?'

'Who knows?'

Sam stopped stroking her arm.

'What's wrong?' she asked.

He took a moment. 'Are you concerned about us?'

'In what way?'

'Are you concerned what the judge might make of the two of us?'

'No.' Grace paused. 'I mean, I hadn't even thought about it.'

'Maybe you should.'

Grace sat up and switched on her bedside light. Sam's face was turned away, towards the window. 'Please look at me.'

He turned, slowly. His expression was deadpan.

'Okay,' she said. 'Is this something we need to talk about?'

'Only from the standpoint that I don't want to be the one to wreck Cathy's chances,' Sam said. 'Not when she's come this far.'

'You're concerned about what? That the judge might be a racist?'

'The judge doesn't need to be a grade A racist or even white to be one of those people who isn't happy about exposing young people to mixed-race situations.' Sam shrugged. 'Any number of black judges might feel exactly the same way.'

'But we don't agree with that, do we?' Grace said.

'No, we don't.' Sam left the *but* unsaid.

'And I thought we'd already dealt with the morals side of things.' A few strands of hair were in her eyes and Grace pushed them back impatiently. 'I mean, we've agreed that we'd have to be more careful about sex if Cathy did come here – I guess that would be a fair point for a judge to be *concerned* about.' She paused again, looking straight at him. 'Anything

more than that, Sam, I don't know about you, but I'd fight
like hell.'

At last, Sam smiled.

'That, I'd almost like to see.'

CHAPTER SIXTY-EIGHT

TUESDAY, JUNE 30, 1998

'Grace came yesterday,' Cathy told Dr Parés when he called in to see her after she'd finished her shift in the laundry.

'How is the lady?' he asked.

'Pretty cool, the way she always is.' Cathy smiled. 'Almost always. She worries too much – she was upset this time in case I got my hopes up and things went wrong.'

'She's quite right,' the doctor agreed. 'It's wiser not to have unrealistic expectations, Cathy.'

'I know,' Cathy said, still smiling. 'It's better to stay calm.'

They were alone in a locked room with a table, two chairs and an old, battered vinyl couch, not far from the infirmary. Privacy was a concession that Parés had won since he'd persuaded the governor that his relaxation therapies were likely to make the prison staff's lives easier all round. Lucille had been scathing about what she called 'hocus-pocus', but the older woman had come around to some degree, glad that Cathy had been able to find some measure of inner peace without turning into a hophead.

'Much better.' Parés sat down in a chair close to Cathy's, picked up his bag and set it on his knees. 'I have more vitamins for you.'

'Aren't I taking enough? I don't like taking too many pills.'

'Just one more.' The doctor opened the bag and took out a small white envelope. 'Actually,' he explained in his soft, attractively accented English, 'these are mineral supplements rather than vitamins – equally important to you as long as you're starved of good food, fresh air and sunlight.'

'I guess I can quit taking them once I'm out of here.'

'Not right away,' Parés told her. 'Your body will need a few weeks to grow accustomed to the changes.' He paused. 'And you mustn't expect everything to go entirely smoothly just because you leave this place.'

'You mean because they could still re-arrest me?'

'Precisely.' Parés paused. 'You've learned many hard lessons, Cathy. You know by now how tough life can be. That's true even out there, with all that freedom.'

'I know what freedom means to me,' she said, softly.

'Tell me.'

'It means running, as far and as fast as I want to.' Her eyes were hazy with longing. 'It means stopping and buying a Dr Pepper or some Ben & Jerry's when I feel like it.'

'That's fine,' the doctor said, 'and it's true, as far as it goes.' His dark eyes grew more serious and for a second or two he stroked his small, neat beard. 'But one of the lessons I hope to teach you is that it's wise in life to learn to recognize one's enemies—'

'I don't want to think about enemies,' Cathy said. 'I'd rather think I don't have any.'

'But you know better than that, don't you? For instance, whoever put you inside this place is your enemy, don't you agree?'

'You mean the guy who killed my parents and the others.' All the light-heartedness had left Cathy's face.

'You think it is a man? It could be a woman.'

'Everyone seems to think it could be this Hayman guy.' Cathy looked at the doctor. 'Don't you think it's him?'

'I've no way of knowing anything about that. I just want you to be aware that you need to stay on your guard, even if things go well and you do get out of here.' Parés opened the envelope in his hand and took out a pink pill. 'Take this later, before you go sleep. All right, Cathy?'

She nodded. 'Sure, doc.'

The doctor glanced at the couch.

'Are we going to do some relaxation now?' Cathy asked him.

'I was thinking that you've become so adept at deep relaxation that I might start teaching you some simple self-hypnosis.' Parés saw her forehead crease. 'It's really very

365

simple and perfectly safe, and it will help you when you leave here.' He paused. 'Everything becomes so much easier, Cathy, once you learn how to control your own body and mind.'

'Okay,' Cathy said.

'Are you sure?' Parés checked. 'You know I never want you to do anything you're not comfortable with.'

'I know that,' Cathy said. 'It's cool. I trust you.'

'I hope so,' Parés said.

CHAPTER SIXTY-NINE

WEDNESDAY, JULY 1, 1998

The first performance of the S-BOP production of *Il Trovatore* was on Wednesday night. Grace had seen Sam Tuesday evening, after the dress rehearsal, and it was the very first time she'd seen the man spooked by anything that didn't involve life or death. Yet on the big night itself, when she brought a single red rose to the dressing room he was sharing with Manrico, the tenor lead, and Ferrando, the bass, Sam seemed startlingly calm.

'This always happens to me just before we really get to do a show for a crowd the first time,' he told her outside the room, speaking softly because the other two men were both basket cases from nerves. 'I'm not sure why it is – a lot of singers throw up around this point, but I just get kind of high.'

'Because you love it so much?' Grace suggested, crazy about the way he looked in his captain's costume with all that dramatic make-up on his eyes.

'The other guys love it too,' he said. 'I guess it might be different for me if it was what I actually *did* – I mean, for a living. But singing with S-BOP just feels like a big fat treat for me. Sure I'm scared of letting them down, but mostly I just feel like I'm coming home for Christmas.'

Grace knew virtually nothing about opera, and less about baritones. She had never seen another production of *Il Trovatore*, and now that she knew the plot more or less inside out, she realized that the story was every bit as idiotic as Sam had once warned her it was.

But she also knew that she hadn't heard him sing better than

367

he did that night, when it really counted, and that she had never experienced such excitement and sheer personal *heat* in any theatre. Of course, she accepted, they were probably all pretty great – but from Grace's own, rather more intimate, point-of-view, Sam was simply greater.

She told him so afterwards, when they were partying with the others.

And then she told him again, back up on his roof, when they were partying alone.

He seemed to like the way she told him.

When Hector Hernandez called Sam early next morning, Sam and Grace were still asleep in bed. Sam got his act together swiftly enough to make it through the conversation, but Grace was still fuzzy when he put down the phone.

Sam leaned over and kissed her on the mouth.

'That was the captain.'

'What'd he want?'

'To talk to me off-the-record.'

Grace was waking up now. 'About what?'

'Seems that Phil Kuntz – remember Phil Kuntz, Grace?' Sam's eyes were very dark and unreadable. 'Sure you do. He was the guy who helped fish you out of the ocean back in May, the guy who owned the *Delia*.'

'Of course I remember him.'

'Anyway, it seems that Phil Kuntz phoned up the chief last week to tell him that he ought to give me my badge back because the *Snowbird* capsizing was nothing to do with me, and all I did was save your life and risk my own – I'm just quoting now, okay? – and risk my own life to try and save Hayman.'

Grace sat up, pulling the top sheet up over her breasts. 'That's good news, isn't it? And it's all true.'

'So anyway,' Sam went on, 'the chief called Hernandez and talked to him, and then the cap called up Kuntz and asked him how come he was suddenly proclaiming Sam Becket – that's me – a hero? And guess what Kuntz told the captain?'

'Beats me,' Grace said, quietly.

'Kuntz told Hernandez that the cute blonde shrink – ring any bells? – had come down to the Keys to see him, told him what had happened to me, reminded him what a big hero I was.'

He stopped. Grace said nothing.

'So?' Sam waited. 'Grace?'

She looked him in the eye. 'So are you going to make a big deal of this, Sam? Are you going to tell me I did something bad?' She dropped the sheet that had been covering her.

'Dirty pool, Grace.'

'All's fair.'

Sam looked at her for a long moment.

'Oh, my,' he said.

'Okay?' Grace asked, still very softly.

'Guess so,' Sam said.

'So what's the situation now? What else did Hernandez say?'

'That though I'm still a much bigger sapbrain than he gave me credit for, I'm also a halfway decent detective and he'd rather not lose me permanently if he can help it.'

'That's wonderful,' Grace said, waves of pleasure coursing through her.

Sam held up his right hand, palm forward. 'Don't get too excited. He also said that if – *if* – I do get my badge back, I'll probably be reassigned to desk duty for a while.'

'Which means what exactly?'

'What it sounds like. I won't be allowed out on the street – I'll have to sit in the office, man the phones and do everyone's dirty work.'

'But that wouldn't be forever?'

'I hope not,' Sam said.

'Of *course* it won't be forever – not after what Hernandez said about not wanting to lose a fine detective.'

'He said halfway decent, not fine.'

'Oh, Sam!' Grace flung her arms around him and squeezed tight. 'It's going to be all right – I'm so happy for you.'

Sam hugged her back, then drew back just far enough to kiss her mouth. 'He said I'd have a letter of reprimand on my file.'

'Is that terrible?' Grace said, her lips still hovering close to his.

'It's not good, but it's not permanent suspension either.'

'So how long is all this going to take?'

'Hernandez wasn't saying.' Sam shrugged. 'My guess is they'll make me sweat until something goes down and they need all hands on deck.'

Grace laid her index finger over his mouth.

'No sailing jargon, please.'

On the Hayman/Broderick front, there was no big news. Martinez told Sam that he'd learned, after the event, that the Monroe County officers had found a stash of prescription drugs in the study of the Key Largo house – nothing that would have been out of keeping for a practising psychiatrist. Except that Peter Hayman had told Grace that he seldom saw patients. And since there was every likelihood that he'd never qualified, if he ever *had* treated patients, he had not been legally entitled to do so.

Still, posing as a doctor might be illegal, Martinez pointed out to Sam, but it was hardly in the same league as multiple homicide.

'Answer me this,' Sam said. 'Aside from the incident in Dania, have there been any more scalpel attacks in doctors' officers or anyplace else since Hayman fell overboard?'

'Not that I know of,' Martinez answered.

'So all we need is a little goddamned luck.'

'Not to mention a lot of goddamned proof,' Martinez said.

CHAPTER SEVENTY

FRIDAY, JULY 17, 1998

It took another two weeks of investigation and reports – by two independent forensic adolescent psychologists, by the governor of the Female House of Detention, by Dr Parés and by Dr Khan – before Jerry Wagner got the powers-that-were to agree to listen to his submission: that even at this early stage in the search for the truth about the so-called Dr Peter Hayman, there were more than enough grounds for believing that the wrong person had been charged with the murders of Marie Robbins, Arnold Robbins, Frances Dean and Beatrice Flager, and with the attempted murder of David Becket.

The last-named victim gave evidence in the form of a magnificently persuasive letter written from his perspective as the physician who'd taken care of Cathy, first in the immediate aftermath of her parents' murder, and again after her collapse during police questioning following Beatrice Flager's death. Given Grace's previously given guarantee that she was prepared to act as Cathy's temporary guardian, her report as the prisoner's psychologist was not admissible, though Grace, too, had been permitted to write a letter affirming her absolute continuing belief in Cathy's innocence.

The judge agreed with Jerry Wagner.

Cathy was released into Grace's care just before five in the afternoon of Friday, the seventeenth day of July.

They both wept as she walked out of the courtroom straight into Grace's arms, and after they'd run the gauntlet of reporters and photographers, it was straight home to the house on Bay Harbor Islands for Cathy's requested dinner: a thin

371

and crispy pizza with roast chicken and caramelized onions from Liberty Pizza in South Beach – with her own tub of whatever was the *most* obscene ice cream in Grace's freezer. Harry, always a perfect gentleman, greeted Cathy like a longlost lover, and even pretended, when she dropped tiny pieces of chicken on the floor, that he was hanging around her feet for her company rather than food.

Sam stayed away that first evening. He telephoned and talked to Cathy for a couple of minutes, but though she tried hard because Sam was Grace's friend and because she'd always said that Sam seemed pretty cool – and because she had now learned that he was currently on suspension from the police department – he was, when the chips were down, still the cop who had arrested her right after Harry had dug up the murder weapon in her own backyard.

'Did Grace tell you' – Cathy said to Harry right after the call was over – 'that I said to say I didn't blame you for digging up that thing?'

Harry wagged his short tail and licked her hand. Cathy looked up at Grace, and her eyes were shining.

'He knows I'm innocent, too, doesn't he?'

'No doubt about it,' Grace said.

Grace soon realized that David Becket had been right about the disruption to her everyday life. A judge had been persuaded to order the media to keep away from Cathy, but still, it was *not* easy having her to stay. Perhaps that was part of the problem – they were both so aware that she was with Grace as a short-term guest, not really to *stay*, not to live. If they had been able to say that Peter Hayman's guilt had been proven beyond a reasonable doubt, that this was now *absolutely* the start of Cathy's new life, then maybe she might have been better able to set about the business of settling down, of re-establishing herself and some tenuous new roots. But neither she nor Grace could safely see any further than a few weeks into the future, and frankly Grace thought they were both badly affected by the uncertainty in different ways.

Sam was great about it.

'This is a really shitty deal for both you ladies,' he told them one evening while they were all waiting for a table at

Hy-Vong in Little Havana, mouths watering as they caught the aromas of spicy Vietnamese food. 'You're both scared about what's going to happen. *You're* scared,' he said to Cathy, 'because it's you it's just possibly going to happen to all over again – and Grace is scared because she wants so much for this all to be over for you – and you're both spending most of the time skirting around how scared you really are because you want to spare each other's feelings.'

The line of waiting people shifted a little.

'He's right,' Cathy said to Grace. She had, by now, forgiven, if not forgotten Sam's role in her arrest and arraignment.

'I know,' Grace said.

'What's up?' Sam asked her.

'Nothing.'

'I can see something's up,' he said. 'What did I say wrong?'

'Not a thing.' Grace winced. 'That's what's wrong. I'm supposed to be the psychologist, but you're absolutely right, Sam – I haven't been allowing either Cathy or myself to face up to our feelings.'

'That's because you can't shrink your own head,' Cathy said.

'She's right,' Sam said to Grace.

'I know,' Grace said again.

They moved a little closer to the head of the line.

'Do you want to see another psychologist?' Grace asked Cathy suddenly. 'Maybe Dr Khan – you liked him, didn't you?'

'He was okay,' Cathy said, but her face had fallen.

'It doesn't have to be Dr Khan,' Grace said swiftly. 'It could be anyone.'

'I don't want to see anyone.' Cathy's voice had grown suddenly loud, too loud, and her cheeks were hot. 'I don't want anyone but you, Grace.'

'But I'm not sure I can be any real use to you as a therapist right now.'

'I don't *want* you as a therapist – I want you as my *friend*.' There were tears in her eyes. 'I know things can't be normal, I *know* that, but I want us just to be ordinary, even if it's only for a while.'

Grace felt Sam's hand touch her right arm, gripping her gently but firmly. She understood his message, wanted to go with his instincts. She wanted nothing more than to give Cathy a big hug, hold her close, *be* the friend she wanted, maybe more. But she was still scared: of crossing a border she had no right to cross, into the territory that had belonged to Marie Robbins.

'Okay,' she said, praying that the simplicity of the word would be enough.

'Is it?' Cathy searched her face. 'Do you get it, Grace?'

'Of course I get it.' Grace compromised, reached for her hand, held it, not too tightly. 'I want that too. Normality.' She glanced at Sam, saw that he was conscious of her predicament, knew that he thought she'd failed, or at least that she'd copped out.

'Well, I know what I want, guys,' he said, helping out again. 'I want spring rolls and fish with *nuoc man* sauce.'

'What's that?' Cathy asked.

'Lime and garlic.'

'You better have that, too, Grace,' Cathy said, grinning.

'Why's that?'

'You know.'

'Do I?' Grace was all innocence.

Cathy giggled. It felt great to hear and watch. Grace knew they were back to game-playing, to skirting around things, but suddenly part of her – the regular woman part, not the psychologist part – felt that maybe it wasn't such a wrong way to go. After all, she wasn't really sure what the hell *point* there was in analysing their feelings right then. Yes, they were both scared, but they both knew that. Sam was right on the button about reminding them to admit to it now and again, but even if the worst happened and this period did turn out to be all too brief, it might – if it was handled in as relaxed a way as it could be – at least provide a comparatively happy interlude for Cathy, another good time for her to hold on to.

She fascinated Grace more and more. Some of the time she was so grown-up, made grimly streetwise by her losses and by her time in prison; other times she seemed to revert to being much younger than her years. And yet, beneath it all, Grace could still see the nice, highly intelligent, perfectly *normal* young person who had both impressed and touched her the first time they'd met.

Grace remembered that first time. She remembered Cathy's composure, the slightly bland expression that Grace had soon realized was part of her blocking mechanism. Cathy still did the same thing now and again, but with Grace, at least, it happened less and less. If one positive thing had come out of the last several roller-coaster months, it was, Grace thought, that Cathy had come to trust her.

It did disturb her that Cathy was so up and down. Her moods were mercurial and extreme, with explosions of rage and bravado, followed by longer periods of depression, followed, thankfully, by times of contentment and optimism. Sam was good with her, *for* her, when he was around – though he and Grace were still, despite Cathy's clear encouragement of their relationship, being circumspect about intimacy. Over and over again, Grace saw what a great father he must have been, would have been, had Sampson lived. Would, God willing, be again some day in the future.

David and Judy did their best, too. David came to visit a couple of times, on his own – which went well – and Judy invited them to dinner one Friday evening, the end-result of which was less of a success.

'Mrs Becket doesn't like me,' Cathy commented later, when she and Grace were back home alone. 'She isn't sure about me, anyway, is she?'

'What makes you think that?'

'It was obvious. Didn't you feel it?'

'I don't think so.' Grace had actually thought that Judy had made a special effort to put Cathy at her ease.

'I felt it,' Cathy said quietly. 'She was okay some of the time – I mean, she was kind to me, and I guess she was trying not to let it show too much, but every time I tried talking to Saul, she was there, in my face, you know? I think, if she could have, she'd have gotten right between the two of us.' She paused. 'It was like she thought I was going to hurt him or something.'

'I honestly don't think she thought that at all,' Grace said, appalled.

'I do,' Cathy said, quite calmly.

CHAPTER SEVENTY-ONE

THURSDAY, JULY 30, 1998

On the penultimate day of the month, Susan Pitlow, a senior nurse in a private hospital in Spokane, up in Washington State, recognized a photograph on a flier pinned to the bulletin board on the administrative floor. She seldom visited that part of the hospital, or else she would have seen it earlier and identified the child in the photograph. Pitlow had nursed more children than she could count since she'd seen that little boy. She had grown fifteen years older, married, had two sons of her own and relocated. But that particular child had been at the centre of a case that had haunted her for all those years.

His name had been Thomas Harding, and she'd met him when she'd been a young emergency room nurse at a hospital in Portland, Oregon. He had been brought in by his father suffering from abdominal pain and vomiting and had died several hours later from a heart attack. Thomas had been a sweet, stoic little boy even in the midst of his agony, Pitlow now told the FBI agents who came to interview her in Spokane, and his father, Paul Harding, had appeared distraught throughout. When Pitlow had enquired, a few days after his death, into the cause of Thomas's illness, she had learned that he'd apparently eaten poisonous berries. What was causing some disquiet was that Paul Harding – a young widower who had come to Portland three years earlier with his son – had taken so long to bring Thomas into the ER. Further investigation had unearthed one previous emergency visit to that hospital, and two more to another emergency room in the city.

Susan Pitlow was not the only person in Portland who remembered little Thomas Harding. The medical examiner on his case had raised the possibility of Münchhausen's Syndrome by proxy as cause of the child's sufferings and indirect cause of his heart attack and death. Paul Harding had been questioned by the Portland police at length, and the boy's hospital records had been gone into in as much detail as possible, but nothing had been conclusively proven. Harding claimed that Thomas was a curious child, always putting things into his mouth; he admitted that on two other occasions he'd had to induce vomiting in his son because he'd been afraid that he'd swallowed pills, thinking they were candy. Harding seemed eager to help at first, gave plausible answers, then, as things progressed, became increasingly outraged. No one succeeded in breaking him down, and a couple of months after his son's death Harding had sold his house and gone away – after Thomas had been laid to rest beside a stranger, a woman named Agnes Brown, one row away from the plots belonging to the Tully family, also strangers to the five year old, in a cemetery just outside the city.

Of the three mountains visible from Portland, Oregon, the one in the photograph that Peter Hayman – now identified as Paul Harding – had taped to the underside of his bed in Key Largo, was Mount St Helens.

They discovered more about Harding. They learned from his brother, David, that as children living in Seattle, Paul and he had both been MSBP victims, courtesy of their mother. Alice Harding had suffered a nervous breakdown when the brothers had been aged three and five, after which their health had returned to normal. No one had put a name to the bizarre torments she had put her sons through, and until he heard about his nephew's death in 1983, David had believed that Paul had put the past successfully behind him, just as he had. Had the Portland police interviewed David at the time of Thomas's mysterious death, they might not have let Paul Harding go free, but no one had talked to David, and if any dark doubts had troubled him, he had pushed them away.

Now that he knew the whole story, David Harding agreed with the FBI that there might even be grounds for wondering if Paul's wife's early death might also have been suspicious.

*

Everyone agreed that it explained a lot. It certainly explained why Harding had taken a new identity and moved thousands of miles to Florida. It clearly accounted for Peter Hayman's fascination with psychiatry and his obsession with MSBP. It also ruled out any possibility that Hayman and John Broderick had been the same man.

It did not, however, explain why he had kept the photographs of three of the scalpel victims and of Cathy Robbins and Grace Lucca in a locked room in his house. Neither did it present the police with any clear or rational explanation as to why he might have turned into a bloody multiple killer.

Grace went to Captain Hernandez and made another statement reiterating what Hayman had suggested at their first meeting back in April.

'He was trying to get me to link up the Robbins murders with MSBP. He invented another case history – the St Petersburg shootings – to illustrate his point. That a parent might be so twisted, so sick, as to get people to believe their child was mentally disturbed enough to kill.'

'To frame their own child,' Hernandez said.

'Exactly,' Grace said.

'But Hayman – Harding – wasn't Cathy's father,' the captain pointed out.

'I know.'

'So how does this follow through, Dr Lucca, in your opinion?'

'I don't – I can't – form a solid opinion,' Grace answered quietly. 'I can only hazard guesses at this stage. Maybe after Harding turned himself into Hayman, the psychiatrist, he thought up bizarre ways of deviating from MSBP. Maybe he had other victims through the years.' She paused. 'Maybe, at some time we don't yet know about, Harding somehow latched on to Cathy and her family, and took it a step further.'

'A big step,' Hernandez said.

Grace read the scepticism in his voice and eyes. 'I know,' she said.

'Isn't there another possibility, Dr Lucca?' The captain paused. 'Isn't it possible that after he met you at the seminar, he became obsessed by you and your involvement with Cathy

Robbins? Isn't it possible that Harding was never actually involved with the murders at all?'

For a moment, Grace closed her eyes.

Back to square one again for Cathy.

She felt, and quickly suppressed, an urge to scream.

She opened her eyes again and faced up to Hernandez.

'Of course it's possible,' she admitted, quietly.

CHAPTER SEVENTY-TWO

WEDNESDAY, AUGUST 5, 1998

They waited for the other shoe to drop.

Grace and Cathy had come to an agreement to be honest with one another, especially when it came to their anxieties over the case. Every day after Grace's conversation with Hernandez, they waited for any indication that Cathy was going to be re-arrested. It didn't come, but they were both increasingly jittery, and Sam was troubled for them both.

It hadn't been all roses to begin with, and it didn't get rosier.

Three things happened in the first week of August – things that Grace hadn't anticipated at all.

The first occurred on Wednesday morning while she was downstairs on the deck with a patient and Cathy was, to the best of her knowledge, reading a book she'd borrowed from Grace's general fiction shelves – Ayn Rand's *The Fountainhead* – not exactly light and easy escapist reading, but still a wonder to Grace, and Cathy had seemed to be immersed in it, too, when Grace had last seen her in her room.

Grace was with Gregory Lee, a seven-year-old sufferer of night terrors, and they were really starting to get somewhere when for some reason Gregory looked up at the outside of the house and grinned. Grace looked up too, and saw what had made him smile.

Harry was out on the tiny balcony off her bedroom.

Standing right at the edge of the narrow parapet.

Grace stared for a second, then got up slowly.

'Gregory, please wait here. I'll be right back.'

She tried not to run, fighting down her panic, aware that if she scared the boy, he might start to make a noise and startle Harry into falling. Once inside and out of Gregory's view, she flew up the stairs and into her room.

Cathy was in there. Sitting on the edge of the bed, looking out at Harry on the balcony.

'What are you *doing*?' Grace's voice was half hiss, half shriek.

Cathy turned to look at Grace. She seemed surprised to see her.

Grace said nothing more. She passed Cathy, moving towards the balcony.

'Hey,' she said, in her softest, calmest voice, to Harry, praying he'd either stay exactly where he was and let her pick him up, or jump down on the inside of the parapet and come to her. 'Hey, Harry, what're you doing?'

Harry wagged his tail, but stayed where he was.

Grace got to him in less than a second, grabbed hold of him, held him close. She could feel his heart beating fast, smell his doggy scent against her face.

'What were you doing out there, Harry?' she said, and then, slowly, giving herself time to calm down, she turned around to face Cathy again.

She was standing now, still beside the bed.

'Is he okay?' Her voice was strained.

'He's fine,' Grace said. 'What happened, Cathy?'

'I don't know.'

'How did he get out there?' Grace paused. *What were you doing in my room?* She stopped herself asking that question. She hadn't made any rules, hadn't declared any parts of the house off-limits, with the exception of her computer, which she had explained housed confidential patient files.

'I don't know,' Cathy said again. 'I was in my room, reading, and I got this feeling.' She stopped.

'Go on.'

'I don't know why I came in here.'

'Maybe you heard Harry?'

She shook her head. 'I don't think so. I just came in, and saw him.'

Grace remembered Gregory Lee. She *never* left young children alone on the deck for more than thirty seconds at a time.

Quickly, Harry still in her arms, she moved across to the window and looked down. He was sitting exactly where Grace had left him. He looked lonely.

She turned back to Cathy. 'I have to go back down.'

'Do you want me to take Harry?'

'Gregory was missing him,' Grace said, as easily as she could. 'Harry's always been at our sessions before.'

'He's good that way, isn't he?' Cathy said, just as easily.

'Let's get out of here and close the door,' Grace said.

They were in the narrow hallway and Grace was about to head downstairs when she turned again. 'Why were you just sitting watching Harry?'

'I didn't know what else to do,' Cathy said. 'I was afraid if I went outside on the balcony he might get scared and fall.'

'You were probably right,' Grace said, still holding Harry.

'I was talking to him,' Cathy said, 'asking him to come inside.'

'I have to get back down now,' Grace said again, and walked down, not too fast, not too slow. 'See you in a while.'

'Okay,' Cathy said.

Grace heard the door of her room open and close.

She put Harry down on the floor and watched him head for the deck, in his usual, untroubled way. Then she stood in the downstairs hall for another few moments, trying to compose herself. She didn't know how much use she was going to be to Gregory for the rest of their session. Her nerves were still jumping, and she guessed that after the interruption the child would probably be focusing most of his attention on Harry, who wouldn't be arguing.

One thing was clear in her mind. When she'd gone into her bedroom and seen Cathy sitting on the bed, she had *not* been talking to Harry, not even softly. That alone didn't bother Grace too much. She might still have been confounded about what to do for the best.

What really bothered her was how the hell Harry could have gotten up on to the parapet at all? He had short legs and was a poor jumper at the best of times.

Marie's goldfish.

Grace tried not to think about them, tried to push the image out of her mind. After all, she and Sam had just about convinced themselves that John Broderick had got into his former wife's

382

house and dispatched the unfortunate fish himself.

Back to work, Lucca.

Grace stirred herself, and returned to her patient.

It was Dora Rabinovitch who discovered the next thing while she was doing some work for Grace two days later, on Friday afternoon, while Cathy and Grace were out doing some shopping together at the Aventura Mall.

Dora told Grace later that she'd known almost immediately after switching on the computer that someone had been using it, and that she'd been surprised because Grace had told her she hadn't had time to turn it on for more than a week.

'You can see right away the heading for the last document,' Dora said.

Grace understood that much herself. She nodded, but said nothing.

'Your house guest's been using it,' Dora said.

Grace knew that Dora still felt much the same as Claudia did about Cathy.

'Is that a problem?' she asked, lightly.

'I thought you'd told her she wasn't allowed to use the computer.'

Grace bristled a little. 'I said I'd rather she didn't.' She paused. 'This isn't a house of detention, Dora. I want Cathy to feel at home. Kids are so accustomed to computers these days – I think they feel cut off without them.'

'Just the same.' Dora wasn't giving way. 'What she did was sneaky.'

'What did she do?' Grace wasn't sure she wanted to know.

'That's just it – I can't tell you.'

Grace was confused. 'You've lost me, Dora.'

She saw a patient expression come across Dora's face. The older woman often ended up being that way with Grace when it came to discussing computer-related matters.

'I can't tell you what she did because she gave it a password.' Dora took Grace's silence to mean that she hadn't understood. 'You know about passwords,' she said, encouragingly. 'We've used them on confidential files.'

Grace did know all about passwords. She had persuaded Dora, some time back, to let her have a small notebook containing the passwords for any files she might need to access in her absence. They'd argued about it for a while. There was no point having passwords in the first place, Dora had pointed out, if they were going to leave them lying around for anyone to pick up. Grace had said that she hadn't planned on leaving them lying around. Dora told Grace she should put them in her safe. Grace said that she didn't have a safe. Thinking back, Grace remembered that she'd had to get as far as reminding Dora that while confidentiality was a matter of real importance, nothing in her files had any bearing on national security. Finally, Dora had handed over the notebook.

Grace knew about passwords.

She remembered Sam telling her about Cathy's password-protected journal entries. The ones they had persuaded themselves might have been doctored by John Broderick.

'Did she give the file a name?' she asked Dora, quietly.

'Every file has to have a name.'

Grace wasn't in the mood for tutoring.

'What name does this file have?' she asked, a tad too crisply.

She knew what Dora was going to answer before she opened her mouth.

'*My Journal*,' Dora said.

Sam called less than an hour later, asking if Grace and Cathy might feel like going to the show that evening. He always referred to it that way; it might be opera, he said, but any opera company that would have *him* singing a major part *definitely* put on shows, not performances.

Grace told him she was snowed under, which was fine because she'd already happily sat through two shows since the first night, and so she knew Sam wasn't going to be upset.

'I don't suppose Cathy would want to come,' he said.

'I think Cathy's all opera'd out,' Grace said apologetically.

'Any chance of getting together after the show?'

'I don't know. I have a headache building, and by the time I've finished doing my paperwork ...' Grace let the sentence trail off.

'You okay?' Sam sounded concerned.

'I'm fine,' she told him. 'Call me when you've taken your last curtain call. Maybe I'll feel better.'

384

'Don't worry if you don't. I'll call anyway.'

Grace wasn't certain why she hadn't said anything to him about the computer thing. Probably for the same reason she hadn't yet told him about Harry being out on the parapet.

She didn't want to have to think about it.

She wanted to bury her head in the sand until she knew it was all innocent and meaningless.

The journal entry was probably entirely meaningless. Cathy had, after all, kept a legitimate journal for a long time, under that simple, no frills heading. It had only been those incriminating entries that she'd denied creating.

And that password.

Grace remembered that one without checking in any notebook.

She waited until after Dora had gone for the day and Cathy had gone out for a run. She went into the study and closed the door, leaving Harry standing guard outside. She sat down at the desk, reached for the switch, and turned on the computer.

She waited while it went through its opening convolutions. Dora had trained it to move through its incomprehensible (to Grace) pre-op checks without operator assistance, so that when she was the one using it she could just switch on, wait a few seconds, and get right to work.

It was ready for her now.

Grace pressed the F-key that Dora had taught her was the fastest route for commencing a file retrieval. Dora had not said which directory the entry had been filed under and Grace had not asked for the information. *SUNDRIES* seemed the most likely port. She pulled the directory down onto the screen.

It was there. *MY JOURNAL*.

Grace asked the computer to open the file. As she had known it would, it refused to do so. Instead, it asked for the password.

Grace took a deep breath. She felt shaky.

She typed it in.

H-A-T-E.

And hit the return.

And wished she hadn't.

Cathy's Journal
Tuesday, August 4, 1998

Know your enemies. That's what Doc
Parés says I should do. He says it's just
as important as knowing who to trust.

It's hard though. I want to trust her. I
sometimes even think I can trust him,
too, but then I remind myself what he
did to me.

Know your enemies.

Grace closed down the computer, found Harry still waiting outside the door, went and poured herself an early glass of wine.

She needed it.

She took it out on deck, kicked off her loafers, sat on the edge, Harry up close, dunked her feet into the water and took a drink.

She was disturbed. No two ways about it.

Putting aside all other considerations – for a while, at least – she was greatly disturbed by what Cathy had written about Dr Parés. Grace had become aware that the doctor had been exerting considerable influence over Cathy during her last weeks in prison, but it had seemed, on the whole, to have been such a *beneficial* influence that she'd seen no good reason to intervene.

Not that anyone would have listened to her if she had tried to.

Grace drank a little more wine, and thought about getting in touch with Parés, but then she began to wonder what she would say if she did reach him. She did not, for one thing, want to risk antagonizing a man who might, at this still crucial time, be in a position to influence the State Attorney or a judge, or – if things did become worse again – a jury. And Parés had written one of the reports that had contributed to getting Cathy out of prison and into Grace's care.

Conscious that Cathy was likely to get home any time, Grace began trying to analyse what she'd written in her journal. Was it really so disturbing?

Know your enemies.

Parés' advice, apparently. And under the circumstances, maybe not such bad advice at that. A teenager accused of monstrous crimes, locked up in a potentially dangerous environment with adult offenders of all kinds, would almost certainly have been well advised to recognize who was an enemy and who was a friend.

Certainly not a good enough reason to get on the phone to Eric Parés and give him a hard time.

Grace moved on to what she knew had troubled her – shocked her – the most.

The fact that Cathy still didn't know whether to trust her or not.

387

That she might still, beneath her increasingly easy exterior, be uncertain about Sam, was not all that surprising. He might be on suspension, but that had come about because of Sam's fears for Grace, not because of his doubts over Cathy's guilt. He was, no matter what, the man who'd brought her in. Sad, but true.

Cathy's uncertainty about *her* was deeply upsetting.

And above it all, of course, was the fact that with Grace, and with Sam, Cathy had apparently been acting out a role. Pretending to trust them.

She was, after all, capable of deceit.

Absently, Grace ruffled the fur on Harry's head and he pressed closer.

'That leaves the big question, doesn't it?' Grace told him softly.

Had the events of the past few months made Cathy that way? Or had she been like that before Marie's and Arnold's deaths?

Big question.

Cathy came home about ten minutes later, flushed and with eyes sparkling, greeted Grace and Harry with breathless enthusiasm, drank three glasses of bottled water and went upstairs to shower and change.

Grace cooked comfort food that evening. Pasta with her own home-made clam sauce. If Sam had been there, she would have opened a bottle of wine, and Lord knew she was tempted to use another glass or two for anaesthetic purposes, but instead she toughed it out and drank Coke with Cathy.

'Are you okay?' Cathy asked her once, just after they'd started eating.

'I'm fine,' Grace told her. 'A little tired, maybe.'

'Did you work hard?'

'Very.'

'How was Dora?'

'Same as usual.'

'Glad I wasn't around?' Cathy pulled a face. She'd told Grace before that Dora didn't trust her. She had, of course, been right.

Know your enemies.

*

388

Sam called just after ten-thirty. He sounded exhilarated.

'Only another two shows,' he said.

'You'll miss it.'

'You bet I will.' He paused. 'You're beat.'

'Afraid so,' Grace said.

'Cathy okay?'

'Fine. She went for a long run, seemed to enjoy it. We ate pasta and watched a movie and now we've both gone to our beds.'

'Which movie?'

Grace frowned. 'I can't remember.' She honestly couldn't. 'Tom Cruise was in it, but I think I fell asleep about five minutes in.'

'You really are beat.' Sam sounded sympathetic.

'And you're ready to party, aren't you?' She felt horribly guilty. 'Oh, Sam, I'm sorry.'

'What for?'

'For being such a drag.'

'Not exactly the word I'd use to describe you, Grace.'

She could not tell him what she really felt guilty about. She would tell him – she knew she would – but tonight she just wasn't ready.

'Sure I can't come over?' he asked. 'Stroke your hair while you sleep?'

Grace was more than sorely tempted.

'My headache's still nagging at me,' she said. 'I think I'm ready to sleep now.'

'Okay,' Sam said. 'Sweet dreams.'

'You, too, when you come down.'

'Oh, I'm already down, baby. Opera used to be the only thing that could get me high as a kite.' Sam paused. 'Now it's you, Gracie.'

Grace remembered quite liking it when she'd heard Teddy's friend Ramon calling her that. She liked it even better coming from Sam.

She told him goodnight, watched Harry burrow down as usual near her feet, then turned out the light and lay still in the dark. Thinking, of course. Mulling it all over. The thing with Harry on the balcony, and the journal.

She was only just beginning to allow herself to acknowledge the worst aspect of all concerning the latter.

The fact that Cathy was still using the same password.

The ugly word they'd hoped had been part of Broderick's creation.

Grace thought she would never go to sleep.

And then she was gone.

She dreamed she was back in Hayman's guest room and that he was in the room again, standing in the dark looking at her.

Grace woke up.

It wasn't a dream.

Except that it wasn't Hayman.

It was Cathy staring down at her.

Grace sat up. 'Cathy, what's wrong?'

She didn't answer. Grace fumbled for the light switch, turned it on. Cathy blinked, but didn't say anything. At the end of the bed, Harry was still lying down, but he was alert, ears cocked, eyes darting between Grace and Cathy.

'Cathy, why are you in here? What's the matter?'

Slowly, very slowly, Cathy shook her head, and then, still not saying a word, she turned around and walked towards the open door. Grace watched her turn right, heading for her room; her heart pounded as she got carefully out of bed and followed.

Cathy had got back into her bed and was lying down, eyes closed, lids fluttering slightly. Rapid eye movement. Breathing even.

She was asleep.

Which seemed to indicate that she'd been sleepwalking.

Grace knew better than to wake her now. As quietly as possible, she crept back through the door and closed it. And went back to her own bed.

'Cathy's a somnambulist, Harry,' she told her wise old dog.

He grunted.

Grace lay back against her pillows.

She was remembering Frances Dean telling her, a few days after her sister's and brother-in-law's death, that she'd woken one night to find Cathy staring down at her. Two weeks later, Frances had been dead too.

Grace didn't know if that meant a damned thing.

Except that she had read about cases where murderers had claimed that they'd been sleepwalking.

'For crying out loud, Lucca,' she muttered harshly.

Talk about the power of imagination.

Except that if it was all just her imagination working over-time, why the *hell* did she feel what she was feeling?

Afraid.

CHAPTER SEVENTY-THREE

SATURDAY, AUGUST 8, 1998

Grace called Sam just after six a.m. and arranged to meet him for breakfast at eight-thirty. It was Teddy's morning to clean the house, so she had no qualms about telling Cathy that she had to leave her and go out on an appointment.

Not too many qualms, anyway.

Sam had suggested meeting in the Garden Café at the Sheraton, Bal Harbour, just across the Concourse on Collins. Grace's first, instinctive reaction had been to feel that it was too pleasurable a location for the meeting she had in mind – but then she remembered that she'd let him down the night before, *particularly* by not sharing the truth with him, so she kept quiet and figured it would be a miserable enough breakfast, so maybe a waterfall and tropical garden wouldn't hurt.

Sam was hungry, as always, and ordered just about everything. The fact that Grace asked for simple coffee and toast, probably combined with the look in her eyes, was more than enough to warn him that something was wrong.

She told him. Three in a row.

He took it all on board, ignoring his breakfast when it came.

'Okay,' he said. 'First things first. Are you having real doubts about Cathy's innocence?'

'Of course not,' Grace said vehemently, then sagged a little. 'I don't think I am. I hope I'm not.'

'So how are you explaining these things away?'

'I'm not,' she said. 'Not just like that, anyway.'

Sam thought for a moment. 'Do you think everything that's

happened to Cathy may have created some new emotional problems?'

'I think that's a real possibility.'

'Except we know she had a miserable time as a little kid, too, don't we?'

'Yes.' Grace looked into Sam's face defensively, afraid she might be about to see some gung-ho policeman materializing out of the gentle father-type she'd thought she'd been spending time with, falling in love with. But all she saw now was sadness and deep anxiety.

'Would you be easier if she went into foster care or a home?'

'Absolutely not.' Grace was positive of that much, at least. 'If I abandon Cathy now, I'm not sure she'll ever recover.'

'Okay,' Sam said. 'In that case, there's only one other thing to do.'

She was apprehensive again. 'What's that?'

'I start sleeping at your place, and the hell with circumspection.'

If Sam had expected Grace to fight him on that, he was out of luck.

CHAPTER SEVENTY-FOUR

SUNDAY, AUGUST 9, 1998

Murphy's Law ruled.

Sam's unofficial moving-in day coincided with that so-long-awaited call from Captain Hernandez telling him that a sudden onslaught of the 'flu had laid low half of his already depleted department, which was why the chief had agreed to Sam's reinstatement. Effective immediately, Sunday and house-moving notwithstanding.

'Are you going to be okay?' Sam asked Grace after he'd told her.

'Of course I am. It's wonderful news, Sam.'

'I guess moving's going to have to be a night-time thing.'

'Don't worry about that – you may still be working tonight.'

'It's desk duty, Grace, no heavy action.'

'Well, that's good, I'd say, with your back the way it is.'

'My back's not so bad.'

'Is that why you're seeing the physio twice a week and taking medication every night to get to sleep?'

Sam smiled at his end of the phone line, hearing her dryness. 'I can't believe that they're doing this *exactly* when I want to spend as much time with you as possible.'

'Don't worry about me,' Grace said.

'Can't stop me worrying.'

'You'll still be sleeping here,' she said, softly. 'Even if it's an hour a night, that's going to make all the difference to me.'

Grace meant what she said. Twenty-four hours did seem to have taken the edge off most of her personal anxieties over Cathy. If she looked hard enough and long enough, she was certain that she would find a rational explanation for everything that had gone on – even if that did end up meaning that Cathy had been traumatized into doing uncharacteristic things while sleepwalking. It was a weak kind of diagnosis that Grace would ordinarily have had some problems with, but for the time being, while she was still being guardian and woman over and above analytical psychologist, it had to be good enough.

The department aside, Sam still found an hour and a half – aided by Martinez – to move all the stuff that mattered into Grace's place on Sunday afternoon: jeans, T-shirts, shorts, shaving gear, medication, and his favourite opera recordings.

'How come Sam's moving in?' Cathy had asked an hour or so earlier.

Her tone had been flatter than of late, her eyes unquestionably wary. It was clear to Grace that the change of status was making her uncomfortable, even suspicious. *Know your enemies*. Evidently it was one thing being pals with Sam when he came over for supper or they all went out someplace fun together, but having him as part of their small, uneasy family was another matter altogether. Grace didn't blame her. If the events of the past week had not occurred, it was the very last step she would have taken at this time. More disruption to Cathy's shrinking, tilting, precarious world. Suddenly, Grace almost wanted to take the teenager in her arms and tell her that if she wasn't happy about Sam coming to stay, she would tell him to go away again.

Only almost.

At six p.m., Sam called to say that he was going to be late. Paper work, he growled into the phone, that was all Sergeant Kovac had him working on: reports, statistics and more damned reports. All part of the chief's rich disciplinary tapestry, Sam told Grace, and Kovac *loved* it – it was probably the departmental version of a dozen Hail Marys, but who the hell knew if Sam Becket was ever going to get absolution.

'You okay, Gracie?'

'I'm great. How's the back holding up?'

'Sore from too much deskwork.'

'You're just itching for action,' she told him.

'I know what I'm itching for,' Sam said. 'I gotta go – Kovac's looking for any excuse to get the cap to chew my ass some more. If I don't watch out, they'll give me the graveyard shift.'

'Don't worry about us,' Grace said. 'Cathy and I are fine. She's been for her run and we're going to have some supper and hang out.'

'I'll be home soon as I can, but don't wait up.'

'So long as you promise to wake me when you do get in,' Grace said.

Less than a half-hour later, Grace's line rang again, and it was the admissions clerk over at Miami General telling her that one of her patients, Joey Miller, whom she and his parents already knew to be a pyromaniac in the making, had been admitted with third-degree burns, and was asking to see her.

Grace told Cathy what had happened.

'I won't go if you'd rather I stayed home with you,' she said.

'You have to go,' she said.

'I don't if you're not happy with being alone,' Grace told her firmly. 'There are other people who could see this boy, and I could catch up with him tomorrow.'

'But he asked for you, didn't he?'

'Yes, he did.'

'Then you have to go,' she said again. 'Anyway, I won't be alone – I'll have Harry for company.'

'Are you sure, Cathy?'

'I know what that's like,' the girl said, softly. 'I remember how glad I was to see you when I was in that place.'

Grace reached for her hand, and Cathy let her squeeze it, though she didn't squeeze back. Grace let her go again.

'I'll write my cellular number on the pad by the phone in the den,' she said, 'and if you can't reach me on that, the hospital number's in the book. Call me if you want me.' Grace paused. 'And you can get Sam, too, any time.'

'He's busy,' Cathy said.

'He'll be there for you if you need him, Cathy.'

Cathy didn't answer.

396

CHAPTER SEVENTY-FIVE

Cathy was heating up a bowl of home-made minestrone in Grace's microwave oven when she heard the doorbell, followed by Harry's barking.

'Who is it, guy?'

She went to the front door, looked through the spy-hole, recognized her caller and opened the door. 'This is really weird, you know – I was just thinking about you.'

Eric Parés stood on the threshold, tall, trim and elegantly casual in chinos and, in spite of the warm night, a navy blue blazer. 'Hello, Cathy. May I come in?'

'Sure you can.' Cathy stepped back to let him through, and closed the door. Harry trotted forward, sniffed at the visitor's slacks and loafers.

'Is this an inconvenient time?' Parés asked. 'Is Dr Lucca preparing dinner for you? I smell cooking.'

'It's just some soup I was heating up,' Cathy told him. 'Dr Lucca had to go out on an emergency. There's no one else here.'

'You're all alone?'

'That's no problem,' she said.

'You shouldn't be alone in the evenings,' the doctor said.

'I never have been till tonight,' Cathy reassured him. 'Grace has been fantastic – when the hospital called, she said she didn't want to go, but I told her she had to.' She paused. 'I wasn't expecting you, was I? I mean, I hadn't forgotten you said you were coming or anything?'

'Not at all,' Parés told her. 'I was in the neighbourhood, and I wanted to bring you some new vitamins.'

'Really?' Cathy was surprised. 'I still have plenty left.'

'Not like these.' The doctor took an envelope out of his blazer pocket. 'These are new and enriched – a great improvement on what I gave you before.' He stooped to look into her face. 'You're looking strained, Cathy.'

'I'm okay,' she said.

'Are you really?' Parés looked concerned. 'I would be very upset to think you were slipping back.' He held up the envelope. 'All the more reason for you to start on these new capsules immediately.'

'You mean now, before dinner? I've been taking the others at bedtime and first thing.'

'These can be taken now, before food,' the doctor told her. 'And then, if you have a little time, perhaps we could do a little more deep relaxation, and you can show me how well you're managing your self-hypnosis.'

'Oh,' Cathy said. 'Okay.' She remembered the soup. 'Would you like some minestrone? It's Grace's own, home-made – it's really good.'

Parés shook his head. 'Not for me, Cathy. But you go ahead – take two of the capsules first, though.'

'No, it's okay,' Cathy said. She didn't much like the idea of eating the soup while the doctor waited so they could do the relaxation exercises afterward. She'd really been looking forward to having the house to herself for once – she'd planned on eating in front of the tube with Harry – he was *the* best company, and he didn't expect anything of her ... Still, maybe if she got the hypnosis stuff over and done with, she could get rid of Doc Parés and then have a while alone before Cathy or Sam got home.

'Where can we go that's comfortable?' the doctor asked her.

'There's the living room or the lanai,' Cathy suggested.

'Or maybe we should go to your room and you could lie on the bed,' Parés said, 'and then perhaps when we're through, you could go straight off to sleep.' He looked at her face again. 'You look as if you could use some early nights, too, Cathy.'

She shrugged. It was no skin off her nose where she did his exercises, though if Parés thought she was going to go right off to sleep when he was gone like some little kid, he was mistaken. She'd had enough of obeying orders, and more than enough of lock-down and lights-out to last her a lifetime.

Still, the hypnosis was usually pretty cool, and the doc had been right when he'd told her she'd feel really calm and in control afterwards. She always did.

They went upstairs.

CHAPTER SEVENTY-SIX

When Grace got home, a little after ten-thirty, she found Cathy sound asleep in bed.

Harry seemed even happier than usual to see her, bouncing up and down, following her up the staircase and making the small, piercing sounds of joy that were generally reserved for when Grace had been away on a trip without him.

'What's up with you?' She picked him up, but he wriggled, so Grace put him back down again. 'Did you think I was leaving you?'

She went to her bedroom – now, of course, or at least for the time being, *their* room, hers and Sam's – to take off her clothes and run the shower so it would be hot when she stepped in. Some people swore by cold showers, especially in the humid Florida climate, but hot water still worked best for Grace.

She was drying off when, from downstairs, she heard the front door close. For just a second Grace froze – and then, just another split second before she heard Sam's voice, she remembered that she'd given him a spare key.

'Gracie, I'm ho-ome!' he sang out in his best Ricky Ricardo style as he came up the stairs.

Grace came out of the bedroom wearing her towel.

'Great outfit.' Sam wrapped her in a major bear-hug.

'You're earlier than I thought you'd be,' she told him.

'Is that a complaint?'

'Are you kidding?' They kissed, long and hard. 'I only just got home myself.'

*

She told him in the kitchen, over a glass of red and a couple of omelettes, about the call from Miami General, and about Joey Miller, who'd been in pretty bad shape when she'd gotten there to see him, though awful as it was to find a young boy in so much pain and terror, a part of her had registered that an early burning accident – one that might have been infinitely worse, as it turned out – might just *possibly* be the kind of chastening experience that could stop Joey's career as an arsonist before it really got started.

'Your back's bad, isn't it?' She could see him shifting around, trying to get comfortable. 'What's your chair like at the office?'

'Forget it,' Sam said, cutting off the thought. 'If you think Hernandez is about to fork over for special needs furniture for me right now, you're crazier than I thought you were.'

'I didn't know you thought I was crazy.'

'Did you or did you not let me move in with you?'

'I guess I did,' Grace said.

'Crazy,' Sam diagnosed.

'For the time being,' she qualified.

'And then what? You figure I'm going to be easy to get rid of?' He shook his head. 'Definitely crazy.'

They took Harry for a walk, then got ready for bed.

'Don't forget your medication,' Grace reminded Sam just before he climbed in beside her.

'I don't need medication – I have you to rub my back.'

'You can have both. You need both.'

'You sound like a wife,' Sam remarked on his way to the bathroom.

'You sound like a big kid.'

He came back a couple of moments later. 'Now you get to rub my back.'

'Only if I get a massage, too,' she told him.

'Any time,' he said, and got in bed with her.

'Where's Harry?' Grace asked, suddenly.

'Probably boycotting me.'

'Shall I go find him?'

'Only after you've healed my back,' Sam said.

They thought they were going to make love. As it turned

401

out, halfway through rubbing Sam's back, Grace realized he was already two-thirds asleep and that she wasn't far behind him.

'Sweet dreams, Sam,' she said, softly.

'You, too, Gracie.'

CHAPTER SEVENTY-SEVEN

He had watched, listened and waited.

It had taken forever for them to finish their food and wine and wash their dishes and take the damned dog for his walk, and then it had taken another eternity for them to get themselves into their bed.

Black and white.

Black Jew cop, white Guinea shrink. The kind of people who were allowed to take charge of young girls. Instead of their own father.

Another obscenity.

He'd gotten very good at waiting. He'd gotten good at a whole lot of things over the years, had refined many useful skills, but maybe the ability to wait, patiently, stoically, was his greatest gift. He could wait out a tortoise in a marathon if he wanted to.

He could wait forever for the right payback.

It wasn't as if he hadn't had fun along the way. Oh, he'd had heaps of fun. It hadn't been what *they'd* had in mind for him – not that bitch and her daughter. *Bitch kitty and baby kitty.* One dead now, the other having it tough.

About to get tougher.

Nothing she didn't deserve.

She'd screwed it all up for him, after all. From conception through to rejection. Her doing, as much as her mother's.

Bitch kitty's sister had called him a power maniac. Because he liked being in control of his wife and child. He showed *her* who was in charge when the time was right.

He'd had plenty of time to think about power. Everyone wanted it. Not just the strong or rich or wicked. You saw it everyday, everyplace, in all shapes and sizes. The infant, controlling its mother. The adolescent tyrant. The raging teenager. User of sexuality. Hungry lion flexing his jaws in the cities. Workaholic exec driving her staff to breakdown. Bus driver slamming his door on a latecomer. Judge dispensing justice. *So-called* justice. Moaning wife. Sick patient.

The desire for control was a human need. No one was too young or too old. They all craved it, all used it. It was just that some were better at using it than others.

Control. Power.

He loved it all right.

He'd watched, listened and waited some more.

And now they were all sleeping.

Even the mutt, thanks to him.

He began to move, quietly, from his hiding place, into the main body of the house. Even in the dark, he knew his way. He'd been here a few times now, and he'd always had a razor-sharp memory for detail. So he knew where the kitchen table was and the chairs, and the doorknobs and handles, knew where each creaking floorboard was on the staircase.

His heart was pumping. He was sweating just a little.

It felt great.

His feet were silent on rubber soles as he passed the sleeping dog and entered the girl's room.

She was dreaming, eyelids, arms and hands moving.

Bad dreams. He knew that for sure. Awful nightmares. The kind of wild, crazed, violent dreams likely to assault an individual who'd taken a large enough dose of methylphenidate mixed with diazepam.

It was exactly as he'd calculated.

Soon, very soon now, she would wake up, and if he'd got the dosage right – and he always did, didn't he? – she would be someplace between a trance and a full-blown, paranoid psychotic state.

He bent over and whispered into her left ear.

A little something he'd prepared earlier. Courtesy of good old Aesop.

'Enemies' promises are made to be broken.'

She stirred. Her eyelashes fluttered.

'Grace and Sam don't believe in you anymore,' he told her. 'It's just a matter of time now until they put you back in jail.'

She moaned, stirred again.

'Unless you stop them,' he said into her ear. 'You can stop them, Cathy. You know you can.' He paused, one more time. 'You have to stop them, Cathy, before they destroy you.'

With his latex-gloved right hand, he took the scalpel out of his blazer pocket, and placed it in her hand, closed her fingers around it.

And stepped back into the shadows.

Cathy woke up, shuddering, sweating, heart hammering.

She sat up. Slid her feet out of bed and on to the floor.

Stood up.

The scalpel fell out of her hand. She stared down at it.

'Pick it up, Cathy.'

The voice came out of the darkness, out of the night.

'Pick it up, Cathy.'

She picked it up. It felt cool in her hand. Smooth.

'Now go and do what you have to, Cathy.'

She couldn't tell if the voice was in her head or coming out of the walls. Her heart was pounding so hard it was hurting her. There was a great pressure inside her skull, in her brain.

'It *hurts*,' she whimpered.

'They're your enemies, Cathy,' the voice told her.

She put her hand, with the scalpel, up to her temple. She thought her head was going to burst. 'But it *hurts*.'

'Go and finish them, Cathy, and the pain will stop.'

'But I—'

'*Now*, Cathy. Do it to them before they do it to you.' Pause. 'It's your last chance, Cathy. Your only chance.'

He watched as she lowered her hand from her head, still gripping the scalpel, and turned towards the door.

She moved slowly. He could see her trembling from where he stood.

Watching.

Waiting.

405

CHAPTER SEVENTY-EIGHT

Grace didn't know what woke her.

It could have been the door opening, or the movement towards the bed.

It might have been the small whisper of wind fanning her face as the scalpel drove down in a perfect arc towards her naked throat.

The brain works in mysterious ways.

She felt the air, saw the blade in the light from the window, jerked her head to the right as she registered the danger. The blade missed her neck and sliced into her shoulder instead.

She screamed.

Sam, lying beside her, groaned but didn't move.

Grace screamed again.

And managed to hit the light switch.

Cathy was standing motionless beside the bed, a scalpel covered in Grace's blood still in her right hand.

'Cathy?'

Grace could see from the immense pupils and confusion in the young woman's blue eyes that she was drugged. *Not sleep-walking*, Grace registered for the record, and wasn't *that* nuts, slipping into shrink-mode now?

'Sam.' She pushed at his back with her right elbow, not taking her eyes off Cathy's face for a second. '*Sam.*'

'Don't stop now, Cathy.'

A man was walking into the room. A stranger.

Tall, slim, dark-eyed, with receding black hair and a tidy beard.

'You have to go on, Cathy,' he told her. 'You have to finish it now. You'll never have another chance if you don't do it now, believe me.'

Cathy wasn't looking at him, but Grace could see her eyes reacting, moving rapidly, the irises flicking wildly back and forth.

'They're your enemies, Cathy,' the man told her in his soft, husky, compelling voice.

Grace knew who he was.

The accent was gone, but she knew this was Eric Parés, purveyor of vitamins and relaxation therapies – and that had to be why Sam wasn't waking up, because Parés had been in the house and had put something in Sam's anti-inflammatory pills – and Christ knew what he'd given Harry, too, because otherwise the terrier would have been barking his head off by now.

'You're Broderick,' she said, and now her head and eyes were moving back and forth between him and Cathy, and she didn't know what she was supposed to do next. 'You're Parés and you're Broderick, and you've done all the killing, and you've done this to your own daughter.'

'Go on now, Cathy.'

He took no notice of Grace at all – she might have been invisible and mute.

Stop the bleeding.

Moving slowly, Grace took a handful of sheet and pressed it against the wound in her shoulder, knowing she had to play for time or *do* something.

Under the sheets, she kicked Sam with her right foot. For the second time, he gave a dull groan, but nothing else. She kicked him harder.

Parés was still focusing intently on Cathy.

'You're doing so well,' he told her, 'so *well*.' His voice was honeyed now. 'Just a little farther, not far to go. If you stop now, Cathy, you know what will happen to you, what they'll do to you. You'll be sent back to that place – Grace and Sam will make *sure* you never come out again.'

Same game, Lucca. You have to play the same game.

Grace's eyes swivelled down to check her shoulder. The blood was oozing through the white sheet, but at least it wasn't gushing, and although she was shaking like a jello in an earthquake, she didn't think she was going to pass out quite yet. She looked back up at Cathy's face, saw absence and wildness and bewilderment in her eyes, and knew that whatever mind she had left right now was trapped in some internal firestorm beyond her understanding.

'Cathy.' Grace tried to make her voice as soft and compelling as his, praying that the girl wasn't too far under to respond to her. 'I know how hard this is for you. I know you don't want to kill me or Sam. You don't want to hurt anyone, Cathy, and you've never killed anyone. I know that – Sam and I both know that – and if you put down that thing in your hand, just drop it on the floor, then everyone else will know it too, and all this pain will be over.'

Keeping her eyes trained on Cathy, Grace heard Parés move closer, heard his breathing speed up a little, then slow again, calm again, and she knew, she just *knew* he was getting closer to what he saw as the climax of the horror game he'd been playing.

'Put it down, Cathy.' Grace's voice was shaking again – there was no *way* of maintaining the illusion of calm. She sounded as desperate as she felt. 'For God's sake, Cathy, you have to *listen* to me before it's too late.'

'It already is too late, Cathy,' Parés said, less softly now, more commandingly, 'if you don't do what I tell you to do. You'll be finished – *through* – unless you do it to them first. Just lift your arm again – just raise it – yes, that's right—.'

Grace watched, horrified, as Cathy's right arm lifted into the air.

'It's getting lighter, isn't it, much lighter – and the steel in your hand is an arrow with a golden tip. It's your passport out of here, Cathy ...'

Grace saw Cathy's fingers clasp more tightly around the instrument. Beside her, Sam slept on, dead to the world, and the blood was still flowing from Grace's shoulder, and she knew she was getting weaker ...

'Drop the scalpel, Cathy,' she said suddenly, loudly, with all the strength she could muster. 'Drop the goddamned *scalpel*, Cathy, or all you'll be is a *murderer*, the way he wants you to be – a *killer*.'

Cathy dropped it. Grace lurched forward, trying to get to it, but Parés was there before her, snatched it from the rug, grabbed Cathy around her waist. Grace saw her head loll, heard the reflexive, gasping intake of her breath as Parés tightened his grip around her middle.

'Let her go,' Grace begged him. 'Hasn't she been through enough?'

'Not enough,' he said. 'Not yet. And don't kid yourself that it matters if she's the one who kills you, or if I do it myself, because I'll be long gone when you're found, and she'll be the last one to die.'

Beside Grace, Sam gave another groan. Silently, she slid her right hand beneath the bedclothes and dug all her fingernails into his side. He yelped in his sleep.

'And later, much later,' Parés went on, 'when they do her postmortem, they'll find quite a cocktail in her system – all kinds of nasty stimulants and sedatives – and they'll know it's all stuff she probably got hooked on inside, the way so many of them do.'

'You dirty son-of-a-bitch,' Grace said as loudly as she could, and dug her nails back into Sam again, knowing she desperately needed to hurt him enough to bring him back to consciousness. 'You used to be a *doctor*, for God's sake, a *real* doctor.' She clawed Sam's stomach, and this time, she thought she felt him trying to get away from her nails, and oh, *Christ*, she hoped he was hurting, she hoped he was hurting enough to come *back* to them before it was too late—

'Oh, yes, I was a doctor,' Parés said. 'A damned fine doctor, before my bitch of a wife and her tight-assed sister wrecked my career, after they and this little baby girl' – he was still tightening his hold around Cathy's body, and any second now Grace was terrified she was going to hear the cracking of her ribs – 'told the powers-that-be that they didn't *want* me anymore.'

'Cathy was just a little *girl* when Marie got that court order,' Grace cried out. 'She was just an innocent little *child*!' Cathy's head was lolling a different way now, and Grace could see her eyes rolling and her lips were starting to turn blue. 'Let her go, please – you have to let her *go*!'

'I don't have to do *anything*,' Parés spat. His eyes were filled with loathing. 'She screamed at me whenever I touched her! She hated me from the moment she came into this rotten, stinking world!' He gulped for air, and now his expression was exhilarated. 'So I took the power for myself, didn't I? I knew I was smarter than they were, than *any* of them were, so I ducked out of the picture for as long as I needed to, and look what happened, I got even smarter.' He was flexing his right hand now around the instrument. 'Oh, the things I learned, Dr Dago Shrink, the things I *learned.*'

Beside Grace, Sam moaned, a new, different kind of a sound. 'Sam!' Grace turned and shook him by the shoulders, yanked at his hair. 'Sam, you have to wake up now!' He moaned some more, so she slapped his face, and she didn't even have to steel herself to do it, it was just life or death, as simple as that. '*Sam*, you have to wake *up!*'

It was the first time Grace had taken her eyes away from Parés since he'd grabbed Cathy, and it was a second too long.

'Grace, watch *out!*'

She spun around to see that Cathy had wrested herself free, and Parés was coming at them, at the bed, and the scalpel was coming down again, and this time it was coming straight for Sam—

Grace screamed again as she used the last of her strength to shove him clear, but she wasn't fast enough, and the blade scythed into Sam's side. With a shriek of agony, he came to and kicked out reflexively with both feet, catching Parés in the stomach and knocking him off balance. Grace tumbled off the bed and was almost beside Cathy when she saw that the girl had the scalpel again, and instantly Grace knew what she was going to do.

'*No*, Cathy!' Grace couldn't let her do that, couldn't let her destroy herself completely. She grabbed the first thing that came to hand – a book from her bedside table. 'Cathy, get clear!' she yelled. 'Get *away!*'

Grace threw the book as hard as she could at Parés' head, heard the dull, sickening, infinitely *satisfying*, sound of it hitting, heard him cry out, clutching his temple, watched him stagger. And then she saw that Cathy had dropped the scalpel again, and Grace dived for it – and suddenly for the first time, *she* was in control.

'Grace, *don't!*'

She only half heard Sam's voice, but she wasn't listening,

and now *she* was raising the weapon, and it felt good in her hand, powerful – and Parés was still stumbling around, holding his head. And for one long moment it wasn't Parés or Broderick that Grace was seeing – it was Frank Lucca, her own monster father, and it wasn't Cathy he'd been half-killing, it was Claudia, and Grace didn't think she knew anymore, or *cared* anymore, which father she was going to kill, so long as she *finished* him, finished the *nightmare—*

The first shot exploded past her head, crunched clear through Parés' hand, ricocheted against the wall beside the bed, made Grace drop the scalpel and sent Cathy, shrieking in terror, crawling away while her tormentor squealed like a wounded animal.

Grace turned and saw that Sam had dragged himself off the bed and had his .38 in both his shaking hands – Grace hadn't even seen him bring the hideous, horrific, wonderful gun *into* the house.

'Grace, get down on the floor!' Sam commanded. 'Get *down*!'

Grace got the hell down, but Sam's hands were trembling violently, and his eyes were screwed up as if he couldn't see properly, and Grace realized that the drugs inside him were interfering with his vision.

'He's got it again!' she heard Cathy shriek.

The explosion of the second bullet grazed Parés' left cheek.

He put a hand up to touch it, wiped away the streak of blood and laughed, a cold, harsh sound. And then he began to move back towards Grace.

The third explosion slammed clean into his chest.

Eric Parés, once known as John Broderick, fell backwards lightly on to Grace's bedroom rug, the scalpel still in his right hand. His body hitting the floor seemed to make no sound at all, though maybe it was because the thunder of the shots was still ringing in Grace's ears.

She stared up at Sam. He was saying something to her, but Grace couldn't hear him. She turned around again, searching for Cathy, saw her over by the door, huddled, head down, with her arms around her knees.

Very slowly, very painfully – as Sam bent to take the weapon out of her father's hand and then pulled the phone on to the floor to call for back-up – Grace crawled towards her.

411

CHAPTER SEVENTY-NINE

TUESDAY, AUGUST 11, 1998

Bogeymen are tough to kill.

John Broderick had made it through surgery at Jackson Memorial into intensive care, and, according to his doctors, there was no reason to doubt that he would survive to face justice. Grace's and Sam's wounds had been superficial. Cathy, David Becket and his colleagues at Miami General said, was going to need careful observation for several days at least while a series of tests – physical, neurological and psychological – were run to determine that no permanent damage had been done by the long-term drug and hypnotic abuse she had suffered.

The greatest concern voiced by the teenager during the early hours had been for Harry, and nothing would convince her that he was perfectly recovered from his own drugs ordeal until David Becket talked the hospital management into letting Teddy Lopez bring the dog in for a brief visit on the second day.

'Better now?' Grace asked Cathy, after Teddy and Harry – bright-eyed and bouncing and no worse off for having napped his way through the ordeal – had gone back home.

'Aren't you?' she said, lying back against her pillows.

Grace smiled. 'Of course.'

'How's your shoulder?' Cathy asked.

'Not bad.' Grace was sitting in a wheelchair, orders of the hospital.

'What about Sam?'

'Getting better. Complaining more about where I scratched him to try waking him up than about the cut in his side.'

Grace waited for Cathy to ask about Parés, but she didn't, which was no real surprise. She considered playing it Cathy's way for a while longer – acting as if he didn't exist – but there was one crucial element that Grace felt Cathy needed to know, and to *believe*, as soon as possible.

'Parés is going to make it,' she said. 'But he's in a maximum security ward at Jackson Memorial.' Grace paused, watching Cathy's face. 'There's no way on earth for him to escape.'

'Like he did before, you mean,' Cathy said, quietly.

Neither Sam nor Grace had been certain how much she had taken in of Sunday night's happenings – Grace hadn't even been sure if Cathy had realized that Parés was really her father. Now she knew.

'So you know who he really is?' Grace said, just as softly.

Cathy didn't look at her, kept her eyes trained on a fold in the sheets on her bed. 'I heard everything,' she said. 'It was all muffled and weird, like I had a blanket over my head or something, but I heard every word you and he were saying.' She paused, still looking down. 'Don't ask me how I feel about it, Grace, because I don't know.'

'I'm not going to ask,' Grace said. 'Not yet.'

At last, the blue eyes turned back her way, and they were pools of confusion and disbelief. 'Is it true?' Cathy asked. 'Is Dr Parés really my father?'

'It seems that way,' Grace answered. 'We don't have one hundred per cent confirmation yet, but there's really very little doubt.'

Cathy was silent again for a few seconds.

'So he killed my mom and Arnie,' she said. 'And Aunt Frances.'

'Yes.'

'And Beatrice Flager.'

'It certainly looks that way.'

'And he would have killed us, too, if ...'

'I think he might have.' Grace seldom saw any good purpose in lying.

Cathy looked away again. 'I'm sorry,' she said, softly.

'What for?'

'Because he's my father.'

Quiet rage seethed through Grace. She leaned forward in the wheelchair. 'You are not responsible for anything he's done, Cathy. It's the other way around.' She had to swallow hard to contain her anger. 'Don't you ever forget that, not even for a second.'

'He said he blamed me for everything.' Cathy's voice was flat again. 'I heard him. He said that I screamed whenever he touched me. He said that I hated him.'

'He isn't a rational man, Cathy.' Grace's right hand clenched the arm of her chair. She wanted to weep for the girl. 'I don't know exactly why, but I'm not certain that he ever *was* rational.'

Cathy looked right at Grace again, and her eyes were suddenly wet. 'I didn't hate him, you know. Mom did – and Aunt Frances.' She shook her head. 'But I don't think I ever did.'

Grace didn't speak.

'I do hate him now, though,' Cathy said.

Thank God for that, at least, Grace thought, but refrained from saying.

She believed it, though, with all her heart. Hate had its place in the scheme of things, she'd often thought. She knew it wasn't a Christian way to think – she knew that if she weren't such a badly lapsed Catholic, she would probably have felt compelled to raise the matter in the confessional.

But Grace did believe in hate, just as she believed in evil.

It existed, all right.

If she hadn't been sure of that before, she was now.

CHAPTER EIGHTY

MONDAY, AUGUST 17, 1998

It took some time to put together.

As soon as the man who'd called himself Eric Parés was out of the ICU and it was deemed decent to go to work on him, they took dental impressions and X-rays and had John Broderick's dentist up in Tallahassee confirm that Parés and Broderick were one and the same. They had already ascertained that he wore brown contact lenses and dyed his hair, and they'd found fine scarring around his ears from where he'd had help from a plastic surgeon to lessen the roundness of his face. More X-rays proved that his large nose had been reduced. The scars on the insides of both wrists and on his throat had been left to nature; probably, the consensus of opinion was, Broderick had feared that asking a plastic surgeon to rid him of those might have drawn excessive attention to himself.

The day after Broderick had been brought into Jackson Memorial, officers from the City of Miami Police Department had entered the apartment that Parés had given as his address when he'd fraudulently applied for his part-time job as physician to the inmates of the Female House of Detention.

The apartment was a one-bed in the Latin Quarter just off the Tamiami Trail. It was small, clean and tidy – a place for everything and everything in its place. The search was meticulous. The officers went through every piece of paper in every file in a two-drawer cabinet – only half filled – and found no trace of anything referring to either John Broderick or the Robbins family. To all intents and purposes, it *was* the home of Eric Parés, MD – the only true strange-

415

ness about it being that none of Parés' papers dated back past May that same year.

'Broderick isn't talking,' Sam told Grace. 'He knows we know who he is and what he's done, but he's not playing ball.' He paused. 'Oh, yeah, and he said – and I quote – that if the "nigger Jew cop comes anywhere near him, he'll shut up tighter than a coffin".'

'Nice,' Grace said.

They were home from the hospital, had been for a few days now, though Cathy was still there, growing stronger but still being monitored for after-effects. It was evening, and they were out on Grace's deck with Harry.

'Not that I can talk to him anyway,' Sam said, 'since all he's charged with so far is filling Cathy with drugs and wounding the two of us.'

'They will break him down, won't they?'

'I'm not a betting man,' Sam said, 'but I'd say they will, given time. We already know a few things about Broderick. When he gets mad, he spews it out – and he likes bragging about how smart he is.'

'But he likes power more,' Grace pointed out quickly. 'And so long as he's not talking, he keeps that, doesn't he?'

'To a degree.'

'What happens if he doesn't confess and we can't prove what he did?'

'We will prove it.' Sam was definite.

'But what if we can't? Isn't there always going to be a chance that Cathy could still get blamed – maybe for doing the killings under hypnosis, or sleepwalking?'

'No State Attorney's going to take that before a jury, Grace.'

'Maybe not,' she said. 'But we need a resolution to this. An ending. *Cathy* needs an ending if she's ever going to get through it all and move forward.'

CHAPTER EIGHTY-ONE

TUESDAY, AUGUST 25, 1998

Broderick was out of hospital and in prison.

Within a few days of his settling down in his maximum security cell, he made it known to his lawyer that he might now be willing to start talking, but that he had one condition.

Sam thought about going over to Grace's house to break the news to her, but he was on duty and he knew it was too important to wait till evening – and besides, there was no way of softening the impact of Broderick's demand.

'He wants to see Cathy,' Sam told Grace on the phone.

He knew, more or less, what she was going to say. Cathy had only been back home for a few days. She was in good shape physically, but emotionally she was fragile. How could she not be?

'Over my dead body.'

'The chief says we have to ask her.'

'The hell we do.'

Sam gave her a moment. 'You could be with her.'

'I don't want her to be put through that, Sam,' Grace said.

'I know. Nor do I.' He paused. 'And I don't want to say what I have to say next, either.'

'Please tell me it has nothing to do with Broderick's being her father?' Grace's voice was very strained.

'That's what he still is,' Sam said quietly. 'I hate it as much as you do.'

'Then please stop this from happening.'

'I don't think I can do that.'

'Sure you can – just tell the chief that we're not going to ask Cathy.'

417

'If we don't, someone else will.'

Grace said nothing.

'Maybe it'll help,' Sam said.

'How could seeing that monster possibly *help*?'

'What's that word you used – when you talked about going back to Chicago for your mother's funeral?' Sam searched for it. 'Closure.'

'I think that what I told you,' Grace said, coolly, 'was that I didn't think I had achieved closure.'

'But I think you said that your sister seemed to have.'

Grace opened her mouth to retaliate, then shut it again. He was right, God damn him, he was *right*.

'Oh, Sam.'

'I know.'

She took another moment, fighting for composure.

'I'm only going to ask Cathy. If she says no, then that's it. Okay?'

'Of course,' Sam said.

'He really is a monster, isn't he?'

'Certainly seems that way.'

Cathy shrank away a little at the words, but then, just as Grace was starting to tell her that no one was going to make her go to the prison, she said that she wanted to see Broderick.

'I think maybe I have to,' she told Grace.

'Sweetheart, you don't have to do anything you don't want to do. You've been through more than enough – no one's going to force you to see him.'

Cathy said nothing for a few seconds.

'But if I don't, I'm always going to have that last picture of him in my head.' Her eyes were cloudy, the way they always were when she was deeply burdened. 'He was trying to kill you, Grace. And he *laughed*.'

'I know,' Grace said, very softly.

'I think –' Cathy stopped.

'What, Cathy?'

'I think, maybe, I need to see him to be sure.'

'Sure of what?' Grace asked, gently.

'That I'm not like him,' Cathy said.

'Oh, Cathy.' Grace couldn't stop her dismay showing

418

through. 'You're *nothing* like Broderick – you must never think that way.' She knew, even as the words were out, that she was wholly wrong and that, as a psychologist, she ought never to have allowed such folly to slip out, because of *course* Cathy was going to think that way – how could she *not*?

Cathy put it perfectly simply.

'He's my father, Grace. I'm his daughter.'

Grace brought herself back under control.

'You're also Marie's daughter,' she said. 'And Arnie's.'

'I know that,' Cathy said, and her mouth quivered. 'But still, I think I do have to go see him.'

CHAPTER EIGHTY-TWO

FRIDAY, AUGUST 28, 1998

Cathy had been jittery and pale from the moment they'd left home. Grace had asked her twice if she wanted to change her mind. The first time, Cathy had said no, but her eyes had, to Grace, seemed to be yearning to say yes. The next time, Cathy had snapped at her and the look of yearning had gone. Grace had known better than to ask again.

Inside the prison, she got worse, jumping every time a door clanged shut. Grace took her hand a few times, and in response Cathy's fingernails dug into her flesh so hard that it hurt, but she held on and said nothing. Grace knew she could not begin to imagine what Cathy was going through. Just coming back into a prison of any kind after the last few months would have been a nightmare. Coming into this place to see Broderick had to be hell on earth.

Their visit had been well-prepared for and there were no significant delays to make the tension worse. When the moment came for them both to be frisked, Grace was all set for Cathy to break down, but she seemed, superficially at least, to have become almost calm.

'Holding up?' Grace asked her quietly.

Cathy nodded. 'You?'

'I'm fine, too.'

They were, they were told, using the lawyer's interview room. It was long and narrow, with four chairs fixed to the floor within partitions, set about six to eight feet apart, a small area of counter top before each one. A window stretching from wall to wall and from the counter tops up to the ceiling divided them from a similar set-up on the other side. There

420

were circles cut in the thick plastic window with narrow slits for them to speak through. A folding chair had been placed beside one of the fixed seats.

'You take that one.' Grace indicated the chair bolted to the floor.

Cathy sat without a word.

They waited.

His red prison jumpsuit and handcuffs aside, Broderick already looked startlingly different. Grace had only seen him as Parés that one time, that night, but she could tell that this sight of him was a fresh shock for Cathy.

No hair dye in jail, Grace thought.

That was part of it. There was already about a half inch of new growth at the receding hairline, more greying than the blond she knew it had been.

No lenses.

That was the biggest thing. Parés had had brown eyes. Broderick's were blue. Grace wished with all her heart that they were a different blue, but they were almost identical to Cathy's colour.

Only the colour. Nothing else.

Broderick was the first to speak.

'I told my lawyer I wanted to see you alone.' He spoke directly to Cathy, ignoring Grace. 'But now I have these gentlemen' – he jerked his head in the direction of the two guards standing near the door behind him – 'and I have her.'

'I wanted Grace with me.' Cathy's voice trembled just a little.

Don't let him get control, Lucca.

'We told your lawyer that my presence was not negotiable,' Grace said.

'I know you did.' Still, Broderick did not look at her.

'Why did you want to see me?' Cathy asked him.

'Why do you think?'

'You tell me,' she said.

The fear almost left Grace then. She had thought for a long time that Cathy was a remarkable person. She had not understood till now, till this instant, just how very brave she was.

421

Broderick seemed to read her mind. For the first time, he looked at her.

'Cathy still living with you, doctor?'

'That isn't really your concern,' Grace answered.

'Sure it's my concern.' First flash of anger. 'She's my daughter.'

Grace didn't speak.

'Perhaps you think you're her new mother?' Broderick said.

He's trying to get control again. Don't let him.

'Grace is my friend,' Cathy said.

Broderick was still looking at Grace. 'If you're planning on playing Cathy's mommy, what does that make your boyfriend? Her daddy?'

Grace took a breath. 'Mr Broderick, what is it you wanted to say to Cathy? We're not going to be here for very much longer.'

'My name is *Dr* Broderick.'

'Whatever,' Grace said.

Broderick turned his attention back to Cathy. 'How are the relaxation exercises going, Cathy, dear?' He was calm again.

Grace felt Cathy flinch. She had an almost overpowering urge to grab her by the hand and pull her out of the room.

'How could you do those things?' Cathy asked.

Her composure, her *strength*, almost blew Grace away again.

'What things are you talking about, dear?' Broderick enquired.

'You know what things.' Cathy's voice faltered slightly.

'I don't know,' he said, 'unless you tell me.'

'Cathy.' Grace touched her right arm, gently. 'Don't put yourself through more than you have to.'

'Fuck off, *Mommy*,' he said.

'Watch your mouth, Broderick,' one of the guards near the door warned.

Cathy started to rise, then sat down again. 'There's just one thing I want to tell him,' she told Grace, 'and then we can go. Okay?'

Grace nodded. 'Whatever you want.'

Cathy turned back to look at him.

'I never did hate you, you know. Before, I mean.'

422

'Gee,' Broderick said.

'I didn't know how to hate back then.'

'But you've learned, haven't you, daughter?'

She nodded, slowly. 'Yes.'

'Is that it?' Broderick leaned forward in his seat until his forehead was almost touching the window on his side and his breath misted the plastic.

'Yes,' Cathy said. 'That's it.'

'Then I have something I need to make sure you know, little girl.'

Grace felt Cathy go rigid.

Broderick leaned back again a little, then directed his voice right at the slatted circle in the window, making sure he was going to be heard.

'I don't forgive you for anything, Cathy,' he said, loud and clear. 'And I do hate you. I hated you from the instant you were conceived.'

Grace stood up. 'Come on, Cathy.'

'You wrecked my marriage and then you and your mother destroyed my career, and you wanted to destroy my life, too.' The hatred wasn't really visible in Broderick's eyes or tone now, only his pleasure. 'I want you to know that – and I want you to understand that you *are* responsible for your mother's death, and for all the others.' He smiled through the plastic into her eyes. 'They may have let you out of prison, Cathy, but I know the truth and it's only right that you should know it, too.'

Cathy got up, too. She was shaking visibly.

'That's right,' he said. 'You run, both of you.'

Cathy turned to Grace. Tears swam in her eyes.

'That's all I wanted you to know.' Broderick was still seated. 'That I still blame you and hate you. And I always will.'

Grace took Cathy's hand and walked her towards the door.

Neither of them looked back.

They were almost at the outer gate of the prison when Grace heard a man calling her name, halting her. It was one of the two guards who'd been on Broderick's side of the window, the one who'd rebuked him when he'd sworn.

'A word, ma'am?' he said to Grace.

'Yes?'

'Alone, if you don't mind.' The guard paused. 'It'll only take a second.'

Grace looked at Cathy. She nodded.

The guard walked about six feet back in the corridor. Grace followed him. He was a large, overweight man with close-cropped brown hair and narrow grey eyes.

'What is it?' she asked. 'I really want us to get out of here.'

'I understand, ma'am, and I'm real sorry to hold you up.'

'That's all right.'

The man's eyes were very intense.

'We just want you to tell the young lady – if you think it's right, that is – we want you to tell her that we're real sorry for her pain.'

Grace looked at him, surprised. 'Thank you,' she said. 'It's kind of you.' She started to turn away.

'There are men in here' – the guard's voice stopped her again – 'who don't like what he's done to her, and who aren't going to like what he's still tryin' to do.' He paused. 'That's just for you to know, doctor. It's maybe better she doesn't know that.' He paused again. 'Just tell her not to fret too much. Okay, ma'am?'

Grace looked into the meaningful eyes and felt a cold shiver creep up her spine.

'Okay,' she said.

CHAPTER EIGHTY-THREE

Grace heard about the new find later that evening.

Sam was waiting at the house to greet them when they got home from the prison, his eyes anxious.

Cathy looked at him for just a moment after they'd walked in the door, and then she went straight into his arms and let him hold her.

Grace watched Sam's face, and was grateful beyond words.

He waited till Cathy was asleep in bed.

'They found Broderick's real home today. A boat named *Healer*.'

Grace was listening intently.

'Seems she's been anchored off Key Biscayne, just sitting there waiting for someone to find.' Sam paused. 'Another boat anchored close up to her yesterday – a family on vacation. You know, meals on deck, swimming around, hanging loose.'

'And?' Grace urged him on.

They were sitting in the kitchen. Sam waited for a moment, listening, wanting to be certain Cathy wasn't awake and coming downstairs.

'They smelled something bad. They told the Marine Patrol that they thought it was something in the water. They kept waiting for it to shift along with the current, but it never did. Finally, they realized it was something to do with the other boat anchored nearby.'

'The *Healer*,' Grace said.

For the second time that day, she shivered.

*

The cabin cruiser had told the police much of what they'd wanted to know about John Broderick, and more besides.

Shelves and cubbyholes crammed with drugs, legal and illegal: sedatives, hypnotics, amphetamines and hallucinogenics; an array of psycho-control weapons ranging from AMF and DOB, through Quaaludes, Ritalin, cannabis and LSD, down to chloral hydrate, morphine and a whole range of benzodiazepines. An obsessive, amateur psychopharmacologist's paradise playground. More than enough dope for Broderick to have played all the mind games he needed with Christ-alone-knew how many others – and maybe himself – and certainly to have sedated his victims in various ways to make it seem feasible that someone unthreatening – like Cathy – had been able to move in close enough to stab them.

They had found the cause of the bad smell, too.

There was a body on board the *Healer*.

Peter Hayman's – Paul Harding's – body.

'He was tied up,' Sam told Grace quietly. 'Bound and gagged and probably stuffed with dope, according to the ME's first report.' He paused. 'He thinks Hayman – Harding – was almost certainly alive when Broderick left him there.'

'Or else why bother to tie him up?' Grace murmured, feeling sick.

'Or Broderick may have realized he'd died and just not bothered untying him,' Sam said. 'Either way ...' His voice trailed off.

Grace closed her eyes for a moment, then opened them again.

'How are we supposed to feel about this?' she asked.

'You're the doc.'

'Not right now I'm not.'

'I know,' he said.

They decided on a stiff drink.

'I don't know if we're supposed to feel better about Hayman or not,' Grace said after a few sips of whisky. 'Less guilty.'

'We are less guilty,' Sam said.

'Because he didn't drown?' she said ironically. 'Because Broderick finished what we started?'

'Partly, yes,' Sam said. 'Mostly because we know what

Harding did to his own son and maybe to a few others.'

'I'm not used to being an executioner, Sam. I'm just a psychologist.' Grace took another drink. 'I'm supposed to *help* people like Paul Harding.'

'You thought he was trying to kill you,' Sam reminded her. 'So did I.'

'Yes.'

'We still don't know that he wasn't.'

They both drank some more whisky and were silent for a while.

'What does it mean?' Grace asked, finally. 'I mean, what's the connection between them? How did Hayman get to be on Broderick's boat?'

'We don't know about the connection yet,' Sam answered. 'But it seems that, for whatever reason, Broderick must have been watching the *Snowbird*. We know he was at the detention centre early that afternoon, but that still gave him enough time to get down to Key Largo. There were a few other boats around, remember, when the coastguard got to us on Kuntz's boat? Broderick must have picked Hayman – Harding – up after the capsize, stashed him on the *Healer* and then gotten out of the way.'

Grace nodded, slowly. 'Watching. Waiting. That's what Broderick's been doing all these years, isn't it?'

'Care to know Martinez's verdict on the Broderick-Harding link?'

Grace nodded again.

Sam's grin was wry and bleak.

'One sick fuck attracts another,' he said.

The *Healer*, they learned, had been registered for the past ten years to one James Brody, supposedly a resident of West Palm Beach. Broderick, the police concluded, had planned well, simply sailing away from his own pre-arranged capsize off Pensacola and moving on shore whenever it suited him.

Sam had predicted ten days or so earlier that sooner or later Broderick would want to talk, want to brag about his achievements.

He was talking now.

*

427

They asked him about Peter Hayman. He said that, much as he would have loved to have taken credit for actively *creating* that particular scenario, he could only claim to have taken advantage of the situation that had presented itself to him so conveniently. He'd been keeping an eye on Grace Lucca ever since she'd first gone to Frances Dean's home in Coral Gables to see Cathy. He was, as they'd already figured out, an avid watcher – an opportunist he supposed they'd call him. It was one of the entertainments that had kept him going during his years of waiting: observing those who had no idea they were being observed. Broderick recalled two instances when he'd seen Grace sense someone watching her – once in Saks close to home in glitzy Bal Harbour; the other time right after the black Jew cop's little brother's barmitzvah, on the road to the Keys to visit with her sister. He'd noted the way she'd squirmed in the department store, the way she'd had to keep checking the rearview mirror of her Mazda, and he'd enjoyed the power it had given him over her.

Broderick hadn't known that Peter Hayman, psychiatrist and published expert on MSBP, had even existed before he'd watched him drawing Grace aside that day at the Westin in Key Largo, but after that he'd made it his business to find out all there was to know about him – and oh, it had been almost *blissful* to learn how much there *was* to know. That was when he'd decided to turn himself into Dr Eric Parés, he told his team of interviewers – at that time including Detective Martinez for the Miami Beach Police Department, Sergeant Rodriguez for the City of Miami and the State Attorney. And, of course, after that it had been just a matter of time before Parés had been ready to apply for his job in whichever prison facility the girl had ended up in. After all, everyone knew how hungry they were for qualified physicians in those miserable places, and doctors willing to put up with low-life patients, lousy conditions and pay were hard to come by. It had suited him, though, in many ways. His daughter aside, he had found those women fascinating, to watch and to treat and, when it was safe, to play his games with.

'He wanted to know if we could guess why he took the name,' Martinez told Sam later, back at the department. 'He knew we couldn't guess – the slime was smirking all over his face.'

'It's an anagram,' Sam said.

'You got that?' Martinez looked surprised.

'Grace got it,' Sam told him. 'Last night. She was doing some reading on MSBP, and suddenly she remembered the guy who'd turned the original Baron Münchhausen's tall tales into a book.'

'Rudolph Erich Raspe,' Martinez contributed.

'That's the guy.'

Martinez shook his head. 'Arrogant sick fuck,' he said.

Many things became crystal clear as Broderick went on spewing up his secrets like a magician entertaining a rapt audience. Other things remained mysteries, might always be destined, Sam and Grace feared, to be guessed about and never confirmed. The things, for example, that had happened during the week before Broderick had launched his final attack, the things that Cathy had apparently done that had so unnerved Grace and brought Sam into her house as lover and bodyguard.

Had Cathy actually *done* those things? Had she, driven by – virtually *controlled* by – Parés' drugs and hypnosis programme, personally composed that last H-A-T-E password-protected journal entry on Grace's computer, or had Broderick slithered his way into the house without their knowledge? On the afternoon Grace had been down on the deck talking with Gregory Lee, had Cathy perhaps dozed off while reading, and then sleepwalked her way – perhaps under some kind of hypnotic suggestion – into picking up Harry and placing him up on the parapet outside Grace's bedroom? Or had Cathy always been a sleepwalker, even as a young child? There was no one credible left alive to ask.

Broderick stopped talking after a while. He began trying to make deals again. A new confession for a computer in his cell. Another for books of his choice. Something really '*big*' in exchange for regular trips to the library. No one was impressed. Even the FBI profiler now visiting him was confident that he would find it tough to stay silent for long.

Either way, they had most of what they really needed.

He'd confessed to – boasted about – drugging and killing Marie and Arnold Robbins, and Beatrice Flager.

He'd confessed to letting himself in and out of the Robbins' house over the last two years whenever it had suited him. He'd talked about doping Cathy with cannabis and cutting the heads off Marie's goldfish – and about, on the night of the first murders, burning one of Cathy's voile nightgowns in the outside incinerator for the police to find. He'd also admitted to the attack on the other female prisoner in the House of Detention and to the planting of the potato peeler in his daughter's cell.

He had admitted freely to the manslaughter of Paul Harding.

He had refused pointblank to confess to any of the scalpel attacks in doctors' offices – even the one on David Becket. And he had also, thus far, refused to admit to creating any of the entries on Cathy's computer, or to killing Frances Dean, or to burying the silver scalpel and rubber kitchen gloves in the backyard at Pine Tree Drive.

'That's just for the hell of it,' Sam said to Grace. 'So that the game doesn't have to end yet. Maybe so he still gets to have his trial.'

'And so that Cathy gets to go on suffering,' Grace added.

No one was being naïve enough to imagine that Broderick's confessions and incarceration would bring an end to Cathy's pain.

That was going to run and run.

Even she agreed that she was going to need therapy for some time to help her get through. Her personal first choice for a therapist was still Grace, but she accepted now that that was impossible. Not just because Grace had become much too close, but because the Department of Children and Families was considering her application to become a long-term foster parent to Cathy.

For now, though, there was still John Broderick to contend with. Still getting his jollies from setting people in motion, like mice in a maze with a lump of cheese at the centre. He hadn't needed drugs to set Grace in motion – he'd found other ways of manipulating her. Broderick's disease might have started out with jealousy and hatred and a desire for revenge, but these days Grace believed that he was getting genuine gratification from the mind games he was so gifted at playing – from setting people against each other.

Fine sport for a dead man.

And opportunities galore still to come on Death Row, if that was where they ended up sending him.

CHAPTER EIGHTY-FOUR

WEDNESDAY, SEPTEMBER 9, 1998

Two days after Labor Day, Jerry Wagner called Grace.

'You're not going to believe this,' he told her straight out, 'and you're going to like it even less.'

'What now?' Apprehension hit the pit of her stomach.

'Broderick's instructed his lawyer to try and block your application to foster Cathy.'

'He can't do that!'

'He's not likely to succeed,' Wagner qualified, 'but he can certainly create problems for you. Hate it or not, he's still Cathy's father—'

'Who's confessed to murdering her mother.' Grace's voice was loud with outrage, making Harry, over in the corner of her office, twitch his ears. 'Who's stated, in front of witnesses, how much he *hates* his daughter.'

'No question about any of that, Grace,' Wagner agreed.

'Well, then?'

'You still need to be prepared,' the attorney told her.

'For what?' Outrage simmered down to unease.

'Broderick's told his lawyer that he won't allow his daughter to continue to be exposed to "an immoral and unsuitable relationship". His words, Grace, obviously.' Wagner sounded embarrassed.

'Obviously.'

'I'm sorry to have to load you with this, just when things looked like starting to settle down for Cathy.'

'Not your fault, Jerry.' Grace paused. 'He can't win on this, can he?'

'I find it highly unlikely.'

'Not impossible?'

'*Highly* unlikely, Grace.'

'But not impossible.'

'Nothing's impossible,' the lawyer said.

Grace closed her eyes.

'I'd like to kill him, Jerry.'

'Off the record, Grace,' Wagner said, 'you're not the only one.'

CHAPTER EIGHTY-FIVE

FRIDAY, SEPTEMBER 11, 1998

The note was waiting for Sam when he and Martinez walked into the big white police department building just after lunch. Sam's return to full duty had been granted two weeks before, and the detectives were both feeling relaxed after successfully helping to tie up a series of assaults around Indian Creek Drive.

'Know who left this for me?' Sam asked one of the uniformed guys at the desk as he started to slit open the envelope.

'No idea,' he said. 'It was here when I came on duty.'

Martinez saw the expression changing on Sam's face as he read. 'What?'

Sam folded the small sheet of paper back in half. 'You don't want to know.'

Martinez laid a hand on Sam's arm and steered him over to the far side of the lobby. 'I got a feeling I do want to know.' He paused. 'Share, man.'

'It's heavy.'

'Is it from Broderick?'

Sam shook his head. 'Not exactly.'

'Share,' Martinez said again.

Sam handed him the note and envelope.

Martinez read, his face a mask.

> *Dad's getting offed unless someone moves*
> *him fast. Otherwise this one's for her.*
> *Brothers in lo-places.*

He said nothing, just folded it again and put it into the envelope.

'What do you think?' Sam asked.

Martinez took a moment. 'About what?'

'What do I do about the message, Al?'

Martinez's eyes were grim. 'I don't see any message.'

The two men looked at each other for several more seconds.

'How about I buy you a cup of coffee?' Sam asked.

'We just ate.'

'I want another cup.'

Martinez nodded and gave Sam back the envelope. 'Let's go.'

They walked back outside into the hot sunshine, strolled down the broad stone steps and turned left along Washington until they reached the corner of 13th Street.

'Got a light?' Sam asked Martinez.

The other detective pulled a matchbook out of his pocket.

'If this boomerangs,' Sam said, 'it's on me, okay?'

'It won't.'

'But if it does.'

'Light the match, Becket.'

'I mean it, Al,' Sam said harshly. 'You never saw this.'

'Just do it,' Martinez told him.

Sam lit a match, touched the flame to the corner of the envelope and held on to it until the small blaze was almost at his fingertips. It swirled silently down on to the concrete sidewalk and turned into ash.

'God forgive me,' Sam said, 'but I think I hope they mean it.'

Martinez put the sole of his right shoe over the ash and scuffed it around.

'God forgives you, man.' His dark eyes were sharper than ever. 'If I know anything about anything, I figure He's probably cheering.'

CHAPTER EIGHTY-SIX

SUNDAY, SEPTEMBER 13, 1998

It went down on Sunday afternoon.

No one parted with dope easily in that place.

For Broderick, it seemed, a few of them made an exception.

A handful of condoms, stuffed with a contaminated blend of smack, coke and dust, and forced down his throat.

Then, when the time was right, a few sharp blows to the abdomen.

He had to have screamed while he was dying.

But no one heard.

Or came.

It had, the guards agreed later, to have been a far more agonizing way to go than anything the hot chair might ultimately have offered.

It seemed, they reckoned privately, a fitting kind of an end for a real piece of scum like John Broderick.

Retrieve File

Filename:	<u>My Journal</u>
Current Dir:	c:\wpwin\sundries
File Info:	19411 Bytes
11/23/98	23.10

File Password Protected

File: c\wpwin\sundries\jrnl

Password: L-O-V-E-&-H-A-T-E

        OK   Cancel

Cathy's Journal
Saturday, November 28, 1998

Know your enemies. That's what he taught me. It was a good lesson in the end.

I remember he once said the same thing about friends.

Thanksgiving was hard this year. I missed my mom and Arnie and Aunt Frances. But Grace and Sam are the best. She says it's too soon to say if they'll stay together for ever. I guess they have a lot to think about.

I don't think I'll ever understand why he did what he did. Grace says there are some things we can't ever expect to understand. She says it's okay for me to hate him, so long as I let myself move on. She says we all have to take things a day at a time.

I still get scared sometimes, and there are things I don't think I'll ever get used to again. Like knowing people are watching me. And being in the dark. Sometimes I'm scared to go to sleep. I haven't told anyone about that – I don't want Grace to know. I worry about bad stuff, too, like how I could have done what I did to Harry that day. Grace and my new shrink say that wasn't really me. I wish I could be sure of that.

I try not to think about it too much. I try to think about how lucky I am. I know I'm lucky to have Grace and Sam. But it all still comes crawling into my head at night in the dark. I can't seem to stop it.

More than anything else in the world, I hope Grace is right about one thing. I hope I'm not like him.